The Horror at Pooh Corner

Other Works by Joe Monson

Anthologies (as editor)

A Universe of Stories

The Horror at Pooh Corner

LTUE Benefit Anthologies (with Jaleta Clegg)

Trace the Stars

A Dragon and Her Girl

Twilight Tales

Parliament of Wizards

A Hero of a Different Stripe

Troubadours and Space Princesses

Dog Save the King (forthcoming in 2025)

For Glory and Honor (forthcoming in 2026)

***Legacy of the Corridor* (as editor)**

The Florilegium of Madness (D. J. Butler, w/Callie Butler)

Dragon Soup for the Soul (Emily Martha Sorensen)

Down the Arches of the Years (Lee Allred)

Sharks in an Inland Sea (Lehua Parker)

The Bacillus of Beauty (Harriet Stark)

In the Haunting Darkness (Michael R. Collings)

Interplanetary Edition and Other Tales of Tomorrow (Emily Martha Sorensen)

All the Monoliths in the Universe (Michael C. Goodwin)

Waiting for Elephants (Jaleta Clegg)

The Chrestomathy of Desire (D. J. Butler, w/Callie Butler, forthcoming)

Other Collections (as editor)

Thin Air: The Cosmic Crime Fiction of Gustavo Bondoni

THE HORROR AT POOH CORNER

EDITED BY
JOE MONSON

ILLUSTRATED BY
LEILA MAY
MEREDITH DILLMAN

HEMELEIN PUBLICATIONS

Managing Editor: Joe Monson
Publisher: Heather B. Monson
Published by Hemelein Publications, LLC. — hemelein.com

First Edition
First Hemelein printing (Kickstarter), August 2024
First Hemelein printing (general), October 2024
10 9 8 7 6 5 4 3 2 1

ISBN (Kickstarter):
    Hardcover: 978-1-64278-043-7 (gen.rel.), 978-1-64278-066-6 (signed)
    Trade: 978-1-64278-045-1 (gen.rel.), 978-1-64278-065-9 (signed)
    Ebook: 978-1-64278-047-5
ISBN (general release):
    Case laminate: 978-1-64278-044-4
    Trade: 978-1-64278-046-8
    Ebook: 978-1-64278-048-2

Library of Congress Control Number: 2024937867 (Kickstarter)
Library of Congress Control Number: 2024937868 (general)

To Alan, Ernest, and Howard—

Your imaginations and creativity
continue to inspire
authors and illustrators to this day.

Thank you
for sharing yourselves
with all of us!

SIGNATURE PAGE

Esther M. Friesner	Kary English
D. J. Butler	Alex Shvartsman
Cedar Sanderson	Eric James Stone
Brad R. Torgersen	Janci Patterson
Jonathan Maberry	Julie Frost
Jody Lynn Nye	Gustavo Bondoni
Jaleta Clegg	Leigh Saunders
Michaelbrent Collings	Steve Diamond
Joseph Capdepon II	Lee Allred
Lehua Parker	Jessica Douglas
Leila May	Meredith Dillman

Contents

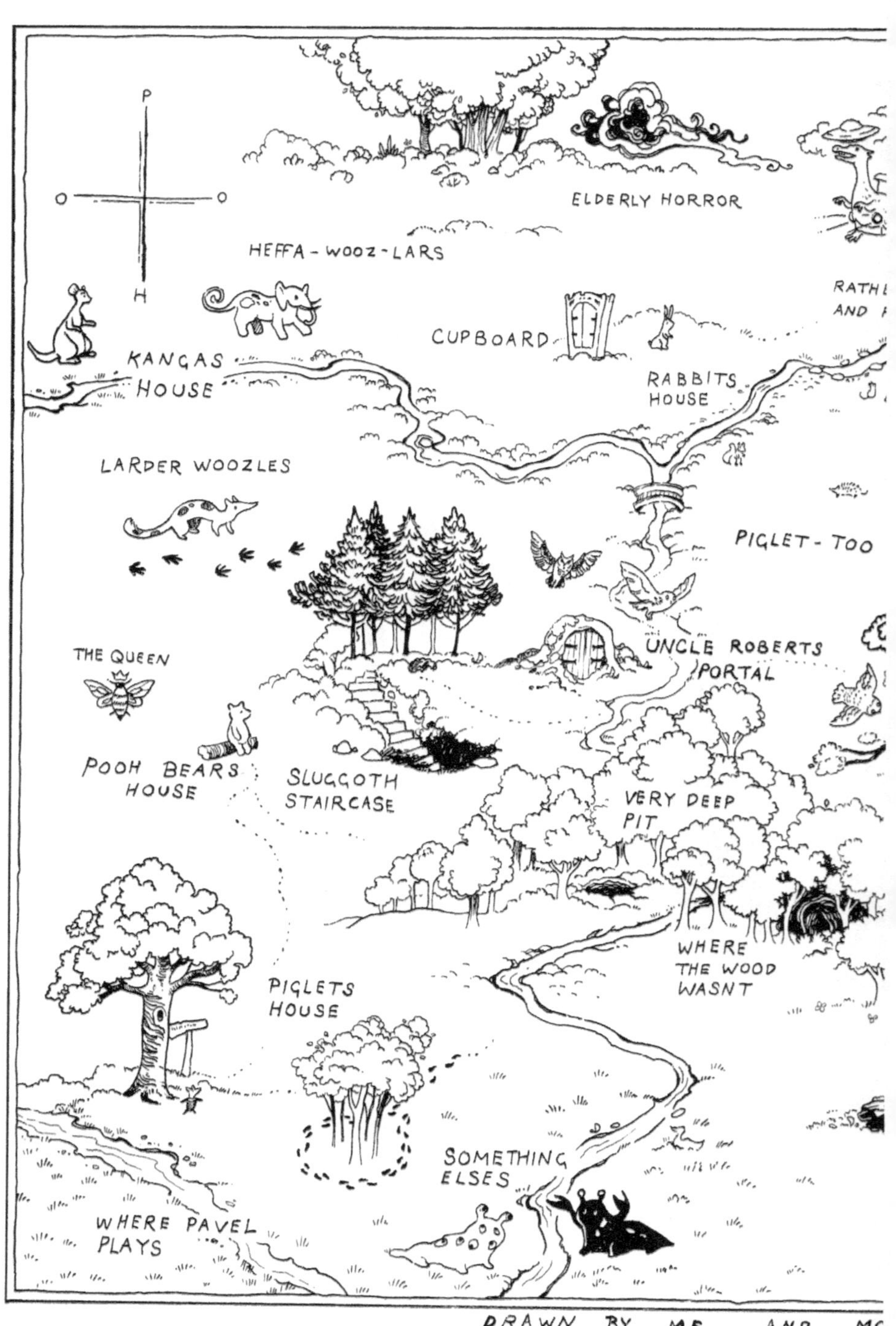

P
H
ELDERLY HORROR
HEFFA - WOOZ - LARS
CUPBOARD
RATHE
AND
KANGAS
HOUSE
RABBITS
HOUSE
LARDER WOOZLES
PIGLET - TOO
THE QUEEN
UNCLE ROBERTS
PORTAL
POOH BEARS
HOUSE
SLUGGOTH
STAIRCASE
VERY DEEP
PIT
WHERE
THE WOOD
WASNT
PIGLETS
HOUSE
SOMETHING
ELSES
WHERE PAVEL
PLAYS
DRAWN BY ME AND MS

ER STOMPY
ROARY
BEE TREE
PIGLETS INAUGURAL FLIGHT
MY HOUSE
JAR COLLECTION
OWLS HOUSE
WHERE THE WOOZLES WAS
GALLEONS LEAP
WHERE PIGLET DID A GREAT THING
NECRO COMIC CON
EGG-NOG
1000 500 100 AKER WOOD
EE YORES GLOOMY PLACE
LURKING LOG
DILLMAN HELPD

We Begin with a Bear of Little Brain

Joe Monson

Great stories often start with very ordinary characters. In this case, all of these stories were inspired by an unassuming bear of little brain who burst into the world as "Edward" in a poem published in *Punch,* a British humor and satire magazine, in February 1924. He was later featured in a story published on Christmas Eve 1925 in the *Evening News,* a newspaper in London. This led to a collection of stories, *Winnie-the-Pooh,* being published in October 1926. A second collection, *The House at Pooh Corner* (the inspiration for the title of our collection here) was published almost exactly two years later in October 1928.

Skip ahead almost 94 years to the beginning of 2022, and Joseph Capdepon II and I conceived an idea after an online discussion. I believe the original idea was his, but we worked together to come up with what became the anthology you now hold in your hands.

I think most of us, when we were very young, while learning to put on our shoes and stockings in order to show our independence, likely had the Winnie-the-Pooh stories by Alan Milne read to us, or we heard of them through other sources. Milne, with the help of Ernest Shepard's wonderful illustrations, had a way of capturing the essence of childhood and presenting it in a way that both young and old could thoroughly enjoy it and immediately identify with it.

I doubt I will ever tire of reading the Pooh books or Milne's poetry volumes. There's a simple pleasure in reading those works, and they bring a smile to my face every time I read them. It's especially fun to read them to a young audience and watch the delight and wonder sparkle in their eyes as their imaginations are ignited by the antics of the inhabitants of the Hundred Acre Wood.

As we grew older, many of us began to read various scary stories (some more scary than others!), including some either by or influenced by Howard Lovecraft. For the latter, I was not one of those who read Lovecraft when I was younger. I read plenty of other stories that would be classified as horror (to varying degrees) or dark fantasy, but I never really found much horror that stuck with me outside of stories that I knew were related somehow to Lovecraft and his worlds. For whatever reason, I never got around to reading anything actually by him until twenty or so years ago.

I'm not a big blood and gore, grimdark kind of reader. I've never enjoyed the slasher genre. Instead, I tended toward the more suspenseful, esoteric horror. Stuff like that found in the original *Twilight Zone* television series, which often left much of the horror to the imagination of the watcher, only hinting at it. I also liked comedic horror, like the *Addams Family* comics (I also liked the original television series as well as the two-film series from the 1990s).

That's what I tried to gather for this anthology. Here, you'll find an eclectic mix of cosmic horror, humorous horror, a little really creepy horror, and everything in between, all set in the occasionally idyllic setting of the Hundred Acre Wood.

Instead of going the normal route for a small press and doing a royalty-share anthology, Hemelein Publications decided to dip their collective toes into the crowdfunding pool and run a Kickstarter. Because the campaign was successful, we were able to pay above professional rates to our authors, which we love to do. We were also able to attract some very-well-established authors to participate in this little venture. You'll find both those and some newer authors who've all written some excellent stories here. I'm very excited to be able to finally share them with all of you.

None of this would be possible without our Kickstarter backers, all 490 of those who followed through and honored their pledges. Thank you so much for your support and patience as we worked through the almost two year process of planning and putting out this volume for you.

Here's the list of all our wonderful supporters, in order of pledging. Names are as the backers requested:

Henry, Josh & Harrison Herz, Cass Smith, andrew greeson, T. Alan Horne, John Haines, James Jaehnig, Jacqueline Johnson, Candice, Elizabeth, The Creative Fund by BackerKit, Brian McMurray, Mark Froom, Jacob Barlow, Amy Claflin, Trevor Holyoak, Dave Ellingwood, Cherise Papa, Jacob Barnhill, Kelly Hopkins, John R. Arpin, Jeffrey Shabel, Diann T. Read, Thlor Mungpupple, Glen Vogelaar, Liam Hall, Katherine Cowley, chibiamy, Jeff Creer, Robert West, Manuel M Lopez, Elijah Jacob Mears, David Batson, David, Debbie Mumford, and Ed.

Christopher Potts, Scott McNeil, LJ Kutten, Michael Hanson, Angela Lamb, Jennifer Perry, jchawley, Hana Correa, Leaf the nymph, Elizabeth Langill, Jonathan, Rachel Lewis, Laura M, Algie Lane, Kevin Harsip, Holly Hamlyn-Harris, rick levy, Joab Stieglitz, David Giusti, Tim Heintz, Allan Lynn, Ralph Donatelli, Ryan, Kristina Kugler, Joseph Wojciechowski, Pavel Nazartsev, Angel Sianez, Edward Stapleton, Jon Nials, Chris Boyle, and Nick Gardner.

Kris Olsen, Joe Ficklin, Robert Dean, Cam, Tessa Hatlelid, Joey Logan, TDNicol, Eilish Higgins, Frank Auge, Shannon Shaneyfelt, Mary wolverton, Alexander Luthy, Brandy Pastore, Ron Beiswanger, Jade Wildy, John Richard Ellis, Marc D. Long, Dan Stufflebeam, Eric Elko, Sarah Louise, Camryn, James Webb, Jim B., Henry Belizaire, earlywinterair, TheyPaints, Christopher Welshan, Pluto, Joe Kelly, Julie Donohue, Lydia Leonard, Benjamin Carlson, Theric Jepson, Jason DeLong, Liam, Brook West, Geoff G Turner, Kyle Marsan, David 'slick' Sellers, Kirby Richard, Charles Fout, and Kurtis Donald Klunder.

Matt Krish, Atomic Twills, jess smart smiley, Krisda Jirochvong, Jacqueline Skelton, Jeff Auser, Heather23, Ethan Skarstedt, Andy Donald, Bryan R Stahl, José Fernando Ornelas, Scott Casey, Ashley Childs, Kimberly Majernik, Eric W. Brittain, Annamae Nedrow, Greg Tippmann, David Tang, Robert D. Matthews, Kasey Sargent, Robert Betterly, Jon Saul, S. Darby, Matthew Conner, Adriana, Torrie Marsh, James, Danny Ham, Andrew Foxx, Josiah Stockton, Michael Whiteman, Mark N., Michael D. Albert, Chris, Ethan Slack, ruthcatrin, and Marc Santosuosso.

Armond Netherly, Mark Lucich, Lisa Crumbley-Murphy, Warren Bennett, Anna D, Sheryl Christopher, Logan Kearsley, Katina Stanley-Brown, Pasquale, moises rodriguez, FirstAidKitster, Frank Lewis, pakhet, Pyndan, William McCullough, Tiffany Ross, Kenneth Hamer, Dave Slavens, crashonhead, Dennis Lee, Tara Rose Palumbo, terry gene, Jim Cebulka, Rachel Meibos Helps, Adrian Bustamante, Chandler Scott, Felix, Christopher, Beth Lobdell, Michael Bloom, Susan Kroupa, Rob Avery, Kevin Wasden, Nathan, Karl Morini, and Carl Duzett.

Nathan Mitchell, Michael Feir, Robert Renken, G Thicket, Kathleen Heinlein, Hal, Adam Hinrichs, Michael Johnson, Sean, Michael Pigoni, Brent Kreinop, Phyllis Gibson, Sam Wayman, Randall York, Luke W. Henderson, Devin P., Keba Jackson, Fabian, Nick Roethlisberger, AR Brennan, Kurt Lambert, Ashlee Montelongo, Lawrence Lee, Kimberley Butson Dunbar, David DiCarlo, Kim Jonasson, Lance and Jennifer Empey, Greg Radabaugh, Kate, Andrew Rector, Chris Padar, Ross Hathaway, and Leah Ning.

"Filkertom" Tom Smith, Scott Mills, Kenzi Stephens, Paul Popernack, Kathryn Fay, Bill Riley, ATH, Kelvrek, Gunnar Santelman, Wulf Moon, Katie Hunsaker, Tiffiny Felix, Ryan Munn, Just Mike, Kurt Lucero, Cathy Witbeck,

Ashleigh, Tim, Asphodel, Wesley Adams, Alexander Nirenberg, Jacob, Jafo, Roberta Santillo, R.W. Wallace, Lorna Hansmann, Benji Smith, Astra Carter, Erik Poulsen, Walter Koegel, Brooks Henry, Kendra Augustine, Tim Lonegan, Björn Bengtsson, Michele Shaw, Robyn Miller, Michelle Swenson, Martin Rye Thomsen, Chelsea, Robert, Jeff T, Ernie, William D Colburn, and Lenore Wagner.

Evan Loehle-Conger, Rowan North, Nick, Akis Linardos, Lilly Ibelo, Bill Ginger, Desiree Dunbar, Morty303, Pernille Thede Jakobsen, Megan Scrivens, Michael, fatolliecat, Greg Davis, Cassidy Plummer, Adam M, Tommy Guisgand, Guillermo Sanchez, William, Cassie Ford, Christopher Cardionale, DG Fletcher, Sheryl Welch, Catelynn Webster, Michael O'Connell, Matt Newcomb, Marychain, Richard O'Shea, Jennifer, Carl Willis-Ford, Ian Concepcion, Crystal DeTemple McNeel, Douglas Vaughan, Melanie Briggs, Lacey L Amann, Povolam, and Maegan Cooper.

Lynn Moore Gietz, Brittney, Boris Veytsman, Michaela, Lindsay V., Andrew Robinson, Keith Bowden, T. Everett, Penny Haspil, Nemonemoo8, HighRiseCode, Charles R. Cox, Joseph, Carol Henderson, Aaron Thomas, Kate Moon, Patrick Coyle, john s shelton, Jill Vance, WarOrdos, David, M. T. Hall, Joseph H, Jessie Conz, Sean Richardson, Rosamaria Cirelli, Jo Peitz, Fen Eatough, Augustine, Tayler, An Valara, Maria Poldson, Simon Mark de Wolfe, James Norton, alex adrian, Andrea Monson, grimrasp, Becky, Jane R., and John Fletcher Pasquini.

AcesofDeath7, Mina Kincaid, Geneviève, Lunaro, Lisa, Leslie OBrien, Tara, Robert Isaac, James Martinez, Joey, CottonPop, Sherry Mock, Robert Hull, Crystal Weese, Karla Laliberte, Visi Gothnut, Lauren Hazel, Luis Roncayolo, Troy, Michael Elliott, Patrick Stansfield, William Rutherford, Thecatbro, Deanna Joy Drummond, David Groo, Ed Surrett, Eric Bergstresser, Christopher L Smith, Benjamin Kanten, Mike Durkin, Jake Stohr, Jack Mc, John Mion, James Wright, Daniel Dunlap, James Norsworthy, Earl Gensolin, Steven Bastien, Steve S, Eron Wyngarde, and Tod Casasent.

Brian Hill, Mike Stoumbos, Joshua Locke, Derek Stevens, Eric B., Jerrod, Wendy Mills, ryan english, Greg Gagnon, Matt Egbert, Rostow, Kvothe, Harriet Rankin, Kirk Keller, Lawrence Person, chris baumgartner, Richard Skripek, Nick Agon Kresky, Marshall Bautista, Daniel Chen, Lila Holley, Tiffany George, Samuel Spradley, Dawn Jaekel, Damon & Peni Griffin, MiJin, Jens Troeger, John Davidson, AlderBeez, Ross Ingle-Finch, Zoe, Garrett Bowling, Jacky Chan, Beth Newhouse, Darrell Winkler, Colleen Feeney, John D. Payne, and James Brown.

Don Juneau, Asenath Waite, Dylan Humphreys, Myron Fox, Cassandra Eisch, Lyn Worthen, John Ver Linden, Adam S., Kirk P, Violet Jijing Covey, Jessica Enfante, Marc, Bryant Gonzalez, Bear Putnam, Boh, Chris Basler, David

Shadoin, Billy Rodriguez, Ted Lai, Annabel, Nicholas K. Fowler, Crackleknees, Talakai, Jared Tallis, James Preston Parham, Annette Evans, Jessica, Holly Iossa, Taszilo, Jenna, Nathan D Howell, Heather Curtiss, Tim Jordan, Kevin Trainor, LakkinHobo, Joy Kristen Allen, Allred, Ariane Beauparlant, Jessica mace-ball, and Justin Fuqua.

Josh Reynolds, shannon, Sean Niemeyer, Dan, Sergio, Paul G, Adam Bargmeyer, AdVocem, Bear McG, Rachel Spina, Dan Polley, Vulpecula, Rebecca L. Garcia, driquelmy, asmallman98, Martin L. Shoemaker, Nina DiPinto, Jennifer Cameron, Lori Bowers, Benjamin T. Smith, Charlie Sullivan, Anthony Hall, Joseph Nell, Sydney Lawrence, Eliza, Keith Haus, Julia Ashley, Marc Adkins, James Hamilton, Dorothy, Ian, Henry Gibbons, Ronin1677, Eben Waters, Amanda Shuman, and Gary Fewkes.

That's a lot of people, and we appreciate each and every one of you. You made this project possible. We were able to get some fantastic, commissioned artwork by Jessica Douglas for the Kickstarter cover. She really had a lot of fun creating it, and it was a delight to work with her. Leila May had a great time coming up with the illustrations for each story, and I think she captured a little bit of both Shepard and Lovecraft in these illustrations. Meredith Dillman did a fantastic job on the brand new map. You'll notice that it has quite a few different notations than those found on the original Shepard (I mean, Christopher Robin) map. All three of our artists were a pleasure to work with.

It was a delight to work with Esther M. Friesner, Kary English, D. J. Butler, Alex Shvartsman, Cedar Sanderson, Eric James Stone, Brad R. Torgersen, Janci Patterson, Jonathan Maberry, Julie Frost, Jody Lynn Nye, Gustavo Bondoni, Jaleta Clegg, Leigh Saunders, Michaelbrent Collings, Steve Diamond, Joseph Capdepon II, Lee Allred, and Lehua Parker on the stories and poems collected here. All of them were a joy to work with, and very professional.

So, thank you from me and from Hemelein Publications to our authors, artists, and our amazing backers supporting this project. We were able to able to assemble such an amazing crew of talent! Everyone who contributed a story or artwork to this anthology is a true professional, and I hope to work with all of them again in the future. What an amazing project, from start to finish!

Thank you. You are all awesome.

I hope you enjoy this volume.

Joe Monson, Editor
July 2024

In Which We Encounter the Shadow Over Grandfather

Esther M. Friesner

Christopher Robin studied the long table in just the way he had seen Nanny peer at the arrangement of cups and plates and spoons before the two of them sat down to tea. He was not exactly certain about what he was looking for, but he was determined to find it. After all, it was not every day that the inhabitants of the Hundred Acre Wood came together to celebrate the return of two of their number from an Expotition of Great and Magnificent Perils. Christopher Robin was particularly looking forward to hearing what sort of Great and Magnificent Perils these had been, as the guests of honor had yet to tell anyone more about it beyond, *We're back.*

It was a sweetly sunny day, one that might well have been made to order for such a festive gathering. The trees of the Hundred Acre Wood rustled and murmured old melodies to which only they knew all the words, although they shared just a bit of that arcane knowledge with the chorus of songbirds perched upon their outspread branches. Cries of cuck-oo-cuck-oo, tea-cher-tea-cher, chiff-chaff-chiff-chaff, kaah-kaah and *ph'nglui mglw'nafh! ph'nglui mglw'nafh!* haunted the woodland and drifted out from those brooding shadows to cast a tenuous pall over the open ground now spread with picnic cloths.

"Tut, tut. This will never do," said Christopher Robin with a frown much like Nanny's. He then moved one of the spoons from the right of the plate to the left and nodded. "Yes, now it will," he said with much pride in a job well done.

He heard a grumble of impatience behind him and turned to see that the guests had arrived. Simply everyone was there: Eeyore and Owl and Tigger and Kanga and Baby Roo and Rabbit, with all of his friends-and-relations in tow, and so many others! If we were to mention them all we would be doing so long past tea time, and that simply would not do to a far more serious degree than a misplaced spoon

"Hullo, everyone," said Christopher Robin. "Please come in. The table is for me and our guests of honor, but there are cloths spread on the grass for the rest of you."

Eeyore the sad donkey counted the number of chairs and sighed. "One too few. I might have known," he said. "Not that I ever expected to be seated at a table like an Animal of Great Importance. No, no, just a thin scrap of cloth spread over the cold, wet ground is more than enough for me, it seems. I suppose I should be grateful to have this much notice paid to me. After all, I might never even have been invited in the first place."

He chose a spot at the roots of a great tree and slowly lowered himself to the ground with many a badly muted groan. "My apologies," he said. "I have an ache in my legs from the damp." He pressed one foot into the soil and studied it. "I see," he said. "My place is not merely damp; it is almost sodden. I suppose I shall pay dearly for this later. But never mind me."

"Is he done yet?" one of Rabbit's numerous friends-and-relations demanded loudly.

Eeyore swung his head slowly in that direction, but before he could reply, Christopher Robin insisted that the melancholy donkey come and take a seat at the table.

"It will be all right, Eeyore," he said. "Piglet can sit on my lap. I think he'll like that, being able to see more of the table that way."

"Very well," said Eeyore, coming to the table and settling himself in one of the larger chairs. "If I must. I wouldn't want to inconvenience anyone Important."

There was much jostling and chatter as the other guests took their places. They oohed and aahed over the care with which Christopher Robin had made the preparations for this grand event. It was an altogether friendly manner for sorting out the seating, with only one moment of trouble when all of Rabbit's friends-and-relations insisted upon occupying the same small picnic cloth. Fortunately, this was soon settled thanks to Owl and his grave Stare of Disappointment which caused the quarrelers to remember both their manners and the fact that they were discommoding a bird of prey.

When everyone was at last comfortable, there was only one unoccupied place at the head table. "Oh dear," said Christopher Robin softly to himself. "I hope that they haven't forgotten. Perhaps I ought to go and find them."

But before he could do that, a great deal of chatter arose from the crowd as, hand in hand, Pooh and Piglet emerged from the trees and made their way to the table.

"There you are, you silly old bear!" Christopher Robin exclaimed. "I was afraid you'd quite forgotten, and we couldn't have a proper celebration without you." He suddenly realized what he was saying and hastily added, "Nor without you too, Piglet."

"Without me?" Piglet echoed. A small shudder set his entire body all a-quiver. "No, not now. Not anymore. You have me. As you must." He fixed Christopher Robin with quite a disquieting look. "As it is now assured."

Christopher Robin was momentarily puzzled. "Are you all right, Piglet?" he asked, much concerned, for Piglet was such a small and timid animal that often the most ordinary things proved somewhat overwhelming for him.

"I am," Piglet replied. "That is, I am all right as far as I have any right to be, after what was done—what *had* to be done—when we—"

Pooh placed one fubsy paw on his friend's trembling shoulder. "You *are* quite all right, Piglet. You needn't say anything more."

At these words, Piglet's tremors stopped and he gave Pooh a look of great gratitude. Christopher Robin then motioned for the little animal to sit on his lap, an invitation Piglet accepted with alacrity (which is merely how grown-up people would say he did it quickly). Once perched there, he leaned his head against Christopher Robin's chest and closed his eyes.

"Look at that, would you?" said Eeyore glumly. "It isn't everyone who gets such special attention. I know that I don't. But then again, I'm sure I don't deserve it. I'm only a sad old donkey. Nothing special to see here. Move along and leave me alone. The same as always."

The last bit of what Eeyore said was almost missed by the assembled guests, for Winnie-the-Pooh had risen from his chair—in fact, he was standing on it—and had begun to speak.

"Hullo, everyone," he said. "Thank you very much for coming to welcome Piglet and me home again. We are 'strornly glad to be here, having only just barely escaped from the midst of an elderly horror from beyond—"

"Eldritch," said Piglet in a dreamy voice. His eyes were closed and his small face was quite pale. "It was an eldritch horror, Pooh, not an elderly one."

"Oh bother," said Pooh. "I fear I truly am a Bear of Very Little Brain, and what is left of it gets quite a bouncing every time I am taken down the stairs from the nursery. I do wish you might take the trouble to pick me up and *carry* me downstairs once or twice, Christopher Robin."

"I'm sorry, Pooh," said Christopher Robin. "I shan't do it again."

"Many things shan't be done again," Pooh replied. He spoke in such an odd way that it troubled everyone who heard him. It was not at all like Pooh to voice such Somberly Enigmatic Utterances, but before anyone could ask Owl for an explanation or to fetch a dictionary, Pooh held out one paw and began a Hum.

Now most of you who are already familiar with Winnie-the-Pooh's adventures also know that he is a bear who will sometimes make up little Hums, which are songs that are Suitable to the Occasion. He had first done so during the adventure in which he tried to help himself to some honey from a wild bees' nest while impersonating a small rain cloud. It was quite a charming Hum, although it did not work as he would have preferred.

This Hum was entirely different. *This* Hum held no happy thoughts of floating free through the blue sky, nor did it wax poetical (which is how grown-up people talk when they are getting paid by the word) over the sweet taste of golden honey, such as bears delight to eat. It rose and fell like the black, oily waves of long-vanished, ageless oceans. It plunged beneath the convulsing brine to drag the fearful listener down into a realm of ghastly drowned cities. Palaces of unearthly ornamentation and unnatural geometry loomed above the wreckage-strewn sea floor, their cyclopean blocks erected according to the insanity-steeped architecture of some vanished race whose handiwork proclaimed their degeneracy. Most of them were blue.

All of the guests who heard Pooh's Hum were seized by an overpowering, morbid sense of dread that made their stuffing freeze, though they could not for their very lives comprehend why. A few of Rabbit's smaller friends-and-relations began to whimper, and Owl flew up from his place at the table to perch on a branch of the nearest tree.

Cradled on Cristopher Robin's lap, Piglet tensed visibly, as one transfixed by a crawling nightmare from which the sole escape was a hideous yet deeply longed-for death. A series of pitiful squeaks escaped his tiny body.

"No, Pooh!" he wailed. "You said I wouldn't have to revisit that foul place! You swore to me that we would never speak of what we saw, what we did, what—what—" He took a deep breath and released it in a shriek of such primal terror and desperation that several of Rabbit's most expendable friends-and-relations vaporized on the spot. *"You promised Grandfather!"*

At those words, the Hum came to a sharp stop. A grim and foreboding silence fell so heavily upon the table and the picnic cloths that several platters of biscuits disintegrated into pitiful heaps of shards and crumbs. A hedgehog keeled over. Owl took an interest.

Pooh breathed deep and fixed Piglet with the icy stare that a Puritan divine might have leveled on a witch condemned to meet her death at the rope's end. "And what *happened* thanks to your grandfather?" he asked in such a stern voice which, coming from such an otherwise easygoing bear, took all of the assembled guests quite aback.

Piglet moaned.

"Your grandfather?" Christopher Robin echoed. "You mean Trespassers—?"

"—Will," Pooh said ponderously. "Trespassers Will, whose name Piglet has taken such pride in displaying by his house for as long as we all have known him."

"William." Piglet's voice was feeble. "His name is—was—Trespassers William."

"Was it, Piglet?" Pooh said in a queerly cold way. "Was it really?"

Piglet shriveled into an even smaller lump of misery. Christopher Robin's heart was moved to protect the small animal, his highly portable if often ink-stained schoolroom companion who had so often been a source of comfort when he found himself faced with the lurking, soul-devouring madness of fractions.

"I say, Pooh, I don't see why you need to upset poor Piglet this way," he said. "We are all here for a party. Every one of us has missed you and wants to hear about your adventures."

"Mm, yes," Pooh said solemnly. "Every one." An inscrutable look passed over his ursine physiognomy, but was swiftly replaced by his familiar façade of bland cheerfulness. "What ever was I thinking?" he said, shaking his head. "Dear Piglet, I am sorry to have troubled you. Will you have another biscuit? You don't need to say one word more." He leaned nearer to the small, quivering animal and smiled. "I shall tell your story for you."

"*No!*" The desperate cry tore from Piglet's throat with such violence that a shower of withered leaves pattered down upon the table. He took a deep breath. "I will tell." He bent his head as though the weight of ages were upon him. "I will tell all."

Owl swooped back to his chair. He was keen to learn what Piglet would tell them. Being a wise bird, by his own account, he swiveled his head toward Christopher Robin and said, "I don't suppose you would happen to have such a thing as a pen and a bit of paper? I would like to make a few notes about what Piglet has to say."

Christopher Robin apologized for being unable to oblige him, so Owl moved the jam pot closer, dipped a talon, and made a few experimental scrawls on the tablecloth. "Never mind; this will do," he said.

"Ah. Strawberry," said Winnie-the-Pooh, studying the results. "Very red. Very dark. Very . . . suitable."

"Silly old bear," said Christopher Robin fondly.

Piglet spoke: "It's all quite strange, really. Before I came to the Hundred Acre Wood I never thought about my grandfather. In fact, I was never aware that I *had* a grandfather, or even that such things as grandfathers existed."

"But you must have done, Piglet," said Christopher Robin. "Everyone has a grandfather or two."

Eeyore snorted. "Two grandfathers? There's luxury. All right for some, I suppose, though they needn't go flaunting their good fortune out where those of us who can't even afford one grandfather have to hear about it. What next? Grandmothers by the bushel? An uncle or sixteen? Third cousins twice removed, just for show? I shouldn't be at all surprised."

"If I let you have some of my superfluous friends-and-relations, *will* you let Piglet tell his story?" Rabbit snapped.

"Second-hand fourth cousins, no doubt." Eeyore sighed. "Very well. More than I deserve. If anyone cares."

Piglet began: "When I moved into my house, the first thing I noticed—"

"Which no one does," Eeyore finished. Rabbit flung a scone at him.

"—was the sign," Piglet went on. "I thought it was just a piece of wandering lumber decorated with a dabble of paint, but there was something . . . unsettling about it. I wanted to move it as far away from my home as possible, but as you know, I am a very Small Animal."

"You could have asked me for help, Piglet," said Christopher Robin.

"I was going to do that," Piglet replied. "I wish I had. But just as I was going to find you, Owl stopped by to see how I was getting on."

"Quite so," said Owl, puffing out his feathers self-importantly. "One has a Civic Duty to provide advice and good counsel to one's neighbors."

"So you offered to help Piglet by moving the sign that was troubling him?" Christopher Robin said. "Oh, well done, Owl!"

"Move the sign? Er . . . not precisely." Owl's puffed-out feathers subsided. "My strength is more of the schoolroom sort. I *think*, therefore I do not move heavy things. I told Piglet what the sign *said*. To know more is to fear less," he concluded with much restored self-satisfaction.

"But sometimes to know more—" Pooh murmured.

"Did you say something, Pooh?" Christopher Robin asked.

"Me?" Winnie-the-Pooh shook his head and looked innocent. "Oh no, not really. I was just thinking of another little song I was making, but I seem to have chosen some rather bother-ish words. Does anyone know what might rhyme with *Nyarlathotep?*"

Christopher Robin laughed fondly. "That's not a word, Pooh."

Pooh merely smiled and said, "Please go ahead, Owl."

Owl looked at the assembly of eager listeners who were fascinated by what he might say next. He could not help but be pleased. "I told Piglet that his sign said *Trespassers W*, and that I had seen just such a sign before, although that one said *Trespassers Will*. I hoped that would be the end of his misgivings."

"Was it?" Tigger asked around a mouthful of cream bun.

Owl shook his head.

"I couldn't help it," Piglet protested. "*Trespassers Will?* Trespassers Will *what?* Trespassers will come to visit? Trespassers will expect me to serve them tea and little cakes? Trespassers will move into my own dear house and refuse to leave?" His voice rose with each distressing possibility.

"Nonsense, of course," Owl said, putting one foot down firmly. It went straight into the jam pot with a rousing *splot!*

While Kanga busied herself cleaning the mess and Roo helped by alternately licking the jam from Owl's foot and choking on the feathers, Piglet became a bit more calm.

"It was then I remembered that Will is quite often short for William," he said, his voice wobbling only a little. "And so—and so—"

"And so, as you later told me, the sign meant your grandfather, Trespassers William," said Pooh.

Piglet turned to Christopher Robin anxiously. "It is all right that I *decided* to have a grandfather, isn't it? Even if it's not the usual way you go about getting one, I mean?"

Christopher Robin thought about this. "Well, I have heard the grownups talk about people who decide not to *continue* having a grandfather, or some other relative. So I suppose it's all right."

"Quite," said Owl solemnly. "You never know when a grandfather might be needed."

Piglet sighed with relief. "Thank you, Christopher Robin. I feel better now."

"Just as you felt *entirely* better when *I* first taught you what that sign of yours meant," Owl said proudly. He looked to Piglet for confirmation.

He was to be disappointed.

"Knowing what those lines said *was* a comfort," Piglet said slowly. "A small one. Of a sort. At the time." He took a deep breath. "Until the day that *he* arrived."

"He?" Rabbit echoed.

"My grandfather," Piglet replied sadly. "Trespassers Will."

"Now see here!" Rabbit exclaimed. "This is absolutely ridiculous. You never had a grandfather before you decided you did, so how could he have—?"

"I beg your pardon," came a sepulchral voice from the depths of the Hundred Acre Wood. "I little *Byakhee* bird told me that I was being invoked, er, spoken of. My apologies for such a lamentably tardy arrival." A squat, toad-like figure shambled out of the oppressive shade of the ancient and foreboding trees. "I have come far, through ghastly and unholy impediments, on a journey whose route too often bordered on lands where madness ruled from a blood-streaked throne. The traffic from K'n-yan was a biiiiiitttttt—" The creature caught sight of a severe warning look from Kanga and made haste to amend: "That is, it was a maelstrom of horror."

Christopher Robin and all of the guests stared in confusion at this uncanny arrival.

In truth, not all of them did so. Piglet trembled in Christopher Robin's arms, the epitome of terrified misery. For his part, Pooh was the picture of calm, albeit with the air of a barbaric warrior, scion of a ravening, vanished race, one shaped mercilessly by a savage environment.

"Mama! Mama!" cried Roo. "Look at Pooh! Look at him! Doesn't he look like he should be steeped to the elbows in the festering entrails of his friends-and-relations?"

"Don't be silly, Roo dear," said Kanga gently. "Bears don't have elbows."

The stranger shambled closer, ill-shod feet leaving a trail of burgeoning fungi in the wake of every sinister step. He only ceased his shambling when he stood within arm's reach of Christopher Robin and Piglet. "Hello, my dear fellow," he said in a croaking voice. "Haven't you got a hug for your old grand-dad?"

With surprising agility for a bear of his girth, Pooh stepped between Piglet and his *soi disant* (which is simply how grownups say— Oh, never mind) grandfather.

"You are back, Trespassers Will," Pooh said in a voice colder than the merciless winds that scour the icy Plateau of Leng. "We *had* a bargain."

"A bargain as yet unpaid," Trespassers William replied. He raised his arms, which were oddly flexible in several anatomically incorrect places, and began to chant a bizarre litany in a tongue so alien to common mortals that its ululating tones and eerie cadences were sure to reduce the doomed listener to mindless, foam-lipped gibbering.

Fortunately, at this point Christopher Robin's Nanny whisked him away for his bath time and the remainder of those present were not mortals of any sort, so that was all right.

(Should anyone need to know how Nanny was able to withstand such an aural assault on her mental fortitude, the reason is a simple one: She was Scots.)

Trespassers Will continued his arcane intonations. As if summoned from the black gulfs between the stars, a fetid miasma began to creep its way out of the woodland, tendrils of bone-white mist twining themselves around the visitant's weirdly articulated limbs. The animals watched, even though their expressions of frozen panic betrayed their appalling realization that their bodies were no longer theirs to command.

In the midst of the glacial paralysis that possessed their friends, only Pooh and Piglet seemed unaffected. Piglet's felted skin had paled from rosy pink to the dead silver of shattered timbers cast up from ancient shipwrecks that had dragged wretched mariners below the waves to be feasted upon by the crawling, slithering, wriggling monstrosities of the ocean's unknown depths, but he still retained a sliver of self-sovereignty. Ah, but *how* he used it—! He began to moan and mumble twisted syllables of no tongue known to the Hundred Acre Wood. His incantation merged with that of Trespassers Will until their voices wove a moldering tapestry of alarming design on the air.

Pooh calmly stretched out a paw to help himself to more honey. "It begins," he said with great solemnity. "Er, that is, I mean it *recalls*," he added with some embarrassment.

It did. The transparent interstice between those two weirdly bonded chanters grew gelatinous with shadowy images. The captive creatures rooted to their seats were forced to witness the mystic apparition of a phantom Piglet leaning at ease against the door of his home. Then at once this otherwise familiar and comforting sight abruptly mutated beneath a palpable atmosphere of evil as Trespassers Will came into view.

The animals remained unwilling onlookers to his brief parley with Piglet, saw his flabby lips move in unheard words. They could not look away but were forced to see Piglet's image bow his head, miserable, and begin to walk subserviently whither his putative grandfather would conduct him.

The semblance of Pooh obtruded upon the conjured vision. Piglet's relief at his friend's chance arrival was as evident as it was short-lived. Trespassers Will glowered at the inadvertent bear, spoke but a single word, and pointed a pitiless finger at the sign bearing his name. Unable to resist, Pooh turned the sign to its other side. As he touched it, a faint rippling ran up his arms from paws to shoulders, but it happened so swiftly that those who saw it happen questioned whether they had seen anything at all.

Sunlight without warmth struck the now visible characters limned in crimson strokes across the placard's back. Piglet's phantasm gaped at the blasphemous, demoniac inscription thus revealed and uttered a soundless scream.

"Ooh! Ooh! Piglet can *read*!" Roo squeaked. The resilience of youth allowed Kanga's child to evade the paralyzing effect of the conjured vision and make an adorable pest of himself. "He can read the squiggly-iggly red things!"

"No, Roo," Pooh replied. "If he could, why ask Owl for help explaining the *front* of that sign? But there are some things we know at first sight to be drenched in ageless evil. We read such things with our very *souls*!"

"Oh," said Roo. And then: "Can I have a biscuit?"

The wee creature's request was ignored. In the vision, Trespassers Will's batrachian mouth stretched even farther in an unsavory leer. He gestured again at the sign whose letters assumed a noxious glow such as might emanate from the slime of rotting toadstools. A gateway opened in the space behind him. The shapes of towering trees were manifest, their ancient limbs arching over an obscure pathway that—

"I say, isn't that just the Hundred Acre Wood?" Owl exclaimed, his urge to pedantry overcoming his immobilizing fear.

Pooh gave him a condescending look. "I only wish it were. You see before you the appalling passage of our Expotition. This path was—and yet is!—the way *to our wood's One Hundred and First Acre!*"

Before their gaping faces, a pageant of mind-shattering beings filled the ensorcelled scene. Yet worse than this gruesome panorama was the disquieting effect now infecting vision's frame. The tenuous border separating memory from reality began to writhe and deliquesce. The boundaries between the familiar and the unspeakably alien balanced unsteadily on the brink of disappearing, opening the gate for an invasion of horrors. The animals who had managed to cast off some small measure of their terror found themselves sucked back into a frenzy of panic that scraped chalky fingers of primal dread across their hearts. Bunnies screamed as the scenes of blackest shadow enfolded them. Mice gabbled maniacally. Hedgehogs exploded.

"*Now* it begins," said Pooh, very much satisfied.

"If you say so," Eeyore muttered. "You did say so before, but nothing happened. Then again, I suppose it's all too much for someone like me to ask. That is, for things to begin happening when someone much more important than me says they will." He sighed so loudly that the grotesque anomalies now oozing from the trees of the Hundred-and-First Acre Wood stopped and stared with pale, luminous eyes at the chronically dismal donkey.

But there was one figure that did not halt its approach. If what the fear-enslaved remnant of Christopher Robin's guests had seen thus far was dire enough to leave their sanity clinging by a spider's thread, this was a sight to beat the horripilating band.

The hideous image they saw approaching was no *set* shape but a constantly shifting glob of jellied protoplasm. It's midnight bulk undulated forward, studded with countless, wildly rotating eyes. Malformed tentacles extruded themselves from the monster's body as needed for propulsion, to be reabsorbed in the way a child's rosy, ravening mouth slurps up spaghetti. Worst of all was the harsh cry it uttered, a cry whose cosmos-spanning dreadfulness somehow managed to break the barrier between the chant-summoned apparition of the past and the realm of the present.

Tekeli-li! Tekeli-li!

"Behold!" Trespassers Will declaimed. "Behold the Shoggoth!"

The apparition was too much for Piglet, who choked on an *Iä* and had to be thumped on the back. The spell was broken. The vision vanished.

"Good riddance," said Kanga. "That is more than enough of that. Such a messy thing, and messy things are a bad example for Baby Roo. You will not be repeating that sort of thing, at least where we must see it." She gave Trespassers Will a Daunting Maternal Look. "Will you." This was no question.

"Will I?" Piglet's appended grandfather wore a disquieting smile that twitched up at one corner in a repulsively impish manner. "It is out of my hands. For know this: There is no return for the servant of the Elder Things until the bargain has been fulfilled."

"*What* bargain?" Kanga asked in the very voice that oh, so many mothers use when they have decided they are not going to like whatever answer you give them.

"Oh, bug—er, blast—er, I mean, oh bother," said Pooh. "It's no use; it must be told."

"About time," said Rabbit, whose testiness had the same remedial effect as Owl's pedantry and Eeyore's incessant bellyaching when it came to casting off the burden of unremitting if likewise tedious terror. (One can carry a sense of cosmic dread only so far before it becomes humdrum.)

"You all know you were invited here to welcome Piglet and me back from a great Expotition," Pooh said solemnly. "You did not know until now that it was an Expotition into the shadowed lands of—"

"—madness, I suppose," Eeyore's glum voice barged in. "Unless you were about to say terror? Fright? Pandaemoniac possession? The Romance of Travel? All right for those with the leisure to enjoy such romps. I wouldn't know."

Eeyore might have gone on in this vein were it not for the irruption of a muffled *rustling* from within the Hundred Acre Wood, underscored by a hideous *whispering*, an insectoid *buzzing*, and an insidious *shuffling*, all accompanied by even more descriptive terms that sound much worse when set in italics.

"It comes!" Trespassers Will exulted. "The Shoggoth comes to claim the sacrifice!"

"Kanga, what *is* a sacrifice?" Tigger asked. "Is it a kind of cake?"

"No, dear," said Kanga, and there was *that* in her voice that made Tigger decide not to ask any more questions.

But Pooh had overheard Tigger's question and said, "Sometimes, when you are quite as corrupt and depraved and insistent on worshipping hideous abominations before some vile fane that is not the Church of England, you might decide to court the favor of the monstrous deities you have chosen to serve. So you kill someone as a little gift for them. *That* is a sacrifice. I understand that the Great Old Ones, the Deep Ones, and the Elder Things are rather fond of them when they're feeling peckish."

Tigger stared. "Is that what you did, Pooh?" he asked. "Is that why you talk like a Bear of Very Much Brain now? You know, as a thank-you present from the Old Elders for your sacrifice?"

Pooh shook his head ruefully. "I made no sacrifice . . . then," he replied. "But I did save Pooh's dear friend Piglet from becoming one."

"*Pooh's* dear friend" Owl echoed. "But aren't you—?"

"*I am no Pooh!*" the one who wore the loyal bear's guise thundered. A gnarled staff appeared in one paw, serpents of bewitched lightning crackling up and down its length. "I—" he drew a deep breath and thundered: "—am *Wizard Sanders!* Spawn of Innsmouth! Adjunct Professor of Comatose Languages at Miskatonic University! Avenger of those blasphemous souls who dared translate the *Necronomicon* into Klingon! I am the guardian of this bear!"

"Sanders, you loathsome malediction." Trespassers Will's features twisted into a mask of rage. "What reason could you have to keep watch and ward over a battered plaything like that miserable teddy?"

Sanders sniffed with disdain. "You're not the only one with a mysterious sign, Tressie. Verily it is written in the ancient texts that Winnie-the-Pooh lived under the name of Sanders. That name—*my* name—was inscribed above his door *in gold letters*, and from that vantage my presence might descend to follow him wherever he might go. Except for when Christopher Robin dragged him up and down the stairs, bump, bump, bump. I'm no fool. Ouch." He made a face.

"Preen all you wish over your gold lettered sign," Trespassers Will retorted. "I formed the letters adorning the back of *my* sign with the blood of slaughtered Mi-Go from the Himalayan peaks! I wrote those words of power in characters taken from runic inscriptions that were old when R'lyeh still stood above the waves and great C'thulhu ranged at will across the earth!"

"I know," said Sanders. "You misspelled *wgah'nagl.*"

"Vaunting miscreant!" Trespassers Will shrieked. "Mock me all you like, but know this: The Shoggoth comes, and when it does, there *will* be a sacrifice!"

"*You* were to have been that sacrifice." Sanders shot him a deadly look that would have been more effective if it hadn't come from a teddy bear's face. He pointed his staff at the exulting Trespassers Will. "You bought your power at the promised cost of your existence! You dropped out of my class at Miskatonic and completely threw off the grading curve! You trafficked with arcane forces and hideous beings from beyond our galaxy, but when the time came to pay your debt to them with your own life, you would have thrust your own grandchild—"

"He's not *actually* my—"

"—your own *fabricated* grandchild into the chitinous jaws of—"

"*He's* the one who made me his grandfather. I just exploited the opportunity."

"Be still!" roared Sanders. "The point is, if not for me, you would have seen that innocent die to save your own wretched life!"

Trespassers Will shrugged. "And what did you do about it? Substituted a different innocent to take the place of my sacrificial substitute. There, at the basalt altar that stands in the heart of the Hundred-and-First Acre Wood, where I had laid your—that is, the bear's—friend, you spoke the mystic words that released him and bound over another!"

"As you did before me," Sanders growled.

"Bah. When the Shoggoth comes—" Trespassers Will cast his gaze to the forest whence the assorted italicized weird sounds were still emanating. "—and it's taking its sweet time getting here, I might add—what will you do? Fight a monster you have no chance of destroying? Give your own life to save that of the one you so casually named as Piglet's doomed proxy? Or turn aside as the Shoggoth reaches out its tremelloid appendages for Roo and—"

"What." The word fell like the lid of a sarcophagus. "Roo? *My* Roo?" Kanga clutched her baby close, and her expression . . . changed.

In that moment, all of the creatures learned a 'Strornly Valuable Lesson: When it comes to her little ones, a Mamma can go from sweetness and porridge to *EVERYBODY DIES!* in less time than it takes to blow the fluff from a dandelion. (Yes, my dears, *your* Mamma too.)

"Uhhhhh—" None could say whether that wobbly response came from Wizard Sanders, Trespassers Will, or both, for at that very moment the Shoggoth, in the full panoply of its inborn horror, finally got around to emerging from the Hundred and First Acre to claim what was owed.

None would soon—if ever—forget what next transpired.

Kanga firmly thrust Roo into her pocket. He squeaked a protest which she staunched by cramming half a dozen tea cakes in with him. Her eyes flared with rage which she swiftly disbursed to left and right, targeting first Wizard Sanders, then Trespassers Will.

"We will speak of this later," she said grimly. "If there *is* a later for you." She tore the staff from Sanders' paralyzed grip and raised it high.

"*Iä! Iä! Shub-Niggurath!*" she cried. "Hear me! *Iä! Iä!* The Black Goat of the Woods with a Thousand Young!"

The ground quaked. Black clouds seamed with lightning and swollen with thunder raged across the skies. "*Iä! Iä!*" Kanga's call rang out louder than the thunder, and from the deep places of the malevolent woodland an answer came.

A fresh abomination surged out of the forest, making much better time than the Shoggoth. Its dark, tentacled bulk towered over the smaller monstrosity on surreally tiny, goat-like legs, and from its heaving girth there dropped a constant effluence of smaller entities, some of which scuttled back into the trees, some of which rejoined themselves to their terrifying genetrix.

"Great Outer Goddess!" Kanga shouted. "You, too, are a mother! Protect Baby Roo from those who would mock their service to the Great Old Ones by playing tag-you're-it with the call to sacrifice! May your will and your power be visited upon us and your choice be made plain! And it had best be a *good* choice. You can't have Roo. Try that nonsense and I'll smack you with this stick, just see if I won't!" She waggled the staff in the unearthly being's general direction.

Darkness gushed from the core of Shub-Niggurath. It boiled over the assembled animals, the picnicking field, the festive table. A fulminating breath of eternity engulfed them all, reducing each to a shivering husk held captive in the isolation of their own martyred minds.

Then it was over.

"Well, *that* wasn't too bad." Trespassers Will looked around at the tranquil, sunlit scene with visible pleasure, noting the absence of both the Shoggoth and Shub-Niggurath. "Whew!" He dabbed his brow with a wadded handkerchief.

He promptly crumbled into dust.

Wizard Sanders reclaimed his staff from Kanga and poked the granular remains of his nemesis. "So perish all who would cozen the Great Ones of their due. My work here is done."

"Is it over?" Piglet ventured in his piping voice. He stared at his powdered grandfather. "No more sacrifices, yes? Please?" He silently implored Kanga for a comforting reply.

"I would hope so," she said, scooping Roo out of her pocket and setting her paws to the task of wiping his face clean of crumbs. "I must say, I expected more. It's not like the Outer Gods, let alone the Great Old Ones, to be satisfied with desiccating a sacrifice. Dust doesn't scream enough to suit them. They prefer to pick a victim more likely to groan and wail and whinge and bemoan their deadly fate; the longer, the better. They may be mind-shattering horrors from beyond the stars, but they do like to get value for money." She turned to Pooh, still freighted with the inner presence of Wizard Sanders. "Isn't that so, Professor?"

"I *said* my work here is done," Sanders said rather grumpily. "Now if you will excuse me. . ."

Pooh's body began to shake violently. A gray brume that bore with it a charnel reek enshrouded him for the space of three awful heartbeats before he tumbled to the ground. The mist dispersed. The paroxysm upon his limbs departed. Pooh sat up and blinked at the ring of concerned animals who surrounded him, yet still maintained a judicious distance.

"Has there been a party?" he asked, looking about. "Have I missed it?"

"Not in the usual way," said Eeyore. "Not in the Let's Not Ask Eeyore to Join Us way that seems to be how it's always done around here. We can't all be popular like you, Pooh. Not that I ever expected to be. None of the Mad Social Whirl for this old donkey. Never being mistaken for the Life of the Party. None of this madcap Tra-la-la, Penny for the Guy, Burn the Wicker Man, Cockle-Picking, Cheese-Rolling high life for me. But never mind—as if anyone ever does: I'm accustomed to being overlooked. I suppose I should be grateful for that much. Being disregarded is a little better than being shunned outright, although there may have been a few times—"

A dark eye-studded blob shot out of the woods. It threw a double wreath of tentacles around Eeyore and sped back beneath the trees, making hideous noises that left its mesmerized witnesses convinced that sludge could giggle. The unwholesome sound was accompanied by Eeyore's voice, still dragging an unending litany of complaints in its wake until both were too distant to hear.

"Shoggoths," said Kanga with a shrug. "Say what you will about them, they never leave a job half done."

"What happened?" Pooh asked anyone who might listen.

"We have had an adventure," Piglet said gravely. "You were a Brave Bear, even if you were not quite yourself, and you helped me a great deal."

"Did I?" said Pooh. He scratched his head. "Perhaps I should go help Eeyore too."

"You will do nothing of the sort," said Kanga, appearing at Pooh's side. "We are quite done with all that, and I am sure we all hope never to have to hear one more word of such eldritch goings-on again."

"But—" Pooh tried to protest.

"I had rather not repeat myself, Pooh dear."

"Still, Eeyore—"

"Pooh, if you insist on quarreling with me, you'll be setting a very bad example for Baby Roo."

"But the thing that took him—"

"Not. One. More. Word," Kanga said in a Strict and Warning way. "We have had Difficulties. They are done. We will have no more."

Piglet bustled to the table and returned with a nicely filled plate. "Please listen to Kanga, Pooh," he entreated. "Here. Have some cake."

Pooh accepted the offering. "*F'thagn* you very much," he said.

And that, my dears, proved to be One. More. Word.

The Cat and the Dragon

Kary English

Cat, cat, fluffin MacGuffin,
Thought of himself as tough,
But cat, cat, my little muffin,
Really was mostly fluff.

Cat, cat, hurry-foot, furry-foot,
Scurried across the floor.
Cat, cat, should-he-foot, would-he-foot,
Snuck out the cellar door.

Cat, cat, hitherto, whither-to,
Shouldn't be thought of as dense.
For cat, cat, peek-a-boo ingénue,
Hadn't been past the fence.

Cat, cat, too-aloof murderfloof,
Commonly known as Tig,
Thought he could take on a dragon,
If only they weren't so big.

Up roared the dragon, honking and hissing,
Its prominent wings displayed.
And cat, cat, silly puss, little wuss,
Found himself quite dismayed.

Cat, cat, fun-away, run-away,
Turned on his tail and fled.
Cat, cat, hide-away underway,
Rocketed under the bed.

Cat, cat, play at home, stay at home,
Never again got loose.
For out in the garden he learned a great lesson—
The dragon's true name was *Goose*.

In Which Piglet Sings Cottleston Pie

D. J. Butler

"Don't open the door," Pooh warned Piglet. His voice was a hoarse growl, as it had been for weeks. "Even when they knock."

Having been interrupted at tea, both friends wore handsome waistcoats, slightly dusted with the remains of biscuits.

Piglet turned to see the inside of Pooh Bear's front door. It seemed to rattle and shrink from its hinges, though he heard nothing.

"Will they knock, then?" he asked.

Pooh dove into his pantry and rummaged among the shelves. "Of course they will. They must. Three times."

Piglet chuckled. "Not vampires, then. Vampires only knock once." He was telling the joke to try to boost his own courage.

"Not vampires." Pooh sneaked a glittering black eye around the edge of pantry door. "Much worse than vampires." He returned to his search.

"But three times, you say?"

"Three times!" Pooh's sandpaper whisper was barely audible. "With a decent pause between. The laws of hospitality were ancient in this land before Hengest and Horsa ever drew swords. If this were America, they'd already have come down the chimney."

There came a knock at the door.

Piglet's knees wobbled.

Pooh emerged, stuffing a jar into a leather doctor's bag. "Don't stand there like a fool, Piglet. We must go out the back." Pooh opened the door to the back rooms of his house and shoved Piglet through.

Piglet lurched, barely keeping his balance. Leaning against the wall between the larder and the spare bedroom, he chanced to look into the latter and saw what appeared to be the lower half of Pooh himself, protruding through a window. The yellow rump wiggled from side to side and the two yellow legs scrabbled as if trying to get purchase on the wall.

"What?" he squeaked. "What?"

A second knock came at the front door.

Pooh shut the kitchen door behind him and dragged a chair from the larder, leaning it on two legs and shoving its back beneath the doorknob.

Piglet pointed at the legs.

"Stop gawping," Pooh grunted. "That's not me, obviously."

Pooh grabbed Piglet by the hand and dragged him toward the washroom.

"But who is it?" Piglet asked.

"It's not you, either," Pooh said. "Be grateful. And get into the washroom."

Piglet took two unsteady steps into the washroom, which smelled of carbolic acid and blood. "They'll have to knock three times again at the kitchen door," he suggested.

"You idiot," Pooh snarled. "They are creatures of law, not dunces! What kind of numbwit goes about the interior of a house, knocking at every door? Now climb up the back of the toilet and get that window open!"

"Yes, Pooh." Piglet took a deep breath and scrambled up the toilet. He was small, which made it easy not to fall off. He expected the window to be jammed shut by paint, swollen wood, and age, but someone had run a rasp around the window frame recently and the window practically fell open at his touch.

"I shall teach you how an Oxford man pays his bill when in town," Pooh rumbled.

A third knock was nearly swallowed up in the noise that immediately followed it, a thunderous roar and the great cracking of wood, as if the entire Weald had suddenly burst, every tree trunk splitting in half from top to bottom. Piglet shrieked, and so did the person whose legs dangled from the window in the spare bedroom. An unseen force on the other side slammed into the kitchen door, knocking the chair under the knob to the floor.

The kitchen door flung open—

Pooh shut the bathroom door before Piglet could see what was coming. He turned the key, locking the door, then frowned at Piglet. "Must I tell you what to do at every step? You are the worst thaumaturge's apprentice in the history of the Hundred Acre Wood, at least."

"Am I a thaumaturge's apprentice?" Piglet asked.

Pooh grabbed him with both hands and hurled him through the window. The leather doctor's bag followed, and then Pooh himself squeezed through the wooden frame. He pulled the glass shut behind himself, seized the bag, and lumbered toward the spinney of larches behind the house.

"Come!" he growled. "Our solicitor is waiting!"

Piglet was faster than Pooh, but his legs were short, and he was hard put to keep up. Hearing a scream from the side of Pooh's house, he gasped and ran faster.

"Do you mean Eeyore?" he asked.

"First rule of thaumaturgy," Pooh rumbled. "Have a good attorney. You're going to get sued at law by clients, the enemies of clients, neighbors bystanders claiming to be innocent, the mayors of small towns, nuns, and all sorts of other riffraff. Having a solicitor and barrister you trust will save you money in the long run, no matter what his honorarium."

"Only Eeyore is so . . . sad," Piglet said. "And speaks nonsense."

"He's a pessimist," Pooh said. "And deliberate. Like all the best lawyers." He dashed through the spinney, leaping over familiar roots and turning around the knee-hitting rock.

Piglet knew the spinney nearly as well as Pooh, and could run safely through it even in the twilight. Racing after his friend, he came upon the track on the other side and saw a black carriage and a matching black horse waiting. It was Eeyore's conveyance, known all over the Hundred Acre Wood.

"Pooh," Piglet asked. "Are you an Oxford man?"

"Of course, I am!" Pooh snapped. "Did you take me for a Tab?"

"I took you for a bear of little brain," Piglet mumbled.

"Oh, yes?" Pooh guffawed. "Was that what you thought when I transformed Christopher Robin's umbrella into a boat to snatch you from the jaws of watery death?"

"I . . ." Piglet said. "I . . ."

"One of us has little brain, that's for certain." Pooh opened the carriage. "Get in."

A wet, tearing sound behind Piglet drew a squeak from him and sent him scrambling up into the carriage.

Eeyore sat in the rear-facing seat, gazing coolly at Piglet through his spectacles. "Six ones," Eeyore said. He held a large wooden cup with his right front hoof, covering the top of it with his left. Meeting Piglet's gaze, he shook the cup, once, with a rattling sound, then moved his left front leg to look inside. "Not six ones."

When Pooh joined them, lunging into the carriage with a heavy grunt, Eeyore shut the door behind him, seized a cane that leaned against the wall, and rapped it on the compartment's ceiling.

Piglet heard the crack of a whip and the carriage leaped forward.

"You're going to need this." Pooh drew a card from the pocket of his waistcoat and handed it to Piglet.

The card held only the printed words "COTTLESTON PIE".

"I don't understand," Piglet said.

"I gathered that." Pooh peered out the window into the gathering gloom. "Well, your apprenticeship is entering a new phase, I see. The phase in which you realize that you're an apprentice."

"A posteriori," Eeyore. "That's Latin for, 'from one's bottom.'"

Piglet racked his brain to try to remember the term Pooh had used minutes earlier. "Apprentice thermometer," he said.

"Thaumaturge," Pooh told him. "The current crisis is due to the poor honey season. I can't sing, obviously, so you're going to have to."

"What?" Piglet said, cleverly.

"Six ones." Eeyore shook his cup. "Not six ones."

"The proximate cause is the poor honey season," Eeyore said. "The ultimate cause is the rise of the cost of housing in southeast England."

"What?" Piglet said, incisively.

"The success of London as a commercial and financial center lies behind that, old chap," Pooh countered.

"Corpus delicti," Eeyore said. "In Latin, that means, 'the body is delicious.'"

Piglet looked at the card again. COTTLESTON PIE. "I'm to sing this? Isn't this one of your songs, Pooh?"

"Be that as it may," Eeyore continued, "scarce housing in the vicinity of the capital led to the firm Brickham and Sons Limited purchasing the forested land adjacent to the Hundred Acre Wood, removing the trees, and building in their stead a row of sagging tenements so dispiriting as to make every owner of a two up and two down on a council feel immensely relieved by comparison."

"Progress." Pooh snorted.

"You laugh," Eeyore said, "but in ten years' time, those tenements will be full of bankers."

Piglet looked out the window. Behind them, a cloud rose over Pooh's house. Within the cloud, lightning flashed from time to time. When it did, Piglet could make out faces within the cloud. The faces were pale and angry. They were deformed, with too many eyes or not enough, too many mouths or a complete, expressionless absence. Most of all, the faces were enormous. Any one of the faces, Piglet thought, could open its mouth and swallow the carriage whole.

For the moment, the cloud of faces seemed not to have noticed them.

"Six ones." Rattle. "Not six ones."

"The sad and relevant fact," Pooh said, "is that Brickham and Sons wiped out the local bee population."

"How is that relevant?" Piglet asked.

"I'm getting there," Pooh said.

"But there's a giant cloud of faces, Pooh," Piglet said. "It's so big, I think maybe it could eat the entire wood. Was that cloud of faces knocking on your door? And what does the cloud have to do with bees and council flats and how many ones in a cup and what comes out of my posterior?"

"Stop looking over there," Pooh said. "If they see you looking, they'll realize where we've gone." To Eeyore, he added, "Perhaps a little more speed."

The donkey rapped the ceiling with his cane again. A whip cracked, and the carriage sped up, noticeably.

Piglet tore himself away from the window and stared at the wall of the carriage. "But . . . bees?"

"I'll get there," Pooh rasped. "You focus on 'Cottleston Pie.'"

"What about 'Cottleston Pie'?"

"You're going to sing it, of course." Pooh cleared his throat. "No bees, no honey. And you know what a problem that is for me."

"You love honey." Piglet smiled.

"Quod erat memorandum," Eeyore said. "In Latin, that's, 'now you get the memo.'"

"No, I don't." Pooh sneered. "I don't like honey, as such. But I must have it, and in industrial quantities, to support all the singing."

Piglet felt that several strands of the conversation had finally wiggled around to be close enough to each other that he ought to be able to understand them. He smiled and contemplated the strands—honey, a thaumaturge, singing, six ones, bees, a memorandum, a cloud of faces, a delicious body, Oxford, half a Pooh in a window, brick tenements—but he could make nothing of it.

"I give up," he said.

"Six ones. You must not give up," Eeyore said. Rattle. "You, of all people, must not give up. Not six ones."

"The only thing the apprentice truly has to offer," Pooh grumbled, shaking his head, "is his utter, bloody-minded unwillingness ever to surrender. Even when traveling five hundred fifty miles per hour and singing his head off."

"Pardon?" Piglet said.

"He won't go that fast," Eeyore said. "That's the muzzle velocity of a ball coming out of a Brown Bess, but Piglet here is much larger than a musket ball. I'd be surprised if he goes a hundred miles an hour, ceteris paribus. That's Latin for, 'fast as a pair of buses.'"

"I'd be surprised if I go any miles an hour," Piglet squeaked. "What are you talking about?"

"Six ones. Not six ones."

"The challenge with turning Christopher Robin's umbrella into a boat, incidentally," Pooh said, "lies neither in the materials nor in the shape."

"No," Piglet said, sagely.

"Ipso fatso," Eeyore said. "That's Latin. It means, 'listen to the fatso.' "

"The simple and obvious fact is that the umbrella does not and cannot possibly displace sufficient water to exceed the weight of Christopher Robin, much less Christopher Robin plus myself. So it should have been obvious to you from the moment you saw us paddling along on the flood that something more than mere nature was at play."

"I suppose I was just grateful to be alive," Piglet said. "Also, grateful that you were taking me away so Owl would stop talking to me."

"Owl!" Pooh snorted. "There's a Cambridge man for you."

"Yes," Piglet agreed.

"Summa cum laudanum," Eeyore said. "It means, 'taking a lot of drugs.'"

"Oh!" Pooh said.

"It's the unofficial motto of the Tabs," Eeyore explained.

"It's a paraphrase," Pooh said. "Pocula sacra, don't you know?"

"I don't," Piglet said. "Or do I?"

"Left turn to Owl's house," Pooh said.

Eeyore rapped on the ceiling. "Six ones!" he shouted.

"He means, 'left turn!'" Pooh bellowed. "Take us to Owl's house!"

"We're going to Owl's house now," Piglet said politely. "Why are we going to Owl's house?"

"He has a hearing trumpet that we shall need," Pooh explained.

Piglet hesitated. "To hear the songs?"

"The songs, yes," Pooh said. "You see, I've been defending the Hundred Acre Wood by singing."

"You sing nonsense," Piglet pointed out.

"Six ones," Eeyore said. "Not six ones."

"Six one whats?" Piglet.

"Just six ones," Eeyore said.

"But then it's not six ones," Piglet said. "It never is."

"It is," Eeyore said, "approximately one time in forty-seven thousand."

Piglet shook his head. "What can a thing be one time in forty-seven thousand?"

"Six ones," Eeyore said. He shook the cup. "I wish I'd had another die. Not six ones. Then it would be once in two hundred eighty thousand."

"We shall make it," Pooh said. "Have confidence. You too, Piglet. Soon you shall be doing the randomizing."

"Per se," Eeyore said. "That means, 'by yourself', in Latin."

"By myself what?" Piglet asked. "Six ones?"

"Not six ones," Eeyore said sternly.

"That's rather the point," Pooh said. "How else do you distract, combat, and ultimately destroy a creature of inflexible law?"

"Yes," Piglet said. "What?"

"They're djinn," Eeyore said. "Fallen angels. Cadit quaestio. That means, 'the questor falls.'"

Pooh nodded. "In Latin."

"Yes," Piglet agreed. "What?"

"The questor meaning, in this case," Eeyore explained, "the angel desiring permanent adherence to all law, even to both of the very first commandments, and even when those commandments are incompatible with each other."

"That is many big words," Piglet said.

"Pacta sunt servanda," Eeyore told him. "That's Latin for, 'don't worry too much about it, just do as you're told.'"

Piglet sneaked a glance out the window. Either the cloud of faces was getting bigger, or it was following the carriage.

Or possibly both.

"But the point is," Pooh said, "the singing. The constant nonsense singing served a couple of functions. In the first place, the echoes of the song created a labyrinth in which the Hundred Acre Wood could lie concealed, completely invisible to these creatures."

Piglet looked at his card. "'Cottleston Pie.'"

"Yes," Pooh agreed. "And also, the sheer chaotic creativity created jagged spikes of energy that wounded the beings whenever they drew near. And the other measures that you and I both took, of course."

"I took measures, Pooh?"

"Your measures were valorous, Piglet." Pooh smiled. "You lived under a sign that said, 'Trespassers W.'"

"Yes I did," Piglet admitted. "And I told people that it was my father's name, Trespassers William, just as you instructed me."

"And you adopted the name Henry Pootel," Pooh added.

"When you told me to," Piglet said.

"It was valorous," Pooh told him.

Piglet considered this. "Was it also valorous that you lived under the name of Sanders, Pooh?"

"It was exactly the same kind of valor, Piglet."

Piglet nodded. "Only . . . what kind of valor was it, then?"

"It was the kind of valor that gave out false names to the djinn," Pooh said.

"False names, and different names. So the djinn saw different Piglets and different Poohs whenever they looked, and had a hard time seeing the real us."

"Oh," Piglet said.

"I'll tell you something else," Pooh said.

"What is it, Pooh?"

"My name isn't Pooh," Pooh said.

"It's Winnie-the-Pooh," Piglet said.

"It's not that, either," Pooh said. "My name is Edward."

"Oh," Piglet said. "How valorous."

"Edward Bear. Which leads us back to the honey."

"What about the part where there are djinn?" Piglet asked. "Fallen angels? Who get confused by our valorous use of different names?"

"Oh, that," Pooh said. "Well, I summoned them."

"You're a hypothalamus."

"A thaumaturge," Pooh said.

"Res ipsa locutor," Eeyore offered.

"Latin?" Piglet asked.

"Latin. It means, 'the race goes to the speaker.' "

"Latin seems a very useful language."

"It is." Eeyore nodded. "You must have quite a large brain to use it properly, though."

"You summoned fallen angels, Pooh?" Piglet felt very small, indeed. He felt that his friend of many years was turning out to be a stranger.

"After the war," Pooh said. "I was with Lawrence in the desert. They were strange times. But the point is, no matter how much these creatures have wished to render me uniform and undifferentiated within their law-bound mass, I have protected and hidden myself and the Hundred Acre Wood and Christopher Robin and even you, my little unwitting apprentice, by singing. Until, of course, the honey ran out."

"Six ones," Eeyore announced. "Not six ones."

"The legs in your spare bedroom," Piglet said.

"Stay focused!" Pooh snapped. "The tenements were built, the bees destroyed, the honey ran out, and I no longer had the wherewithal to soothe my throat from the many hours a day of singing nonsense songs to ward off the djinn."

"Your throat got sore," Piglet said. "There was no more honey, so you couldn't sing, so the fallen angels found you."

"Tea without honey is abominable," Pooh said. "With sugar, it's worse."

"And now you need me to do the singing," Piglet continued.

"Yes," Eeyore said. "And also to bear the randomizers. Fortunately, your waistcoat has pockets."

"Why is that fortunate?" Piglet asked.

Eeyore shrugged. "Six ones." He shook the cup and looked inside. "Not six ones."

"Are those dice you've got in that cup?" Piglet obviously. "Are you shaking dice?"

"Prima facie," Eeyore said. "Which in Latin means, 'about time you faced it.' "

"To save the Hundred Acre Wood," Piglet added.

"Yes," Pooh said, "as we fire you into the cloud of fallen angels using Christopher Robin's gun."

The carriage rattled to an abrupt halt.

"What?" Piglet asked.

"Stay here," Pooh said. "I shall return shortly." He slipped out of the carriage.

"What are the two very first commandments again?" Piglet asked. "Is one of them the one about the donkey?" He remembered that there was a commandment about a donkey, and how you shouldn't cover it, and, as Eeyore was present, perhaps those facts constituted a pertinent connection.

"Have babies," Eeyore said. "And do not eat the fruit."

"Oh," Piglet said. "What?"

"Six ones," Eeyore told him. "Not six ones."

"Do the six ones hurt the djinn?" Piglet asked.

"They are chaos," Eeyore said. "And as they run counter to my stated expectation, they create more chaos. Unless, I suppose, I said, 'six ones,' and then rolled six ones."

"What would happen then?"

"I rather suppose the djinn would eat us."

"Corpus delicti," Piglet said. "The body is delicious."

"There you have the gist of it," Eeyore said. "Perhaps if you decide that thaumaturgy is not for you, you might go into law."

Pooh reappeared, climbing into the carriage. He held an oversized ear trumpet. Before he sat, he banged his fist against the ceiling and called out, "Christopher Robin's!"

The carriage lurched into forward motion again.

"That was fast," Eeyore said. "Owl wasn't in a talkative mood, then."

"Owl is always in a talkative mood," Pooh said. "Tab that he is. So rather than provoke him into gabbing, I simply walked into his house and took what I wanted. Anyway, it's daytime, so he was asleep."

Pooh held the hearing trumpet up against Piglet as he talked, scrutinizing the funnel-shaped device and his apprentice hypothalamus.

"Jus necessitatis," Eeyore said. 'The juice was needed,' in Latin."

Piglet chuckled warily. "You look as if you're seeing whether I can wear that hearing trumpet as a frock, Pooh."

"Yes," Pooh said. "That's a good way to think of it."

"So the angels didn't want to have babies," Piglet said.

"What nonsense have you been telling him while I was gone?" Pooh demanded of Eeyore.

"The boy didn't even know what the commandments were," Eeyore said. "Thought there was a donkey involved. What sort of apprentice is he?"

"He's an apprentice who will fit inside the hearing trumpet!" Pooh snapped.

"Yes," Eeyore agreed. "There is that."

"Look, it's simple," Pooh said. "You remember the story the vicar tells about how God put Adam and Eve in the garden, and he said, 'there's this fruit over here, don't eat it.'"

"Yes," Piglet said truthfully.

"And he also said to them, 'go forth and multiply.'"

"Yes," Piglet said triumphantly. "Yes, Pooh, I remember that."

"Six ones." Rattle. "Not six ones."

"There you go," Pooh said. "Had to choose one or the other, didn't they? Couldn't do both, could they?"

"Ipso fatso," Eeyore said.

"I suppose," Piglet said, not convinced.

"So certain of the angels believe that man has sinned, and must now be punished for that," Pooh continued. "They believe that they continue to enforce the law. Indeed, they believe that God Himself has broken the law."

"God?" Piglet said.

"Because God told Adam that on the day he ate the fruit, he would die. Only he didn't. So God told a porky, you see, so God's a sinner."

"That's not what the vicar said."

"Right," Pooh agreed. "This is what the djinn say. The fallen angels."

"It seems a very strange opinion," Piglet said. "But then, they seem very strange creatures."

Pooh nodded. "And they believe that God and man alike have fallen, along with the rest of God's creation. Only these fierce, law-enforcing, pitiless angels remain true to their charter. And so they hound man like a plague, for being a lawbreaker and for seducing God into breaking his word."

"Only you're not a man, Pooh," Piglet said. "You're a bear."

"That's a detail, Piglet!" Pooh snapped. "Are we here to quibble about theology or save the world?"

"I suppose I'm not sure of the answer to that," Piglet said slowly. "Considering the day I've had so far."

"Save the world, of course!" Pooh bellowed.

"Six ones. Not six ones."

"By wearing a hearing trumpet," Piglet said.

"By being fired from a gun, rather," Pooh told him.

"You said that before," Piglet said. "What does it have to do with djinn?"

"It's all very well and good deliberately to manufacture chaos as a cloak and shield," Pooh said, "so long as the djinn were elsewhere, looking for me. And for Lawrence, of course."

"But the honey ran out," Eeyore said. "Inter alia. That's Latin for, 'plus all the other things.' "

"My voice got hoarse," Pooh said. "I couldn't sing. By the time the trick of the dice occurred to me, the djinn had found us. There's no hiding now. We have to take the fight to them."

"By shooting the fallen angels with a gun." Piglet looked out the window. The faces in the cloud leered at him.

Pooh dragged Piglet back inside. "Don't attract their attention!"

"Six ones. Not six ones."

"You can't shoot a cloud, Pooh," Piglet said. "Only a madman would shoot a cloud."

"I'm not going to shoot the cloud." Pooh laughed. "I'm going to shoot you at the cloud. With pockets full of dice, singing 'Cottleston Pie.'"

"That still seems like something a madman would do."

"It's a good plan," Eeyore said.

But Eeyore hadn't denied that it was the plan of a madman.

"We'll fire the jagged randomness right into the heart of the djinn," Pooh said. "If it doesn't kill them outright, it will disperse them and give us a chance to get our concealing devices back into place."

"What will happen to me, Pooh?" Piglet asked.

Pooh clapped him on the shoulder. "You'll be a hero."

"Oh." Piglet looked at the card again. "But you haven't written any verses here."

"'Cottleston Pie' isn't a song with fixed verses," Pooh told him. "That's the point. You've got to make up the verses each time. That's the creativity, the randomness, the jagged edges and so on."

"I remember a verse about a chicken," Piglet said. "It seemed a nice verse."

"I don't remember it at all," Pooh said. "I have made up a thousand verses to that song. Nay, ten thousand. Now you've got to make some up."

"I'll make up some right now," Piglet said.

"Fine," Pooh agreed. "Only don't say them now. Hold them in your head and say them while you're arriving at the cloud of djinn. If you say them now and then say them again later, you've added order to the world, when what we want is for you to add chaos."

"I see," Piglet said.

"Six ones," Eeyore said. "Not six ones."

"Are you thinking?" Pooh asked.

"Yes," Piglet said. "But I'm having a difficult time thinking of anything."

"Compos mentis," Eeyore told him. "Which is a Latin explanation that says, 'you've got to have compost for your mind.'"

"To be fertile," Pooh said.

"Yes," Piglet agreed.

"So as to have verses blossoming," Pooh added.

"How do I have compost for the mind, Pooh?"

"Compost is rotten eggs and grass clippings," Eeyore said. "Try pondering rotten eggs and grass clippings."

"Yes," Pooh said. "Here we are."

They had reached the top of the forest, and Christopher Robin's house with the green door. The carriage stopped and Christopher Robin leaned in the window.

"Hello, Piglet," Christopher Robin said. "How are you feeling?"

"I'm Henry Pootel," Piglet said. "And I'm feeling valorous."

"That's the spirit," Pooh said.

"I'm thinking about rotten eggs and grass clippings," Piglet said.

"I hope that helps." Christopher Robin handed his gun in through the carriage window. Pooh took it and nodded.

"Christopher Robin," Piglet said, "what happens after one is a hero?"

"Ah," Christopher Robin said. "I can see why this would be on your mind."

"I'm being valorous," Piglet said. "I shall try to be a hero. Then what?"

"Six ones," Eeyore said. "Not six ones."

"Don't bother Christopher Robin," Pooh said. "We have work to do."

"It's only that I'm rather nervous," Piglet said. "And when I'm nervous, I have a difficult time thinking about rotten eggs and grass clippings."

Christopher Robin folded his arms on the carriage window and rested his chin on his arms. Piglet tried not to notice the sound of howling wind, wind with voices in it.

"Well, Mr. Pootel," Christopher Robin said. "My understanding is that an ordinary person becomes a hero precisely by not thinking about what's going to happen after the moment when he does his heroic deed."

"Ad hoc," Eeyore said. "Which is Latin, and means, 'even to the point of being a hawk.' "

"Does it?" Christopher Robin asked. "I rather thought it meant something like, 'made up on the spot.' "

"Have you considered a career at the bar?" Eeyore asked.

"I have far too many other things to do, I'm afraid," Christopher Robin said. "Good luck, Mr. Pootel. You are indeed valorous, and you are the hero we need for the times we live in."

"Thank you, Christopher Robin."

"Six ones. Not six ones."

Pooh rapped the ceiling of the carriage with the gun and shouted something, but Piglet was too distracted to hear what.

"Prepare the projectile," Pooh said. He pulled the jar from his doctor's bag. It had the word LARD printed on it.

"Prepare what?" Piglet asked.

"Er, prepare Mr. Pootel," Pooh said. "For his inaugural flight."

Piglet looked at the card. "Cottleston Cottleston Cottleston Pie," he intoned.

"Don't you dare waste any verses," Pooh snapped. "Think them in your head, prepare, but do not say them aloud. Wait until you are launched. Ideally, until you are in the cloud." He took the lid off the jar, reached in, and removed a dollop of white fat. He smeared this fat around the narrow end of the hearing trumpet. Then he wiped his paw on his waistcoat.

Piglet looked out the window. The cloud of faces seemed to rage directly above the carriage. Lightning flashed in their eyes and along their teeth.

"If I stop rolling the dice," Eeyore brayed, "the djinn may see us."

"They shall see us soon enough, regardless!"

"Habeas corpus," Eeyore said. "They shall have the body."

The donkey reached into his cup, extracting one large ivory die at a time and tucking them into pockets in Piglet's waistcoat.

"They are rather large dice," Piglet observed.

"You have rather small pockets," Eeyore countered. "Would you consider swallowing just a few of the dice?"

"Could I hold them in my hands?" Piglet asked.

"You'd likely drop them," Eeyore pointed out. "And if you keep them in your mouth, you won't be able to sing. Just two dice, look, the other four fit into your pockets."

Piglet sighed, but swallowed two dice. They felt very chunky and angular, going down his throat.

Pooh, meanwhile, jammed the narrow end of the hearing trumpet down into the barrel of Christopher Robin's gun. He twisted the trumpet tighter and tighter, until it would no longer move, and the gun now opened in a funnel-like shape.

The carriage stopped.

"No time to lose," Pooh said. "Don't vomit."

He and Eeyore spilled from the carriage, dragging Piglet after them. They stood on a mound of earth capped with a large stone. "What is this place?" Piglet asked.

"I think of this as the Cottleston Stone," Pooh said, "though it isn't."

"It isn't?"

"Properly, it has no name. But I have sung many verses of 'Cottleston Pie' here, so the echoes should be propitious."

"The echoes will help me?"

"They may hide you. Make it harder for the djinn to see you."

Piglet looked up into the cloud. Faces stared back at him, faces that overlapped and stretched across the sky. They were smeared and distorted faces, larger than hills.

They opened their mouths, revealing teeth the size of houses.

Pooh stood beside the Cottleston Stone and laid the gun on it, pointing the funnel toward the cloud. "Get him into position, counsellor."

"Up you go." Eeyore hoisted Piglet up onto the rock.

"Is it too early to sing, Mr. Sanders?" Piglet asked.

"Wait until launch, Mr. Pootel. And, ah, it's best if the verses don't make too much sense. Now kindly oblige me by seating yourself in the trumpet."

Piglet got in. "It tickles my a posteriori a little bit."

"As it should," Eeyore said. "Bona fide. That's Latin for, 'this is for real now.'"

"Yes it is." Piglet looked at Pooh sighting up along the barrel of the gun, then squeezed himself as far down into the hearing trumpet as he was able. He looked up at the faces. They howled and stretched their jaws wide. He saw a tongue as big as the Hundred Acre Wood wagging at him, lightning crackling all along its length. "I shall be a hero now, and not think about what comes next."

"You're already a hero," Eeyore said. "Res judicata. That's Latin for 'a race that has already been judged.'"

"Three," Pooh called, "two, one . . ."

The gun kicked with a loud boom and Piglet launched into the open mouth of the cloud of djinn, singing.

> Cottleston Cottleston Cottleston Pie
> Pooh is a wizard and neither am I
> A face is a friend unless it's in the sky
> Cottleston Cottleston Cottleston Pie

He patted his waistcoat, feeling the dice. The wind struck him in the face with great force as he raced upward, and the dice seemed to be spinning. He looked down and saw Pooh and Eeyore watching him, hands shading their eyes. He smelled ozone and felt the little hairs on the backs of his hands and arms stand up.

> Cottleston Cottleston Cottleston Pie
> Tea without honey is not fit to try
> A gun and a trumpet can make a pig fly
> Cottleston Cottleston Cottleston Pie

"Six ones!" he shouted into the oncoming gray faces. "Not six ones!" He felt the dice in hie belly tumble and thought it might make him feel ill if it went on too long.

His vision went dark and the air turned chill and damp and he plunged into the cloud of djinn.

> Cottleston Cottleston Cottleston Pie
> I've dice in my belly and I don't know why
> But Pootel's a hero with no fear to die
> Cottleston Cottleston Cottleston Pie

Lightning flashed about him.

In Which Christopher Robin Visits the In–Between Places

Alex Shvartsman

Look for me in the in-between places, Chris recalls having been told by his childhood best friend. At least, he thinks he recalls it. Memories from the time of the Haze are not to be trusted.

The memories of Edward's voice and his face are as clear as they are impossible. *Seek me out in the deepest heart of the forest, in the perpetual shadow cast by the mighty oaks,* the stuffed toy bear had told him. This is not helpful, Chris thinks as he walks through a clearing in a wooded area sparsely populated by trees. This is not directions; it's not even a clue. A hundred acres may have seemed like an entire world to a child, but to his adult gaze it is a small, sad patch of abandoned land.

Even so, his quarry is nowhere to be found.

No matter. He can cover all of it, crisscross the Hundred Acre Wood, leave no stone unturned. He picks up the pace, marches through the clearings and the thickets to the accompaniment of chirping insects. He's all alone, walking faster, faster, but he can't outrun his thoughts.

There's no sense of wonder, no majesty. Even the colors aren't the vivid, vibrant palette he recalls. Everything is mundane. Rotting leaves squelch under his feet, and his boots leave muddy imprints in the moist soil. Nothing is the way Chris remembers it, the way he'd seen it through the prism of innocence, through the prison of a few well-placed suggestions, through the hallucinatory haze of mind-altering honey.

They say one can never step into the same river twice—one can never revisit one's childhood. That is fine by Chris. There's no nostalgia, no saccharine memories from the time of his life that couldn't possibly have been, the events that couldn't have played out the way his traitorous brain claims to recall. His right hand shakes until he reaches back and clenches the stock of the old hunting rifle slung over his shoulder. The gun feels cool and smooth, and it calms him somewhat.

His boot makes a slurping sound as he extracts it from a muddy patch of dirt. The imprint quickly fills with fetid water. He forces himself to steady his pace, to pay closer attention to his surroundings, to focus on the sole reason he chose to return to this place:

To kill Edward Bear.

Chris stumbles upon Rabbit's dwelling by sheer luck. It is a hut built of dilapidated wood with a straw roof covered by fallen leaves. It's not the hole in the ground that he seems to recall Edward getting stuck in one time, but the hut sits impossibly low and is built in the shape of a hill. Perhaps there's method to the madness of the memories of the Haze, after all. The structure blends into the background, so much so that Chris would've passed it by had he taken a slightly different path.

He's about to knock when he pauses at the narrow entrance which could well be the mouth of a cave and not a shoddy door built by someone who's had only a passing acquaintance with carpentry. Whatever is on the other side of the door couldn't possibly be a talking rabbit. Talking rabbits do not exist; drug-induced hallucinations do. Rage wells within Chris's gut and he knocks firmly on the door, his knuckles rapping against the rotting wood.

There's a scuffling noise inside. Someone answers, but Chris can't make out the words. Is it Rabbit? Is it one of his many family members—children, cousins, unspecified relations Chris has heard so much about but can't recall ever meeting in person?

"Hello?" Chris calls out tentatively. He struggles to keep his voice even. "May I come in?"

There's another unintelligible response, but Chris can see that the door isn't locked, doesn't even have a lock. He pulls, finds that the door opens inward, then pushes. He steps inside before he can lose his courage.

Chris is a man of average height, yet he has to slouch in order to avoid bumping against the ceiling. The small room inside is illuminated with a lantern. The candlelight flickers and casts long shadows on bare wooden walls. A junk-yard velvet couch stands in the middle of the room.

A skeletally thin, diminutive man of indeterminate age is sitting at the edge of the couch. His pupils are dilated, his gaze constantly darting, as though he's attempting to track several jumping fleas at once. His fingers absent-mindedly stroke the couch cushion as if it were a cat. The couch's color could once have been described as loud fuchsia, but it's been muted with age and dirt. The cushions are threadbare and stained.

This man is Rabbit. Chris is sure of it, even though he has no memories of the man's face. He remembers the twitchy mannerisms. They're the same mannerisms he's seen so often in rehab. The thought triggers a flashback. It's not an image or a sound, but a taste; the sweet, irresistible savor of honey. Chris shudders, and bites his tongue hard. The sharp pain and taste of copper exorcise the ghost flavor.

"Hey, Rabbit," he says. "It's me, Chris. Christopher Robin."

Rabbit's head turns sharply and cocks, like a bird. He stares past Chris with those enormous pupils.

"Christopher," he says in a voice of a person trying on an unfamiliar word. Then there's a spark of recognition and the malnourished man smiles, revealing several yellow, rotten teeth separated from each other by wide gaps. "Pooh's friend."

Pooh. The name triggers memories of honey withdrawal, of sweating and screaming and clawing at his skin. A name he swore he'd never utter again.

Chris grimaces at Rabbit in a failed attempt at mirroring his smile. "Yeah. Edward's friend. That's right." He makes a gargantuan effort to get a grip. "Do you know where he is?"

"Naw," says Rabbit. "Haven't seen Bear in an age."

There's something peculiar to how the addict's jaw tightens, how he pauses for just a moment too long before delivering his response, how his dirty fingernails dig deeper into the couch cushion.

"I need to find him," Chris presses. He takes a step closer. The stench of tobacco and urine emanating from Rabbit overpowers the general smell of decay in the hut. "I've got a bit of money. Help me, and I can give you some, so you can buy something to . . . eat."

He knows exactly how the money will be spent. Rabbit licks his cracked lips, squeezes the couch cushion tight. If it were a cat, he'd be choking it.

"I haven't seen him," Rabbit repeats.

Chris isn't buying that. He knows addicts. Rabbit should have lied, invented whatever story he thought might sound plausible to get his hands on that money. Something isn't right.

He thinks back to the times Edward would visit Rabbit, with young Chris in tow. The two adults would mostly talk of incomprehensible or boring things. And every time Rabbit would spin a story about his many friends and relations, Chris would wonder how come they were never around . . .

"What about your family?" asks Chris. "Maybe one of them knows something?"

Rabbit's gaze darts toward a hole in the back wall. It's much smaller than the already-tiny front door, barely the size of a ventilator window. Except it's at ground level, and the scant illumination from the lantern isn't enough to see where it leads.

Rabbit re-focuses on his visitor just as quickly. "They don't know anything," says Rabbit. "They haven't seen Bear lately, either."

Chris is tired of the lies. Confronting one's past is exhausting. No one should be forced to do it. "Are you sure?" he asks. He points toward the hole. "Why don't we ask them?"

Rabbit leans forward. His entire body tenses. One moment he's a twitchy herbivore, the next he's a predator ready to pounce. "No. I think it's time for you to go, Christopher Robin." There's an almost wistful quality to his words, as though he's deeply sorry to see Chris depart. "You managed to leave Pooh Bear behind once. You should do that again. Before it's too late."

Pooh. The name refuels Chris's rage. A dozen feral cats claw at his frayed soul from the inside like it's a scratching post. He's not going to slink away in the night, not this time.

Chris glares at Rabbit. What's he hiding? Why such a strong reaction? He thinks back to the bad old days, struggles to separate strands of memories from the handful of dreams and the abundance of nightmares.

The hole! That's where Edward Bear had got himself stuck. It wasn't the front door, it was this hole, and Rabbit was none too pleased then, either. Could that be it? Could Rabbit be hiding Edward Bear deep in the bowels of this hovel? Why else would he fail to take Chris's money?

Chris doesn't say anything. He ignores Rabbit, zeroes in on the hole. On where Edward is hiding. He takes several unsteady steps toward the back wall.

Rabbit tackles him from behind. He knocks Chris to the ground. Chris rolls onto his back. Rabbit punches him in the gut, the groin, and the ribs with the manic strength of a junkie. Chris is disoriented, grunts in pain as he tries to block those punches, to shove Rabbit off of him. Up close, the stench coming off Rabbit is overwhelming, making Chris gag.

Something is pressing painfully into Chris's back and he realizes it's his rifle. He contorts and grabs for the gun, his muscles aching in protest. Rabbit mumbles incoherently as he presses his attack, punching and gouging, his overgrown fingernails digging into skin uncomfortably near to Chris's eyes.

Chris strikes and the butt of the rifle connects to his assailant's temple with a soft, sickening *thud.* Rabbit ceases his attack and sits on the ground, dazed. He exhales a wheezing, low groan. Then he leans back slowly, peacefully, as though lying down for a leisurely nap, until the back of his head connects with the unvarnished wooden flooring and he's still.

Chris watches this as though from a great distance. He thinks he should feel something. Pity? Concern? An adrenaline rush that comes with besting an enemy? None of those emotions breach the surface of intellectual thought, of cold detachment. Instead, he finds comfort in the rage he feels toward Edward Bear. He grasps onto it, like an old, abusive friend. Then he crawls toward the hole that leads deeper into Rabbit's dwelling and sticks his head in.

There's only pitch black inside, but Chris has survived far worse things to ever fear the dark. He's thinner than Bear's pudgy ursine frame. Even so, he struggles as he digs deeper, deeper into the ground. The damp cool dirt swaddles him in a calming embrace, but it's not cold enough to extinguish his fury.

He emerges on the other end of the tunnel like a newborn babe, covered in dirt and grime instead of amniotic fluid. There's a cellar under the hut that's almost as tall as the hut itself, which is not very tall at all, and leaves Chris crawling on his hands and knees. He fumbles for a flashlight in one of his pockets and the bright, concentrated beam blinds his eyes, which have already grown used to the meager light from the lantern.

When Chris can finally see, he wishes he couldn't.

All around him are corpses. Stacked on top of each other like firewood logs, the desiccated cadavers line the walls, each wrapped in a burlap sheet. They are old enough for the faces to have rotted off. Empty eye sockets stare at him in anonymous indifference.

Chris scoots backward until he reaches the hole, presses his shoulder blades and the back of his head into the packed dirt above it. The terror, the disgust he knows he should be feeling never breach the surface. Those emotions roil like great pelagic monsters under a sheet of ice, muted and unknowable. All Chris can think of are the childhood memories of the Haze, a stuffed teddy bear having tea with a plush rabbit, the rabbit regaling them both with comfortable tales of his family's adventures.

Those supposed family members, stacked atop each other in a mass mausoleum, tell Christopher no tales of their own.

He wonders if Edward Bear is among the dead, uncertain whether to root for or against such a possibility. Then, another realization dawns upon him, an emotion breaching thick Arctic ice and chilling Chris to the bone.

The decedents are all very small. Too small for any of them to have been Edward.

Children.

Chris can't stand to spend another moment at the bottom of Rabbit's hole. He claws his way out, terrified of getting stuck the way Edward did.

Along the way, his mind conjures scenarios that are marginally more palatable to his heart. Perhaps those are short people. Perhaps Rabbit had cut them off at the knees, the stumps concealed under layers of burlap . . . there are so many of them, fitted into such a small space. When Chris emerges again it's a reverse of the birthing process. He has erected mental barriers, wrapped his mind deep within the womb of the perceived safety of the self.

He stretches out painfully to his full height and bumps his head against the hut's ceiling. When he steps toward Rabbit's body still lying unconscious on the ground it is no longer with any thought of helping the man, of checking his vital signs. Instead, Robin tightens the grip on his rifle with both hands.

A gunshot reverberates through the all-too-mundane trees and bushes of the Hundred Acre Wood like a crackle of thunder. A flock of startled birds takes flight in the distance. Then, all is still again, and the symphony of branches caressed by the wind and chirping insects resumes once again.

It is an overcast afternoon. Clouds pregnant with impending rain hang low in the sky, and bleak sunlight peeks through the occasional jagged rip in the cloud cover. Chris marches through copse and spinney, down open slopes of crabgrass and buckthorn, over rocky beds of streams, up steep banks of sandstone and into the buckthorn again; and so at last, tired and hungry, he stumbles upon a picturesque cottage nestled among pumpkin patches and flowerbeds overgrown with weeds.

This is the Chestnuts Cottage. Chris recalls having visited here several times during the Haze. The paint has peeled in places and lichen climbs the cottage walls. The once-thick growths of blooming flowers are mostly dead, with only a few primroses surviving among the unwanted vegetation. Despite all the changes, this is still the home of Owl that he remembers.

There is a bell-pull and the knocker, and Chris recalls something about an elaborate code Owl and Edward had used. He doesn't know the proper order to use them so instead he bangs his fist on the stained wood door insistently.

"Coming!" A female voice announces from somewhere within the cottage, followed by a soft patter of footsteps.

A door creaks open and a woman in her late forties peeks out.

"What can I do for you, young man?" she asks.

She wears a floral pattern summer dress and her brunette hairdo is streaked with gray. Her facial expression is placid, lips on a verge of breaking into a smile. But her eyes, set deep behind large round glasses, are inquisitive and focused, boring into him with the intensity of a nocturnal predator.

"Owl?" he asks. The only images from the Haze are those of a human-sized bird, wise and non-threatening, perched atop a chair by the fireplace. But those eyes, they're the same eyes he remembers.

The woman laughs softly. "It's been a long time since anyone's called me that. The name's Charlotte." The eyes watch him, unblinking. "And who might you be?"

"Chris," he says. "We met when I was little."

There's surprise in those eyes. She stiffens, but the lips finally spread into a big, welcoming smile.

"Christopher? Christopher Robin? My, how you've grown." She opens the door wide. "What a nice and unexpected surprise." She moves aside. "Come in, come in."

Inside the cottage is neat and tidy and safe in all the ways his childhood hadn't been.

"Sit, sit," Charlotte coos as she ushers him toward the soft, ample armchair by the fireplace. "Would you like some tea?"

Chris is hungry and cold, and his rumbling stomach wins out over his caution. He drinks the aromatic tea with a generous helping of milk and sugar, and scarfs down cucumber sandwiches.

Having cleared the cup and plate, Charlotte sits in the rocking chair opposite him. "Now," she says, "what brings you here?"

"I need to find Edward Bear."

Her placid veneer cracks for only a moment, but long enough for Chris to notice. She takes off those large round glasses, cleans the lenses with a handkerchief, puts them back on.

"You don't want to find him, dear. Trust me on that."

His instinct is to shout, to argue, but what's left of his better angels convince him otherwise. He looks Owl in the eye, his gaunt face reflecting in her lenses. "There's a difference between *want* and *need*," he says evenly.

Owl . . . no, Charlotte. He must use her real name. Charlotte studies him for a time and sighs, the weight of the world on her shoulders.

"You are the boy who left," she says. It's not a question so much as a declaration.

"I am," says Chris.

"It couldn't have been easy."

Chris flashes back to the rehab, to the chills and the nightmares.

"It wasn't," he says.

"You do not remember things as they were," Charlotte says. "You have questions. Curiosity is a relentless taskmaster. It's what drives you to return."

It's the rage that drives him. Rage is the ultimate taskmaster, able to extract any price from its charge. But Charlotte doesn't need to know that, so Chris merely nods.

"There's an ecosystem to the Hundred Acre Wood," says Charlotte. "Your leaving had unbalanced it. It teetered, but with time it settled back into the proper routine, as any resilient system is prone to do. You coming back is no longer necessary, it can't help things. And also, it can't help *you*. I know that you have no reason to believe me, but you should leave and never return here." She sees the expression on his face and raises her hands, palms outward. "I'll help you if you insist, but I hope you heed my warning."

"I need to find Edward," Chris says again.

"Very well," says Charlotte. "I did warn you." She leans in conspiratorially. "You must look for him in the in-between places."

Chris recoils as if slapped. What is this nonsense? Is she mocking him? She looks back at him with sympathy.

"I've heard that before," says Chris. "I don't know where that is."

"You can never find him in this state, not if you search for a lifetime," Charlotte explains. "You must look for him in-between what's real and what's perceived, and there's only one way to achieve that."

She walks into the kitchen. Chris knows what's coming, he can feel his body tense, yearn, revolt, all at the same time. An icy fist grips his heart, a counterbalance to his boiling rage.

Charlotte returns with a small saucer of honey. Chris can smell it from across the cottage; the urge to run out the door and the urge to dash toward the saucer are equally overwhelming. She places the saucer on the arm of his chair.

The honey does not look the way he remembers it from the Haze. It is radioactive-green. A thin coat of foam glistens on its surface. It wiggles with the consistency of gelatin. There's nothing Chris has ever wanted more in his life.

It takes a gargantuan effort for him to look away. "Never again," he whispers the mantra he's repeated so many times in rehab.

"This is the only way you will find Edward Bear," says Charlotte.

Rage wells up, melts the ice around his heart. Chris will do anything to get his revenge. *It's merely an excuse*, whispers the rational part of his brain. *A lie you tell yourself so you can use again.* He disregards those thoughts. His shaking hands reach for the saucer.

Charlotte rests her palm on his shoulder. "We have to get the dosage just right. Too little, and you won't access the in-between. Too much . . ." She pauses, searching for the right words. "Too much, and you'll see the world the way you used to again."

Chris swallows hard. His hands grip the sides of the armchair. He looks up at Charlotte, pleading.

Charlotte smiles at him with her lips, but not with her eyes. "Don't worry, dear. I'll help you."

She leans in close to the saucer armed with a silver teaspoon. A grinning bear face is stamped on the spoon handle's decorative knob.

CHRIS STUMBLES through two different versions of the Hundred Acre Wood. *Blink.* He traverses an ordinary woodland, ground and trees and sky painted in bleak colors. It's beginning to drizzle, tiny droplets of cold rain touching tentatively against his skin. *Blink.* He stumps through a lush forest, vibrant and majestic, sunlight from a cloudless sky warming his face. *Blink.* He forces himself to focus, to seek out a tree here, a hill there that look similar in both versions of reality, and he presses onward in his single-minded pursuit.

A taste of honey is never enough. When it passed his lips, it was a mixture of terror and ecstasy. Only rage, that deplorable taskmaster, had been enough to let him keep his composure, not to devour the entire saucer, not to lunge at Charlotte and grab for it when she took it away. Now that he's had a dose of it, his brain and his body are screaming *more, more, more,* drowning out the sounds of the forest, along with everything else but the rage.

Chris holds on to that emotion like a beacon, and follows it where it may lead. He must sustain it, feed it like a smoldering fire, so that it may burn brighter and illuminate his path. His honey-fueled memories are sharper, more three-dimensional than before.

There he is, dressed in shorts and a plaid shirt that's a size too large, chatting with a gaggle of children. He regales them with tales of talking stuffed animals and of wild woozles inhabiting the East Pole. Some children laugh at him, others listen intently. Finally, a couple of them follow him when he promises to show them a live heffalump. He's a Judas goat, leading others deep into the Wood, toward the Very Deep Pit, where Bear waits.

Bear had made him an addict, which is bad enough. But he had also made him a monster, damned his soul if such a thing exists, and for that there must be a reckoning.

Chris halts abruptly. He grasps on to the slippery, elusive eel of a memory before it can wiggle away. Bear, waiting by the Very Deep Pit. He shrugs off the in-between nonsense, the hallucinations, the doubt. He remembers the where, if not the why, of the pit. He turns and marches in that direction.

The deeper into the Wood he ventures, the more his two realities seem to merge. The trees are closer together, taller, thicker with bright-green leaves. It's getting colder, and sparse heavy raindrops roll down his cheek like tears.

He comes upon a pond, too wide to jump across. The still water is mostly undisturbed by the occasional raindrop. Several slick stepping stones offer a shortcut across.

Chris approaches the edge of the pond and leans in, to gauge its depth and whether it's safe to cross. He sees his reflection.

A stuffed bear stares back at him with beady little sewn-in eyes.

Chris stumbles back, trips, lands on the bed of wet leaves atop the dirt.

This is the honey playing tricks on his mind. On his knees Chris crawls toward the pond. He inches forward with the caution of approaching a chained guard dog that's baring its teeth. He leans forward again. He recoils and screams.

<hr>

CHRIS DOESN'T KNOW how much time has passed before he tries again. He mind roils. His anger wells up within like so much magma that's lost its path, and doesn't know how or if it can ever become lava. Eventually, he forces himself back to the pond's edge and takes a long look.

He wishes desperately to blame it on the trick of the light, on the honey, on anything else, but he knows the truth now. He remembers. He admits it to himself, swallows it like a bitter pill.

He's Bear.

The realization opens the floodgate of memories, and they ooze out like bile and spittle from someone trying to heave on an empty stomach.

Once upon a time, a very long time ago, a man named Sanders had approached a young Christopher Robin and told him about the Hundred Acre Wood. Chris had listened to the stories, mouth agape, and it had sounded like the best place in the world. When Sanders had offered to show him a live heffulump, Christopher had followed him without hesitation.

Chris never knew what motivated Sanders to spare him, feed him honey, adopt him into his dark enterprise. He had been too young to ask questions like that, and his mind was too addled by the Haze. It was only once he got older that he figured it must've been because, unlike all the other children, he too appeared as a stuffed animal once they entered the Wood. The Wood itself had accepted him as one of its own. He became Sanders's protégé, his assistant, his Judas goat. Time and again, he'd lured kids into the Wood, toward the Very Deep Pit where the Bee lived.

Innocence is the secret ingredient, Sanders had told him. *The Bee feeds on it so it can make honey.*

When Sanders died, Christopher had tried to feed him to the Bee, but it had rejected the offering outright. There was no innocence to be had there. Then Christopher had stepped up, taken over Sander's role. He became Edward Bear.

They had been an efficient team of monsters. Everyone had a role to play: Bear had masterminded the operation. Owl had processed and packaged the honey. Rabbit had disposed of the evidence. The others . . .

Chris thinks back to what Charlotte had told him, about the Wood ecosystem healing itself.

After he'd finally marshaled the strength to get out, which one of them had taken his place?

His feet carry him into the deepest heart of the forest, where the Very Deep Pit had been dug in the perpetual shadow cast by the mighty oaks. The rain intensifies, soaking his clothes, washing out some of the mud and grime. *Blink.* He's Christopher, enraged and befuddled, moving forward because, at this point, what else is there? *Blink.* He's Bear, calculating and cold, on a mission to reclaim what's rightfully his.

It's pouring now, water cascading down the crooked branches. Chris can barely see more than a few steps ahead. He stumbles on a root emerging from the ground. *Blink.* Bear finds his way, stepping surely across the drenched forest floor.

Soon he reaches the edge of the pit. It is a yawning gash in the skin of the Hundred Acre Wood, easily several times as deep as Chris is tall. He wipes his face with his sleeve and peers down.

The Bee is at the bottom of the pit. It is a pale, elephantine slug, slick with mucus and rain. A scattering of a dozen eyes and several pneumostomes are interspersed across its albino, semi-translucent skin. The pneumostomes are gaps in the creature's flesh that suck in and release air with a raspy slurping sound audible even in the downpour. Each lidless, cloudy eye is the size of a human palm. Some of the eyes zero in on Chris, and the Bee stirs.

Chris leans in and cranes his neck for a better look. Someone tackles him from behind and he tumbles into the pit.

Chris claws at the packed earth of the steep pit wall and grasps desperately onto the gnarled tip of a tree root protruding from the rain-soaked dirt like the jagged edge of a broken bone. The bandolier slips off his shoulder and the rifle falls to bottom of the pit. He dangles a third of the way down, hanging on to the root with both hands. The skin on his palms is scratched and raw, blood welling along multiple scrapes. Somewhere below, Bee emits a predatory, entirely unslug-like howl.

"You should've listened," sounds a shrill voice from above. "You should've gone home."

Chris looks up at Charlotte's face, framed by the bright-yellow hood of a raincoat. She meets his gaze. There's no apology or regret in the eyes hidden behind those large glasses.

"I told you there's no need for you anymore, dear. Perhaps there never was." Charlotte sneers at him. "The honey should've unsettled you, should've sent you away, but you've always been stubborn. You had to find your way back here, didn't you? But I've already said there's nothing for you here. And now, you won't even make a satisfying morsel for our Bee."

The root is slippery. He's struggling to hang on. A flash of lightning illuminates the pit. Chris blinks.

Bear pulls himself up with both paws, heedless of the pain shooting through his muscles. He digs his claws into the pit wall, climbing upward with the agility of a seasoned mountaineer. There's murder in his black-bead eyes.

Charlotte gasps, takes a step back. A scraped hand, blood and dirt under its fingernails, grasps the edge of the pit. A clap of thunder echoes across the sky on the heels of the lightning. Bee howls again. It makes Bear blink.

Chris nearly slides back into the pit, hanging on with his right hand, trying to find purchase with his left. The muscles of his arms are in agony. He's almost free of the pit.

Charlotte rushes forward and stomps on Chris's hand. She grinds the tip of her boot into his fingers. The bones crunch. Chris shrieks in pain and releases his grip. As he slides into the pit, he manages to clasp Charlotte's ankle with his left hand. They fall together, screaming.

<hr>

CHRIS IS LYING face down in the muck. He must've lost consciousness for a few moments, and he had almost drowned in a puddle of rainwater before coming to. He struggles to his knees and coughs up the vile liquid. He's caked with wet mud. His body hurts all over and his eyes sting. He blinks rapidly to try and get the stinging runoff out of his eyes. His perspective keeps shifting from Bear to Christopher, so fast that it merges into the in-between he's been chasing all this time, but the only thing to be found in the in-between is the same miserable pit.

Chris lifts his head toward the cloudy sky, forces his eyes open and lets the rainwater cleanse them. After a few moments of this, the stinging subsides. He looks forward again, only to find Charlotte, equally covered in grime. She stands facing him, her feet planted firmly in the muck, her steady hands holding Chris's rifle. In a smooth, practiced motion, she points it squarely at his midsection.

His mind races during the fraction of a second it takes for the rifle to point at him. There are flashes of his life as it could've been, of all the different choices he could've made before he ran out of time. He has so many doubts, but if there's only one thing he's certain of, it's that Charlotte will pull the trigger. He wonders in these final moments whether it is better to die as Christopher or as Bear. He suspects that, no matter how much he wishes it were otherwise, there truly is no difference.

Charlotte is about to squeeze the trigger when Bee moves impossibly fast. It slides across the bottom of the pit like a freight train, loud and unstoppable. Charlotte must hear it coming but doesn't even have time to turn around. She's just beginning to shift her stance when Bee slams into her at top speed. Her bones crunch and her body is flung across the pit like a rag doll. She lands a few steps away and does not move again.

Bee comes to a full stop, as abruptly and unimaginably fast as it had lunged. Many of its eyes are focused on Chris. It makes a mewling sound.

Bee has made its choice. It chose Bear over Owl, or perhaps the Hundred Acre Wood made the choice, just like it had chosen to elevate him from victim to predator back when he first followed Sanders into the Wood.

Chris blinks several times, but his perspective is no longer shifting. The rage is gone, and so is his cold detachment. He isn't Christopher, and he isn't Bear. He has achieved a permanent state of the in-between. He understands that much. He knows what he is, but it's still up to him to decide *who* he is. He can be Christopher, or he can be Bear. That depends on what he chooses to do next

He takes a careful step, then another. Bee watches him, but makes no move to stop him. Chris slowly picks up the rifle. If he aims just right, he can end the cycle of abuse and murder, he can kill not only Bear but also Bear's entire world. He moves slowly toward Bee, so as not to spook it, so as not to provoke it.

He's within arm's reach. Bee's mucus-laden skin jiggles as the creature breathes. Heedless of the pain in the crushed bones of his hand, he aims the rifle toward the pneumostome nearest to where he thinks Bee's equivalent of a brain is located.

The breathing pore spasms and excretes a glob of radioactive-green mucus at Chris. The clingy, pungent discharge covers him from head to toe. It gets into his eyes, his nose, his mouth. The taste he's never stopped yearning for overwhelms him, breaks down his defenses. The rifle falls from his limp hands.

Chris gorges himself on honey.

It is a sunny autumn day, warm and breezy like a fond memory that gets better with each time one recalls it. A pair of children—a boy and a girl—are playing in a field of blooming wildflowers.

A well-dressed, pudgy, middle-aged man approaches the children and flashes them a disarming smile. He greets them and begins talking to them. The children, cautious at first, are having a wonderful time. They laugh at his self-depreciating humor and witty anecdotes.

The man launches into a tall tale of talking animals and friends having adventures. He points toward a copse of trees in the distance, and the girl notices that several of the fingers on his right hand are crooked, like they'd been broken and healed wrong. The spell is broken for her and she draws back, but the boy doesn't mind. He listens, rapt, to the stories of what sounds like the best place in the world. A place he finds he'd very much like to visit.

In Which Piglet Falls Out, and Then In Again...

Cedar Sanderson

After a week of dreary drizzle which meant that no-one wanted to be out-of-doors, a momentous morning finally arrived that was crisp and bright and blue.

Piglet said as much to Pooh, when Pooh finally came to the door Piglet had been knocking on. Admittedly, it wasn't a very loud knock, because Piglet was not a very loud person.

"Blue?" Pooh peered past Piglet in his near-sighted way. "I think rather, not so much blue as, er, perhaps yellow?"

"Look up, Pooh." Piglet pointed and tipped his head way back. This was a difficult effort for the rotund bear, but he succeeded after he went all the way out of his house and lay on his back on the path. The path was still rather damp, unless you found a part that was covered in rustly autumn leaves that dried faster than the earth beneath them. Pooh had plenty of those, dropped from the tree that arched over his house.

The sky was indeed blue, clear of any hint of clouds. It was the sort of newly-washed cerulean blue that is rare to see, unless it is in a child's drawing of what the world ought to look like. Children who are happy don't see the clouds.

"I see. It is blue," Pooh agreed. It took both of them some effort, with huffing and puffing, but they got Pooh up on his feet again. "I should look up more often." Pooh contemplated his belly, and just visible beneath that, his toes. "Only, down is easier."

"Sometimes it's worthwhile to do the hard things." Piglet sat on the bench (which was really a big part of a tree trunk, conveniently laid down where it had fallen just next to Pooh's door) and contemplated the day. "I think that today is an easy day, as it's so sunny."

Pooh, who had wandered in his mind from contemplating the sky, to the yellow buttercups by the log, and from there to his golden honey, hadn't really been listening.

"Yes, yes," he said, because that's what you say when there is a pause where it feels like you ought to say something. "I shall check my honey supply."

By which he meant, and Piglet knew it, that he would reduce his supply by eating what would fit in his capacious hunger. You could see how large his hunger was by looking at his tummy.

"I shall go and visit Tigger," Piglet decided, out loud, so Pooh would know what he was thinking. "He will perhaps want to know the day is blue."

Pooh had gone back inside his house, although he hadn't closed the door in his friend's face. Piglet decided that he would leave the door open, it being a fresh air sort of day, and he quietly left again. Behind him, there were slurping sounds, and muffled 'mmms!' of the kind a hungry bear makes.

Piglet strolled along the path towards Tigger's place, humming a little, because it was that sort of day. There were dewdrops on leaves, from the rain yesterday, but they wouldn't last long. This was the season of the year where summer, having fallen to the chills of autumn, came back again for a brief cheery visit before winter crept in to freeze and blacken the earth. Piglet had taken the time to wrap his scarf around his throat before leaving home, as it was wet out even if he stayed on the path, and he was always cautious when there was a danger of damp. Now, he loosened the scarf and felt warm, which cheered him up.

Pooh was *sometimes* up for a quiet stroll, which is why Piglet had gone there first. Tigger was always up for *anything*, but it was never quiet. Piglet preferred a more peaceful companion, he admitted silently to himself. Pooh was peaceful, as was Eeyore. Rabbit made him nervous. Tigger . . .

"Boom!" that worthy announced, standing on Piglet's chest with both his forepaws. "I found you!"

"I knew where I was." Piglet tried to make his voice sound stern. It was not an easy thing to achieve as he was lying flat on his back, rather flatter with a tiger balanced atop him. "I was coming to find you."

"You found me, old chap. What was it you came about?" Tigger bounced back onto his heels, and Piglet sat up with caution, patting all his seams to assure himself he wasn't coming apart after that greeting.

"I came to tell you about what a nice day it is." Piglet got all the way up onto his feet and dusted himself off. "It's a lovely blue."

Tigger flopped onto his back immediately, clasping his hands over his belly. "Yes, 'tis blue. You know what this means?" He bounded to his feet again, a few leaves fluttering up with him.

"No . . .?" Piglet did, in fact, think he knew what Tigger meant, but it wasn't what *he* had meant, that was nearly certain.

"It's the perfect day for an'dventure!" Tigger bounced around, attempted a cartwheel, only to collapse halfway through. He did it again, then again, before stopping. "We shall sally forth into the Hundred Acre Wood and find it's very centre."

Piglet, who had never seen a map of the woods, and who had a slim grasp of how large an acre was, much less a hundred of them at once, clasped his hands behind his back. He rocked on his heels, contemplating.

"Won't it take very long?" he asked, finally.

Tigger was now turning somersaults, having managed one perfect cartwheel. "Wouldn't think so. Not longer than a day."

"Should we take provisions?" Piglet suggested, touching the end of his scarf, which was hanging loose now that the day was warm.

"We shall! We shall indeed!" Tigger dove into the hollow tree he called home, and reappeared a moment later with a bag in one paw, and a bottle in another. "Fizzy lemonade, and some buns, only a little squashed. We shall call the ones with raisins in 'em dessert."

He shouldered the bag, after some scuffling about in it, to put the bottle below the buns (mostly, but they had already been squashed, so it did very little harm in the end) and took Piglet firmly in paw.

"Seems to me there's a marching song, Piglet, do you know it?"

Piglet did not, and they set out in the general direction of the deeper-in woods accompanied by Tigger muttering and humming in a somewhat melodious fashion.

Tigger went faster than Piglet, who fell further and further behind. Piglet was beginning to feel rather hot, and just a little cross, when a thornbush snatched his scarf off entirely.

"Oh!" Piglet jumped away from it. "Tigger!" He shouted as loudly as he could, but the warm drowsy humming of a very nice day damped his voice. "Tigger, wait!"

Tigger, being far enough away that he was no longer in sight, might have waited. He didn't come back to Piglet, which is what Piglet *really* wanted. So Piglet seized the end of the scarf and gave it a tug. The springy wood of the bush tugged right back, and Piglet nearly fell into the thorns.

"Bother." He borrowed Pooh's word, and dug in his heels. "Give. It. Back!" He put a little shimmy into his last pull, and the scarf broke free with an abruptness that had him rolling end-over-end before he had a chance to prepare. He wound up lying on his back looking up, the scarf clutched firmly and safely out of the thorns.

The scarf didn't seem so important now, because the sky above him wasn't blue any longer. It wasn't cloudy, either, like a storm would come, with something as expected as rain. It was a peculiar color that Piglet couldn't put a name to, and it pulsed, like strands of grass in the stream under the bridge where they played Poohsticks. Lights and shadows chased themselves across the . . . Piglet decided he wasn't going to call it sky, any longer. Sky was something insubstantial, this was a great deal more solid. Solid, and moving. He sat up and looked around.

The thornbush was gone. So, too, was the rest of the wood. There wasn't anything, other than a rumble. Piglet put his hand on his stomach, and felt the rumble.

"Nearly as loud as Pooh," he said out loud, to test his voice. It didn't sound right. He cleared his throat and tried again, with "Tigger? Tigger, can you come here please?"

There was no response. There were shadows, twisting out of his sight when he moved his head, but nothing to cast the shadows. Piglet got to his feet, swaying a little, and gulped. Without the trees, the land looked very strange. It wasn't brown, like you'd expect it to be, but a funny sort of purple that had some brown if you angled your head . . .

He stopped tilting his head. The way the colors changed when he did made him feel like he was standing in a boat or something that didn't have a proper up and down, but moved when you didn't expect it, and never in a direction you wanted. There was a sheen on everything, like a rather nasty puddle rising up on tarmac.

Piglet took two steps forward. Well, he thought it might be forward. It wasn't clear any longer where his front was. Things just got less clear the longer he stood still, he thought, and moving might help with that. So he took two strides, right foot, then left, right, and then . . . something threw him down on his back. It wasn't as violent a throw as the thornbush, which had catapulted him quite a distance, but it was enough to knock the breath out of him.

He lay there, feeling a squirming underneath his body that he didn't want to think about. Instead, he tried to see who had grabbed his hand and pulled him over. He looked, and realized he was holding tightly onto his scarf, still. The other end of it, the one he wasn't holding, stretched tightly out and simply ended in midair, with the fringes on the other side of . . . something.

Piglet stood up and this time, he used the scarf to pull himself towards that.

"If I fell down," he reasoned, "perhaps I can get back up again to the thornbush."

He was feeling charitably inclined towards that familiar prickly companion at this point. It seemed like thorns were far more reasonable to understand than this strange place. His eyes were watering, as the sky and the earth or whatever they were, tried to invert themselves. The ground kept squirming from under his feet, and there was a whimper now and again. That might have been from him, like the rumble, but he didn't want to stop and investigate.

He kept pulling, hand over hand. The scarf hadn't been this long when he put it on that morning, he was sure.

Was the ground-stuff moist? He hadn't meant to think that; it was because he was thinking about why he put on the scarf. The matter under his feet suddenly got squelchy, and pulled at his every step, clinging in an awful way, building up more and more when he put his feet down.

"If I can't move my feet any longer, I shall have to pull myself along," Piglet said out loud, defiantly. "I must not stand still here."

His feet felt as though they weighed more than the rest of him, but he managed to lift one and swing it forward, clump, clump . . .

Piglet tried to take a deep breath, but the air here was strangely heavy, and his chest ached. Still, he put one foot in front of the other, afraid to stand still for too long. What if he fell down again? Would all of him become covered in the goo that balled around his feet, like clay on a wet path?

The scarf suddenly started to unravel in the middle. Piglet squeaked in alarm. Frantically, he reeled in the wool towards him, struggling to keep his feet moving in the direction of the now-vanishing scarf end. He was so close he could almost touch it, and row after row, it got smaller and smaller. He hurled himself towards it, knowing that if he fell down, now, into the slime pooling around him, he'd likely never be able to get up. As his paws caught the knot of the fringe, there was a vast heave, and then . . .

The ground was brown and green with moss, and a few leaves again. Piglet gasped. Until he'd taken this breath, he hadn't realized there was such a difference in the air. Here, it was sweet and cool, and there, it had been greasy and foul. He coughed, then coughed again, feeling his chest burn with the effort of getting it all out. Wherever he had been, whatever that place was, it wasn't good for him.

"Piglet!" Tigger bounced into view. "Piglet?"

"You found me!" Piglet said, his voice faint after the coughing fit.

"Where were you?" Tigger tilted his head, "Why are you in the middle of . . . the middle. And where is the rest of you?"

"The rest of me?" Piglet twisted around. He was aware of a constricting feeling around his center, now, and he couldn't move very well, so he couldn't see his toes. Or anything below his belly, now that he was looking.

Tigger walked around, contemplating, his paw cupping his chin, fingers stroking his whiskers. "Piglet, how do you feel?"

"A bit sick," Piglet admitted. "I can feel my toes, and wiggle them." He did so, realizing that Tigger was standing behind him at that moment.

Tigger came around to stand in front of him, and Piglet felt a little disoriented. He was looking Tigger in the face. Tigger's dark eyes were narrowed in concentration, and Piglet could see little golden flecks of sunlight in them. Normally, he would be looking up at Tigger, tilting his head back until his neck strained, if they were both standing. He looked down at the ground, with its wonderful bits of moss, and the curled fawn of beech leaves scattered here and there.

"I'm not sure what happened." Piglet said.

"You can feel your toes?" Tigger reached out and touched the wadded-up yarn Piglet was still gripping tightly, all that was left of his scarf.

"Um, yes?"

"I can't see 'em." Tigger peered at Piglet. "I can only see half of you, and there's a bit of peculiar color wound round the middle of you, hard to make anything out there. There should be half a piglet, the bottom half, trotters and all. There's more like a disk, then there's the rest of you."

Piglet kicked his hinds, as hard as he could. "Can't you see that?"

"Nope. I can see you wriggle, is all. What were you doing?"

"Kicking. I can't feel anything . . . I mean, there's nothing to push against. I'm stuck."

"I can see that. Would you like me to pull?" Tigger offered.

Piglet recalled an incident with Pooh, too much honey, and Rabbit's doorway. "Yes, please. Or maybe go get the others."

"I'd better give it a go." Tigger reached out. "Can you drop the wool?"

"Oh, yes, of course." Piglet discovered that this was easier to say, than to do. His fingers cramped painfully and didn't want to uncurl from what had been his lifeline out of that place. Tigger unraveled him, uncharacteristically quiet and patient.

"Tigger?" Piglet hated to bother his friend, who was focused on the yarn, head bent over Piglet's small, rather grubby hands.

"Hmm?" Tigger didn't look up as he unwound another bit of the yarn.

"I can't feel my toes any more."

Tigger grabbed Piglet's hands in his own paws. He threw himself backwards, feet planted against the dirt on the ground. Piglet, looking down, his shoulders stretched to their breaking point, saw Tigger's big feet leave small furrows as his heels pushed and pushed against Piglet's inertia.

"Hang on," Tigger let go, and seized Piglet under the arms. "Hold on to me."

Piglet tried to get his little arms around Tigger's neck. The tightness around his middle was much more so. "I'm . . ."

He didn't finish his thought before Tigger hauled on his arms again, this time his shoulders didn't feel it, but now his midsection felt as though it were being squeezed through a very small pipe.

"Ouch!" Piglet squeaked.

"Sorry," Tigger mumbled in the vicinity of his ear. "One, two," he didn't get to three before he was yanking on his little friend again. Piglet felt rather sick, but his nethers weren't hurting. Some little part of his mind was gibbering that he should be hurting a lot more, not to mention the midair position of his whole self.

"Better get help." Piglet said, gasping, after the third try by Tigger to pull him out of the place he'd fallen into. Or had he fallen out of the woods, into that place?"

"No time," Tigger was panting, and Piglet could feel how his arms, wrapped around his own torso, were trembling. "I can see your tail, it's lost its curl."

That was reassuring.

"Almost out, then."

"Manner of speaking, better out than in." Tigger braced his feet, which was about all Piglet could see. "Piglet . . ."

"Yes?"

"If things go wrong, what would you like me to tell everyone?" Tigger sniffled. "A few last words for Pooh, perhaps?"

"Is it that bad?" Piglet shivered, his head on Tigger's shoulder. He was squeezing his eyes tightly shut, so he didn't have to see what was happening. Then he changed his mind, "no, don't tell me. I don't want to know. It was a horrible place, with a smell."

Piglet tightened his grip on Tigger. "I don't want to go back in there! Just pull!"

Tigger leaned back, his feet digging deeply into the forest floor. There were small trenches under them from his efforts. Piglet felt a pain.

Tigger let go and sat down all of a heap on the ground. He looked up. "Oh, dear."

"Don't tell me." Piglet begged, his voice a faint gasp. "I don't want to know."

"I won't tell you, then." Tigger looked up at him, and his face was sad. "Still can't feel your toes?"

"I can't feel anything any more." Piglet drooped. He'd been pulled back into there, whatever there was. He could feel that by how he was being held up at the chest instead of below the belly. "You tried. It's all right."

Tigger glared at him, then bounced back up to his feet. "I'm not giving up. I just needed to take a breath."

He wrapped an arm over Piglet. "Let's try a wiggle, then."

Piglet squeaked in protest as Tigger threw his weight against him, pushing him to the side. Then Tigger bounced, pulling this time, shouting as he did.

"Heave! Ho!" He chanted. Piglet flailed for a grip on something, anything, and wound up with one of Tigger's fuzzy ears in his hand. He clung to it as Tigger bounced back and forth. "Heave! Ho!"

There was a peculiar sucking noise, and then Piglet felt a little like a cork popping out of a bottle. It was wet, or slimy—perhaps both—and then the two of them were rolling over and over through the moss and leaves and dirt before winding up in a tangled heap.

Piglet looked up at the blue sky.

"Whew." Tigger let go, and flopped on his back.

"I'm in again." Piglet lifted a foot with an effort. "All of me."

His foot looked strangely shaped and pale. He wiggled it with a painful effort. It flopped at the end of his leg.

Beyond it, the sky was very blue.

"Piglet," Tigger said in a very thoughtful voice. He paused, to think some more. "Piglet, I think you found the middle of the Hundred Acre Wood."

"I fell into something . . . somewhere." Piglet shivered in spite of the warm sunshine. He didn't feel like getting up from the nice solid ground, and the twig poking him in the ribs was pleasant, after being in midair for so long. "It was a very, er, hungry place."

Tigger sat up, and stroked his chin. "You were almost swallowed up and digested."

"I feel like I was chewed on." Piglet looked up at Tigger. It was better to not look into his friend's worried eyes from such a small distance, there was no avoiding the look in them when he was this close. "And then spat out again."

"Piglets don't agree with the middle of the woods." Tigger was well on his way to recovering his buoyancy.

"My scarf is ruined, though." Piglet let out a mournful sigh. "All pulled to pieces . . . Tigger?"

"Yes, Piglet?" Tigger turned to look at what Piglet was pointing towards, with shaking hand.

There was a strand of wool, a bit frayed, leading from the messy wad of tangled strands on the ground near them, in which only the knots of the fringe could still be identified as useful bits of a craft. The line of it led up, and into the blue of the sky from their perspective so close to the ground. And there, in the middle of nothing special at all, it vanished.

As they watched, the wool twitched a little.

"Tigger, I want to go home now."

"Me too, Piglet. Let's go back to Rabbit's and get some tea." Tigger was already on his feet, and scooping up his little friend. He was starting to run before Piglet could object to being carried.

Behind them, unseen, the thread of yarn moved, slowly. The snarled wool rose, carrying with it sticks and leaves and more than a little dirt. It went up, and up, and then, it went into the blue.

After that, there wasn't anything left at all. But by that time, Tigger and Piglet were sitting at Rabbit's table having biscuits and tea. Piglet wasn't doing any of the talking, and if his teacup rattled against the saucer with every drink he took, no one mentioned it, politely.

For a long time after that day, Piglet stayed home. When Pooh came to visit, Piglet just said that he liked to have a roof over his head.

"Will you ever come out again?" Pooh asked, opening a cupboard and looking into its emptiness.

"Maybe." Piglet closed the other cupboards Pooh had looked into, and left open when he was done inspecting them for honey. "Perhaps on a nice cloudy day. But not too far from home."

Tigger visited, and made sure that there was food in the cupboards, on different days.

Christopher Robin came round, with a soft new scarf.

"Oh, no thank you, it's not . . ." Piglet started to object, with mixed feelings. He knew how close it had been to both saving him and dooming him.

"Nonsense." Christopher Robin had a warm hand on Piglet's head. "You'll get a chill when it's damp." He wrapped it around Piglet's neck. "Nanny knitted it up out of an old sweater she pulled apart after the moths had been at it. Nasty little moths just eat and eat, she says."

Piglet shivered.

"Now, then, what did I say? You need a warm scarf."

Christopher Robin went away again, sure that his little friend would be warm all winter, while the woods slept beneath a comforting blanket of soft white snow.

Piglet sat in the chair by his tiny fire, and watched the flames eating away at the wood, and knew that somewhere, in the centre of it all, was an appetite. One that you couldn't see, but that didn't mean it wasn't there. That didn't mean that you couldn't fall into it. Only getting out was much harder.

Some days, he wasn't sure he had gotten out. Some nights, he woke up with a cold wet blanket wrapped around him right around his middle and his sweat soaking through. He grew thinner, and rarely ate. The hunger gnawed inside him, and he put a hand on his stomach to feel the rumble. It was very real and present and reminded him that even there, where he'd fallen in, he'd been able to hear himself.

The worst days were when the sky was blue and clear. He pulled his curtains tight, and sat on the floor as close to the fire as he could, listening to it and feeling the warmth soak into his body, even if it never reached his centre.

In Which You Never Can Tell with Bees

Eric James Stone

On a warm spring morning, the sun shone brightly over the trees of the Hundred Acre Wood. The beech trees were bedecked with new green leaves. Edward Bear, known to his friends as Winnie-the-Pooh, was on his way with Piglet to visit Christopher Robin's house when they came across that Old Gray Donkey, Eeyore, his head slumped toward the ground.

"Good day, Eeyore," said Winnie-the-Pooh.

"Unlikely." Eeyore shook his head from side to side. "Unless you mean it's a Good Day to Meet our Doom."

"I don't think that's what I meant," said Pooh. On seeing Eeyore slump a little more, he added humbly, "But perhaps it was."

Eeyore perked up a bit at that. "Yes, a Good Day for Armageddon."

"Indeed," said Pooh. "A good day for Almond-Getting. Perhaps Christopher Robin has some almonds we could get."

"We are going to Christopher Robin's house," explained Piglet. "Do you want to come with us?"

"You will most likely get lost along the way," said Eeyore.

Pooh was about to reply that he knew the way very well, but he was distracted by a buzzing-noise, and being a Bear of Little Brain, he forgot what he was going to say. Instead, he began to think about buzzing-noises.

And that led him to think of bees.

And that led him to think of honey.

And that led him to think he was hungry.

"I wonder," Pooh said, "whether those are the *right* sort of bees for honey."

They were nowhere near the Bee Tree with the bees he had determined were the wrong sort.

"They sound like they are getting closer," said Piglet.

"Maybe," said Pooh. "You never can tell with bees."

But Piglet was right: a swarm of bees streamed over Eeyore's Gloomy Place and into the trees near Owl's house.

As the buzzing-noise faded, Pooh said, "If they're going *to* their honey, then I suppose it is well guarded. But if they are coming *from* their honey . . ." He licked his lips and looked toward where the bees had come from. It was rather boggy. Did bees like bogs? "Eeyore, do you think there is a bee-hive over there?"

"I doubt it," said Eeyore. "It's far too noisy, what with all the buzzing-noise all day and all night." He yawned. "I haven't slept in days."

Pooh thought that sounded very much like a lot of bees, and where there were a lot of bees, there might be a lot of honey. If they were the *right* sort of bees. "You don't mind if I just take a quick look, do you?"

Eeyore sighed. "If you must."

"But, Pooh," said Piglet, "we were going to Christopher Robin's house."

"We shall," said Pooh. "After I see if there is a bee-hive in the bog with the right sort of bees for honey."

"But what if they are the wrong sort of bees?" asked Piglet.

Pooh wrinkled his nose, remembering his last encounter with the wrong sort of bees. But he did *so* like honey. "I think I shall be all right as long as I do not climb any trees or use any balloons."

"I am scared to get stung," said Piglet.

"It might be best if you stay here safe with Eeyore, then," said Pooh. Then he set off into Eeyore's Gloomy Place.

As he squished through the bog, the buzzing-noise grew louder and louder.

Finally, he reached the other edge of the bog, where the ground firmed up and there were more trees. By now the buzzing-noise was so loud he could hear nothing else. "It is a good thing I am a Bear of Little Brain," Pooh said to himself, "for such a loud sound would make it hard to think big thoughts."

The buzzing of the bees flowed in a rhythmic pattern. It almost sounded like words being shouted in Pooh's ears, but they were no words he knew: *C-uln Stho-anog ch-nglui ph`shogg, c-sll'ha Stho-anog wgah'n shugg.*

When he suddenly happened upon a clearing in the woods, Pooh realized that Eeyore had been right: all the buzzing was far too noisy for there to be a bee-hive. But it was just the right amount of buzzing for there to be six very large bee-hives, nestled in the hollows of six trees equally spaced around the clearing.

In the center of the clearing, a large swarm of bees appeared to be building Something. Something that was most definitely not a bee-hive.

A swarm of bees flew over Pooh's head into the clearing and joined the swarm at the Something.

Since all the bees he could see appeared to be occupied in building the Something, Pooh decided to check if the nearest bee-hive had any honey. Fortunately, these bees had built their nests in hollows at the bottom of the trees, so he would not need to climb. He began to think that these very much were the right sort of bees to make honey for bears to eat.

When he got close to the nest, he was sure he could smell the honey. He could almost taste it.

As he went to stick his paw into the nest, however, the rhythmic buzzing changed to a steadier tone that grew in intensity.

Pooh froze in place. He could tell the bees were suspicious. He withdrew his paw, and the buzzing-sound returned to its rhythm: *C-uln Stho-anog ch-nglui ph`shogg, c-sll'ha Stho-anog wgah'n shugg.*

These were not the *right* sort of bees after all, Pooh decided, and he carefully backed away from the bee-hive and out of the clearing.

As he made his way back to where he had left Piglet and Eeyore, he sang a little song to himself. It went like this:

> Cool as though Egg-Nog
> In this gooey, fussy Bog.
> Buzz! Buzz! Buzz!
> 'Cause I'll have the Egg-Nog
> Or I'm going to shrug.

"That's a funny song for me to make up," said Pooh. "It must be because of all the buzzing. But it does make me thirsty for egg-nog."

He sang it a few more times, and the buzzing-noise around him seemed to keep rhythm with him, even as it grew fainter. By the time he rejoined Piglet and Eeyore, the words seemed to be a constant refrain in the back of his mind.

"Did you find some honey?" asked Piglet.

"They were the wrong sort of bees," explained Pooh.

"Of course they were," said Eeyore.

"*Now* can we go to Christopher Robin's house?" asked Piglet.

"Yes," said Pooh. "Would you like to come with us, Eeyore?"

Eeyore shook his head. "No point, really. Stho-anog will arrive soon, and then comes eternal night."

Pooh looked up to the sky, where the sun still shone brightly in the east. "Well, then, there's plenty of time to come with us to see Christopher Robin before Stho-anog arrives, isn't there?"

Eeyore sighed. "I suppose it doesn't matter."

So the three of them set off for Christopher Robin's house.

There was no answer when they knocked at the green door.

"I told you there was no point," said Eeyore.

"Perhaps he has not yet woken up," said Pooh.

"Yes, he has," said Piglet. "I can hear him talking."

Pooh listened closely, and he thought he could faintly hear Christopher Robin's voice, though he couldn't make out the words. So he knocked again, harder this time.

They listened and waited, and still no one came to the door.

Finally, Pooh opened the door and stuck his head in. "Hallo! Christopher Robin? It's Pooh Bear."

He could definitely hear Christopher Robin's voice now from upstairs.

"I think he's in his bedroom," said Pooh.

"Let's go find him," said Piglet, and he scooted through the doorway and climbed the stairs.

Pooh followed, and as he reached the top of the stairs, he could now, just barely, make out the words Christopher Robin was repeating, over and over again: *C-uln Stho-anog ch-nglui ph`shogg, c-sll'ha Stho-anog wgah'n shugg.*

"He must have learned that from the bees," said Pooh.

Piglet stood in the doorway to Christopher Robin's bedroom. "He looks like he's asleep, but he's talking."

Pooh joined Piglet in staring at Christopher Robin, who lay on his bed, eyes closed, as the strange words came from his mouth.

"Should we wake him up?" asked Piglet.

"If he's asleep, it's not very restful," said Pooh. He marched forward and put his snout next to Christopher Robin's ear. "Christopher Robin, are you awake?"

Christopher Robin did not react. He just kept repeating the words.

Pooh lifted Christopher Robin's arm and shook it. When he let go, it fell limply back to the bed.

"I think there's something very Wrong here," said Pooh.

"Will he be all right?" asked Piglet.

Pooh did not know how to answer him. Pooh did not know what to do, and knowing he was a Bear of Little Brain, he did not think he could figure it out on his own. "I think we should go see Owl," said Pooh. "If anyone will know what to do, Owl will."

Down the stairs they went, and out the door to rejoin Eeyore. The three of them made their way into the Hundred Acre Wood until they reached The Chestnuts, Owl's residence.

Pooh climbed up to Owl's front door and knocked (there no longer being a bell-rope to ring a bell, of course, since it had been nailed back in its rightful place on Eeyore) and then called out, "Owl! It's Bear speaking. There is something Wrong with Christopher Robin!"

After a few moments, the door opened, and Owl looked out.

"Hallo, Pooh," said Owl. "You say there is something Wrong with Christopher Robin?"

"He won't wake up," said Pooh, "and he is saying strange words in his sleep."

"Well," said Owl, "that could be a febrile delirium."

Pooh nodded. "It could be. How do we cure a Feeble Delicious?"

"First," said Owl, "we must find the Cause."

"There's a crow near my house that caws," offered Piglet.

"There's another one near my house, too," said Pooh, "unless it's the same one."

"The Cause—the source of the febrile delirium—is not likely to be a bird," said Owl.

Despite his being a Bear of Little Brain, an idea came to Pooh, and he thought it was a good one. "Could it be bees? You never can tell with bees."

"It is not likely to be bees, either," said Owl.

"No, of course not," said Pooh. "It's just that he's saying the same words the bees are buzzing."

"Christopher Robin is buzzing like a bee?" asked Owl.

"No," said Pooh. "It's more like the buzzing of the bees beyond Eeyore's Gloomy Place sounds like talking."

"What are they saying?"

"The same thing Christopher Robin is saying," said Pooh. "That's why I thought maybe the bees were the cause."

"Perhaps I should examine these bees for myself," said Owl, "in order to better hypothesize regarding their potential to influence Christopher Robin's febrile delirium. Beyond Eeyore's Gloomy Place, you say?"

"Just follow the buzzing-noise," said Pooh.

Owl took flight toward Eeyore's Gloomy Place.

"What should we do while he's gone?" asked Piglet.

"I shall go home," said Eeyore, "to Pass the Time until our Inevitable Doom takes us."

"I shall go back to Christopher Robin's house," said Piglet, "to keep him company till he wakes up."

Pooh nodded. "And I shall go to my house, to see if there is still some honey in my pot. If Christopher Robin has Feeble Delicious, perhaps some honey will make the Delicious less Feeble."

So they went their separate ways.

After Pooh arrived home and entered through his door under the name of Sanders, he went straight to the larder, stood on a chair, and from the top shelf took down a pot with HUNNY written on it.

Alas, it was empty, as if someone very hungry had licked every single drop of honey from it. Which he had done, yesterday.

"Bother," said Pooh, sitting down on his chair. "Christopher Robin needs honey to get better. Now, where can I fill this pot with honey?"

He was certain he had smelled some honey earlier that day. Being a Bear of Little Brain, it took him a few moments to remember that it was at the bee-hives in the clearing beyond Eeyore's Gloomy Place.

Pooh also remembered there were a lot of bees there. Suspicious bees.

Pooh's plan of floating under a blue balloon to get to the bee-hive high up in the Bee Tree had not worked. But *these* bee-hives were near the ground. He did not need a balloon this time, which was good, because Christopher Robin was not awake to give him a balloon.

On the other paw, these bees had already shown they were suspicious of a bear near one of their nests. So he needed to not look like a bear.

His disguise as a little black cloud had not worked on the bees of the Bee Tree, so there was no point in trying it with these bees. In any case, a black cloud near the ground would be very suspicious.

"What would not be suspicious near the ground?" asked Pooh of himself.

"A flower!" replied Pooh. "But I would make a very large flower. I think the bees would suspect something."

"How about a puddle!" suggested Pooh. "But how could I disguise myself as a puddle? Get myself wet? I would just look like a wet bear. Although if it was a mud puddle, I would look like a black bear." He remembered rolling in the mud to create his disguise as a black cloud, and felt silly for having thought that would fool the bees.

"What about . . . a mound of dirt?" said Pooh hesitantly. "If I cover my woolen blanket with mud and hide under it, I would look like a mound of dirt. And if I move slowly, the bees may not notice that I've moved."

"I think that's a good idea, Pooh, especially for a Bear of Little Brain," said Pooh.

"Thank you kindly, Pooh," replied Pooh.

So Pooh took the woolen blanket off his bed and carried it, along with his honey pot, to a very muddy place – the very same where he had disguised himself as a cloud. Within a very short time the blanket was blackened with mud.

Pooh spotted some daisies that had bloomed nearby. "If I stick some daisies in the blanket," Pooh said, "perhaps the bees will be distracted by them." So he picked some daisies and threaded their stems into his blanket.

Then he pulled the blanket over himself to test out his disguise.

And then he pulled the blanket off himself because he could not see what he looked like from inside the blanket. Instead, he put it over a tree stump.

It looked somewhat like a mound of dirt with flowers on it.

"That will do, I think," said Pooh. It could almost fool him, and while he was a Bear of Little Brain, bees had even littler brains, he supposed. Unless you added up the brains of the entire hive, that is.

With that, he picked up the blanket and headed toward Eeycre's Gloomy Place.

As he passed The Chestnuts, Pooh checked to see if Owl had returned, but he was not at home.

The sun, which had been shining brightly all morning, seemed to dim. Pooh looked up to see that a giant circular cloud had formed overhead and seemed to be spreading out from beyond Eeyore's Gloomy Place.

"Bother. I hope it doesn't rain and wash the mud from my blanket," said Pooh.

He found Eeyore standing, head drooped, in his Gloomy Place.

"Hallo, Eeyore," said Pooh. "I'm just going to pop on past your bog to get some honey for Christopher Robin."

"*C-uln Stho-anog ch-nglui ph'shogg, c-sll'ha Stho-anog wgah'n shugg,*" said Eeyore.

"Oh, dear!" said Pooh. "The Feeble Delicious got you, too. I guess I'll need some honey for you as well."

Pooh continued into the bog. The rhythmic buzzing of the bees grew louder, and the song that had been throbbing in the back of his mind this whole time came from his mouth again:

> Cool as though Egg-Nog
> In this gooey, fussy Bog.
> Buzz! Buzz! Buzz!
> 'Cause I'll have the Egg-Nog
> Or I'm going to shrug.

Pooh stopped singing and thinking about a delightfully cool cup of Egg-Nog as he noticed a clump of feathers on the ground ahead. As he grew closer, he realized it was more than just a clump: it was Owl.

"Hallo there, Owl," said Pooh. "Why are you lying on the ground? Did you find the Caws of the Feeble Delicious?"

"*C-uln Stho-anog ch-nglui ph'shogg, c-sll'ha Stho-anog wgah'n shugg,*" said Owl.

"Oh, Owl, the Feeble Delicious has gotten you. I hope Piglet is all right with Christopher Robin!" said Pooh. "But he may have gotten it, too."

"I . . ." said Owl, feebly. "I cannot resist its Cyclopean power. *C-uln Stho-anog ch-nglui ph'shogg, c-sll'ha Stho-anog wgah'n shugg.*"

"I suppose I shall also be coming down with the Feeble Delicious soon," said Pooh. "Unless I can get some honey."

Pooh looked down at Owl. "I'll get some for you, too."

After a few minutes, when he could see the clearing ahead, he stopped to put on his disguise.

"I'm just a mound of dirt," said Pooh quietly. "Nothing to worry about."

Slowly, he crawled toward the clearing.

Peeking under the edge of his blanket, he saw that the Something the bees were building was glowing blue in the darkness from the cloud overhead.

Suddenly, the rhythm of the buzzing-noise changed, and for a moment Pooh thought the bees suspected his mound of dirt was not a mound of dirt. Instead, the strange words from the buzzing changed: *Shoggothth Stho-anog-nythth nog geb ng-ah.*

The blue glow increased until it was almost blinding, and then a clap of deafening thunder shook the ground.

By the time Pooh had recovered his senses, he saw that the blue glow had mostly faded. In the clearing, surrounding the Something, were large black glistening globs. As they undulated, their multiple eyes looked in all directions.

"Bother," said Pooh. "Bees were bad enough. But now there are Heffalumps."

But there was no other choice if he wanted to get the honey to save his friends: he had to continue with his plan.

The bees returned to their previous buzzing rhythm: *C-uln Stho-anog ch-nglui ph'shogg, c-sll'ha Stho-anog wgah'n shugg.* But now, instead of working on the Something in the middle of the clearing, they circled it.

The Heffalumps, meanwhile, worked on the Something, rearranging parts of it and expanding it.

Pooh moved a few inches toward the nearest bee-hive, then stopped and waited.

The bees ignored him.

The Heffalumps ignored him.

So Pooh moved another few inches and peeked out.

And another few.

And a few more. He was getting close.

The Heffalumps stopped their work and backed away from the Something, which started to spin on its axis. It also began to glow dimly in a color Pooh could not recall having seen before. Despite not being very bright, the color almost hurt to look at. As it grew brighter, Pooh shut his eyes and tucked his head between his paws beneath his blanket.

The buzzing-noise grew louder in its rhythm, joined disharmoniously by an eerie musical piping.

The strange-colored light flashed so bright Pooh could see it through his blanket, through his paws, through his eyelids.

A giant thunderclap shook the ground.

Then came absolute silence.

After a few moments, Pooh dared to lift his blanket a little so he could peek out.

The Something still glowed brightly in the strange color, shooting a beam up toward the center of the cloud overhead. A giant opening in the cloud was growing, but instead of showing the sun, darkness seemed to radiate out from it.

And in that darkness, a giant tentacle undulated outwards.

The Heffalumps were motionless in the clearing.

And the bees – the bees had all fallen to the ground!

Pooh did not know if the bees were dead or merely asleep. But now was his chance! Pooh wriggled forward until he was right next to the bee's nest in the hollow of the tree. He set his honey pot upright, ready to receive the honey he would pull from the bee-hive.

Slowly, he stuck a paw into the nest. He broke off a piece of honeycomb. Slowly, he brought it out and placed it in the honey pot.

No bees buzzed angrily.

Ever so carefully, he brought out piece after piece of the honeycomb, until his honey pot was almost full.

From nearby, a musical, piping voice said, *"Kn'a shoggoth grah'n hupadgh shugg."*

Pooh froze in place.

He heard a Heffalump squish along the ground closer to him. It smelled awful. *"Kn'a shoggoth grah'n hupadgh shugg,"* it repeated.

All Pooh could think of to say in reply was "Buzz buzz buzz."

His blanket was lifted away by the Heffalump's pseudotrunk. A dozen eyes the Heffalump's eyes stared at him.

Another pseudotrunk extended, wrapped itself around Pooh's honey pot, and lifted it away.

"No!" shouted Pooh. "I need that to cure my friends from the Feeble Delicious!" And he jumped up to take the pot back.

But he failed to get ahold of it. Instead, he knocked it upside down while it remained in the pseudotrunk's grip. Pieces of honeycomb fell out onto the Heffalump. Eyes sprouted out to look closely at the pieces.

Pooh had lost the only chance to save his friends. Now, he could only try to save himself.

Pooh turned to run and immediately tripped over a tree root and fell facedown to the ground. His right paw, sticky with honey, smashed into the dirt.

The Heffalump squished after him.

Pooh rolled over and looked up to see the Heffalump looming over him. In the sky beyond it, a fourth tremendous tentacle began to emerge from the darkness at the center of the cloud to join the other three that undulated, reaching out as if toward the ends of the Earth.

A faint buzzing-noise arose.

The bees were waking up.

The buzzing-noise grew louder.

The bees were suspicious.

The buzzing-noise became almost deafening as it closed in on Pooh.

The bees were angry.

Pooh shut his eyes and curled into a ball, anticipating the stings of thousands of bees trying to punish him for stealing their honey.

A shrill piping-noise joined in cacophony with the buzzing-noise. Unlike before, there was no rhythm that seemed to form words—just angry buzzing and . . . shrieking?

Pooh dared to open his eyes.

The bees were swarming over the Heffalump, which had pieces of honeycomb stuck to its skin. The Heffalump had withdrawn all its eyes into its body to protect them from stingers, and now it was blindly rolling about, crushing some of the swarm under its bulk. It crashed into one of the bee's nests, getting even more honey on itself in the process. This seemed only to enrage the bees even more.

The Heffalump's gyrations took it to the center of the clearing, where it collided with the Something. Part of the Something broke off with a crack, and the part flew across the clearing to smash into another of the bee's nests.

The Something began to wobble.

The other Heffalumps rushed toward it, reaching out with pseudotrunks to steady it, but it was spinning too quickly.

The Something exploded. The shock wave knocked Pooh off his feet.

When Pooh stood himself up again, he saw that the Something's explosion had shattered his honey pot into small pieces. It had also shredded the Heffalumps into small pieces, some of which were still undulating.

Looking up at the sky, Pooh saw the giant tentacles pulling back into the darkness at the center of the cloud, which was rapidly shrinking.

Within a few minutes, the sun shone brightly in the clear blue sky. The bees resumed their buzzing.

Pooh worried that the bees would smell the dirt-covered honey on his right paw and come after him, but they left him alone as they began rebuilding their nests.

Pooh shrugged and said, "Like I always say, you never can tell with bees." He walked back the way he had come.

Owl was asleep on the ground where Pooh had last seen him. Pooh's right paw still had some dirt-covered honey on it, so he wiped a little on Owl's beak.

Owl woke up, sputtered, and said, "Pooh, what are you doing?" He looked around and saw where he was, and said, "What am I doing here?"

"It worked!" said Pooh. "The honey cured your Feeble Delicious."

He set off to cure the rest of his friends, and hopefully to find a cup of Egg-Nog, perhaps sweetened with honey.

In Which Christopher Robin Faces the Hundred-Acre Monster

Brad R. Torgersen

The light in the sky was fading. I'd just finished the five-pointed star within the circle I'd previously sketched in the soil—using the narrow end of a tree branch scavenged from nearby—when my fiancé came walking up. At other times and on other days she'd have had a smile on her face. But not this evening. She was all business. Which, I suppose, suited the mood. It had been almost twenty-five years since I'd stood in this particular spot on this particular edge of this particular patch of woods. Not a forest, per se. But plenty dense enough for the undergrowth to quickly fade to black as I chanced a glance along the path that led into the trees, then looked back at my fiancé as she held out the large duffel in both hands.

"You found it," I said, staring at the old olive-drab bag which had seen me through military training. At a time in my life when I'd been eager to shrug off childish things.

"Of *course* I found it," she said, "but why you made me drive it all the way out *here,* and as the sun's about to quit, I have no idea. Wait. Dear God, Christopher, how come you drew a pentagram in the dirt??"

I sighed. This was going to be the hardest part to explain. I'd kept this specific bit of my childhood mostly hidden from Teresa during the six months we'd been engaged. Oh, she'd seen the stuffed animals in the duffel before. Lumped in the closet under the stairs. Back at my condo. And she'd only discovered them because she'd been helping me slowly clean things out in preparation for us to move in together—once we were married, and ready to begin a family.

"Probably better if I just show you," I said to her, and reverently took the duffel out of her hands. Then began laying out the contents at each of the five points of the star. First, the donkey. Then, the pig. Followed by the tiger. Then the kangaroo—with a little stuffed baby kangaroo still tucked into her pouch. And then the bunny. After which I pulled out the five short, thick, red-wax candles I'd tucked into my backpack after an unplanned stop at the dollar store. And placed one candle at the head of each of the stuffed animals.

"Seriously creepy," Teresa said, her arms folded across her chest, and her hands tucked under her biceps as she fidgeted in the gloaming.

"I agree," I said. "It's been a long time since I did anything like this."

"If I'd known you were into witchcraft I might have reconsidered your proposal," she said sarcastically.

I stopped, and stared at the shadowy shapes laying inert on the ground. The sky was now becoming illuminated by the first, bright stars of night.

"Yeah," I said, "I can't blame you for being weirded out. But there's a good reason for this. You'll understand in a minute."

We weren't far from civilization. It was only a few hundred yards back along the trail to the empty parking lot. Well, empty except for my motorcycle, and Teresa's battery-powered electric car. Then it was just ten minutes down the road to the first stoplight on the outskirts of town—the same small city where Teresa and I had met, each of us trying to put our lives back together after separate divorces. No kids in the mix for either of us, yet. We'd talked about having a baby. She wasn't yet forty. Her biological window wasn't shut, and I felt like I was finally grown up enough I could handle having a son, or a daughter. Maybe more than one? They say the odds of twins go up, the older the mother gets.

"Well?" Teresa demanded. "It's getting cold, Chris. And I only have my sweater. I didn't bring a coat."

"Right," I said, snapping out of my reverie.

The last stuffed animal to come out of the duffel, was the bear. Oh, how use-worn he'd become. His shabby little green shirt was stained and faded, and parts of his legs, arms, and ears had been rubbed raw of the yellow fuzz which otherwise covered his whole body. I felt his little polished, black button eyes with my thumbs as I gently placed him in the middle of the five-pointed star. I reached into my jacket pocket and pulled out the box of kitchen matches I'd also bought at the dollar store.

Teresa's eyes were wide as I lit the first match and illuminated her face. I bent down and touched the lit match to the wick on the candle sitting at the kangaroo's head. Once that one was going, I quickly moved to the next candle. For the third and fourth candles, I had to light a new match, and then again for the fifth and final candle. Each time, I blew out the burnt ends of the matches and scrubbed them under a heel.

The six stuffed animals lay face or belly-up in the flickering light provided by the candles. There was just enough to see by now, but not so much that the light was comforting. Rather, the entire scene had become even more eerie than when I'd first laid it out. And in my mind, I remembered as a child conducting the ritual. The chant suddenly came back to me like I'd been saying it daily ever since.

I stood at the edge of the pentagram, raised my arms above my head with the palms facing upward to the sky, and shouted, *"Honey! Honey! Honey! Sweet as can be! Oh, cuddly Pooh bear, won't you talk to me? Fire burns red, night like black pitch! The ceremony's begun, I am your witch! Honey! Honey! Honey! Sweet as can be! . . ."*

And so on, and so forth. I repeated the mantra seven times, my eyes locked on Teresa's as she stared at me like I'd gone crazy.

"Dammit, Chris, I just—*OH NO!*"

The bear in the center of the pentagram sat up. No longer the mere stuffed childhood toy he'd once been. He was now fat, round, and easily three times his original size, and he rubbed at his eyes with two doughy fists which lacked fingers. Just hands like mittens, with big thumbs. When he took his hands away, he looked up at me with those black eyes, the candlelight shining in them as he blinked, then he spoke—a curious voice, almost like an old man's, with a gentle quality at odds with the dark strangeness of the scene.

"Christopher," the bear said. "Do you know how long it's been?"

"I know, old friend," I said, trying to smile, despite the fact I was unnerved by Teresa's reaction. She'd backed several steps away from the pentagram, her hands clutched to her mouth, and her eyes now wide with fright.

"What is it? Chris, what . . . *tell me what you did!*"

The bear turned his head and looked at her.

"You never brought a human friend before," the bear said. "I'm afraid I don't have anything sweet to share with you, dear. In fact, I think it's safe to say I don't even have a home anymore. Not like I used to. Christopher could tell you."

"I'm sorry about that, Pooh," I said.

"You should be," the bear remonstrated me, but gently. "All these years and you never thought to include me or the others in your life. Were we not good enough for you anymore, Christopher?"

"It's not that at all," I protested, my hands now shoved into the pockets of my jacket. "It's just . . . well, for people at least, we grow up, you know? By the time I was in high school, it became clear that I was going to need to move on."

"But we had such magic together," the bear said. "You never worried about it when you were twelve. Not even when you were fourteen."

"I know," I said. "It's really hard to explain."

The bear turned his attention back to Teresa, who remained frozen in place, her mouth still covered, and her eyes staring.

"I make her afraid," the bear said sadly.

"I should have prepared you," I said to Teresa. "I just did *not* know how to tell you about this. There wasn't any way that'd make sense. And, honestly, I never thought I'd be doing this again. Not after I was out of my mother's house. Every year went by, and I just got involved with my life, and then there was getting married to Megan, and all the trouble we went through, moving around the country, and finally I came back here once the divorce was final. I remembered this place. Was tempted on occasion to visit. But decided not to, just because that part of my life was so far in the past."

"So, what the hell changed your mind?" Teresa managed to stammer, still staring in horrified fascination at Pooh as he turned his attention from her, to me, back to her, and then back to me finally.

"I got the message," I said, looking at Pooh.

"Took you long enough," the bear said.

"What message?" Teresa asked.

"Difficult to explain that, too," I admitted. "Any time Pooh wanted my company, he had a way of letting me know. Once I shipped out to boot camp after high school, the messages came several times, until suddenly, they stopped. And I just put it out of my mind, being where I was, and unable to do anything about it anyway. Then, today, I got it again. And it was so strong, I knew I couldn't ignore it. I figured it was because I was back home again. Or at least in the vicinity, with you and me about to get married and everything. Maybe Pooh could sense it?"

"What the hell *is* 'Pooh'?" Theresa demanded, daring to take a step closer, and lowering one arm to aim a finger directly at the bear's face.

"I am *Winnie* the Pooh," the bear simply said, smiling the same smile he'd smiled at me the very first time I'd seen him move, on this very spot, all those years ago. Then the bear looked at me, aimed one of his mitten-hands in my direction, and said, "And this is Christopher Robin. And that is Tigger. Up, now, furry tiger, up!"

At once, the inert stuffed toy that looked like a tiger, became three sizes larger, and also began rubbing his eyes.

"And Piglet, and Ms. Roo, and Rabbit! And of course, Eeyore," the bear said, pointing his mitten-shaped hand at each of them in turn. And in each case, the stuffed animals were suddenly alive. Not nearly the size of real animals, but still much larger again than their stuffed selves. All rubbing at their eyes as if they'd been asleep for a long time, then looking around them—to take stock of the situation. Even the little baby kangaroo in its mother's pouch.

"They don't look quite real," Teresa said, daring still another step toward the pentagram.

Eeyore—the donkey—was closest to her. He was on all fours now, blue coat with a mane of black hair. His eyes were large, with a sad expression.

"First new human we've seen in forever," the donkey moaned, "and she doesn't even like us."

Perhaps it was the forlorn tone in Eeyore's voice, or perhaps it was the fact he still looked very much like his formerly stuffed self, including his silly bow-tied tail. Teresa reached out a shaking hand to touch him. Ever so gently. Her fingertips delicately dipping into the black hair of his mane, and then instinctively moving to scratch gently at one of his big, floppy ears. To which Eeyore uncharacteristically leaned in, saying, "Awwww, maybe she's changed her mind?"

"He's soft, just like a stuffed animal should be," Teresa said, marveling. "But he's *not* a stuffed animal! Chris, this is . . . okay, I know I'm not drunk, and I'm not high. So, you'd better tell me just what this is all about, and in a hurry."

"I wanted friends," I said simply. "I was a kid, I was lonely, and I wanted friends. And I found this old hand-written notebook in our attic, and in the notebook were a bunch of . . . well, I am not sure what to call them. Spells? Rites? The notebook had belonged to my great-grandmother. Or at least it had her name signed inside the cover. I found it buried amongst a bunch of keepsakes one day after school. And one of the rituals described in the book said it could bring inanimate things to life. But had to be done far away from where grown-ups could see. So, I came out here with all of my stuffed animals one evening—told mom I was doing a sleepover at one of my friends houses—and performed the ritual. And *voila*, it worked precisely as great-grandma's notes described."

Teresa continued to experimentally rub the top of Eeyore's head and ears.

"Unbelievable," she said.

"Believe it!" Pooh said, pushing himself to his feet—which, like his hands, were not fully formed in the manner of peoples' feet. Rather, they were shaped roughly like feet should be shaped, just with no toes. With a doughy quality. And uncanny lines where the edges of the fabric that was his skin were sewn together. Even though he was now much bigger than he'd been when he'd been in the duffel. And his coat was no longer bare along the friction points. He was all fuzzy and new and yellow, and his shirt had become its bright, original green color again.

"Who's that, mama?" asked the little baby kangaroo from its pouch.

"I don't know, dear," the adult kangaroo—standing far smaller in stature than an actual kangaroo might—said, "but it's nice to be awake again after such a long time. Christopher Robin, I'd give you a good talking-too, young man, if you still *were* a young man. But you're not. And that's why Pooh called you here."

"For what?" I asked.

All six of them turned and looked at me, and I felt a chill run down my spine.

"Something's in the woods," Pooh said, and each of them aimed a mitten-hand at the trail that led back into the now-dark trees. "Something new. Something *bad*. We don't know what it is. But if somebody doesn't do something about it, it might threaten everything!"

I gulped. This wasn't what I'd been expecting. When I'd been a boy, the animals and me had enjoyed our share of adventures. When you're a child, even a hundred acres of trees, bushes, and a stream, can seem like the whole world. I'd lost entire afternoons in that place. So happy that I had companions to go exploring with. And who talked to me, just like I talked to them, but they understood me better than any adult ever had. Even my mother, and she'd understood me better than most. Even to the point I'd confessed to her that I was coming out here to play with Pooh and the others. And my mother had just smiled at me, and put my chin between her finger and thumb, and said, "Of course you are, Christopher, I used to do the same when I was a little girl!"

And that had been the end of it. She had humored me. As a parent might.

Or had she? The notebook had been in the family for generations. Surely I wasn't the only one who'd discovered what was inside. Maybe there'd been more to my mother's statement than I'd then known?

And now for the very first time, it occurred to me. If the ritual worked for me and my toys, what was to say it wouldn't work for someone else and their toys? Or did it even have to be a toy at all?

Again, I felt a chill run down my spine.

"Somebody's brought bad things to life," I said, once the implication hit me.

"Yes," Pooh said. "We don't know who, and we don't know what, but we *know* it's here, Christopher Robin. And if you can't stop it, now, before it gets any worse, there might not *be* any stopping it!"

I pulled a hand out of my jacket pocket and rubbed my face with it.

"It would help a great deal if I knew what 'it' is," I said.

"We don't know," the big kangaroo said.

"You're going to have to find out," the rabbit emphasized. "None of the rest of us have been around to watch this thing. We only know it's around, now, because it comes from the same place in the universe *we* come from—and to where we go back, when our person is done with us."

"Your 'person'?" Teresa said. "Like, Chris is your owner?"

"We're *not* pets," the donkey said emphatically, continuing to enjoy Teresa's gentle head-scratching. "We have minds that think. We even have souls like people do. Except, our souls exist in a different place when we're not here. And we can only be here when a person calls us to be here. Once that person calls us—Christopher did, once upon a time—we're his for the duration."

"It's like make-believe," Teresa said, "except somehow it becomes real."

"More or less," I said.

Teresa pulled her hand away from Eeyore's mane and put both palms over her eyes and face.

"Can't be happening," she said. "Just can't. Nope."

"It is," I said, stepping over to where she stood, and pulling her hands down, so that they were clasped firmly in each of mine. "I'm sorry I never explained this to you before. I wanted to. But now you know. And if Pooh and Kanga and Rabbit are insisting there's something dangerous here now—something that could threaten the world outside of these hundred acres—then I'm going to have to do something about it."

"Like what?" Teresa asked. "You're a computer geek. That's even what you did for the Army when you were still in. How are you supposed to fight something, especially if you don't even know what it is?"

"You're not asking any questions I'm not asking," I said, and looked into her eyes. I still saw a lot of fear there, but I also saw that she trusted me.

"We should come back when it's light again," she insisted. "I didn't even bring a flashlight. Do you have your gun?"

"Of course I have my gun," I said, patting the in-waistband holster where the Ruger model SP101 five-shot revolver pressed against my pelvis. The .357 Magnum cartridges loaded in the revolver's cylinder would instantly kill a grown man twice my weight, with proper shot placement. And the flash and boom from the short barrel would frighten anyone unfamiliar with such fireworks. But would it be enough against . . . whatever it was Pooh and the others were afraid of?

"There isn't much time," Kanga cautioned.

"No time at all!" the little kangaroo in her pouch cried. "We have to go tonight!"

"Wait," I said to them all. "She's right. We're being foolish if we go tromping around in the trees, in the dark, at night, trying to find something we're not even sure about."

"We'll know it when we find it," Pooh said. "And so will you, Christopher Robin. Of this we're certain."

I looked at Teresa, and was tempted to try to just forget the whole thing, take her away from this place, convince her it had all been a delusion. Or even a bad dream. But she was looking at Eeyore, who was looking up at her, and I could tell she'd already made her decision.

"Sounds like they're depending on us," she said.

"On me, you mean," I corrected her.

Teresa turned her head to look me square in the face, and said, *"Us,* honey. If there can't be an 'us' at a time like this, when will there ever be an us?"

I opened my mouth to argue, but found I didn't have the words. She was completely right.

So, I went back to my bike, dug out the emergency hand-held LED lantern that I kept in case I was ever in mechanical trouble somewhere at night, clicked it on, and returned to where the candles continued to burn at the points of the pentagram.

"Do we have to leave those going?" Teresa asked. "They could start a fire."

"No, once the ritual is done, they can go out," I said.

She doused them. And now my friends—the former stuffed animals become real—were illuminated by a harsher, modern light. It had been so long since I'd seen them I'd forgotten how odd it was, looking at living creatures who still seemed so much like the toys that they were. Or had been. And would be again, once this—whatever it was we were getting ourselves into—was all over. They looked at me hopefully, clustered together, about as big as I'd been when I was eleven years old, and seemed to be waiting for me to take the lead. Which I did, heading down the path into the thick blackness of the woods. A path I'd taken many times as a youngster, but which could be going any which way, now. Since it had been so long. And I had no idea whose feet had worn, or changed, its course, since mine had followed it.

A few night crickets still chirped quietly. It wasn't quite cold enough yet for them to have been silenced. But it soon would be. I took my jacket off and wrapped it around Teresa's shoulders, then held the LED lamp from one hand aimed out in front of us, my other hand resting on the SP101.

I'd never drawn my weapon on a human being. Had never fired a shot in anger during my Army days, even, despite spending time in the Middle East. Teresa was right. I'd spent my life working with computers and computer equipment. There wasn't a whole lot for someone in my occupational specialty to do, except run network cable, set up secure wireless hotspots, and re-image mil-spec laptops. A trade I'd later turned into a nicely-paying profession, once I was out of the service and into the civilian working world.

But that wouldn't help me now.

The more constricted the path became, the more I curled my fingers around the pistol's grip.

"Like Luke going into the cave, on *Empire,*" Teresa mumbled as the path ahead grew more foreboding.

"Way to make me feel better about doing this," I replied sarcastically, then realized we were both talking in hushed tones.

"Why are we afraid of it?" I suddenly said at full voice. "Maybe we should make it afraid of *us!*"

A chorus of shushing came from behind.

"Courage and folly go hand in hand!" Rabbit whispered.

I frowned at them, then faced back down the trail, and continued walking. Not slowly, mind you, but not fast, either. My eyes continually scanned for . . . something. Anything. And kept seeing nothing at all. Which I found frustrating, and not just a little annoying. Trying to feel our way forward despite the gloom was an exercise in aggravation.

Then, suddenly, we were coming out of the trees into a small meadow.

The sky opened up overhead, and we could see the stars again.

The light from the LED lamp was absorbed in the blackness, though I could make out the treetops in the distance at the meadow's edge.

I stopped, and leaned back.

"Rabbit, is this—?" I began to ask, then Rabbit hissed.

"Yes," Rabbit finally said. "But they're not here now. Gone! All gone!"

"Who's gone?" Teresa asked.

"Rabbit has a rather . . . extended family," I said to her.

"But we can't see a thing," Teresa said. "How can the rabbit tell—"

"I can feel it," Rabbit said forlornly. "And you forget, human, I have a rabbit's ears. I would be hearing them if they were still here. Except, they're not. I fear whatever evil it is that's upon the wood, it's already been through here, and gone away."

"That's terrible!" the pig said, stuttering slightly, and clinging to Pooh Bear's arm.

"Oh no, Piglet! Oh no, oh no!" was all Pooh could say, over and over again.

I stared into the blackness, annoyed that the harsh, artificial light of the LED lamp showed me nothing, then realized I was violating one of the cardinal rules of conducting a night operation. I used my free hand to switch the light off, then whispered to everyone that they needed to follow me. Holding hands.

I proceeded carefully, letting my eyes adjust to the dark. Teresa was directly behind me, her hand closed around mine like it was made of iron, and her other hand was closed around Pooh's, who in turn was linked to Kanga, then Tigger—who was being unusually quiet, which was quite out of character considering his ordinary bravado when faced with danger—then Piglet, and finally Eeyore, who had one of his large, floppy ears grasped tightly in Piglet's fist.

"What are you looking for specifically, now?" Teresa asked me in a whisper.

"I'm so stupid," I said. "That lamp gave away our position like a beacon the moment we came out of the tree line. Now I'm taking us along the tree line, toward the stream you hear in the distance. When we hit the bank, we'll follow that. And no, I still have no idea what it is we're looking for. But I am hoping we might now see it—whatever it might be—before it sees us."

"I hope you're right," Teresa said, and squeezed my hand.

We hit the edge of the stream fairly quickly, and then I began to lead us perpendicular to the way we'd come. I was very careful with my steps, working as hard as I could to pick a sure path, since the others were trusting me to find the way. All the while, I kept my ears tuned for the sound of anything unusual or out of the ordinary. It had been a while since I'd done anything like this at night, and the murmur of the stream flowing over the rocks made it difficult. But I was still waiting to hear *something* not right. A noise, or noises, that didn't match what my young ears had grown accustomed to in this place, decades ago.

It didn't take me long to pick out the wrong sounds.

I froze in place, and instinctively ducked down, taking a knee. Teresa felt me go down, and did similarly, with the others doing the same.

"Why did we stop?" Piglet asked, stuttering his words, which were full of fright.

"Do you hear that?" I whispered to Teresa, who whispered it back along the line.

"No," Pooh said, coming up to crouch next to me.

"Just wait," I said.

And then, very far off, there it was. A slightly mechanical sound, like a rusty hinge, but knocked down several octaves, so that it had a grinding, base quality.

"What is it?" Teresa asked.

"A dragon!" squeaked the little kangaroo from his mother's pouch.

"D-d-d-dragon?" Piglet said, now sounding truly terrified.

"Lemme at 'em!" Tigger suddenly shouted, and I felt him—rather than saw him—spring over the top of all of us, and suddenly go bounding—or was it bouncing?—off in the direction of the sound we'd been hearing.

"Oh no!" Eeyore said. "There goes our chance to stay hidden from the dragon!"

"Tigger!" I half-shouted. "Come back, you idiot! You have no idea what's out there!"

But my toy tiger, at once cowardly *and* courageous, depending on which way his mood swung, had suddenly turned manic. And I remembered from my childhood days that once Tigger was off the chain, there was no telling what he might do.

"Great," I said to Teresa. "Well, we might as well follow him."

"We can't even see where he went!" she protested.

I decided to click the LED lamp back on, and pointed to the tracks on the ground.

"Holes?" she said, confused.

"Tigger tracks," I said confidently. "He bounces on his tail."

"What?" she said, incredulously.

"Come on!" I said, and got up to quickly follow where Tigger had gone. There was little need to worry about subtlety now. Tigger would announce our presence for us. But, I also thought, Tigger might keep the—dragon?—busy while we approached, too. He could be a foolhardy tiger, but Tigger was also rather durable. One didn't live so recklessly as Tigger had done, when I was younger, without having all nine lives kept ready. Perhaps Tigger still had a life or two to give for the cause?

We reached the bridge where I expected it to be—not nearly in as good a shape as I remembered it, but the wood was still weight-bearing—and crossed to the other side. As we did, the hinge-like, grinding, base-tone noise suddenly echoed across the night like a bellow. Or a roar? It was followed by the crashing and smashing sounds of trees being knocked down. And I no longer doubted little Roo's guess that we were indeed facing a dragon.

Now it was my turn to feel the terror which had set Piglet to quaking.

"Let's go back!" he wailed.

"Not while Tigger needs our help!" Kanga said emphatically.

I led them a few hundred yards more, past new rows of trees, until suddenly we could see *and* hear the beast out of nightmares.

It was as if someone had taken a Tonka backhoe, dump truck, and fire engine, then kitbashed them with several different species of toy dinosaur, topped off with what looked like a toy flying saucer for a head. Except, this was no toy. The Frankenstein's monster of a behemoth was two stories tall, and almost seemed to be growing taller right before our very eyes. Several spotlights shown out of the saucer head and down onto the ground, where we saw Tigger springing about, dodging either the behemoth's smashing fists or smashing feet—its limbs and torso being a combination of mechanical and dinosaur parts, with scoops for hands, treads for feet, a bizarrely reptilian torso, and again, the saucer-shaped head. Which seemed to be looking this way and that, trying to discern what it was on the ground which was antagonizing it.

One of the beams from the spotlights traced across a cluster of huddled individuals who cowered beneath a low bluff. They were on the opposite side of the action from us, but I could see what appeared to be most of Rabbit's family, and also what seemed to be three humans. Or, rather, teenage boys. Young teenagers, by the look of them. They cowered with the rest, afraid of the monster which towered over them.

"What in the *hell* is that thing?!" Teresa exclaimed, as it attempted to stomp Tigger flat, missed again, then tilted back its flying saucer head and let loose with the most strange and unsettling kind of mechanical shriek. And with every move it made, the base-level grinding sound of metal could be heard. Its kitbashed joints complaining loudly against the movement, as its imperfectly and grotesquely-made body fought its attempts to keep up with Tigger as he bounced deftly around at the behemoth's feet.

I stared up at the thing—which blessedly had not noticed our little group, yet —and had no idea what to tell my fiancé. Then I looked again at the three young teenage boys cowering along with Rabbit's extended family. And it hit me. My initial speculation was correct.

"Come on," I told her. "We have to move while Tigger's keeping it distracted."

I led our group around the edge of the clearing the behemoth had razed. Tigger—still manic as he could be—continue to shout at the thing, and spring around energetically on both his tail and all fours.

"Missed me again, you lumbering lummox!" Tigger exclaimed with his characteristic lisp, laughing and taunting as he moved.

We eventually reached the low bluff where Rabbit ran to his relatives, and Teresa and I both grabbed the boys by their shirts.

"It was all innocent fun until you gave it life!" I shouted into one of the boy's faces. The largest, and oldest, by my reckoning.

"Who are you?" he asked, looking both exhausted and scared like he'd never been scared before.

"Someone who thinks he knows exactly what you did!" I shouted over the shrieking of the behemoth, who kept attempting to turn Tigger into a bug on a windshield.

"We didn't mean it!" exclaimed one of the other boys. "It was Terry's idea!"

"Shut up!" said the third boy. "I just brought the toy parts!"

"I did it," the largest boy said. "I saw the charm on-line. Saved it to my phone. I thought it would just be something fun to do. Kinda cool. And kinda scary, you know? I didn't in a million years think it would actually work. We drew the pentagram, with the candles, and spoke the charm. And then *that* became real."

"But why is it so huge?" Teresa demanded. "None of the rest of the toys became monstrous!"

I stared up at the thing, wondering the same. And then it hit me. This wasn't a single toy. It was components from many different toys, which had been owned by many different children. Summoned to life by three boys at once, versus just one, and all that combined, youthful energy had made it big. As well as powerful. And now, seemingly as it raged in the night, its fury made it even stronger. It literally towered over the trees. There'd be no stopping any such thing with my little concealed-carry revolver.

But we wouldn't need that. I knew precisely what could be done, even if the boys didn't.

"You don't know how to make it stop, do you?" I said to the largest boy.

"No," he admitted.

"I do," I said, glancing at Pooh, Kanga, little Roo, Eeyore, and Piglet, who still clung to Pooh.

"You have to remember that it *is* a toy. Or, at least, toys. You have to remember that when you walk out of here, that thing can't walk out with you. It exists as long as your imagination *allows* it to exist."

"I don't understand," the boy admitted.

"Like this," I said, looking at Pooh specifically. Then added, "I'm sorry, old friend."

"I think I understand, Christopher," the bear said. "Do what you must. Save the wood!"

As I stared at my old bear, I remembered all the times I'd finished up playing. In time to get back home for supper. And my bear, my donkey, my bunny, all of them simply reverted to their ordinary selves. So that I could tuck them away in my little house I'd cobbled together for myself on the other end of the wood, or push them into my backpack and take them back home with me. In each and every case, it hadn't been an act of will, but merely a switching of the mind. From the freedom of play and imagination, to the pragmatics of needing to get home in time to wash up and be at the table when food was about to be served.

I explained as much to the three boys, and emphasized to them that they had to do it together. One of them doing it on his own wouldn't be enough. The three of them had to realize that play time was over, they were long overdue for getting home, and if they would just stop letting their fear of the behemoth rule them, the rest would take care of itself.

As proof of concept, I looked at Pooh and the others, then simply allowed myself to switch modes—in my heart—from the reality of them being fully animated beings, to the reality of them being my stuffed animals whom I had loved and cherished ever since I was a boy. And in that moment, all of them—including Rabbit's many relatives—instantly transformed back to what they'd been originally. Including Tigger, who's diminutive stuffed toy self was promptly crushed by the behemoth, which now began striding mighty strides toward us.

"Do it!" I screamed at the boys. "It's not real if you don't *let* it be real!"

The behemoth shrieked one last time, raised a leg to drive one of its treaded feet down on top of us as we stared up at it . . . and then, suddenly, it was a three-foot-high glued-together contraption of various toy parts, jerkily waddling around on the dirt, its flying saucer head making strange, alien, outer-space noises, and flashing colorful lights, while the inexpertly-joined arms, legs, and torso, both shuddered and flailed—the mechanisms inside never quite working correctly.

The boy named Terry shakily stepped over, and turned the thing off.

Teresa and I slumped against each other, breathing a sigh of relief. Suffice it to say, we walked out of those hundred acres that night a rather changed couple. We got the boys back to their homes—all three of them incredibly apologetic for what had happened, but grateful for the ride in Teresa's electric car. And if the parents had raised eyebrows, well, Teresa was a Jr. High School counselor, and could truthfully state she'd had to rein in a truant or two in her day. What were three boys more? Even if they weren't from her district specifically?

All three of them promising me they would *never* try the "charm" again. Not knowing what they could unleash, if they weren't careful to respect the powers they'd unwittingly unleashed in this world. The very real damage the thing had caused—it was in the news the next day, and the park service was quite at a loss how to explain the fallen trees and tracks from what appeared to have been a caterpillar tractor run amuck—was enough to convince them all not to tempt fate twice.

As for Pooh and the rest? Teresa made me promise not to keep them under wraps for decades again. We'd build a window nook for them at the new place. And Teresa sent the pieces of Tigger to get stitched back up at her mother's place. In anticipation, Teresa said, of there being a very real need for toys in our not-too-distant future. Which just made Teresa's mother beam.

In Which Pooh Discovers Woozles in the Walls

Janci Patterson

Winnie-the-Pooh was just sitting down to a large pot of honey when he heard the buzzing coming from the walls. These were not just any walls, of course, but his own walls, in his house in the forest where he lived under the name of Sanders. By which, of course, he meant that the name of Sanders stretched across the door above him and he lived underneath it.

Pooh paused with his paw over the large pot of honey. It was emptier than he had remembered, and for a moment he wondered who had eaten all his honey, but then he recalled that he'd opened the jar for an afternoon snack so he supposed it must have been him, after all. His tummy rumbled, and as it did, the buzzing sound through the wall grew louder.

Pooh thought to himself that this buzzing noise must mean something. After all, you didn't get a buzzing noise like that, just buzzing and buzzing, without it meaning something. If there was a buzzing noise, then someone was making a buzzing noise, and the only reason Pooh knew of to make a buzzing noise was because you were a bee. And, of course, as he had long thought, the only reason for being a bee was to make honey, and everyone knew that the purpose of honey was for it to be eaten by Pooh.

"That's awfully considerate," he said to himself. The tree was so tall, it took a great deal of effort for Pooh to climb to the top of the tree to get that honey, and last time he'd tried he'd unfortunately fallen a great distance and landed in a gorse bush with prickles in his nose.

It was all so very inconvenient, the way one fell so much faster than one climbed. The more Pooh thought about it, the sillier it seemed, given that climbing was so much more useful than falling, especially when it came to doing the most important task of getting honey out of trees. Nevertheless, falling was fast and climbing was slow and therefore it would be most considerate of the bees to relocate themselves to the much lower position of the inside of Pooh's walls.

Pooh left his pot of honey—which was large but not *so* large that he wouldn't be needing another in short order—on the table and moved over to the walls, listening carefully. The buzzing was loud, and sounded as if it were just beyond the surface of the wall, directly on the other side of the wallpaper.

And this is where Pooh encountered a problem. It *was* very convenient for the bees to pick such a nearby location to make their honey, but while Pooh *did* know how to climb a tree, he didn't have the first idea of how to get to the inside of the walls. And if he couldn't get in, then how did the bees?

It occurred to Pooh that perhaps the bees only *sounded* like they were coming from the inside of the walls. Perhaps the sound was traveling out of his larder, so he opened the cupboard and checked, but the larder held nothing but a few empty pots, none of which contained bees.

"If they really wanted to be considerate," Pooh said to himself, "the bees might just make their honey right here in my honey pots." Though then when he went to reach for the honey, he might come up with a pawful of bees, so maybe it was better that they not be *too* considerate after all.

Pooh returned to the walls, listening again to the deep, resonant buzzing. The longer he listened, the more of a draw he felt to stand there with his ear pressed to the paper, continuing to listen to the sonorous buzzing, as if it were trying to whisper something to him.

If there were bees making honey in his walls, there had to be a way in, and if there was no way in on this side of the wall, it only made sense that Pooh check on the other. So Pooh, with a longing sigh, left his pot of honey on the table and wandered out from beneath the name of Sanders to check on the outside of the wall.

Pooh lived beneath a large tree, and as Pooh pressed his ear to this side of the wall, all he heard was the rustling of the trees overhead. The wall was silent, which wasn't very nice, now that Pooh thought of it, to be silent when a someone was trying so hard to listen. The wall might at least have offered him some kind of "how do you do" or "how are you today" when he was straining to hear anything at all. But there was no reply from the wall, not even a bit of the buzzing that had been so present and loud from the other side.

"Bother," said Pooh. If the bees had gotten into the walls from the outside, they must have already retired for the evening, and unless one decided to take an evening walk, he wouldn't be able to determine how they'd gotten in.

So Pooh returned to his kitchen, where he listened again to the buzzing in the walls. There were quite a lot of bees in there, it seemed, which meant, Pooh could only imagine, that they must be making quite a lot of honey. He sat down once again with his honey pot, which now seemed more empty than ever, and indeed when it was empty, Pooh hardly felt satiated at all. So it was that he went off to bed with the rumbling in his tummy drowned out only by the continuous roar of the bees.

It was hard to sleep, with the bees buzzing so loudly. They were inside the walls by Pooh's bed, and indeed, seemed to be inside the other walls as well. Pooh thought about trying to count them to put himself to sleep, but being a bear of very little brain, he was unable to count to the truly colossal number of bees that must have taken up residence in his walls, even if he could have begun to separate one buzzing sound from another. As the night progressed, it seemed as if the mighty swarm grew larger and louder, as if the walls themselves were alive with the cacophonous sounds. In the light of his candle, Pooh thought he saw the walls begin to shake with them, each flower of the wallpaper undulating wildly, seeming to execute a singular dance of death.

The bees continued their nauseous dance with such a force against the wall-paper that their bodies began to draw trails of motion, so that Pooh could now determine their singular direction. The bees, it seemed, were all flying *down*, from somewhere near the top of the wall to someplace below.

"Bother," said Pooh. His tummy continued to rumble, and if the bees were making their honey somewhere down near his floorboards, it was so close he could nearly taste it. It wasn't considerate of them at all to bring him honey so close at hand and yet in so utterly inaccessible a place. And so he resolved that in the morning he would go directly to someone with more experience at getting into tight spaces.

So IT WAS THAT, in the morning, Pooh went directly to visit his friend Rabbit at his home in the hole in the sandy bank. When he came to the hole, Pooh stuck his head directly in. He had learned that if he called out to Rabbit, someone would answer who was *not* Rabbit and who would insist that Rabbit was *not* at home. But then it always seemed to turn out that Rabbit *was* home, after all, and so Pooh had given up announcing his arrival entirely.

"Hallo, Rabbit," called Pooh.

"Rabbit who?" Rabbit replied. He had already set out a plate for his breakfast, though to Pooh's great disappointment, his breakfast did not seem to involve even a morsel of honey.

"Rabbit you," Pooh said. He knew he had come to ask Rabbit a question, but he was so distracted by the rumbling in his tummy that he might have forgotten had it not born such a striking resemblance to the buzzing of bees.

Ah yes. That's right. "Rabbit, have you ever thought about how you would get inside the walls of your house?"

Rabbit took a look at the sandy walls of his hole, considering this question. "I suppose I would dig," Rabbit said, "except I wouldn't because I like my walls where they are, thank you."

"My walls are in a very fine place," Pooh said, "but there are bees making honey in them, and I don't know how they got there."

"Are you sure that they *are* there?" Rabbit asked.

Pooh was quite sure, having seen the rippling of them through the paper, and heard the insidious buzzing well into the night, though it did seem to have quieted very much this morning. "Yes," Pooh said. "So if you wanted to get into the walls—not at your house but at mine—how exactly would you go about it?"

"I wouldn't," Rabbit said. "If there were bees in your walls, they must have a way of getting inside. But they're so much smaller than you that you'd hardly be able to get in the way they did. And none of it matters because there *aren't* any bees in your walls, and even if there were, you wouldn't be able to follow them."

Pooh didn't like this answer at all. "What kind of house," Pooh said, "has walls containing honey that you can't get into to take the honey out?"

"Pooh," Rabbit said, "did you *see* any bees in the walls of your house?"

"No," said Pooh. This was beginning to remind Pooh of that time Roo met that Strange Animal in the woods, who he insisted was real, though Rabbit was certain Roo had made the entire thing up. "But while I was trying to sleep, I saw them pressing against the inside of the wallpaper, all flying down at once."

"They did this one time?" Rabbit asked.

"They continued doing it most of the night," Pooh said. "And then when I woke up, they hadn't left me any honey for breakfast."

"See now," Rabbit said, "how could the bees fly *down* all night without ever taking the trip up again?"

Pooh scratched his head. This was a very good question. One fell down fast and climbed up slowly, but if one didn't climb up at all, one could only fall to the bottom on a singular occasion. Even a bear of very little brain knew that.

As Pooh was thinking about this, Rabbit continued. "Pooh, there aren't any bees in the walls of your house."

"There aren't?" Pooh asked.

"There certainly aren't. There's nothing wrong with your house or your walls. And there isn't anything wrong with my house except that there's a bear with his head poked in."

"Oh," said Pooh. Rabbit was right. It was a very nice house, and there *was* a bear with his head poked in.

"I don't think you're thinking straight today," Rabbit said.

"I never think straight," Pooh replied. "It's so much better to think roundly, wouldn't you agree?"

"I'd agree," Rabbit said, "if your thoughts brought you round to going back to your house, where there isn't anything wrong at all."

Pooh couldn't argue with that. His stomach, which was rather round, was beginning to ache more sharply than before.

"Thank you, Rabbit," Pooh said. And he pulled his head out of Rabbit's hole and started wandering through the woods, trying to think.

As Pooh wandered through the Hundred Acre Wood, thinking as he went, he came across his friend Piglet, who was doing some thinking of his own.

"Oh dear," Piglet said as he walked. "Oh dear, oh d-dear."

"What's the matter, Piglet?" Pooh asked, forgetting, for the moment, what he was supposed to be thinking about.

"I was looking through some of the papers that belonged to my late grandfather, Trespassers W," Piglet said. Piglet had inherited his house beneath the beech trees from his grandfather, and had a sign with his name on it to prove it. "And I found a strange sculpture made out of clay."

"Oh," Pooh said. "That doesn't sound so bothersome. Was it a sculpture of your grandfather?"

"N-no," Piglet said. "It was a sculpture of a Hostile Animal that was made by a friend of his."

"So it was a present," Pooh said. "That doesn't seem so bad at all. Don't you like presents, Piglet?"

"N-not this one," Piglet said. "I didn't like the look of that Animal. The note I found with it said that creature is dreaming under the ocean, and now I'm afraid it will rise up and eat me."

Pooh nodded. He knew how unpleasant it was to be afraid. Like having a rumbling in your tummy that you could never stop, no matter how much honey you ate. "Have you ever been to the ocean?" he asked Piglet.

"Well, no," Piglet said.

"Then why would you be frightened of something under it?"

"I didn't like the look of that statue!" Piglet said. "And now it's in my house, so I think I need to find somewhere else to stay. Oh dear, oh dear."

If Piglet needed someplace to stay, then a place should surely be offered to him. Rabbit was particular about who he let into his hole, while Kanga and Roo had gone off on an Expotition to examine that rock that fell out of the sky, and Pooh hadn't seen or heard from them since. He and Tigger had been meaning to go on an Expotition of their own to find them, but then Tigger had to travel to visit his cousins in the town of Ulthar, where apparently they were having some kind of trouble.

Pooh didn't know much about rocks or cousins or statues or Hostile Animals, but he did see there was only one thing to do in this situation. "Come home with me, Piglet," he said. "You can stay at my house, because there is nothing wrong with it whatsoever. Rabbit told me so."

"Well, okay," Piglet said. "If you're certain it's all right."

So it was that Pooh and Piglet spent the afternoon thinking and walking, walking and thinking, and then Piglet returned home with Pooh, where Pooh found a half-full honey pot on the highest shelf of his larder where he had quite forgotten it, and they both had honey for supper. The honey must have been forgotten for longer than even a very forgetful bear was accustomed to abandoning it, because it was dark amber in color and quite thick, clinging to his paws and sticking to his nails, coating his teeth so that lick and lick as he might, he could never quite get them clean again.

Once they had eaten, Pooh made Piglet a bed next to his out of two blankets and a dresser drawer, and then they both settled down for an early sleep.

It was then that the buzzing began again. First, it was a distant hum, so much that Pooh thought he himself might be mumbling a tune, and listened closely to himself to try to figure out what song he was humming.

"Pooh," Piglet said, "what is that sound?"

"It might be me humming," Pooh said, though it kept buzzing even as he talked, and he'd never been able to talk and hum at the same time before. "Or maybe my tummy is rumbling again. We only had half a honey pot's worth for supper, after all."

But then the buzzing grew louder, rising to first a grumbling and then a roar, until Piglet had to fold down both his ears, burrowing down into the blankets in fright.

"Are you sure that's your tummy?" Piglet asked.

Pooh *wasn't* sure, though if it wasn't bees in his walls, he couldn't think of what else it could be. "It must be nothing," Pooh said. "Rabbit said there weren't any bees in the walls of my house, and there was nothing wrong with my house at all."

"B-bees?" Piglet said. "Why would Rabbit say anything about bees?"

"Because I asked him how I might get their honey out of the walls," Pooh said.

"But Rabbit said there was no way into my walls, and even if there were, there weren't any bees in there anyway."

"You said there was nothing wrong with your house!" Piglet said, shrieking now to be heard over the raucous buzzing.

"There isn't," Pooh said. "Rabbit said so."

"Then what is that noise, Pooh?" Piglet asked.

That was a very good question, and one that Pooh paused to consider. If there were no bees in the walls of his house, then what *could* be causing the noise?

"I don't know," said Pooh, and he listened carefully as the buzzing grew louder than he'd ever heard it before. The roaring rose and fell, until it almost sounded as if something behind his wallpaper was chanting.

"Oh dear!" Piglet shouted as the strange words took form, rumbling themselves along like thunder from a storm cloud. "Oh dear, oh dear, oh dearie dearie dear!"

Pooh sat up in bed and watched as his walls once again began to roil with the outlines of thousands of bees, all pressing little divots into the wallpaper and falling purposefully and unstoppably *down*.

"Well," Pooh said. "I suppose it's possible Rabbit was, well, not *wrong*, exactly, but at least partially misinformed. It certainly *looks* like there are bees in the walls."

"I've never seen b-bees do anything like that!" Piglet said. He had his snout tucked under the blankets, with only his eyes protruding, and the other blanket pulled down tight over his ears to block out the noise.

The longer Pooh listened, the more the buzzing *did* sound like chanting. He listened closely to make out the words. "Ya," it sounded like the bees were saying. "Yayaya—"

"Do you think it might be a Heffalump?" Piglet cried. "Or—" he paused to take a desperate gulp of air, "—Woozles?"

Ah! Perhaps that's what it was. Not "yayaya" but enthusiastically "wawawa!"

"If there are Woozles in my walls," Pooh said with a sigh, "then there isn't any honey in there at all."

"It certainly sounds like there's *something* in there!" Piglet cried, watching where the ripples behind the wallpaper began to bulge along the floorboards at the edge of the wall, creeping farther and farther into the room and then sliding their way toward the door. All the while the shape of the words became more and more clear in Pooh's mind.

"Wawawawizzle wawawawoozle wawawa—"

If Rabbit said that everything was fine at Pooh's house, then clearly Pooh needed to speak to someone who knew things. He would have asked his friend Christopher Robin, but just last week Christopher Robin had found a silver key and run off to have an adventure with it from which he had not yet returned, so it must be a wonderful adventure indeed.

It was just as well, because if anyone knew anything about anything, it was Owl who knew something about something. In fact, one might even say Owl frequently seemed to know too much.

Pooh resolved to speak to him first thing in the morning.

FIRST THING IN THE MORNING, Piglet ran home, telling Pooh that perhaps the statue he'd found wasn't so bad after all, and he should like to finish reading the notes his grandfather, Trespassers W, had left him on the history of the thing.

Upon Piglet's departure, Pooh set immediately out to visit his friend Owl.

Owl lived in The Chestnuts, in a house in a tree with a gambril roof. Pooh didn't know what gambril meant, but he knew it described Owl's roof because Owl had described it to Pooh in just that way on far too many occasions.

Pooh approached the door of Owl's house, which had both a knocker and a bell-pull, and a sign above both that said "P.GETAE. PROP . . . TEMP . . . DONA . . . L. PRAEC . . . VS . . . PONTIFI . . . ATYS" which meant "Please ring if an answer is required," which Pooh knew very well because Owl had told him.

"Owl!" Pooh called, after both knocking the knocker and ringing the bell. "I require an answer!"

Owl poked his head out of the door. "Hallo, Pooh," he said. "What answer do you require?"

"There are Woozles in the walls of my house," Pooh said. "And maybe a Heffalump. Possibly a Wizzle or two, but *definitely* a Woozle."

"A Woozle, you say," Owl said. "How curious. What made you arrive at this conclusion?"

"Piglet and I heard it," Pooh said. "It was making a buzzing sound in the walls, and pressing against the wallpaper. I thought it was bees, but Rabbit said that it wasn't, and then after that it began to talk."

"And what did it say?" Owl asked. "Tekeli-lil, tekeli-lil, something like that?"

The words sounded strange and made Pooh feel rumbly in his tummy all over again. "Not at all," he said. "It was a chant of sorts, a kind of wawawa—"

"Ah," said Owl. "Which brought you to the inevitable conclusion that what you were hearing was a Woozle."

"What else could it be?" Pooh asked. "And how do I get the Woozle out of the walls of my house?" He didn't like the idea of having to find a new house. He quite liked living under the name of Sanders, even if his larder was less full of honey at the moment than he would have liked. He couldn't imagine why anyone would have left the house, though someone had surely lived in it before he had, for they'd left behind the bed and the table and chairs and had never returned for them.

"How indeed," Owl said, and Owl began to talk and talk, all about things that lived under the sea and some friend of his who went by the unlikely moniker of Him Who Is Not To Be Named. Pooh tried to pay attention, but Owl went on, using longer and longer words, until at last he came back to where he started, and he suggested that if someone was trying to talk to Pooh from within the walls of his house, the only polite thing to do would be to answer it back.

"Oh," Pooh said. "Of course. How rude of me not to think of that."

"And be sure you apologize for the oversight," Owl said. "I'm sure it will forgive you. Only so much can be expected of a bear, after all."

"Thank you, Owl," Pooh said, and he set out for home again, thinking extra hard as he composed his apology.

POOH WAS SO INVOLVED in how exactly one should apologize to Woozles in the walls that one has previously slighted and ignored that he made several circles around the Hundred Acre Wood before he arrived back on the path that would lead him home again. And just as he was about to round the last bend that would bring his home into view, who should he come across but his friend Eeyore, the Old Grey Donkey, his tail swishing along behind him.

"Hallo, Pooh," Eeyore said. "Where are you off to?"

"I was going home to speak to the Woozles in my walls," said Pooh. "I'm afraid I've offended them."

"It's an easy thing to do," Eeyore said gloomily. "No matter what you do, people will be offended. Nothing to do be done about it."

"No, no," Pooh said. "It's my fault. The Woozles were trying to speak to me, and I didn't have the courtesy to answer. I do hope they weren't trying to tell me anything important!"

Now that he thought about it, the purpose of the Woozles seemed more obvious than ever. Something had been making the buzzing in the walls, and where there was buzzing, there were bees, whatever Rabbit said. And if there were bees in the walls along with the Woozles, then the Woozles had certainly been trying to give him directions to get into his walls to get to the honey. Here Pooh had been, bemoaning the fact that he couldn't get into the walls, and the Woozles had been trying to give him the answer all along.

"It probably doesn't matter what you say," Eeyore said. "Might as well just keep on ignoring them."

"I rather think I'm going to ask them to forgive me," Pooh said. "I was just going home now to speak to them. Would you like to come with me?"

"Might as well," Eeyore said. "I haven't anything better to do."

And so it was that Eeyore followed Pooh back to his house under the name of Sanders, where they both sat at Pooh's table and waited for the buzzing to begin again. On several occasions Pooh was certain he heard it, only to discover that this time it really was his tummy rumbling, and his larder was all out of honey. So Eeyore went home for a pot he'd had stored in his cupboard, as he liked to keep one there in case he received a visit from Pooh. It must have been a great long time since Pooh had last visited him, because this honey was thick and gritty and so deep an amber color that was almost red, as if it had been mixed with several cupfuls of blood, but they both ate until Pooh's tummy was no longer distractingly rumbly.

That evening, the buzzing began again at last, first as a whisper, then as a hum, and then as a grumbling so loud that even Eeyore had to admit that it certainly was coming from the walls.

"Hallo, Woozles!" Pooh called above the din, just as the words began to form that inevitable chant of "wawawa" that seemed to vibrate in Pooh's bones. "I'm terribly sorry for having ignored you. Do you know how I might be able to reach the honey the bees left inside my walls?"

"You'd probably have to put holes in the walls to get to it," Eeyore said. "And then next time it rains all the rain will come in."

This was a very good point, and a very good reason to hear out the Woozles before Pooh did anything rash. Pooh continued his plaintive apology and Eeyore continued to listen with no further acknowledgment but the swish-swish-swish of his tail under Pooh's table.

At first, the Woozles gave no reply that Pooh could recognize, only continued their inevitable chant of "wawawa" as the wall paper began to ripple again, and then the floorboards to bubble, as the Woozles or the bees or some terrible combination of both pressed against the inside of the room. And just when Pooh was certain that he'd offered too great an offense and the Woozles would never bring themselves to forgive him, Pooh noticed that, after falling to the floor, the tiny, bee-sized bubbles were traveling along the floorboards in the direction of the larder.

Alarmed that the Woozles might be after his honey, Pooh threw open the larder doors, remembering only then that there wasn't any more honey in the larder, only empty honey pots. "Bother," he said, though he consoled himself that at least if he had no more honey, there was no more honey for Woozles to steal.

The tiny ripples in the floor ran beneath Pooh's feet, tickling the pads of his paws, and Pooh jumped, watching as they ran into the corner and circled, like they had found some residual honey remaining in the jars there. If there was even a morsel of honey, Pooh wanted to save it from the vengeful Woozles, so he lifted the pots up into his arms, balancing them precariously one upon another, all the while hopping from foot to foot as the tiny ripples tickled his paws.

Eeyore stood in the doorway, surveying this sight and saying nothing until at last he mumbled, "What is that down there?"

Pooh looked down and noticed for the first time a small door in the corner of his larder that he never remembered seeing before. It was square, and made of the same wood as his floorboards, and was now being circled by the thousands of rippling bees from the other side of the floor, before they popped out of sight as if they'd swirled around a whirlpool and then slipped down some kind of a drain.

"Wawawa," the Woozles continued to chant, and Pooh thought they had perhaps answered him after all. He'd asked where the honey was, and had been immediately directed to this door. The two had to be related.

And so it was that Pooh found himself dumping the honey pots in the opposite corner and prying up the door in the floorboards to see what was on the other side.

Beyond the door, Pooh found neither bees nor honey nor Woozles, but a set of narrow wooden stairs spiraling down into the dark.

"What do you think is down there?" Pooh asked Eeyore.

"Probably nothing," Eeyore said. "Certainly not any honey."

But Pooh pondered, and as he pondered, he remembered wishing that bees would make their honey somewhere *down*, because it was so much easier to go *down* than up. "Come on, then," Pooh said to Eeyore, and he collected a candle, stepped onto the stairs, and began to descend.

It wasn't easy for a bear with such a round shape to fit down through such a small door. Pooh had to scoot and shuffle, and for a moment, he was afraid he would become stuck as he once had in Rabbit's front door.

"I guess you'll have to stay up here after all," Eeyore said. But with some urging from Pooh, Eeyore finally consented to put his front feet on Pooh's shoulders and stuff him down into the hole, and Pooh fell down onto the stairs with a plop. Once he was past the doorway, Pooh was able to continue down the stairs, and so he and Eeyore traveled down, down with the candle, much slower than Pooh had fallen out of the honey tree, and he was very grateful for that.

"It's very dark down here," Pooh said, as the darkness seemed to press in around his candle, the shadows dancing just beyond its reach.

"It's always dark everywhere," Eeyore said. "Especially places under the ground."

Pooh supposed that it must be, though Rabbit managed to keep his hole well-lighted enough.

Down here, the chanting of the Woozles was even louder than before, and Pooh thought he could understand things from the rhythm of the "wawawa" that he had never comprehended before. He felt as if he were crossing a barrier into some strange land where no brave bear had gone before, home to the Lord of All Woozles, the key and the gate, the One-in-All, the lurker at the threshold. And surely anyone who was both a key *and* a gate and lurked there with frequency must know where the bees had hidden the honey. The buzzing was so loud, so urgent, so close, it sometimes seemed to be coming from inside the bear's own mind, and so the honey must be incredibly close as well.

As they traveled down, Pooh remembered a rhyme and began to sing it to himself in time with the chanting.

Wa wa wa
If Bears were Bees
Wa wa wa
They'd build their nests at the bottom of trees
Ya ya ya
If Bees were Bears
Ya ya ya
We shouldn't have to climb down all these stairs.

And still, Pooh was so relieved to be climbing down rather than up that down and down and down he went, his mouth salivating at the thought of all the honey he was bound to find at the bottom, accompanied by the rumbling buzzing. The walls of the stairwell began to ripple around them again, as if the bees were passing them by as they sank into the abyss. The air was cold down here, and had a strange, sticky sweetness to it.

The honey must be very close now, and yes, Pooh was beginning to see it dripping from the walls, running down over the tops of the ripples like so much ichor. But as he reached for it, the honey dripped just out of his reach, beckoning him always downward. The walls of the tunnel were jagged and chipped, and where the unattainable honey dripped from the ragged edges of the passageway, Pooh noted from the direction of the sharp edges that it appeared the tunnel had been painstakingly chiseled from *beneath*.

"Eeyore," said Pooh, "how do you suppose this tunnel came to be here?"

"It was probably always here," Eeyore said. "Why wouldn't it be?"

Pooh couldn't argue with that, particularly because the passage did *feel* like it had always been here, even though he had only come to know of it now.

"It feels," said Pooh, "like something I had always known, even before I knew it."

"It probably was," Eeyore said. "Things are always making themselves known only when it's too late."

"Do you think so?" asked Pooh. "And what do you suppose it's too late for?"

"For everything," Eeyore said.

Pooh hoped that Eeyore was wrong about that much at least. He hoped there was still time to recover the honey from the Woozles. They had gone very far down now, much farther than Pooh had fallen from the honey tree, and was glad for the stairs which kept him from falling all this way, because he wasn't certain there was anything even as soft as a gorse bush at the bottom. Pooh's tummy was rumbling very loudly now, and the air felt thick with honey, but as he stuck out his tongue and tried to draw it in, he could never get enough of a mouthful to quite taste it.

The stairs opened up upon a large forest, composed not of trees, but of stone. Pillars rose from the floor, set in strange circles, dwarfed by tall monoliths that towered between them. The stones stretched on and on before Pooh's eyes, so much that he wondered if it wasn't larger even than the Hundred Acre Wood. Buildings, once erected against the sides of the stones had fallen into ruin, and all around and over them grew thick patches of a strange yellowish-white moss.

No, Pooh realized as he reached the bottom of the stairs. Not moss. *Stuffing.* Great piles of it, billowing up from the ruins, heaped at the centers of the pillars of stone, blowing gently in the strange, sickly sweet breeze that wafted from farther down in the great chasm.

Some of the stuffing almost took on the shape of animals. Pooh thought he saw the outline of a rabbit here, and a bird there, and over there, on the far side of one of the monoliths, a wad of stuffing roughly in the shape of a pig. Some of the stuffing was of higher grade and looked almost pristine, while other piles were ratty and matted or nearly disintegrated, turned to a kind of ephemeral fluff that floated in patches through the air.

Pooh's stomach continued to rumble, joining now in time with the chant. It seemed as if his stomach was no longer grumbling but now singing the inescapable "wawawa" and "yayaya", and Pooh began to search through the piles of stuffing for the shapes of Heffalumps, of Wizzles, of Woozles, of all the Hostile Animals that must live in a place as topsy-turvy as this.

"It wasn't honey after all," Eeyore said sadly. "How predictable."

But Pooh wasn't certain that was the case. There might still be honey, hidden somewhere under all this fluff. Eeyore followed behind Pooh as he searched through piles of stuffing, many of which reached far, far over his head. Pooh thought he could make out the terrible shapes of Woozle and Heffalump alike, but they were always at the edges of his vision, and when he turned his head, disappeared in the tangle of fiber and fluff. Pooh reached into the stuffing, pulling it aside to see what terrible secrets the Woozles were hiding, and as he did, one of the floating bits caught on his tongue.

The stuffing seemed to melt there, like the finest sugar, spun up into cotton, and Pooh stuck his tongue out farther, tasting the nearest pile of fluff. It tasted of the finest honey, laced with something darker, and Pooh grabbed fistfuls of the stuff, shoving them into his mouth. The sweetness was overwhelming, and Pooh began to feel wobbly, staggering on his feet as he took in more and more, first with his paws, then breathing the stuff in, sucking it as if through a straw, pulling the fluff into his being in time with the constant "yayaya."

There were miles of the stuff. Acres of it, and Pooh hungered to swallow it all. And why shouldn't he? The Woozles had drawn him here, after all, beckoned him, *given* him this great hoard of sweet lusciousness, and Pooh intended to eat his fill. He devoured the pile that looked like a pig, and tasted of fat and weighed heavy on his tongue. Pooh wondered why he'd never thought before to eat a pig, or a bird, or a rabbit, or even an Old Grey Donkey. Pooh lost himself then, becoming one for a moment with the Woozles and their world of endless floating fluff.

When he came to himself again, sitting atop one of the lower stone pillars, his tummy rounder than ever and finally satiated, he did not know how long he'd been down in the stuffing city with the Woozles. He could not remember how much he had eaten, as, fortunately for Pooh, ultimate horror so often paralyzes the memory in the most merciful way.

The chanting had died, and the buzzing returned to a low hum that reminded Pooh of a song he used to sing when he was young. He remembered his friend Eeyore, then, and looked around, calling his name, but even though he wandered for what must have been hours, searching for Eeyore before at last finding the stairs upward again, the only trace he could find of his friend was his tail lying lost and forgotten at the base of one of the monoliths.

"Eeyore will surely be missing this," Pooh said to himself, and he picked up the tail, and carried it with him to the stairs, thinking he must have lost Eeyore somewhere in the abyss of the stuffing, and perhaps his friend had headed up to bed without him.

And so, with a heavy step, his body lethargic from his great feast, Pooh began to ascend.

POOH HAD NOT CHANGED his opinion, he decided, that going down was much easier than going up. The stairs seemed to ascend forever, and while Pooh knew they must have a top, since his larder was located above it, it seemed that the ground had fallen forever under the name of Sanders, as if the stairs were carrying him downward at a greater pace than he ascended, and he feared he might be walking forever.

He'd lost his candle in the great forest of stuffing, but he'd found that his eyes had somehow accustomed to the dark, even though there was no light to speak of. So he could see how very alone he was here, with only Eeyore's tail to cling to, the bees and the Woozles having abandoned him all.

The stairs didn't continue forever, as it turned out, for Pooh eventually reached the top of them and scrambled and squeezed and squished himself until he managed to pop from the opening in the floor of his larder and land on the bare floorboards, which were still now, and no longer rippling.

Pooh stumbled to his kitchen table and sank into his chair. He called for Eeyore several times, but received no reply, so he lay Eeyore's tail on the table next to the honey pot Eeyore had brought for them to share, where he would remember to return it to Eeyore when he saw him next.

Pooh's tummy was feeling especially rumbly after the long climb, and he picked up the honey pot to see what was left.

There was more than a morsel of honey in the bottom. Several fistfuls, in fact, all crawling with bees. The bees buzzed lightly, scurrying over the stuff, and Pooh reached in and coated his paws in thick honey and crawling bees, first one paw, and then the other. He held them up, admiring the way the honey dripped down his arms, and then he stuffed both paws into his mouth, honey, bees, and all, relishing the way the honey flowed onto his tongue, punctuated by the occasional crunch. He hummed to himself, a constant "yayaya" as he ate until every drop of honey was gone. In his last fistful, he encountered something stringy that required a few extra chews, and when he finished, he put the pot on the floor and licked his paws clean and then laid them before him on the empty table.

His stomach ached, now, churning as if a great maw had opened inside him and was sucking out all the honey, the bees, and his stuffing, too. And Pooh had a sense that something terrible had happened down below, something unspeakable, unnameable.

It wasn't his fault, he decided. Whatever had happened down there, it wasn't the sort of thing a bear with any amount of brain could have anticipated. It was bees who had first called him with their incessant buzzing, and the Woozles who had beckoned him down, ever down, into that great place of horror. It hadn't been Pooh's idea, no, never, not at all.

It wasn't him; it was the Woozles. The Woozles: the Woozles in the walls.

Bump, Bump, Bump!

Kary English

Bump, bump, bump, shall I ride a heffalump?
Or shall I ride a camel just to sit astride the hump?
The saddle's way too high for me, and so I'll have to jump.
Bump, bump, bump, shall I ride a heffalump?

Howl! Howl! Howl! There's a woozle on the prowl.
They aren't very nice, and their stench is rather foul.
Lock up all the chickens, and tell the dogs to growl.
Howl, howl, howl, there's a woozle on the prowl.

Skit, scat, scale, I found a donkey's tail,
Out behind the garden hidden 'neath the water pail.
So I dunked it, and I swished it, and I dried it on a rail.
Skit, scat, scale, I washed a donkey's tail.

Slurp, burp, bunny, when I have a little money,
I buy a little something, and the something's always hunny.
It's sticky, slicky, licky, and Piglet thinks it's funny.
Slurp, burp, hunny, when I have a little money.

In Which Eeyore Tries to See Forever...

Jonathan Maberry

I

"Oh, I've lost my tail again," said Eeyore.

He sounded most distressed. Even more than Winnie-the-Pooh had ever heard before, and Pooh had heard Eeyore sound very distressed indeed many times. Many, many times. Many times on the same day, and many ways on different days.

Eeyore was good at being distressed.

Or maybe it was that he was so frequently distressed that he had become good at expressing it. Winnie-the-Pooh did not know which and it befuddled his bear brain to decide the right answer.

So, to understand, he asked, "Oh . . . ?"

He had something cleverer in mind, a better question, but that's what came out. Just "Oh . . . ?"

Eeyore was standing near a clump of newly flowering bog asphodel, but he was turned half around to look at his bottom. Winnie-the-Pooh could clearly see that there was no tail at all, not anywhere to be found. There was barely even a mark from where the last one had been pinned.

"Oh dear," gasped Pooh. "Your tail is most completely and totally gone."

"It is," moaned Eeyore. "Will you help me look for it?"

"Of course!" cried Pooh. "I will help you at once. I'm very good at finding things."

Eeyore looked doubtful about that but did not comment. It would be rude to do so when a helper was so enthusiastic.

"Where have you already looked?" asked the bear.

"I think I've looked everywhere," said the sad old donkey.

"Everywhere? Hmmm," mused Pooh. "Then we shouldn't look there. But where else is there to look?"

"Everywhere else?" suggested Eeyore.

"Then let's start there," agreed Winnie-the-Pooh.

2

EEYORE AND POOH began by walking in a spiral that moved around and around and outward and outward from the asphodel where Eeyore had been standing. They did not find the tail because it was one of the places the old donkey had said he already looked.

So they wandered about, going here and sometimes there, and occasionally way over there. Looking and looking. They peered behind bushes and up into trees; they leaned their faces into creeks and asked the fishes, but fishes being fishes they swam on. They had, after all, their own tails and were busy using them to get away from bears and donkeys.

They disturbed a snoozing family of chipmunks, and Mr. Chipmunk had some very unkind things to say about donkeys and bears, while Mrs. Chipmunk tried to settle the little ones back down for their mid-morning nap.

"Sorry," said Eeyore mournfully. "It's just that I lost my tail and I very much need to find it."

"Maybe if you paid more attention to it, you wouldn't lose it," scolded Mr. Chipmunk. He was only a little bigger than a hamster, but he had a growly voice, even if it did squeak. He shook a stern finger at them. "And why would you look for a donkey tail in our neighborhood? Why look for one in our front garden? Do we look like the kind of animals who need or want donkey tails?"

"It has a pretty pink ribbon on it," said Pooh, hoping that would help.

Mr. Chipmunk put his tiny hands on his tiny hips and gave them both a tiny but very angry glare. "And what does that matter? I mean, it's still a tail, is it not?"

"Why . . . yes, but—" began Pooh but he was cut off before he could get out even a quarter of a thought.

"A *donkey's* tail, unless I am very much mistaken."

"Is it, but—"

"Do we *look* like donkeys?"

"No, but—"

"Do you see any donkeys in the vicinity?"

"Just my friend, but—"

"Can you see even one donkey tail—with or without a ribbon—anywhere around this neighborhood?"

"Not as such, no, but—"

"Then good day to you both," snapped Mr. Chipmunk. Then he turned his back on them and stomped back to his hole in the ground, stamping his little feet as hard as such tiny feet could be stamped, which was not very hard at all. He had no door over his hole, but Mr. Chipmunk did his best to slam the clod of grass that was handiest.

Eeyore and Pooh retreated to the other side of the path to consult.

"I don't think my tail is in the chipmunk part of town," said Eeyore. And by 'town' he meant that small part of the Hundred Acre Woods.

"Maybe we had better look elsewhere," said Winnie-the-Pooh.

Eeyore drew in a deep breath and let it out as such a long sigh Pooh thought his friend was completely deflating.

"I suppose," said the old gray donkey.

And off they went.

———

3

NEITHER POOH nor Eeyore was at all aware that they were being watched.

A small shape clung to a branch of a high oak tree, listening intently to their conversation. It watched as they trudged away, and soon it came down from the tree and followed.

It was not a bird nor a rat or a cat nor a bat. It was not a bug or a slug. It moved like smoke and made no sound at all.

But all the time it followed—through stalks of slender grass and between green flower stems and over cool moss and around gray stones—it smiled and smiled and smiled.

Had Winnie-the-Pooh or Eeyore seen that smile they would have agreed that it was not a happy smile. No, not at all and not in the least. Not happy at all.

And yet the thing that followed them was very happy.

In its own way.

In its own very particular way.

———

4

POOH WAS CONCERNED that his friend looked so down. More so than ever before. So he tried to tell some jokes, but he could never remember the punch lines, and so they landed like badly inflated balloons. Just soft thuds, and each time, Eeyore looked even sadder.

"Hey," said Pooh, "I know a song about finding lost things."

This was not entirely true, but Pooh was better at making up songs than he was at telling jokes.

"Shall I sing it for you?"

Eeyore twitched a little, or maybe it was a wince. But then he said, "If you think it will help . . ."

Pooh walked a few steps before he found a starting place.

"Something's lost and must be found," he began. "Something's lost and wants to be found. Where oh where can it be, be, be? Something's lost and needs to be found."

After a considerable pause, the donkey glanced at him. "Is that it?"

"Well, there's more, I think."

But Pooh had no more ready to hand, so he sang those lines again.

"What do you think?" he asked.

Eeyore tried to smile. He was never very good at it and didn't try very often. When he did, he showed his buck teeth in a way that looked more like the way Christopher Robin looked that time Piglet had dared him to eat a lemon. All wincey-wrinkled-scrunchy.

"It's . . . great . . . ," lied Eeyore.

"Do you really think so?"

"It's the best searching for lost things song I've hear all morning," said Eeyore. That much, at least, was the truth, for he had heard no searching for lost things songs all day. Nor yesterday, for that matter.

Pooh puffed out, feeling proud of himself. He sang the song several more times, then stopped and saved his breath for running because Eeyore had suddenly picked up his pace and was far ahead.

———

5

THE THING from the tree followed them, but never too close.

Oh no, not too close.

Not yet.

Sometimes it slithered like a snake, and sometimes it hopped like a toad. It ran for a while on little rat feet, but when it didn't need rat feet anymore it stopped having them and went ahead on skittery bug legs.

It passed by Piglet, who was sitting on a stump eating an early lunch—or perhaps a very late breakfast—and reading a book about planting dandelions. Piglet was very deep into his book and so did not notice the thing that passed. But he suddenly shivered as if the wind was cold, which it was not.

When Piglet looked around, there was nothing to see. But he frowned at the nothing anyway and shivered once more.

The strange little thing glided on, moving now like shadows, if shadows had a hundred little bug legs.

———

6

THEY WERE SEARCHING a patch of sunflowers where Eeyore said he had been standing earlier.

"Why were you standing in a patch of sunflowers?" asked Pooh.

"Why wouldn't I stand in a patch of sunflowers?" asked Eeyore.

Pooh had no answer to that and just accepted that standing in a patch of sunflowers was something one does. He decided that he might try it himself some-day. The fact that there were plenty of bees flitting about made the thought even more appealing, since bees meant beehives, and beehives meant honey, and honey was Pooh's favoritist thing in the world.

"Did you have your tail when you were here?" he asked.

Eeyore considered, then nodded slowly. "I believe I did. I remember swishing it to shoo away a bee, or perhaps two bees."

"Maybe that's when it fell off," said Pooh, brightening. "The pin might have been loose, and all that swishing could have have made it fall."

That seemed reasonable to both of them, and so they looked and looked.

They found a few pennies that were old and covered with smudges of blue-white gunk that Pooh thought might have been bird poop, but Eeyore said was only rust.

"It's oxy-day-shun," explained the old donkey.

"What's that?"

"It's when pennies get old."

"Oh," said Pooh, and did not know where to take that conversation. So they kept looking.

At the very center of the patch of sunflowers, they found an old log that neither of them ever remembered being there.

"That's new," said Pooh.

"Is it?" asked Eeyore, trying to care. "Oh, I suppose it is. Though it looks very old."

"Can't it be old but new here, too?"

"That would mean somebody brought it here after it was old," said the donkey.

"Maybe. It looks heavy."

"I daresay. It's part of a tree."

"There aren't any trees close by," observed Pooh. "Somebody would have had to go to a lot of trouble to move it here."

"Some people have nothing better to do," said Eeyore. "People who haven't got stray tails to find, I mean."

"Why a log?" wondered Pooh. "And why here?"

"Why not a log?" said Eeyore. "And why not here? It's as good a place as any. And by that, I mean it's just an ugly old log, so what does it matter where it is?"

"It *is* rather ugly," observed Pooh. "It's all gnarly and knotty and has wood-pecker holes and bumpity-bumps. Maybe someone put it here because they didn't want to look at it."

Eeyore tried to shrug, but donkeys don't have the right kind of shoulders for shrugging, so it just looked like a twitch.

"Or," said Pooh in a suddenly hushed voice, "maybe somebody put it here on purpose."

"That's what I said," Eeyore replied.

"No, not to keep it out of sight because it's ugly."

"Then why else?"

"Maybe to hide it where no one else can find it."

The donkey looked at the log and back to Pooh. "I don't know what that means."

"Well," said Pooh, "just look at it. It's creepy and strange and it kind of just . . . just . . . well, I don't know the right word. What do you call it when something just stands there kind of glaring at you?"

"You're saying the log is lurking?"

"Lurking!" cried Pooh. "Yes, that's the thing. It's lurking here."

Four or five entirely different expressions seemed to march across Eeyore's gray face. His big, sad eyes looked bigger and sadder.

"This is all very well," he said dolefully, "but it's not helping me find my tail. And I rather miss my tail. It's the only thing that makes me happy."

Pooh thought about that. Something about the gnarly old log bothered him, but in a way that made him curious rather than made him want to run away. Though there was a little bit of 'run away' floating around in his fuzzy bear brain.

"Perhaps," he said, "whoever brought this log in found your tail and took it with them."

Eeyore honked in alarm. "Would they *do* that?"

"They might."

"Why would anyone take my tail? It's mine. It fits me and no one else."

"Why," said Pooh, "I don't really know. Maybe because it's pretty."

"Well . . . it *is* pretty," agreed the donkey. "But if someone took it, then how will we find them?"

Pooh walked around the log as he pondered this. He stopped at the far end of the log because, unlike the other end, that end was hollow. It might have been rot, because there was a lot of that in the woods. Trees fall and limbs fall, and sometimes trees were cut down by beavers. If they were left to their own devices, the wood-chomping bugs would bitey-bite the wood until it was all filled with holes.

He bent down and peered into the hole, hoping he would see the tail with its bright pink bow.

"Well now," he said, "would you look at that? Come and see what I found."

"Is it my tail?" cried Eeyore in the happiest, most hopeful voice he had.

"No, I'm sorry," said Pooh, bending low and leaning into the open log. He grabbed the thing and pulled and pulled and it didn't want to come. He felt it move a little, but then it seemed to pull back. And that was odd, because it wasn't the kind of thing that either pulled or pushed or did anything just on its own.

"Show me," said Eeyore, still hoping that whatever it was Pooh was wrestling with, his missing tail might somehow be involved.

"Ouff!" said Winnie-the-Pooh as he struggled with it. "Oh bother! Stop fighting me. Ow!"

"Did it bite you?" asked the donkey.

"I don't think so," said Pooh. "But it tried to."

He gave a last furious pull and then he was tottering backward on his heels, fighting for balance, losing that fight pretty quickly, and then falling down hard on his bottom.

"Owwww!" he said again, though he was really more surprised than hurt.

The thing he had pulled out of the log was big and old and heavy and dusty, and cockroaches and worms fell from it and fled back into the shadows. Eeyore came and stood looking down at it.

"What is it?"

"Why," said Pooh. "It's a . . . a . . . a book."

"I can see that it's a book. But who would hide a book in a tree?"

Pooh gave him a mysterious look. "Maybe it was a hobbly-gobleton."

"A what?"

"You know, those creepy old hobbly-gobletons that they say live in places like dead trees and mossy old caves."

"I don't know about hobbly-gobletons," said Eeyore in a way that meant he didn't care about them. "Are they known for stealing donkey tails?"

"Christopher Robin says hobbly-gobletons get up to all kinds of trouble. Hiding keys and stealing one sock but leaving another."

"What about tails, though?"

"I don't know," admitted Pooh, who really just loved to say *hobbly-gobleton*. "Anyway, we have a book now."

"But what kind of book?"

It was well known that the old donkey was not the best reader among all of Winnie-the-Pooh's many friends.

Pooh peered at the cover. It was made of some kind of very old leather, and although there was a title engraved in it, it was written in a very fancy and flowy style, and he could not understand a word of it.

"I don't know."

"Open it and see if maybe someone used my tail as a . . . what do you call it when they put something in to mark a place?"

"A bookmark?"

"That's it," said Eeyore. "Though," he added glumly, "I suppose it won't be there."

And that was true enough. There was one bookmark, but it was made from ratty old black cloth and was attached to the book itself. Pooh looked at the writing, but except for a few words —mostly 'a' and 'and' and suchlike—it was too adult for him and he could make neither heads nor tails of it. Certainly not donkey tails.

"Look," Pooh said, pointing to the margins on several pages, "someone has written in the book. That's pen writing, not book printing. I know the difference."

They considered it.

The sun was overhead now and the mild day had become quite hot. They were both tired and thirsty from all of the tail searching.

"I know," said Pooh, brightening, "why don't we take the book to Rabbit? He reads a lot and he's nearly always home. And his burrow is cool and he often has honey cakes and jam."

"Will he help me find my tail?" asked Eeyore, looking doubtful.

"Maybe that's what this handwriting is about," said Pooh encouragingly. "Rabbit can read that stuff, too."

"I guess," said the donkey, and off they went toward the north-central part of the Hundred Acre Wood, where Rabbit owned a tidy little house filled to the rafters with books.

———

7

THEY PASSED RIGHT by the shadowy creature, who was busy looking like a hairy vine on an old elm. But as soon as the two passed, the hairs melted back into its black skin, and it pulled its fake vine parts into its body as it dropped from the tree.

It followed them, now looking like a black dog with a lolling black tongue.

The thing enjoyed being many things at different times. It loved to see and not be seen. Or to be seen and not be seen as what it was.

It trotted along behind them, careful not to make a sound.

———

8

AS IT HAPPENED Rabbit was home and was reading a book when he heard the knock.

He set his book down and peered out of a small window to see if his visitor was someone worth stopping his reading for. When he saw that it was Pooh and Eeyore, he took a moment, remembering how much he was enjoying his book—all about sailing ships and pirates. Then he saw that Winnie-the-Pooh had a book tucked under his arm.

"Well, well, well now," he said, and he opened the door.

———

9

"RABBIT!" cried Winnie-the-Pooh. "We're so glad you're home."

"And why is that?" asked Rabbit, looking up at Pooh's face and then down at Eeyore's.

"I've lost my tail," said Eeyore, making it sound like the worst thing lost in the history of lost things. After all of their searching that morning his glum face had become very much glummer.

"Oh dear, not again," said Rabbit. "Where have you looked?"

"We looked everywhere," said Pooh, "and some places twice."

"It's lost forever and I will never have a tail again," moaned Eeyore.

"Hmm," said Rabbit, ushering them in. He set about putting the kettle on. "We'll have to devise a better plan for finding it. I have some good maps of the woods and we can create a search pattern. I'll call all of my friends and relations to help in. It'll be quite like a quest, and who doesn't like a quest?"

"I don't like quests," said Eeyore, but his friends pretended not to hear.

"Now," said Rabbit as he placed some carrot slices and pieces of radish—bright white inside and glorious red outside—on a tray and set it on the table, "I cannot help but notice that you have a book under your arm, Edward Bear." He sometimes called Pooh by his formal name, which almost no one else ever did.

Winnie looked down at the book with surprise on his face as if he had somehow forgotten he was carrying a rather large book.

"Why yes!" he cried. "We found it while looking for Eeyore's tail."

"Seems to me like an acceptable exchange," mused Rabbit.

"Not to me," said the donkey. "I don't much like books, but I do love my tail. Tails don't need to be read and I can't read very well." He sighed. "I can't do anything very well. I can't even keep my tail pinned on."

"True, true, you make a fair point," said Rabbit quickly. "But for the moment, let's take a look at this book you found. Lay it on the table and let's see what we can see."

Pooh did so and Rabbit bent over it, peering carefully at the leather binding. Then he traced the lettering on the cover, making frequent remarks like *"Hmmmm-mmmm"* and "Well now."

"Can you read what it says?" asked Pooh.

Without looking up, Rabbit said, "I can pronounce it, but I can't tell exactly what it is."

"I tried to pronounce it," said Pooh, "but it befuddled my tongue."

"Yes, yes, it would, it would. It's not in English, you see?"

"No," said Pooh, "I don't see. I can't read anything *but* English, so how would I know it's not written that way?"

Rabbit looked at him for a moment. "Because it's not *in* English."

Before Pooh could reply to that, Rabbit went and fetched a magnifying glass and used it to study each word. He sounded them out individually, frowning a bit and twitching his whiskers.

"De Vermis Mysteriis," said Rabbit aloud, pronouncing each syllable slowly.

"What does that mean?" asked Pooh, totally perplexed.

"Why . . . I don't quite know," admitted Rabbit. He shrugged and opened the book to the title page. "Ah!" he cried. "Someone else must have had this book first and did our work for us. Look . . . do you see?"

Pooh bent forward with enthusiasm and Eeyore with barely feigned interest. There on the title page, written it what looked like old brown ink, was a translation of the title. Pooh read it out.

"*Mysteries of the Worm*," he said. "Funny old title."

"I like worms," said Eeyore. "They never make fun of me. A worm would never steal my tail."

"Which worm do you think it means?" asked Pooh.

"A very old worm," said Rabbit. "This book is the oldest I think I've ever seen, and I've seen a few. I have a very old book on manners on one of my shelves, and it looks like it's been around forever. Though, come to think of it, it's probably lasted this long because it isn't read very often. No, not often enough."

"But what does it mean?" asked Pooh. "Why would there be a book this big and this thick if it's all about worms? How many mysteries can worms actually have?"

"Enough for a whole book," said Rabbit. He began turning the pages.

"I saw other notes in there," Pooh said, trying to be helpful. "Written in the margins."

"Let's see what they say," said Rabbit. "Oh, here's one. Hmmmm. It's a kind of rhyme."

"A poem rhyme or a song?"

"I don't know. Let me see if I can read it. The handwriting is very shaky."

He read . . .

> *When need and fear do bleak the heart*
> *And shadows crawl behind*
> *Look for the thing that takes the part*
> *Of every crawling kind.*

"That's a very strange song," said Pooh. "Or a stranger poem."

"It rhymes," said Rabbit. "So there's that."

"What's it mean?" asked Eeyore. "And does it have anything to do with finding lost tails?"

"Not . . . as such," said Rabbit. "Though it seems to offer help of some kind."

Pooh frowned. "How does one 'bleak' a heart?"

"Losing one's tail will do it, I can tell you that," muttered Eeyore.

"Let's keep looking."

"I wish there was something in there that *would* help me find what I lost," said Eeyore. His big eyes were filled with unspent tears of sadness. "I miss my tail very much indeed."

When he said the word *wish* a strange thing happened. Well, two things, to be precise. The door, which Rabbit had sensibly shut, blew open, and it let in a breeze that rifled the pages. They all three jumped, though Eeyore less so because he was too sad and depressed to be enthusiastic even when startled.

Pooh, who was closest, hurried over and shut the door, jiggling the handle to make sure it was quite properly closed now. As he did so, he thought he saw something dart in past him, but when he turned to look, there was nothing.

"That's funny," he said, but then he forgot about it and went back to the table.

"That breeze was a lucky one," announced Rabbit, who was using radishes to hold down the pages in case there was another breeze. Pooh looked at the book and saw that this new page had lots of writing on it. All in the same flowing script and the same dull brown ink.

"What's it say?" asked Pooh, caught up in the fun and mystery of the strange old book.

"Well, well, well," said Rabbit. "It starts with a warning not to read what is says."

"That seems sensible," said the donkey to himself.

"Bother!" huffed Pooh. "How can you be warned about something if you aren't allowed to read the warning? It's like saying 'don't climb this tree' but on a sign at the top of a tree."

Rabbit glanced at him. "You're actually right," he said. "That makes it a special day."

Pooh, not realizing this was a slight, smiled proudly.

"It must have been written for someone else a very long time ago," said Rabbit. "Because it couldn't have been written for us."

"No it can't. Go on," urged Pooh. "Read it."

Rabbit set himself into a proper reading posture and began . . .

The Spell of Seeing and of Finding

To Tsathoggua, the Sleeper of N'kai we pray
He grants us the eyes to see and the heart to find
What is our deepest desire.
From his place of dreams eternal
His wisdom and grace stretch out across
The infinite realms of waking and dreaming
For without him, that which is most treasured
That which is sought most desperately
Can never be found
But to the seeker true of heart
That which is desired will be made manifest

As, through Tsathoggua's eyes, all that is in
The vault of forever may be discovered
Hold Tsathoggua in your mind and make your wish
With witnesses to bear your truth.

He stopped reading and looked at his guests.

"Now," he said, "what should we make of that?"

Eeyore looked at him. "What's a Tsathoggua?"

"I have no idea," admitted Rabbit.

"Maybe it's a kind of hobbly-gobleton," suggested Pooh. "I hear they're very strange."

Rabbit sniffed. "I've never seen a hobbly-gobleton," he said. "Though I have heard of them. From you, Mr. Winnie-the-Pooh, I believe."

"Oh, they're everywhere," insisted the bear. "Always hiding in the shadows. Much like woozles and gelfumplies, though not as common."

Rabbit tilted his head to one side as he thought about it. "I wish Owl was around. He's quite good at puzzling out puzzles, and this is a very puzzling puzzle. But he's off visiting his cousin, Barn Owl, over by the south edge of the wood."

Pooh said, "It seems to be about finding something lost. Does that mean it'll help us find Eeyore's tail?"

"Yes," said the donkey. "It seems to me that's what it says."

Rabbit looked at the inscription again. "Well . . . that might be the case."

"But how can we know it will work?" begged Eeyore.

"Well . . . ," said Rabbit.

"Ummm . . . ," said Pooh.

"Squeak . . . ," said a small black rat.

———

10

THEY ALL TURNED around in surprise to see that there was, in fact, a small black rat sitting on the arm of Rabbit's favorite reading chair.

"It's a rat," said Pooh, which he did not need to say because they could all see very well that this is what it was. Small, but plump and rather . . . well . . . *ratty.* His fur was all messy and seemed to move as if he was standing in a hot breeze, which of course he was not. Rabbit's door and windows were all shut and there was only a small fire in the hearth.

"Is he a friend of yours?" asked Eeyore.

"He may be," said Rabbit uncertainly. "I have a large number of friends hereabouts. Perhaps he is a relation of one of my other rat friends."

"Do you have many rat friends?" asked the donkey.

"More than a few," said Rabbit, "though fewer than a lot."

The rat looked at them and squeaked again.

Winnie-the-Pooh stepped closer to the rat. "What is your name?"

The rat's eyes were small and very black and as shiny as stars. It began to speak, or tried to speak, and kept stopping as if it was not at all familiar with how to do it.

"I . . . ," it began in a voice was a deeper and more growly than a rat's usually is. It stopped, twitched, shivered, and tried again. "I . . . am . . . shoggoth . . ."

"Shoggoth?" asked Pooh. "That's an unusual name."

"Shoggoth," repeated the rat, and saying it a bit more firmly now. To Pooh it sounded as if it was not at all used to saying that name out loud. "Shoggoth is . . . me. Shoggoth is what I be."

"Bear is what I be," said Pooh. "And my name is Edward, though nearly everyone calls me Winnie. Winnie-the-Pooh, in fact. So, I guess that makes you Shoggoth-the-Rat."

"Shoggoth," said the rat. It looked down at its paws and for just a little part of a small moment the paws seemed to lose their shape and almost look like wiggly black worms. Then the moment passed and they were paws again. "Shoggoth . . . the Rat."

"It is very nice to meet you, Shoggoth-the-Rat," said Pooh, giving a small and rather formal bow. "This is my friend, Rabbit, and this is his home."

Shoggoth-the-Rat looked at Rabbit with those glittering black eyes. "Rabbit . . ." he said, though it came out very odd. It sounded more like "*Raaaah-hhbittt.*"

"That's me," said Rabbit, though he seemed a bit taken aback. "And, although I don't recall inviting you, I will do the polite thing and welcome you to my home. We probably have many friends in common. I have lots and lots of friends in these woods."

"Woods," said Shoggoth. "Dark woods."

"Um, well, sometimes, I suppose," said Rabbit. "Not now, though. It's only a quarter past noon."

"Dark under leaves . . ."

"I suppose that's true."

"Dark in holes," said the rat.

"As a rule, yes."

"Dark in hollow logs."

"Wait!" cried Pooh. "That's it . . . I've found it out. You were in that hollow log where Eeyore and I found the book."

"Booooooooook," squeak Shoggoth. "Yes. Book."

"Mysteries of the Worm, as I recall," said the donkey. "But I don't remember it mentioning rats."

"Tsathoggua's book," whispered the rat.

"Is that who owns it?" asked Rabbit.

"Or is that who lost it?" asked Pooh.

"My tail is lost," said Eeyore, though it was likely clear that everyone, including the rat, knew this by now.

"Book knows where lost things are," said the small black rat.

Everyone stopped talking and looked at him for a moment. The room seemed very quiet.

"The book . . . ," began Rabbit.

". . . knows . . . ," said Pooh.

". . . where lost things are?" finished Eeyore.

"Oh . . . yes . . . ," said Shoggoth-the-Rat.

⸻

II

THEY SAT around the table with tea and crunchy vegetables and a small slice of very nice cheese for the rat. The book lay open in the center of the table.

It was a bit difficult, they found, to have a conversation with the rat and in a quiet aside, Rabbit suggested to Pooh that it was likely English was not the rat's usual language.

"Rats travel on ships quite a lot," he said.

"Oh, yes, I've heard of ship's rats," agreed Pooh, who had, in fact, heard about that from Christopher Robin, who knew everything about ships and sailing and pirates and desert islands and lost treasures and all of that sort of thing."

"How will we ever find my tail?" whined Eeyore, who was getting even more frustrated and depressed.

It was the rat who answered. "Book," he said. "Book finds."

They all three looked at him. "But *how* does the book find things?" Rabbit asked. "I checked, and there is no index in the back and no table of contents in the front and there are a lot of pages. How, then, are we to learn how it will help us find anything, let alone a donkey's tail?"

It was a fair question, and better phrased than what Pooh would have said, so he just nodded. Beside, he had a mouthful of carrots and was crunching so loud he could not hear his best thoughts.

"Book knows," said Shoggoth-the-Rat. "Book *sees*."

"Sees?" echoed Eeyore. "Can it see where my tail is?"

"Yessss."

For once the old donkey looked quite excited. Then doubt clouded his eyes and he asked, "But how do you know?"

"I know," said the rat. "Shoggoth know."

"But how?" asked Eeyore and Pooh together.

The question momentarily confused the rat, and he sat there pondering. His little tail was not pink or gray like most rats but was instead a curious shade of black. So black that it had almost no detail, as if it was made of something like oil and smoke and shadow all mixed together and straightened into a rat tail. His fur was not much different, and even though Pooh could see the hairs, they looked like a lump of shadow with little tips of hair sticking out of it. Very odd and, Pooh thought, just a bit strange. Strange in the way things are on windy October nights near Halloween. Not the way they usually were in a comfy little house in the Hundred Acre Wood on a fine and bright afternoon in the early summer.

Rat caught him looking and—Pooh was never quite certain about this later, though it often came into his mind—made himself look more rat like. The tail went a bit paler and now Pooh could see the little bumps along it; and the hairs were more hairlike.

And . . . did the rat smile just a little when that happened?

But, no, it was less a smile and more of a fake smile. A sad smile, thought Pooh.

The rat kept looking at him, then he lifted a paw and touched his own chest. "Rat," he said.

"Yes, of course," said Pooh.

"No bat or cat or muskrat," insisted Shoggoth.

"That's very true."

"Not snake or spider or slippery eel," continued the rat. "Not goose or moose or snarly bear. Not rhinoceros or stegosaur or night gaunt or . . . or . . ."

He stopped and Pooh was alarmed to see that large tears had formed in the rat's eyes and slowly fell, vanishing into the tiny bristling hairs of its face.

"Rat," said Shoggoth.

"Rat without a doubt," said Pooh, feeling that it was somehow important to agree that Shoggoth was indeed, and indisputably so, a rat. "And a very handsome rat, too."

Shoggoth studied him with suspicion. "You see rat?"

"Why of course."

"*Real* rat?"

"As real as can be."

"Not fake rat?" asked Shoggoth, a plaintive tone in his voice. "Not nasty rat or fake rat or very bad rat? Not slimy, shifty, sneaky, nasty, mean, horrible, do-bad-things rat?"

"Oh, not at all," insisted Pooh, aware now that Rabbit and Eeyore were watching this conversation with great interest. "You are, without a doubt, a very fine rat. A gentleman among rats. Isn't that right?" He directed this last part to his friends.

"By all means," said Rabbit quickly, catching on that there was something sad and insecure about their guest. "I have a good number of rats—as well as many mice—among my friends and you are, without any little bit of doubt, a very fine example of a rat. The very thing, when it comes to rats. Wouldn't you agree, Eeyore?"

"I suppose so," said the donkey with absolutely no trace of conviction. Pooh nudged him under the table with a foot. Eeyore twitched, then began nodding. "Oh yes, the very best kind of rat, to be sure."

"There you are," said Pooh. "Shoggoth-the-Rattiest-Rat of them all."

The small black rat's expression slowly changed from one of anxiety to something like pleasure. He even managed to smile, as well as any rat could smile, that is. There was a twitch of whiskers and a lot of teeth.

"Rat," he said, pawing away his tears. "Real rat."

"Yes."

"Real."

"Really real," they all agreed.

"Um," said Eeyore, "about my tail . . . ?"

12

SHOGGOTH WALKED over to the book and crawled onto the page.

"The book sees all," he said. "The book sees forever."

"I don't need to see forever," said the donkey. "I just want to see far enough to find my tail."

The rat looked at him. "To find tail . . . or anything . . . say the words and look forever."

"Um . . . what . . . ?"

"I think," said Rabbit, "that *you* have to read the same passage I just did."

Eeyore gave him a despairing look. "It's a lot to read."

"We can help," said Pooh brightly. "With the hard parts."

"All of it's hard."

"So, we'll help you with all of it."

The rat nodded.

"Wait a bit," said Rabbit, "if reading that passage makes you see forever—or at least as far as something lost—why didn't *I* see that far?"

They all thought about that.

Then Pooh said, "Is there anything you're missing?"

"Me? Dear me no. I gathered my vegetables and I know where my books are and where are my friends and relations are. I haven't lost anything."

"That is why," said the rat.

And all three of them—Rabbit, Pooh, and even Eeyore—said, "Oh."

"Well, that explains it perfectly," said Pooh.

"Have you lost anything?" Rabbit asked him.

"No . . . not that I can recall," said Pooh after giving it a bit of thought.

"Well *I* have," said Eeyore. "And we still haven't found it."

"We will," promised Pooh. Then he glanced at Shoggoth. "What about you? Have *you* lost anything?"

Again there was a flicker of pain in the little creature's eyes. "Lost . . . me . . ."

"But you're right here!"

The rat sniffed. "No. Never *found* me. Not *me* me."

"I don't understand."

"Always . . . other. Cat or bat or dog or tarantula or pterosaur or . . ." His little voice trailed off. "Never me."

"But you have," cried Pooh. "You're Shoggoth-the-Rat and you have found yourself here. Right here in the nicest house in the woods. And you found friends."

Shoggoth stared at him. "Friends . . . ?"

He spoke as if the word was entirely new to him. He even mispronounced it once or twice before he got it out in the right shape.

"Friends," he said again.

"Why, of course," said Rabbit, being a very good host. "We're all friends here. Well met, well fed, and all together."

"Maybe my friends will help me find my tail," complained Eeyore.

The rat turned to him. "Friend?"

The donkey gave him a long, sad look, but then he said, "Yes. We're friends." He paused. "Will my friend help me find my tail?"

The rat straightened a bit. "Yes," he said. "Shoggoth-the-Rat will help his friend."

And so they set about it.

"What do we have to do?" Asked Pooh.

The rat crawled further onto the book and squatted there, scratching at the handwritten words. Not the first line, not The Spell of Seeing and of Finding.

Instead, Shoggoth touched the line below it.

"With me," he said. "See forever. See everything."

"See my tail?" asked Eeyore hopefully.

"See everything."

But Eeyore hesitated. "I still can't read all of that. It's the . . . um . . . handwriting."

Pooh and Rabbit exchanged a look. They loved Eeyore very much, but even Pooh, who was not nearly as smart as Rabbit nor a tenth as smart as Owl, knew that Eeyore was a very good donkey but not a very smart one. Or, perhaps, he was just too depressed to be good at concentrating on things like reading.

"Shoggoth," asked Pooh, "would it help if we all read it together? Out loud, I mean?"

The rat's black eyes sparkled strangely. "We . . . can try . . . ?"

There was just a bit of doubt in the way he said it, but Pooh was determined to have their tail-finding adventure end happily. And Rabbit always loved a happy ending to any story.

So, with Shoggoth-the-Rat and Rabbit leading the way, with Pooh following close behind and Eeyore doing his best, they began reading from the *Mysteries of the Worm* there in Rabbit's comfy little house.

* * *

1 3

Now it must be clearly understood that no such group of creatures had ever read that spell together. In all of the years since the book was written, and all the years since that spell was handwritten onto the printed page, no two people—or animals, for that matter—had ever read the spell together. Never. Never ever.

But they were determined, and they were friends, and as friends they plunged ahead. Friends often do things that any single person—or animal—cannot do alone. That was, as Pooh understood things, how it all worked best. His many adventures with Christopher Robin and Piglet, with Kanga and Roo, with Owl and Tigger, and all the others in the Hundred Acre Wood got things found and got things done and found ways to be happy in each other's company while doing it.

So, together they read . . .

> *To Tsathoggua, the Sleeper of N'kai we pray*
> *He grants us the eyes to see and the heart to find*
> *What is our deepest desire.*

When those lines were said, the air in the house seemed to change somewhat. It was both cooler around the edges and warmer there at the table.

> *From his place of dreams eternal*
> *His wisdom and grace stretch out across*
> *The infinite realms of waking and dreaming*

The flames in the fireplace leaped up and coughed sparks onto the stone hearth.

> *For without him, that which is most treasured*
> *That which is sought most desperately*
> *Can never be found*

Pooh saw that Eeyore's eyes seemed darker and they sparkled much like those of Shoggoth-the-Rat.

> *But to the seeker true of heart*
> *That which is desired will be made manifest*

The rat himself seemed to be struggling with himself as if he was having some kind of fit. Pooh saw—or thought he saw—Shoggoth's tail grow strange and thick and nearly shapeless. And all the hairs on the rat's body jerked and twitched as if each was alive, as if they were tiny armies of worms. But it was hard to see because the flickering fire made the shadows dance on the walls like hobbly-gobletons.

> *As, through Tsathoggua's eyes, all that is in*
> *The vault of forever may be discovered*

"I . . . can . . . see . . . ," began Eeyore, and instead of sadness there was a different quality entirely in his voice. Pooh thought it sounded like . . . wonder. Like amazement. But it was also kind of hollow and far away. "I can . . . see . . . I can see . . ."

Little Shoggoth squeaked at the same time. It wasn't words. Not really. Or, at least not words of any kind Pooh had ever heard. He said, "*Tekeli-li! Tekeli-li!*"

Pooh could not tell if the little rat was excited or alarmed or scared or all three.

> *Hold Tsathoggua in your mind and make your wish*
> *With witnesses to bear your truth.*

The room went completely dark for a moment, even though Winnie-the-Pooh could still *feel* the fire burning. Then there were lights in the darkness. Two clusters of them. No! Four. Two very small ones and two medium-sized ones. Little round bunches of lights. It was like looking up through Christopher Robin's telescope into the night sky and seeing just those stars visible at the other end of the lens.

Somehow, Pooh knew that he was seeing stars in the tiny eyes of the rat and the larger eyes of the donkey. It scared him to see it and scared him to know it. But he was with his friends and scary things bothered him less in such times.

Then the rat said something.

And after that, Eeyore said something else.

The rat spoke in that language Pooh could not understand.

Shoggoth-the-Rat said, *"Y' ahor mgr'luh syha'h."*

What Eeyore said was in English, though somehow Pooh knew that it meant exactly the same thing as what Shoggoth had said.

"I can see forever . . ." whispered the donkey. And he no longer sounded sad.

14

The darkness melted away and the room was just a room again.

The fire in the fireplace was burning quietly. The sunlight glimmered on the windowpanes. The tea in the pot smelled of chamomile and thyme. And the four of them were at the table. Though, to be quite accurate, Shoggoth was on the book that was on the table.

But the book itself was not there.

Instead, laid out flat and neat and clean and with its lovely pink bow, was Eeyore's tail. There was even a fresh, clean pin.

"My tail!" cried the donkey, and the sparkling starlight in his eyes twinkled for a moment longer and then vanished. But Pooh saw that instead of sadness, his friend's eyes were filled with joy. Actual joy, which Pooh did not recall ever seeing there before.

Rabbit hopped off his chair and, with Pooh's assistance, fastened the tail to their friend's behind. Eeyore trundled around in a circle and even ran three times around the table, shaking himself to prove that the tail was not going to fall off.

Then he stopped and looked at Pooh. "You helped me find it, Winnie-the-Pooh."

"Of course! I knew we would."

"You are my friend," said Eeyore. And he gave a little bray of happiness. Then he turned to Rabbit. "If it wasn't for you reading the book for us, and letting us use your house to do this, I might never have found my tail."

Rabbit, who was a little embarrassed by all this, gave an awkward bow. Though he looked very pleased as well.

Then Eeyore turned to the rat, who looked even more like a rat than he had before. And a proper rat. One with a pink tail—almost the same color as Eeyore's ribbon—and very ordinary rat hair on his very ordinary rat body. And though his eyes sparkled, they did not twinkle in that strange way.

"And you helped me see," said Eeyore. "You helped me see forever."

Shoggoth just stared at him.

"You are a good friend," said the donkey.

"I . . . am . . . ?"

"You are a very good friend," insisted Eeyore. "You may be my best friend."

Outside, a cloud passed in front of the sun and for a moment the room darkened, but Shoggoth-the-Rat turned toward the window and glared very fiercely and soon the cloud snuck away and the sun shone brighter still. When he turned back to Eeyore, the little rat's eyes were moist.

"Friends," he said. "Friends are . . . good."

"Friends are the very bestest thing in the whole world," agreed Winnie-the-Pooh.

There is more to this tale, but this is enough for now. After that day, Eeyore was still sad sometimes, and sometimes very down, but not as much and not as often. And he was seldom sad when Shoggoth-the-Rat was with him. They spent a lot of time walking and talking, and if it was sometimes in that strange language, Pooh didn't mind. He was happy that they were happy.

The summer blossomed in the Hundred Acre Wood, and all that season there were plenty of flowers for the bees to visit, and plenty of honey in the hives, and songs to sing and quests to follow, and things to do.

And he was happy there.

With his friends.

In Which Owl Tries to Rescue His Uncle Robert

Julie Frost

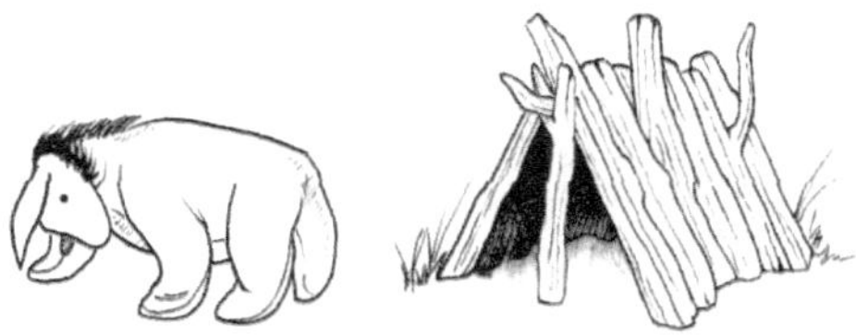

An ancient evil slumbered beneath the Hundred Acre Wood, and Eeyore was the only one holding it there. It was a very big responsibility for a Very Small Donkey, but he shouldered it—not gladly, because Eeyore didn't do anything "gladly" anymore, but it was Duty, and he took it seriously.

Let the others keep their innocence.

Which was all well and good until Eeyore woke up one morning to find his tail missing. Again. Someone had visited, but hadn't even stopped long enough to say "how do you do" or "by your leave" or any of the other pleasantries one normally exchanged when visiting. Just taken the tail and scarpered, and managed to do it without waking him up. Quite Professional. And also a bit Worrisome. The tail was important in ways that no one was supposed to know about.

"Bother," Eeyore said. "I suppose I should ask around and see if anyone's found it."

This would involve leaving Pooh Corner and his comfortable little house and wandering about. But it would give him a chance to strengthen the wards and see to it that all was well.

All wasn't well, of course, because why should it be. The first ward he came to, at the bridge on the track between the Outland and the Forest, had been entirely dismantled. Eeyore shivered. This was worse than he'd thought. More so because he didn't have the correct ingredients with him to set it right again. Christopher Robin had helped him make the ward the first time, because he knew things, but Christopher Robin had left, and no one had seen him for a long time.

Owl knew things as well. Perhaps not the same things, but it wouldn't hurt to ask. And Owl's new house was on the way to the next ward, so Eeyore could pop in and ask in a roundabout way if he had any sage, salt, or chalk lying about, or maybe a candle or two.

Owl was startled when Eeyore knocked on his door. "Oh. Ah! Eeyore. How, ah, lovely to see you. I'm sorry, you've caught me at a bad time. I was just going out. My Uncle Robert has given me a task, you see, and I'm terribly busy."

"I was just wondering—" Eeyore started.

"So sorry! Must fly!" And Owl took wing without even saying goodbye, which Eeyore thought was very rude.

"I suppose," Eeyore reflected, "that Rabbit might have some sage or salt, and with so many friends-and-relations, he could come up with a candle and chalk as well."

The next ward was also broken. There were seven altogether, because seven was a Holy Number, and Eeyore began to think they'd all been broken. By whom was the question. If so, he'd need a *lot* of sage and salt, more than one stick of chalk, and at least four candles if not more.

Prepare for the worst, that was his motto, and he soon came to Rabbit's house. "Hallo, Rabbit," he said. "I was wondering—"

"Oh, hallo, Eeyore," Rabbit said, and Eeyore mused what it was with everyone not letting him get a sentence out today. "Have you seen Small? He's lost again."

Eeyore didn't quite roll his eyes, but it was hard going not to. He still remembered searching for two full days before anyone thought to tell him that Small had been found. "No, but he's bound to turn up somewhere. I say, do you have any salt or sage you're not using lying about? Chalk? Candles?"

"I can spare a little sage and a dash of salt," Rabbit said. "Why?"

"No particular reason," Eeyore said, because Rabbit didn't Need To Know. "But if you could trouble your friends-and-relations for some, that would be helpful." And might save us all, he didn't say, because he wasn't sure how bad it was just yet and didn't want to alarm anyone, least of all Rabbit, who tended to be a bit flighty. "I'm going to see Pooh, so if you could be a good fellow and give me what you can spare . . . ?"

"Of course, of course." And Rabbit soon had a sack ready with some sage and salt, and handed it to him. "And if you see Small, send him my way?"

"I will. Good-bye." And Eeyore took his leave.

Sure enough, the ward between Rabbit's and Pooh's houses was also broken. "That's three," Eeyore said to himself. "I don't like to assume, but I may have to start."

When he reached Pooh's house, he was just in time to see Owl flying off with a pot of honey clutched in his claws. "Hallo, Eeyore," Pooh said. "What's in your sack?"

Eeyore stared after Owl with consternation. "Was that a *full* honey pot?" he asked.

"Why, yes, Owl was quite insistent, something about his Uncle Robert. I didn't like to give it up, but he was dreadfully urgent about it."

Piglet, who lived with Pooh now, sidled up and peered at Eeyore. "I-i-is everything all right, Eeyore?

"No," said Eeyore, "no, it decidedly is not. Pooh, could I trouble you for any salt or sage, chalk or candles?"

"I have candles," Pooh said doubtfully, "but I use them at night."

"If I could just borrow one or two, or six? In here, if you don't mind." And he thrust his bag toward Pooh.

"So many people borrowing so many things today," Pooh muttered. But he went inside with the sack and returned a few moments later. "I only had two. Is it enough?"

"No," Eeyore answered, "but it will have to do, at least for now. Oh, and Rabbit is looking for Small again, so if you see him . . . ?"

Pooh twisted around and looked at his back, which Eeyore thought odd, and said, "Well, he's not there."

"I'm off to Kanga's. If Owl comes by again, try to keep him occupied until I can come back, and send Piglet for me."

"All right, but what—"

"Good-bye!" And Eeyore picked up his sack and trotted off before things got Awkward. "Well. More Awkward." Because now the situation had got Serious.

There were three sacred elements in the Hundred Acre Wood. Eeyore's tail, Pooh's honey, and Roo's Strengthening Medicine, the Extract of Malt. As long as those elements were kept separate, everything was fine.

In combination? Coupled with a Ritual? And a Sacrifice?

Everything was decidedly *not* fine. Dread coiled around Eeyore's heart. It was happening again. He'd barely stopped it last time, and the Gravel Pit, where nothing ever grew, was the result. He had a bad feeling about where Small was, and hoped he was wrong.

He hurried as fast as his stubby legs could carry him to Kanga's house. Owl had beaten him there and was in mid-argument with Kanga, while Tigger and Roo looked on. Eeyore crashed to a halt in a plume of dust and spat the sack out.

"Owl, you must stop at once," Eeyore said.

Owl swiveled his head and speared him with a crazed look. His pupils were blown wide, though it was broad daylight, and his feathers were disheveled. "My Uncle Robert says it's very important."

"And where is your Uncle Robert, Owl?" Kanga asked gently.

"Well, I don't know, do I? But he's speaking to me. He says if I don't do this, he'll be trapped in torment forever."

"That doesn't sound very nice," Tigger remarked. "We found Small, before. Perhaps we should organdize a search for Uncle Robert."

"There's fire and sulfur," Owl said. "And nothing like that in our Wood. He's Beyond where we can go, he says, but if I follow his instructions he can come back."

"Owl," Eeyore said. "I mean this in the nicest way. Your Uncle Robert is dead."

Roo and Tigger looked at him with puzzlement. Kanga closed her eyes and nodded sadly. Eeyore knew she'd barely escaped from Something Very Dreadful with Roo and her life, but she didn't talk about it and he didn't ask.

"I don't understand," Owl said. "What is 'dead'?"

That brought Eeyore up short. How to explain death to people who'd never experienced it, who didn't even have the concept? "Well," he said. And, "Ahem." And, "Think of it like this." He rubbed his ear with his forefoot before continuing. "He's gone away. Forever. To a place we can't follow and can't bring him back from. Whether we follow his instructions or not."

"I refuse to believe that," Owl said. "And so I'll thank you, Kanga, for that Elixir of Malt."

Kanga stepped firmly in front of her door and crossed her arms. "I'm sorry, Owl. I can't give you that, much as I'd like to help in any other way."

"There is no other way!" Owl cried. "He's trapped and hurt. The Elixir is the last thing I need to release him."

"Oh, Owl," Kanga said. "If you managed to release him, I'm afraid you wouldn't like it very much. Trust me when I say that bringing people back from the dead never ends well for anyone involved." A haunted expression crossed her face, briefly. Eeyore wondered what had happened to Roo's Da and decided that was not a question he would ask, ever.

"But if we can help Uncle Robert—" Tigger said.

"He is beyond our help and that's all there is to it," Eeyore responded.

"Thank you all for exactly nothing," Owl said, and flew away in a huff.

Eeyore slumped, partly in relief, partly in sorrow. "I didn't like to break it to him like that. But there seemed no easy way to do it."

"That's all right, Eeyore, dear," Kanga said. "Would you like to come in and have some tea? I just made it fresh. We have lemon tarts."

"Thank you, no, Kanga," Eeyore answered. "I have things I must attend to. But if you have sage, salt, chalk, or candles lying about, if I could trouble you for those, I would greatly appreciate it."

"I have chalk for Roo's lessons, yes, and salt for seasoning. I would imagine you need matches as well. Will that do?"

Eeyore nudged the sack toward her. "In here, if you please."

She came out a few moments later, and the sack was heavier. "I put a lemon tart in there, and some of Roo's Elixir as well, to keep your strength up."

Kanga was wise; Eeyore did feel a bit peckish. He thanked her humbly and headed to the next ward. "Smithereens," he said when he arrived. But now that he had everything he needed to repair it, he supposed he should get to work. It wouldn't be the same as having all seven, but it couldn't hurt and might help.

One couldn't hurry a thing like this, and Eeyore carefully laid everything out before beginning. First the salt, in a circle around a local pebble, to anchor the ward to that spot on the ground. Then a chalk six-sided star around that—two triangles, three also being a Holy Number. A candle lit at the northern point. Sage set alight from the candle and waved, as Eeyore carried it walking a sunwise circle seven times around the lot, whilst humming one of Pooh's songs. Pooh didn't know they were sacred and inspired, but he didn't need to, after all.

Right in the middle of his sixth circumlocution, the very worst point to be interrupted at, an "AHA" sounded from above. Eeyore's head jerked up in time for him to see Owl swoop down, seize the sack in his talons, and fly aloft again. Eeyore lunged, grabbed—

And missed. He landed on his nose, bruising it. "Owl! Bring that back this instant. It has my lemon tart in it."

"Oh ho ho," said Owl. "It also has the Elixir of Malt I need. Uncle Robert told me you might try to replace the wards, so I lay in wait until you were good and distracted. And now you can't fix those either. Farewell!" And he flew triumphantly off to the west.

"Bother!" said Eeyore, along with several other much naughtier words the other animals didn't and shouldn't know. "Well, I suppose that's Torn It." He squeezed his eyes shut for a moment and heaved a heavy sigh.

He wouldn't be able to stop this on his own. He pondered. Rabbit was far too flighty. Tigger too bouncy. Kanga had Roo to take care of, and he wouldn't ask a mother's aid in such a dangerous enterprise in any case.

That left Pooh and Piglet. Piglet was very small, and also frightened easily.

Pooh, though. Pooh was a faithful Knight. Christopher Robin had dubbed him so. And though he had Very Little Brain, he was good at following directions.

Owl's ritual would take some time to set up. Eeyore decided to find him first, and then get Pooh. "No sense both of us traipsing all over." He headed west, keeping an eye on the trees overhead, wary for an ambush. He didn't think Owl would actually hurt him, but he had sharp talons and wasn't completely in his right mind, so it wasn't out of the question.

West, and west, and farther west, until, "Ah." And, "Of course." And, "I should have known." Because Galleons Lap, at the very top of the Forest, was an enchanted place, and just the spot for a Ritual.

Eeyore hid behind a tree and watched Owl for a moment to see what he was up to. Muttering to himself, Owl measured out a quite large five-pointed star at the center of the Lap, and started trimming the grass close to the ground. The elements for the ritual he kept in the center so they were always nearby him, so rushing in and taking them wasn't Feasible. And even if he did, Owl could easily catch him and they'd be right back where they started.

"No, best to get Pooh and then we can stop this together," Eeyore said, and turned and trotted back to Pooh's house as fast as his legs could carry him.

"Hallo again, Eeyore," Pooh said when he got there. "What happened to your sack?"

Eeyore was somewhat out of breath and grouchy about it. "Owl took it. I'll explain on the way."

"On the way to where?"

"Galleons Lap. We must stop Owl from doing a Terrible Thing, and there's no one else for it but you and me, because Rabbit is too flighty and Tigger is too bouncy and Kanga is a mother and Piglet is frightened of everything." He snorted out a breath. "It's little enough I have to work with, you being a Bear of Very Little Brain, but you were dubbed a faithful Knight by Christopher Robin, and so you will have to do. Come along."

"Will there be Heffalumps?" Pooh asked, balking ever so slightly. "Because I wouldn't much like that."

"I shouldn't think so. This is Different."

And Pooh, who knew Duty when he heard it, followed Eeyore in the direction of Galleons Lap.

Piglet had listened from behind a door, and he stood up very straight. "Frightened of everything!" he said indignantly. "Pooh made up a whole song about how brave I was. Courage! There's always hope. And they might need help, because I'm sure three heads are better than two when it comes to Things Like This. So long as there are no Heffalumps involved, I think I should do quite well. It can't be any more frightening than squeezing through a letter slot."

So he followed behind, but not too closely, in case they saw him and sent him back. It was a long walk for a Small Animal, and he was winded by the time they got to Galleons Lap and found Owl. They couldn't very well send him back now, could they, so Piglet walked up to Pooh and Eeyore and said, "Oh, hallo," nonchalantly, like he'd just been going in the same direction and met them by surprise.

"Piglet," said Eeyore sternly. "You shouldn't be here. It's dangerous."

Piglet peered into the clearing. "What is Owl *doing*?"

"Something that Pooh and I must stop and you should not be anywhere near," Eeyore said firmly.

"Oh, but I daresay I could be of some help, surely?"

Eeyore eyed the clearing. They'd taken longer than he'd thought to get back, and Owl had finished his star, inscribed a circle around it, and placed Eeyore's tail at the bottom point, Pooh's honey to the right of that, and Roo's Elixir of Malt at the left. A jar holding Small sat in the pentagon in the middle, and Owl stood centered between the two empty points.

Singing.

Singing one of Pooh's songs.

Only he was doing it subtly wrong. And out of tune.

> La-la-tra, la-la-tra.
> La-la-tra, la-la-tra.
> Tiddle-um-tum-rum-tum.

Over and over. The ground quaked. A rumble sounded from deep in the earth, like rocks grinding together. Something roared, far away, but coming closer. Dark thunderheads gathered overhead, flashing lightning.

"Pooh!" Eeyore shouted. "You grab the honey and the Elixir. Piglet, you rescue Small. I'll stop Owl." And he charged into the clearing without waiting to see if the other two would follow his lead.

Pooh and Piglet stared at each other, wide eyed. The quake became a definite shake, the rumble became a thunder, and the roar became a screech. Lightning split one of the sentinel trees. Before they could take a step into the clearing, the Forest floor flexed like an ocean wave and threw them off their feet. Eeyore fell backward, rolling and rolling until he bashed into a tree at the edge of the clearing with a grunt and a very bad word.

Before he could gather himself again, a huge arm, many-jointed and black as night, bigger than the trees, twice as big as the trees, who would have thought an arm could be that enormous or have a hand with claws that long or be covered in that much chitin or be dripping that much ichor, burst forth from the center of Owl's star. Owl stuttered to a stop. "You aren't my Uncle Robert," he said, rather stupidly, Eeyore thought, because that much was Obvious.

The hand grabbed the jar holding Small and smashed it like an eggshell. Small also went smash, squirting green goo and screaming. Another arm joined the first, grasping toward the sky, the claws clicking together in a pattern Eeyore was quite sure wouldn't be good for anyone.

Pooh said doubtfully, "Is that one of Rabbit's friends-and-relations? Seems a bit large."

Eeyore was frankly flummoxed at this point. It would take another Ritual to return this Abomination to its slumber. He would have to come up with one on the fly, he decided. The ingredients were at hand, if he could only get to them across the ground, which was doing a fairly impressive impression of a rumba.

"Piglet," Eeyore said. But Piglet was staring at those arms in frank terror, even as a third one joined the other two. Eeyore shook him. "Piglet! I need you to be very brave now. Can you do that for me? For all of us?"

"I-I-I d-d-d-don't know." Piglet shivered all over. "What do you want me to do?"

"See the Elixir, there, closest to us? You must run and grab it and bring it back here."

"G-g-get near that *Thing*?"

"Gallant Piglet," Eeyore said, turning Piglet's head to look him straight in the eye. "You will not tremble. You will not blinch. Ho for you. Ho."

Piglet took several deep breaths, and his chin rose and his shoulders (such as they were) squared. "All right, Eeyore. I was brave once. I can be brave again."

"There's a good fellow. Pooh?"

Pooh shook himself out of the horrified stupor he'd fallen into. "Yes?"

"I need you to come up with a song."

"Right now? In the face of" —Pooh waved a paw— "*that*?"

"Yes. It's very important." They had to stop the creature before it got its head above ground.

"Will an old one do?"

Eeyore shuddered at the "old one." "No. It must be brand new."

Pooh's eyes got wider and wider. "Does it have to be any good?"

"Just do your best. Owl!" Eeyore shouted across the clearing. "Have you come to your senses yet?"

"Eeyore?" Owl blinked several times. "What . . . what is happening? I thought my Uncle Robert—"

"Yes, well, I tried to tell you and you refused to listen," you cast-iron numb-skull, Eeyore didn't say. "Bring us the honey, if you please, while Piglet and I fetch the Elixir and my tail. Ready, Piglet?"

Brave Piglet didn't tremble or blinch. He instead took off running the same time Eeyore did, heading straight for the Elixir without hesitation across the heaving ground. Eeyore ran toward his tail, timing the rhythm of the waves so he didn't stumble. Owl flew to the honey pot and picked it up.

Piglet grabbed the Elixir and turned to run back to Pooh just as Eeyore got hold of his tail. Eeyore, still timing the rhythm, made it back to Pooh, and Owl alighted beside him. Piglet—

One of the arms flailed down and swatted Piglet aside. The Elixir sailed in one direction.

And Piglet sailed in two directions.

Cut cleanly in half by a razor-sharp claw before all their horrified gazes, he didn't even have time to scream. But Pooh, Owl, and Eeyore screamed enough, even as a fourth arm shot forth from the earth. Pooh and Owl had never experienced something so awful, and they collapsed in shellshocked dismay. Eeyore had, and managed to—barely—keep his feet, but one never got actually used to such things.

He recovered first and inscribed a hurried six-pointed star on the ground while Pooh and Owl gibbered. Then he headbutted both of them. They stared at him uncomprehendingly. "Pooh! Owl! Fall apart later. Concentrate now. We still need the Elixir, Owl, and you must go fetch it as you're the most able. Pooh, do you have a song for us?"

Owl shook himself and took flight. More lightning flashed, and balls of it rolled around the clearing. An arm crashed down toward Owl, but he dodged it adroitly, picking the Elixir up and depositing it next to the honey before landing with a flump and flurry of feathers. "Now what?" he asked.

"Now someone nails my tail back on. We mix the Elixir with the honey. We put a haycorn in the center of the star in honor of Piglet, and smash it with the honey pot. And Pooh sings his song while I stir the Elixir and the honey with my tail. Hopefully before anything else comes bursting from the ground."

"I do," Pooh said, "have a song. It's not. It's not a very grand one. Or long."

"Shorter the better, really. My tail?"

Pooh pounded the nail home while Owl did the honors with the haycorn, the honey, and the Elixir. A fifth arm joined the other four. An antenna followed it, cracking about like a bullwhip.

"Now, Pooh!" Eeyore said, getting his tail well down into the honey pot and stirring vigorously. "Sing!"

And, oh, Pooh sang:

> Owl's Uncle Robert asked him for help
> It's not Uncle Robert, said Eeyore a-yelp
> Owl, please, you must hear
> But Owl didn't listen
> 'Cause Uncle Robert was hissin'
> Terrible words in his ear
> Owl placed things in a pail
> Elixir, honey, and tail
> And took them to Galleons Lap

> And Piglet and Small
> Paid the price for it all
> Before we made the Horror take a permanent nap.

Two of the abominable arms were sucked back into the ground with a wail of disappointment. Eeyore stirred more vigorously. "Again, Pooh!" he cried. "Louder!"

Tears soaking his fur, Pooh sang the song again, using a deeper register, bringing the words up from his chest. When he got to the end, two more arms disappeared. The Horror shrieked and howled, while the remaining arm and the antenna thrashed about, knocking the tops off several trees.

Eeyore's tail was whipping up a froth by now. "I think once more will do it," he said. "Because it's in threes, you see."

Pooh nodded, took a deep breath, and really belted it out. Owl and Eeyore sang along. The ground bucked. Trees cracked in half. The Horror screeched. And the last arm and the antenna slurped back into the earth with a wet squelch and one last indignant but somehow anticlimactic squawk.

Eeyore, Owl, and Pooh fell backward and lay staring at the sky. The thunder-clouds cleared, revealing the sun, which shone down on the triumphant but devastated three.

"Did we win?" Pooh finally asked, tears still leaking from under his closed eyelids.

"Yes," Eeyore answered. "And also no."

They stumbled to their feet in various states of Disheveled. All the grass from the center of Galleons Lap had been churned to mud. Eeyore wondered if it would ever grow back, or become like the Gravel Pit, and decided that Time Would Tell. More than half the sentinel trees had been destroyed in one way or another.

"I didn't mean," Owl said. And, "I'm sorry." And, "I should have listened." And, "Perhaps I don't know as many things as I once thought."

"A voice in your head you immediately took at its word," Eeyore said, rather severely. "I daresay that was a misstep on your part, though not your last. I don't like to say I Told You So, but I rather did, if you recall."

Owl was not often humbled. "I know. And I'm sorry."

"What do we do now?" Pooh asked.

"We gather the others, tell them what happened, and give Piglet a burial with full honors and a posthumous medal."

"I had just got used to him living with me," Pooh said. "The house will seem empty without him."

"I'm sorry," Owl said wretchedly

"As you should be," said Eeyore. "We'll bury Piglet next to your house, Pooh, and his valiant memory shall live on in all our hearts."

Carrying Piglet's remains, the sorrowful trio made their way back to Kanga's house to break the news to her and Tigger. Owl flew to Rabbit's and told him they were having a Meeting. They gathered at Pooh's house in a circle in the yard, with the two pieces of Piglet's body in the center.

They'd all lost a bit of their innocence this day, Eeyore thought. Roo still didn't understand, bless him, and Eeyore hoped he never had to. Tigger was still for once, and Rabbit decided all his Urgent Business could wait.

"We shall have a proper funeral," Eeyore started and then . . .

"Hallo, everyone," Christopher Robin said. "I'm back for a little while. What's all th—" And he stopped short when he saw Piglet. "Oh."

"You missed a lot while you were gone," said Pooh.

"I can see that," said Christopher Robin. He sat down and pulled Pooh into his lap for a hug. The other animals gathered around as close as they could, comforting, and being comforted, as Eeyore laid out the sorry tale.

Owl hung back in the periphery, still ashamed of his role in the whole wretched affair. Eeyore noticed and nudged him inward. "You didn't mean it, Owl," he said. "Just if there's a next time, let one of us know and we'll steer you back on course before it's too late."

Owl nodded miserably. "Piglet was Brave and Stalwart," he said. "Braver than I deserved. Twice."

"We're a forgiving lot, by and large," Christopher Robin said, petting him. "Rabbit, you're good at digging. Can you dig a grave for our Piglet? And I shall make a marker. I've learnt to spell better while I was gone, in any case. And perhaps we can all make bits and bobs for Decoration."

"And what about Small?" Pooh asked. "What happened to him wasn't very nice either, but there's not enough of him left to bury." And Eeyore suddenly felt bad about leaving Small at Galleons Lap and wondered if they should try to find his remains in the mud.

"We'll have a Memorial for him here as well," Christopher Robin said briskly. "Right ho, then, let's all get to work."

Everyone scattered. When they reunited a couple of hours later, each of them had brought a little something and Rabbit had finished digging the grave.

Christopher Robin brought the marker and a blanket to wrap Piglet in, along with a medallion.

Pooh brought a quite large pot of his best honey.

Owl brought the rope that Piglet had used to get out of his house when it had blown over.

Kanga and Roo brought a flower garland.

Tigger brought a bag of haycorns.

Rabbit brought a basket of violets.

And Eeyore brought the bit of balloon Piglet had given him for his birthday.

Christopher Robin wrapped Piglet tenderly in the blanket and laid him in the grave. Piglet's expression in death was serene, as if he knew he'd done a Grand Thing and a Brave Thing and a Right Thing. Which he had, of course. They placed the haycorns and the honey and the rope and the balloon in the grave, and the flowers at the head and foot, and Rabbit filled the grave back in, sniffling a bit as he did.

Christopher Robin said "Poor Small," and set Small's marker in place. It read:

In Memory of Small
He Didn't Deserve
What Happened to Him

"Piglet was the best of us," said Christopher Robin. "May his rest be peaceful." He put down Piglet's marker, which said:

Here Lies Piglet
A Very Small Animal
With a Very Big Heart
The Bravest of Us All

"Oh, gallant Piglet (PIGLET)! Ho!" Eeyore said.

In Which Woozles Attempt to Manifest Themselves in the Midst of a Friendly Gathering

Jody Lynn Nye

Owl listened with growing interest as Winnie-the-Pooh sat on the velvet settee in his sitting room and described his latest dream. Though Pooh was a Bear of Very Little Brain, quite a large part of it could see into the future. Naturally, Pooh had no idea that that was what he was doing. His inner-sense kept him from thinking too deeply.

"Do tell me more about your dream," the sage inquired, sounding as impressive as he could, which was very impressive indeed. He drew himself up and puffed out all his feathers. "Elaborate. Discourse. In fact, inform." The small, golden bear looked as though he was honored to be asked, and gave Owl a smile.

"Four Heffalumps came to take my honey from me," Pooh said. "They chased me and chased me. They kept changing shape and color – perhaps to make me think they were something else, but they still wanted my honey! I jumped into Rabbit's house – he was just about to have his dinner – and closed the door behind me. They reached right through the wall with their trunks! I didn't know they could do that!"

"Yes, hmmm, they can," Owl intoned low through his beak. "Sometimes. When the wind is in the west quarter. What happened then?"

"I hit them with my honey jar. I jumped up and down on their trunks. Rabbit came over with his frying pan and swatted at them. It made a clang! with every stroke, as though they were made of metal, too. The trunks went away, and they howled outside. I was afraid." Pooh shivered.

"And then?" Owl urged, gently.

"I . . . I . . . I woke up. And my honey jar was right there, so I thought," Pooh said, tilting his head to one side with a winsome expression, "that I would make sure everything was all right. And it was! The honey was in the jar! But I had to make sure it tasted the way it ought to taste. So, I sliced some bread and spread honey on it."

"And *did* it taste the way it ought to taste?" Owl asked.

Pooh smiled blissfully. "It did. But eating a snack in the middle of the night made me feel sleepy, so I went back to bed."

"And did you dream again? What did you dream of?" Owl pressed him.

"I dreamt of honey," Pooh said, with a sigh of pleasure. "Ponds and rivers and lakes full of sweet, golden deliciousness, dripping down from the trees, slithering in oozy goodness!" He looked around. "I don't suppose you have any here I could try? To see if yours tastes the way it ought to taste?"

Owl lowered his head so as not to show his amusement. "I don't eat honey, my well-upholstered friend, so I don't keep it in my home."

"But you could keep it for your friends. When they visit," Pooh said, still looking hopeful.

"Do you know, that's not a bad idea." Owl fluttered off his perch and waddled toward the opening of his eyrie. "But I don't have any now. Perhaps you should go home and have some more of *your* honey on bread, even if it makes you sleepy. *Especially* if it makes you sleepy."

He saw the small bear to the ladder that led downward from his very, very tall tree, and watched as Pooh disappeared over the bridge crossing the river, into the undergrowth, on the way toward his own home. Though the sunshine of a golden afternoon lit his way, Owl was all too aware of the shadows that loomed nearby.

When Owl was certain Winnie-the-Pooh was out of sight and out of earshot, he turned to the wardrobe at the end of his sitting room.

"Come out, my friends, and tell me what you think."

Kanga and Rabbit hopped out of the wooden cabinet. Small Piglet scrambled to climb over the threshold, and was nudged upward by Eeyore, who emerged after him. Kanga settled herself on the green velvet pouffe set before the cozy fireplace with Piglet, and Eeyore hunched down beside them, but Rabbit could not sit still. He paced up and back in the small sitting room, throwing his paws about with every evidence of frustration.

"We are all *doomed*," he said. "Our safety – our very existence! – depends upon a Bear of Very Little Brain and Very Large Appetite. He could put us in danger. All this month, the visions have become more dire! What if he forgot one of his dreams, and we were beset? You remember what happened to my cousin and all twelve of his children? They have never been seen again!"

"I forgot about them," Kanga said, with a horrified expression.

Rabbit spun on his large back foot. "That is what happens when the Heffalumps disappear people. Only their closest relations remember them."

"Or my-my-my auntie," Piglet said sadly. "She ran away. I miss her!"

"Rabbit, Piglet, I beg you not to despair," Owl said, although he was just as worried. Time and again, Pooh had given warnings of the unspeakable dread that lay beyond the boundaries of the Wood, never realizing or noticing that the terrors were real. "He has not failed us yet. Pooh has always given warning in plenty of time! In his nighttime musings, he always sees the proper defense. We have defeated the horrors every time."

"But what if I don't hit those Heffalumps hard enough to drive them away?" Rabbit asked, wringing his paws.

"You will," Owl said, with more confidence than he felt. "Pooh imagines Heffalumps only exist in his dreams. And Woozles. And those others." He shuddered, causing his pinfeathers to twitch. "I do not wish to think of what he would do if he knew they were real, and far more threatening than in his visions. We would be overrun by terrors beyond all imagination."

"What if one actually breaks through into the Hundred Acre Wood?" Kanga asked. "What if Pooh actually sees one? They are far more horrible and fearsome in person than they are in dreams." Roo, asleep in her pouch, muttered and twitched at his mother's agitated voice. The female kangaroo stroked her son until he settled down again.

"That we must prevent at all costs," Owl said. He opened his large golden eyes until they took over most of his face. "We must never allow his inner-sense to be lost."

"How did we come to this?" Rabbit asked, his eyes wild. "I never thought that we would be marooned here on a deserted island of safety in the middle of a sea of terror?"

"It's a pretty nice island," Eeyore said, chewing thoughtfully on a mouthful of grass. Owl always had fresh grass for his morose friend. "It's big enough. I don't ever go outside of it."

"Neither do we," Piglet said, his eyes huge. "I haven't wished to go elsewhere for ages. Everything I want is here."

"Except escape!" Rabbit said, wringing his paws. "We do not have freedom!"

"We do!" Owl insisted. "We are more free here than we would outside the bounds of the Wood. Because of our rotund little friend, we have been largely protected. And, in turn, we must protect him."

"What must we do?" Kanga asked. "Give Pooh all the honey he wants?"

"No! No!" Rabbit said. He drummed his long foot on the floor. "His appetite for honey never wanes. The entire forest would run out before he filled up!"

"Fortunately, we have plenty of honey," Owl said. "The bees are most cooper-ative, as are the wildflowers."

"I can keep a close eye on Pooh," Eeyore said. "Not that he ever notices I'm there. No one does."

"Of course, we notice you, my sorrowful friend," Owl assured him, wrapping a reassuring wing around the small donkey's gray shoulder. "And if he confides in you, any of you, you must inform me at once."

"I will!" Piglet said, although he looked very frightened. "I will, too!"

"We all will," Kanga said. The others nodded.

Owl couldn't help but glance out of his door in the direction that Pooh had gone, toward his small house and the sign above its door. Beyond it lay the bound-aries of the Wood, wreathed in dark shadow. That little home and its occupant was all that stood between peace and peril. He shook every feather he had until he was puffed up like a balloon.

"It'll be all right," Kanga said, but even she didn't sound too certain.

IN THE MORNING, Winnie-the-Pooh climbed up the tall tree to Owl's house again. The dream he had had the night before was still vivid behind his eyelids, so much, that every time he closed them, he saw it all over again.

Owl was reading a huge, leather-bound book with many words in it – so many, in fact, that clouds of them escaped from the pages and swarmed around his head like bees. The very thought of bees brought him to mind of honey, and the thought of honey almost made him forget his reason for the visit.

Fortunately, Owl saw him, and clapped the book shut. The words fled inside the pages and vanished.

"My good friend!" the sage said. "Well, well. And how are you on this fine morning?"

Pooh remembered all of a sudden why he was there.

"Well, I am on my way to see Christopher Robin," Pooh said. "And since you are on the way, I thought I would come by here first."

"And why is that?"

"I had another dream, and Christopher Robin was in it," Pooh replied. His round face scrunched up. It hadn't been a pleasant one, Owl could tell.

"Tell me, my friend," Owl said. He opened a cupboard and withdrew from it a small white-and-blue painted crock. "As you see, I have taken your suggestion and laid in a supply of honey. For my visitors."

Pooh beamed with delight and took the lid from the jar.

"This is the right kind of honey, I can tell," he said. He put a paw into the container, pulled out a sticky golden mass, and shoved it into his mouth. "Mmm! Gooh!"

"About your dream, Pooh Bear . . . ?"

"Um, yeh," Pooh said, around the mouthful. "Moh Woo'el! Puhul oh-ed uhnh. Eih oh wehf!"

"More Woozles, you say? Purple-spotted ones? Eight or twelve?' Owl translated, tapping a claw on the floor. "And what did you do?"

Pooh gave a mighty swallow and began to lick his paws. "I hid," he said. "Christopher Robin and I had to hide away from them because there were too many. The sun disappeared! Then I heard a terrible buzzing noise! When we looked up, the sky was black with bees. The Woozles exploded with a mighty boom! Except one. It ran away." He turned the crock bottom up to scrape out the remaining honey with a thoughtful finger.

"Do you know to where it ran?"

"No. I was, er, doing my best to keep Christopher Robin from being afraid. That is why I am going there now, to warn him about the Woozles!" He examined the jar, and peered up at Owl. "I don't suppose you have any more honey in your cupboard?"

"I'm afraid not, Pooh," Owl said, gently. "I thought it would be enough for a visitor on one visit. Don't you agree?"

"I suppose so. Thank you very much," Pooh added, with more grace than Owl thought he would display. "It was very kind of you to think of it."

"It is my pleasure."

Owl hid his alarm from Pooh. The dream of the night before had come true. Rabbit and the handful of relations that had been visiting him at the time had indeed faced Heffalumps sticking their trunks through his door. As Pooh had foreseen, Rabbit's strong defense with the frying pan had deterred them.

He waited until Pooh climbed all the way down the tree and headed in the direction of Christopher Robin's small house, then took wing toward Kanga's home.

"There will be an escape today," he told Kanga, careful not to alarm Roo, who was playing happily near his mother's tail. "A breakaway. And it involves Christopher Robin."

"What?" she asked.

"A Woozle. A purple-spotted one, no less."

Kanga wrung her hands. "That is the fiercest kind. And they divide into many times their number, one for each spot! Piglet must be warned. Those were the same Woozles who nearly took him."

"That is why he is always afraid," Owl agreed. "This time will be hard for all of us. They are bold enough to attack in daylight. It means they are growing stronger. I will tell the others."

***

He found Piglet visiting with Rabbit, Eeyore, and half a dozen of Rabbit's relations, enjoying a late breakfast. His appearance at the door was welcomed until the party-goers beheld the grave expression on his face.

"Wuh-wuh-what are you doing here?" Piglet asked, nervously clutching his teacup to his chest.

"A warning, my friends," Owl said. "We fear that a Woozle will break free today. Once it begins to divide, we are all in danger."

Rabbit clutched at his ears. "How will we defend ourselves? What did Pooh say?"

"Alas, he didn't. His dream ended before that moment."

"Is this the end of us all?" Piglet squeaked.

"No," Owl declared firmly. "No, it isn't. We will push back the darkness, and we will survive. We always do. Pooh is the key to our deliverance. We need to rally around him and fight back."

"But what is the best way to proceed?" Rabbit asked. "He will be curious as to why we *are* rallying around him."

The others stared at Owl. He thought for a moment.

"A birthday party," he said. "We shall have an impromptu birthday celebration. And monsters can't stand happiness. We will overwhelm them with happiness."

"Who is Impromptu?" Piglet asked.

Owl smiled. "You shall be Impromptu today, my small friend."

Piglet looked all shy for a moment.

"But, but, it isn't my birthday!"

"If you are Impromptu, it is," Owl said. "Impromptu's birthday is any day we say that it is."

Rabbit shot to his feet.

"That's a very good idea, Owl. Very good." He turned to his family. "We start cooking. Let's make a tall, beautiful cake. No purple spots anywhere on it!"

"And you must rehearse a speech," Owl told Piglet. "As long as you can make it."

Piglet blushed. "I'm not good at speeches."

"Make it an Impromptu speech, and it will be just fine." Owl spread his wings. "I must go see how things are faring at Christopher Robin's house."

"Silly old bear," Christopher Robin said. The small blond boy sat on a stump, watching Winnie-the-Pooh try to walk along the fence rail that ran around the flower garden. "I don't believe in Woozles. I've never seen one. Have you?"

"Not in person," Pooh said. He took a careful step and hopped over the first fence post. "I dream about them all the time." Pleased, he made for the second upright. It looked taller than the first. But he was able to get over it without tumbling down. "Almost as often as I dream about honey."

"Then, maybe we will stop for a snack in a little while," Christopher Robin said. He was always happy to indulge his friend.

"When?" Pooh asked, skirting the third fence post and skipping toward the next.

"As soon as you finish walking to the end of the fence," his friend said.

Pooh laughed in delight. But, at that moment, he felt that something was wrong. He stopped.

A picture came up in his mind. In it, he held a big honey jar, bigger than any he had ever seen, bigger than he was, or even his house! A long, sinuous snout came over his shoulder and dipped into the opening. He pushed the snout away, but grasping claws covered in purple spots reached around him and clutched the crock. Trying to keep hold of the honey jar, he lost his balance. Pooh fell off the fence with a thoroughgoing thud.

His vision cleared. Christopher Robin ran to him.

"Are you all right, Pooh?"

Pooh shook his head. He was convinced he was seeing things. The biggest trees in the forest began to move. And grow limbs. And turn colors. The trees turned into Heffalumps! And the Heffalumps started to move toward them.

"Christopher Robin, did I hit my head when I fell?"

The small boy looked him over closely. "I don't think so."

"Then, they must be real," Pooh said. Christopher Robin's lack of concern puzzled him greatly, so he asked his friend. "Don't you see them?"

"Who?"

"Woozles! Dozens of them! And Heffalumps! Green ones with pink-ringed trunks!"

"There's nothing over there. Is this like in your dream?" the small boy asked. He helped Pooh to his feet. "It feels cold, all of a sudden. It felt cold like this yesterday, too. Do you think we need to get sweaters or raincoats?"

Pooh thought hard. It was not so easy when one has a Very Little Brain. How could he explain that he was dreaming while he was wide awake? These monsters couldn't possibly be real, but they were very frightening to look at. And they were getting closer. They were taller than the trees, and they had long sharp claws stretched out toward him. He didn't want to be near them. Christopher Robin was his good friend, and Pooh didn't want him to be scared.

"I think it would be a very good thing to go inside your house," Pooh said, taking Christopher Robin's hand and tugging him toward the door. "Yes, we will go and lock the door, and find many sweaters and raincoats. We should put them all on. They will keep us safe. And warm. We should get inside before the bees come."

"Bees?" Christopher Robin asked. Pooh could barely see him. "Silly old bear, there is no one there!"

"But I see them! They're all around us. They are getting closer!"

The small boy looked in alarm, then an amused but patient look came over his face.

"It's just your imagination," he said. "I have always been amazed by your imagination. It sees things that aren't there."

"But, they are there," Pooh said, in a very small voice.

The monsters loomed closer and closer. Pooh could feel their cold breath gusting at him like an approaching storm. It was too late. The Woozles slithered forward on sharp-toed feet, surrounding them. The Heffalumps loomed over them, cutting off all the sunlight. There was no longer any way to escape toward the inviting little house. Pooh huddled down beside Christopher Robin's legs. They would both be eaten up in a smackering. There was nothing at all to be done to save them. Pooh moaned in fear and covered his eyes with both arms.

"Surprise! Surprise!"

The voices of their familiar friends came from behind the ring of monsters. Pooh looked up. Suddenly, a huge birthday cake came into his view. It was four layers high, and covered with blue and pink frosting. A lit candle tipped at a precarious angle on top. Rabbit held it out to Pooh on a big round platter. And, just as suddenly, the dream in his eyes faded. All the Woozles disappeared. He saw Owl looking down at him, with Eeyore and Kanga at his sides.

"Are you all right, my padded friend?" the sage inquired.

"I . . . yes . . ." Pooh replied, confused. The monsters were indeed nowhere in sight. "I . . . think I was dreaming while I was awake. That almost never happens to me. Do you think that it's cold here?"

"Cold? No!" Owl said, even though he felt the chill permeating the air. "Look here! We have come to have you help celebrate an impromptu birthday party!"

Pooh's eyes widened with excitement. "Who is Impromptu?"

"I . . . I am, today," Piglet said, wiggling through the crowd of Rabbit's many relations.

"How did you become Impromptu?" Pooh asked.

"It was a spur of the moment thing," Eeyore said, his head drooping. "You wouldn't understand."

"Then we have to congratulate you!" Christopher Robin said, hugging the little pig. "Happy birthday!"

"Owl, they're closing in," Kanga whispered.

"I know, my friend. Be prepared." Owl straightened and held himself up to his tallest height. "My dear Pooh, and all of our colleagues gathered here today – " A gust of frigid wind interrupted him and the sky darkened from blue to gray, but he had to make believe that nothing out of the ordinary was going on. " – We are pleased to celebrate a most festive occasion! Our cherished companion, Piglet, is celebrating an impromptu birthday. We must all join hands and dance and sing!"

Cheerfully, Pooh took Piglet's and Christopher Robin's hands. Owl noticed that he was shivering. They were all being affected.

The cold began to penetrate through to his bones. In not too long a time, they would all be frozen solid, and the horrors would pour in unabated from the edges of the Hundred Acre Wood. Sorrow nearly overwhelmed him. He had been in the Wood longer than all the others but Eeyore, who had been its sole guardian in the beginning. He regretted that he would likely be its last, failed guardian. If this worked, all would be well. If. If. If.

Kanga began to sing through trembling lips, and the others joined in:

> "It's a happy, happy birthday,
> A happy birthday day!
> A carefree celebration
> And time to sing and play
> With cake, ice cream, and presents
> Your friends are here to say
> It's a happy, happy birthday,
> A happy birthday day!"

Owl twirled and pranced with the rest of them, but it was no use. The Woozles crept closer and closer. The party was just not festive enough.

"Speech!" he called. "Speech from the guest of honor! Speech!"

Piglet blushed so hard he went from pink to red. The others surrounded him, Pooh, and Christopher Robin, in hopes that they could raise the feelings of joy high enough to drive the monsters back into the shadows.

Closer the Heffalumps came. Closer. Closer still. Where were the bees?

"Speech! Speech! Speech!"

Piglet, egged on by Rabbit and his many relations, cleared his throat.

"Unaccustomed as I am to p-p-public speaking," he began, his voice constricted to a nervous squeak, "I am p-p-pleased to—Oh, I don't know what to say!"

The shadows surrounded them. Owl could feel the claws about to sink into his back.

Then, Pooh stepped forward.

"Well, you could say how happy you are that everyone is here," he said. He beamed at the people in the circle around them. "And how much you like everyone. Because they are very good friends. And how no one could be more grateful for the kindness that everyone always shows in offering their very best hospitality for festive occasions, or even little visits, when they have honey – or other nice things to eat. And presents. Everyone always gives such good presents."

"Good idea, Pooh Bear!" cried Christopher Robin. "I have a very nice present I wrapped up for your birthday, but I think it will be perfect for an Impromptu Birthday."

He started for his door. Owl realized in horror that the boy couldn't see the monsters any more than Pooh could. He flew over and snatched Christopher Robin from the open jaws of a very large red Woozle with purple spots. Out of the boy's line of sight, he raked his talons down the creature's face. It screeched and ran away, rubbing at its eyes, or what was left of them. Owl suppressed a smile. One small victory, though there were many more to be gained. The beasts were waiting for a vulnerable moment to attack.

"Allow me, my young friend," Owl said, setting them both down in front of the bright blue painted portal. He swept the door open with his wing and scanned the room with a keen eye, in case that sanctum had been invaded by dark forces. But, no, nothing was within but the trappings of a small boy with an inquiring mind. A telescope and a magnifying glass stood on a small table near the window. A butterfly net hung on the wall beside a safari helmet, both suitable for expeditions into the woods. The little bed, neatly made, had a quilted counterpane, and was flanked by a well-filled bookshelf and a night table with a lamp that had a fleecy white lamb on the shade. He saw the gift at once, as it was a good-sized box wrapped in blue and white paper with a large green bow on top, sitting on a shelf.

Christopher Robin ran to pick it up.

"It was meant for Pooh Bear," he admitted. "But Piglet might like it, too."

They brought out the gift and presented it to a glowing Piglet.

"Tha-thank you! I-I-I don't know what to say." He blushed again and set to undoing the ribbon. Everyone's eyes were fixed upon him as he opened the box and drew out a large white jar. "Honey!"

"I took it from the tallest tree I could find," Christopher Robin said, proudly.

"A million bees couldn't stop me from getting it. It's the best honey in the Hundred Acre Wood!"

Piglet shook his head. "This is too, too, too much for me. You take it, Pooh Bear."

Pooh's eyes were glistening with greed. "Thank you, Piglet. But this is your birthday!"

"It's an Impromptu Birthday," Piglet said, graciously. He pushed the jar into Pooh's paws.

"Oh, well, we can't let it go to waste," Pooh said, with a pleased smile. He pried open the top.

Kanga gasped, and Roo echoed her. Owl felt Woozle talons plunge through the feathers on his back. They had lost focus! Rabbit fell to the ground, a Heffalump trunk around his neck. Piglet was picked up by a ravening Woozle. Eeyore kicked and bit at a pair of Heffalumps trying to pull him apart between them. Pooh and Christopher Robin were entirely unaware, their attention fixed on the jar of honey.

This is it, Owl thought. *Despite our festivities and frivolities, they have conquered us.* He vowed to protect the innocent ones with the last strength in his body. He spread his wings and prepared to fight.

Then, the sky darkened, going in an instant from gray to black. An unearthly humming descended, nearly deafening Owl's sensitive ears. Clouds upon clouds of black-and-yellow striped insects zipped out of the sky and swirled around and around the partygoers.

"Uh-oh," Eeyore said.

"Bees!" Rabbit declared. "They've come for that honey, Christopher Robin!"

"Oh, no! Oh, no!" Piglet cried, throwing himself on the ground. "Drop it, Pooh Bear, or they'll carry you away!"

But it was not the partygoers that the bees were fixated on. They zoomed angrily around the honey jar, then burst outward, attacking the Heffalumps and Woozles with every stinger they had. Owl closed his wings around Pooh and Christopher Robin, engulfing them in a feathered embrace.

"What are they so angry about?" the small boy asked, trying to see over Owl's shoulder.

"It's the weather," Owl said, evoking calm from somewhere deep within. "Swarming season, you know. It happens every July from April until October."

Behind him, he could hear the sounds of battle, but it was very one-sided. The monsters couldn't withstand the bees' onslaught. With howls and screeches that curdled the blood, each of the stung Woozles and Heffalumps exploded into showers of spots and stripes. As soon as those hit the ground, they dissolved.

In moments, the battle finished. The bees, with a snort and a shrug, flew up into the treetops. Owl released his hold. Pooh immediately examined the jar of honey.

"They let us keep it," he said, happily. He took a fistful of gold and stuffed it into his mouth. "Tha'th tho goo'!"

"The straggler," Owl whispered to Kanga. "We can't let it go."

Kanga pasted on a bright smile. "Hide and seek!" she exclaimed, clapping her hands.

"What?" Christopher Robin asked, his brow wrinkled.

"Games!" Kanga insisted. "It's a party. There must be games. Pooh, you will be the seeker! You have to count to one hundred, then you have to come looking for all of us."

"All of us!" Roo added.

"My word, what a marvelous idea," Owl said. "Pooh, cover your eyes and start counting. Find us and . . . and you shall have yet another prize!"

"Weh, ah ri'," Pooh said, around another mouthful. He shut his eyes, but kept the honey close. "Wuh, 'oo, 'ree . . .'"

The others started running. Christopher Robin made for the Pooh-sticks bridge, and the others headed in the direction taken by the errant Woozle.

The sky had lightened to gray again. Owl took to the air.

"I will find it," he promised.

It didn't take long, as the purple, green, and pink beast tore through the undergrowth as though it meant to tear up every shrub in the forest. Owl spotted it rolling downhill into the gorse patch. He hastened back to the others.

"This way!" he called, winging overhead. Kanga scooped up Roo and Piglet. The others followed her bounding gait all the way to the copse of scratchy bushes.

"We're just in time," Rabbit gasped.

Indeed they were. The Woozle seemed to have expanded to several times its original size. It grew every time it took a deep breath.

"Stop it!" Piglet cried. "It's going to divide!"

"Not if I can help it," Eeyore said. The small donkey charged. He jumped on the Woozle and knocked it over. It tried to claw at him, but Eeyore kicked it again and again with his back feet so hard that his tail fell off again. Roo grabbed it up. The others dove in, rending and tearing at the spotted beast. Rabbit and his relations jumped up and down on it. It shrank with every blow, dwindling in size until it was the size of an apple. Then, it popped.

"Is that the last?" Kanga asked, breathless, brushing away Woozle dust from the top of Roo's head.

Owl took off again and flew on silent wings through the Hundred Acre Wood. The sun shone with abandon, casting rays into places that it had not touched all day. He breathed a heavy sigh of relief, and landed among his friends.

"It was. We must allow Pooh Bear to find us now," he said. "We can't leave him alone for long. He has performed the task that we needed, as we always trust that he can. His inner-sense is preserved. The shadows are driven back. I hope it will take them a long time to build up again into the threat they posed today."

One at a time, they crept back to the woods nearest to Christopher Robin's house. Each of them hid themselves in an obvious place, making sure to allow a hand, or a foot, or an ear to protrude from concealment. One by one, the round bear found them and hauled them out with gleeful exclamations.

Pooh bounded over to the last bush and pointed at a long gray ear.

"I see you, Eeyore! Come out, come out!"

"Aww, you caught me," Eeyore said, in a glum voice. "I guess I lose."

"Never, my friend," Owl said, making sure that Eeyore's tail was pinned properly, and a bow tied around it. "You won today. We all won."

They all came to sit in a circle in Christopher Robin's garden, enjoying the blueness of the sky, and wedges of pink and blue cake, which were delicious in spite of their lopsidedness.

Pooh sighed with happiness.

"I like Impromptu Birthdays," he said. "Can we have another one very soon?"

"If we plan them, they are not Impromptu," Owl admonished him. "You shall have to settle for Real Birthdays."

"Oh," Pooh said. "Do you know, it has been a most unexpected day. I saw so many things that weren't there."

"This is what happens when your dreams get on the outside of your head instead of on the inside," Owl said wisely. "Pooh, you must tidy things up so that they are in the right place. Then, I am sure we can have another party." He looked up at the sky, which was becoming a rather darker blue.

"I should go home, then," Pooh said. "Thank you for the party. Thank you for the lovely present, Christopher Robin."

"You're welcome, Pooh Bear," the boy said, hugging his plump friend. "I have to go to bed now, too. We should have some more adventures in the morning." He went inside and shut the blue door.

"I must also go," Owl said, sketching an elegant bow with his right wing. Kanga hopped over to him and gave him a kiss on the cheek.

"Neither of them saw a thing," she said. "Not hide nor hair of the invaders."

Owl nodded. "This haven shall remain intact as long as I can make it so."

"We're safe again," Eeyore said. "Kinda."

"It *feels* safe," Piglet said, looking hopeful.

"For a while," Rabbit said, gathering his family to depart.

"Yes," Owl said, with a sigh. "But that's all we can hope for. As long as inner-sense exists, we will preserve it and be guided by it."

With a smile for his friends, he took wing and flew off through the Hundred Acre Wood.

In Which Rabbit Investigates Schrödinger's Owl

Gustavo Bondoni

"Don't be ridiculous, old fellow," Rabbit said. "Your uncle Robert is either alive or dead. He can't be both."

Owl blinked slowly. "Did I ever claim he was both alive and dead?"

"Yes," Rabbit replied. "You've told his story five times in the years I've known you." He pointed at the battered portrait which hung slightly crooked on the wall. "Of those times, you've mentioned that he was still alive twice, and that he'd died doing his great deed three times. And the deed has been different each time."

Owl puffed his feathers up, which made him look about twice as big as usual. Rabbit took a step back. They were friends, but Owl had to eat sometime . . .

"Are you calling me a liar?" Owl demanded.

"No. Not at all. The thought never crossed my mind," Rabbit said, holding up his paws. "But you must admit it seems curious that someone with your memory would fall into inconsistency."

Owl deflated. "I understand why you might be confused. But each of the stories is true, and each is exactly as I told it."

"But that can't be. Each is the same story, and each is different. And in some he lives and in some he dies."

"That's how it is. He went through the gate under the Six Pine Trees. In that place, life doesn't dictate the story . . . the story dictates life."

"Nonsense," Rabbit replied. "We should put this to rest once and for all."

"You may do so, but I will not come with you. I am satisfied with what I know."

"But you don't know anything. You're an owl . . . don't you want to be wise?" Rabbit knew it was a desperate ploy, but Owl's pride was legendary.

So, of course, was Owl's capacity to condescend to the other inhabitants of the Hundred Acre Wood. "Sometimes, wisdom is the ability to understand that it's better not to know."

"It will end in tears, of course," Eeyore said. Rabbit had come straight to his house after the interview with Owl.

"It will be a magnificent adventure," Rabbit replied.

"Did I ever tell you how I lost my tail? That was supposed to be a magnificent adventure, too."

"Yes. A dozen times," Rabbit said testily. "Will you come with me or not?"

"I suppose so. Staying or going, tears seem to be my lot."

"That's the spirit," Rabbit said.

"So tell me . . . why are we doing this?"

"I need to know if that blasted Uncle Robert is alive or dead."

Eeyore took some moments to think about it. "I thought he was both at once."

Rabbit glared at him. "Don't you start on me now. He can't be both."

"Why not? Like that cat," Eeyore said.

"Tigger?"

"No. The other one. The one in the box with the poison."

Rabbit cocked his head. "Is this another of the things those voices whisper in your head?"

"I don't know. It might be. They say so many things, that I only recall some of them."

Rabbit shuddered. "Let's get going," he said.

They crossed the stream that separated Eeyore's Gloomy Place from the rest of the Wood, skirted the denser growth of trees—not even the intrepid Rabbit would go in there—passed Owl's house, and approached the Six Pine Trees.

The whispering began as soon as that half-dozen gnarled and lonely sentries came into view.

This wasn't the whispering that Eeyore lived with. It wasn't a gloomy madness of passive acceptance. This was a thing of hate and vileness, that drove deep into your mind and made peaceful creatures that couldn't digest meat want to tear and rend each other with unsuitable teeth.

The whispers were carried on the wind by an unspeakable buzzing.

"The bees are back," Rabbit said, fighting to keep hold on his sanity. Biting Eeyore would only get him kicked, and the donkey probably tasted terrible.

"Yes," Eeyore said gloomily. "I expect they think they can make me fly into a murderous rage. Obviously, they don't know what it's like to live in utter despair."

Rabbit patted his friend. "Thank goodness for your depression," he said. "You'd be hard to contain if the bees' madness sent you on a rampage."

"Small mercies," Eeyore said.

They trudged closer, half of their minds on the bees, the other half alert for what might come out from the Six Pine Trees. Though the entire Hundred Acre Wood was dangerous to anyone unused to its particular quirks, the Six Pine Trees were arguably the most threatening. There was never a good time to run into a Jagular, but probably the worst time possible was while trying to keep one's sanity against the buzzing that drove you closer and closer to the edge of uncontrolled murderous fury.

Especially if the Jagular could feel the buzzing, too.

Rabbit shuddered and took another step. Eeyore, seemingly unaffected—as it seemed he was unaffected by everything—trudged along in his wake.

"Do you hear that?" Rabbit asked, ears twitching.

"The buzzing? We've talked about it already," Eeyore replied. "If you've forgotten, you're probably going mad." He allowed a long, gloomy moment to pass before he said: "it was bound to happen eventually, of course."

"It's coming from behind that tree," Rabbit said, pointing to one of the pines in the center of the formation. "Let's go have a look."

Moving faster, and shaking his head against the buzzing, Rabbit walked between two of the pines and stopped. "Am I going mad?"

Eeyore stopped "Do you see the air shimmering like a heat mirage in front of us?"

"Yes."

"Then you aren't going mad." Eeyore sounded disappointed.

"Was this always here?" Rabbit asked. For a moment, he wished he'd chosen a different companion for this particular journey of discovery. But then he remembered why Eeyore was perfect. His deep gloom was impossible to budge. Not even the strongest calls to madness could shift him from eternal sadness. It would be different with any of the others. The few adult humans that had heard the bees and survived hadn't remained in their original state. They'd become shells of themselves, haunted eyes staring into the empty distance, shattered bodies awaiting starvation.

And with Tigger . . . exposure to the bees could be lethal for any companion. Rabbit knew that, beneath the façade of empty-headed bouncing lurked a flesh-rending predator just waiting for madness to release it from the bonds of friendship.

"I don't know. I try not to come this way," Eeyore said. "I've already lost my tail . . . I'm not terribly interested in losing the rest of me."

"So why did you come with me?"

"Because I'm also not very interested in losing you. I don't have that many friends."

Rabbit shrugged. It was as good a reason as any, he supposed.

The sun was up and the day was bright. Rabbit sniffed the air and tried to fix the good parts of the Wood in his memory. He suspected he was about to experience the bad parts first hand.

"You reckon it's a portal?" Rabbit said.

"It's a portal."

"Where do you reckon it goes?"

"Somewhere awful," Eeyore said. The thought seemed to perk him up a bit. "Are you coming?" he asked, taking a step toward the shimmer.

Rabbit matched him step for step.

The world twisted sideways, and the sunlight turned to night, the trees to mist and the soft scent on the breeze into sharp gusts of icy pain.

"Ah," Rabbit said. "I thought that infernal buzzing would never stop."

They looked around. "The real Hundred Acre Wood is never quite as inviting as the shadow of it we live in," Eeyore said.

Rabbit looked at his companion. In the dim light, the ragged donkey seemed somehow sleeker, the plodding ruminant replaced by something the same shape but somehow more agile, as if a panther had donned an Eeyore disguise.

"Do you really think this is the real Wood?" Rabbit asked.

"It's the way I see it all the time," Eeyore replied. "It's nice to finally share reality with someone else."

Even his voice was brighter in this place. Rabbit shuffled slightly away, not obviously, but enough to stay out of kicking range. He wasn't sure what to make of his companion's newfound energy.

"Any idea which way to go?" he asked.

"No," Eeyore replied. "It's real, but I haven't actually been here before. We'll have to search."

They walked back between the clumps of mist that had replaced the trees, avoiding the white tendrils that seemed to reach out at them. Rabbit heard whispers coming from those white strings. Better not to touch them.

"I think I found where we'll have to go," Eeyore said.

Rabbit looked where the donkey pointed. A squat black structure of rough stone shrouded in dark fog and smoke stood there. Fire emerged from windows in the upper story.

"What is that?" Rabbit asked.

"A reflection," Eeyore replied. "Just a reflection."

"A reflection of what? The only thing in that direction in our world is Pooh's house. And that doesn't look at all like his house."

"We don't always see things as they really are," Eeyore replied as he plodded off toward the forbidding structure.

"Wait. I'm coming," Rabbit said. "And how do you know so much about this place, anyway?"

Eeyore didn't answer. He just walked and, together, they crossed over the familiar terrain. Every little rise and knoll from the other side of the portal seemed to be here, and Rabbit's feet crossed the terrain without thought. He'd come this way countless times in his life.

What he saw, on the other hand, was a dark realm. The sky above was grey and tendrils of mist stretched from one clump to another. Eeyore strode through them, but Rabbit avoided them assiduously. The ground was just black earth—not the black of rich loam, but the black of dead rock.

His feet never missed a step, though, and soon they felt the well-worn path that led to Pooh's house ahead.

But that wasn't Pooh's house ahead.

The door gaped like a missing tooth, the opening surrounded by stone that looked more organic than mineral. Green, veined, as if pus or some other unpleasant humor lurked just beneath the surface.

Eeyore led the way, slowly but without pause.

Inside, the pleasant summer morning in the Hundred Acre Wood was forgotten. Cold, damp air hung in the winding corridor that penetrated deep into the stone of the house. Rabbit felt the path descend below him, leading them deep under the earth.

Eeyore never paused until they came to the first fork in the path.

Both roads were dark.

"Now what?" Rabbit said.

"I don't know."

"You seem to have known where we're going until now."

Eeyore nodded. "Yes. But so far there's only been one path. Now there are two. It's your quest . . . you have to choose."

"How do you know this?"

Eeyore shrugged.

"All right," Rabbit said. He studied the choices. Neither path was quite dark enough to be pitch black. Light came from somewhere, even if Rabbit couldn't see where that might be. Though they looked the same, there was . . . something . . . about the right-hand path that called to him. He led Eeyore in that direction.

As he advanced, the air seemed to get thicker, to slow his progress, and he had to push forward to make headway.

"I don't think . . . " Rabbit began. But when he turned to look back at Eeyore, the donkey had his head down, looking at the ground, moving forward without paying any attention. Rabbit pushed on and, just a few feet further in, felt the resistance end. He imagined something emerging from his body, and flitting off into the distance. Or perhaps he simply felt lighter because the resistance had ended.

"Do you hear that?" Rabbit asked.

"The whispers?" Eeyore said. "Yes. I hear them. More madness, I suppose."

Rabbit stopped short.

"Why are we doing this, Eeyore?" he said.

"I thought you wanted to know what happened to Owl's Uncle Robert."

"I do. But it seems like an awfully silly reason to have come into this dark, awful place where the walls whisper at you."

Eeyore lifted his head. On any other creature, the expression he wore would have passed for the traces of a sad smile. But not on Eeyore. Rabbit knew that his friend never, ever smiled. "Perhaps this is how deep a glimpse into the scarred insanity of the Hundred Acre Wood your mind accepts before it begins to question the twisted nature of the place. Perhaps this is the wakeup call that sets you to asking why we act the way we do . . . why we accept that predators of the forest bounce along with kangaroos, and why a honey-addicted bear is our de facto leader. It's about time you question it."

"And you?"

"I am convinced, always, that those of us trapped in that accursed forest are truly wretched." He showed the half-smile again. "Of course, that's because I'm the only one of us that is sane."

Rabbit preferred not to think of that possibility. "So what do we do now?"

Eeyore moved aside. "See if you can leave."

Rabbit tried, but the air that had resisted him now formed a wall. He felt that he simply didn't have the strength to push it aside. Not only was the air suddenly stronger . . . but Rabbit felt that he was somehow less.

"We're committed," Eeyore said.

"You're enjoying this," Rabbit accused.

"No. I'm just used to it. My life feels this way every day: a long, dark maze with no way out and no good ending in sight."

They walked in silence until the corridor ended and they could go forward no longer. Open doors led into equally murky passages on the left and right.

"How is this helping us find Robert?" Rabbit said in frustration as he peered into the dim light on one side, then the other. I haven't seen head or tail of that Owl yet. Not dead. Not alive. No sign he's been here at all."

"You're following his path, even so," Eeyore said.

"That's impossible for you to know. We'll probably choose wrong every time the path forks."

"That doesn't really matter."

"You mean they all lead to the same place?"

Eeyore shook his head mournfully. "Not at all. But they all lead to Uncle Robert, eventually."

"I don't understand," Rabbit said. "But if that's true, then I can choose whichever of these halls I want and it will make no difference at all." He started to go right, simply because it was closer.

One of Eeyore's hooves stopped him. "No. It isn't the same. You need to choose carefully. The consequences . . . " The donkey shook his head. "Even I'm not prepared for what will happen if we go the wrong way."

So Rabbit concentrated. Once again, he felt one side call him more than the other, so he headed to his left. Once more, the air seemed to resist his passage, and once more he broke through and felt he got lighter, as if losing a thin slice of himself.

This time, then he looked back, Eeyore wasn't blocking the whole entrance and he discerned the backs of two figures entering the doorway opposite. A blue quadruped and the elegant lines of a grey rabbit. Both appeared slightly faded and ghostly.

"Is that us?" Rabbit said.

"Reflections," Eeyore replied. "What might have been. Don't pay any attention to them."

Rabbit recalled the sensation he'd had as he chose the path, the sense of losing something. He shook his head. "No. That's a part of us."

Eeyore sighed. "Leave it alone. There's nothing you can do, no way you can help. Just keep going . . . and choose wisely."

Rabbit wanted to argue, but Eeyore plodded forward and nudged him with his head. Rabbit turned back toward the corridor that stretched before them.

This one seemed to stretch into infinity. In the darkness, it was impossible to judge how long it might be, but it certainly seemed to extend further than the structure aboveground. Sulfurous-smelling water dripped from the roof and pooled around Rabbit's paws. He thought he felt it moving, bubbling up through his fur.

Rabbit shuddered and walked as fast as he could, but now the walls reminded him of veins, of the vascular structure of some recently-dead kill.

But how would Rabbit know that? There were no active predators in the Hundred Acre Wood. Pooh, Owl and even Tigger kept their instincts under control and never attacked their natural prey, no matter how many opportunities the close interaction in the wood afforded them.

Then why did Rabbit look at the wall and immediately think of a fresh kill?

For a second, a vision of running for his life, trying to take cover from death that came from above, flashed through his head, accompanied by a feeling of the deepest terror, a sensation so alien and unimaginable that it took his breath away and he stumbled.

Eeyore, behind him, plodded to a halt. "We need to keep going, Rabbit," the donkey said. "This isn't a good place to stop."

"Are there any good places to stop, Eeyore?"

"Not in the Hundred Acre Wood," Eeyore replied. "But this is a particularly bad one."

Rabbit started up again. He suspected Eeyore was right. In addition to the bubbling water, the corridor's whispers could almost be made out, voices saying things that hovered just under the threshold of intelligibility. Rabbit strained his ears to make out what the voices said . . . but other than a sense of awfulness that left him feeling soiled, he couldn't discern the meaning.

The corridor led onward, never getting any lighter, never getting any darker, never getting any drier. The only thing that became more pronounced was the smell of brimstone.

The hall eventually opened up into a circular room whose far walls were just barely visible.

"Up or down?" Rabbit said.

"You choose," Eeyore replied.

"And if refuse?"

"Then I will choose . . . and we might not survive very long."

"Why would my choices be any better than yours?"

"Because, in the end, you prefer to live, and that colors your choice."

"Oh," Rabbit replied. If one's attitude toward life affected the outcome of one's choices in this place, then it was probably better to avoid letting Eeyore make any decision.

But pressing forward . . . what point was there in more movement in that direction? He felt it—in his bones—that the house would just send them through an infinite number of corridors until it spat them out again, splitting pieces of his soul out and sending them down other paths . . . paths that even Eeyore seemed reluctant to face.

"Up," Rabbit said.

"You haven't stopped to think about it," Eeyore replied, a slight note of urgency creeping into his voice.

In fact, the tug downward was quite strong. "I know. But we will be going up every chance we get. I want to leave this place." He pushed through the resistance before Eeyore had a chance to stop him.

Rabbit turned around. He ignored the figure who looked just like him that went into the stairs going down. "Are you coming?" he asked Eeyore.

The donkey actually shuddered, then groaned . . . but came forth.

As they climbed the endless staircase, Rabbit felt a vibration through his feet. The building was shaking. A soft sound, like a desperate wail heard at a long distance, reached his ears.

He set his jaw and kept walking. Eeyore knew more than he was telling . . . but Rabbit got the sense that he was telling all he dared. The donkey walked behind him, trembling in fear and muttering to himself.

Another image arrived unbidden. The world as seen through a curtain of leaves that concealed Rabbit from view as Tigger, maw red and dripping, stalked past.

He blinked and the image was gone.

The stairs ended at another circular room. This one wasn't empty, but held several contraptions, machines of wood and metal bands and chains that swayed in the air that moved through the passageways.

The machines were stained and worn, dark with dried liquid. Rabbit shuddered.

"I think we should get out of here as quickly as possible," Rabbit said.

Eeyore looked up. "I think it might be too late."

Something fluttered through the air, descending slowly. As it passed in front of his face, Rabbit plucked it out of the air.

A large white feather with brown edges. A feather that would have looked at home on his friend Owl. Or on Owl's uncle. Specks of reddish-brown, a different shade, could be seen on the feather.

Rabbit looked at the machines around him and shuddered. "Up!" he shouted, ignoring the sense that the right way to go, the way he wanted to go, was down.

"No!" moaned Eeyore.

But Rabbit went up. This time, as he pushed aside the resistance in the air, he turned back and watched how a second set of Rabbit and Eeyore, so thin he could see through them, walked across the room to the stairs heading down—a different set of stairs, not the ones that led upward. The blue donkey in that duo looked a lot less unhappy than the much more solid one accompanying him.

"You just saved them," Eeyore said.

"From what?"

"I don't know. I just know that we're going the wrong way. Up is bad."

"Up is out," Rabbit retorted, "and I want out. I don't know what madness possessed me to come in here, but it was a mistake."

Eeyore looked mournfully back to the duo walking down the stairs. "Well, at least one version of us will survive," he said.

"One version?" Rabbit said. "You mean they're real?"

"As real as you or me . . . except that they took the opposite decision we did in every room."

"That makes no sense. I was watching. They came into being after I started walking up the stairs."

Eeyore shrugged. "Things don't need to make sense in order to be," he said.

"You mean there are . . ." He tried to count, but counting wasn't something Rabbit excelled at. ". . . a lot of versions of us, people, things just like us, walking around this place?"

"By now, some of them won't be walking anymore. They chose wrong. And so are we."

"I don't believe it," Rabbit said. "But we need to get out of here."

"You can't decide that. This place will let us go only after it's finished with us. But you need to concentrate on what you came here for. You need to find Owl's Uncle Robert."

Rabbit held up the feather from the floor below. "We know what happened to Robert. He was ground to goo in those machines down there. He's dead. Now we need to get out. And out is up."

"You're forgetting the nature of this place," Eeyore said.

"And how do you know it so well?" Rabbit shot back. "Have you been here before?"

"No. I know it because it's my life. I always feel that, in every decision I take, another version of me took a different one."

"And that version was happier?"

"No. We're both miserable."

"Oh, come on, Eeyore," Rabbit said. "You're just being dramatic. And besides, we both know there's no way you can know what a ghost feels."

"They're not ghosts. They're quite truly us."

"Whatever. We're still going up." Rabbit found another flight of stairs and bounded up the steps three at a time. The next room was completely dark, not dim like the ones before. Rabbit came to a stop. The whispers seemed louder in this place, and almost fully intelligible. Rabbit could tell they were saying awful, awful things.

Suddenly, lightning bisected the room, showing Rabbit the contents for a fraction of an instant. He turned away, appalled, unable to believe what had been revealed in that white exposure.

Only one thing mattered. He'd seen another staircase. The one that went up was along the same wall they were standing beside. There was no need to cross that charnel house of horrors to reach it.

This time he didn't look back to watch their ghostly doppelgangers. Those figures would have to walk through the room to reach another exit. They wouldn't make it . . . and even if they did, they glowed slightly in the dark and Rabbit didn't want to see what they illuminated. The instant during which he'd glimpsed what hid in the hot, humid darkness would give him nightmares forever.

Or worse. A small part of his mind was still screaming at what he'd witnessed. It hadn't stopped since the light had illuminated the scene.

On the next landing, they could see again. Mercifully the room was empty and the roof towered high above their heads. Brown and white birds fluttered among the rafters.

Rabbit craned his head to look. Could it be?

But it couldn't. Among the things illuminated by the lightning below, he'd seen the end of Uncle Robert, his pieces spread among the parts of other poor souls. Had they been torn asunder and recombined into new life forms? The flash hadn't lasted long enough to answer that question. But Uncle Robert was certainly dead.

And yet an owl flew among the rafters.

"Robert!" Rabbit called up.

The bird changed course. It circled one final time and suddenly dove toward them.

Rabbit, confronted with something he instinctively feared—and yet, for some reason, had never experienced in the Hundred Acre Wood—froze. He should have run, should have bolted to the nearest shelter.

But the enormous, rodent-eating monster in the sky scared him too much to flee.

He just watched winged and taloned death approach. As the distance closed, he realized that, whatever the body above him was, the head was something else. An indescribable mass of writhing tentacles, some with eyes on the ends, surrounded a round, toothed maw so dark that it seemed to go on forever.

A large body bumped him aside and the flying death monster slammed into it in a cloud of feathers. Eeyore had saved him. An owl, no matter how horrific, could never carry off a donkey.

The owl-thing slumped to the floor and Rabbit looked around for an exit. The stairs went up, but that didn't matter to him this time. He just wanted to leave.

"Come on," Rabbit shouted.

This time, the stairs were much longer, due to the high nature of the room's roof. They seemed to go on forever, and the words in the background, though still unintelligible called to him. They promised—without words—unlimited wonders and inexpressible pleasures.

A glimpse through the arch at the top of the stairs showed a dark background with pinpricks of light.

The outside!

Rabbit redoubled his pace. He charged forward. And Eeyore, despite his plodding pace, somehow managed to keep up.

Now that freedom was in sight, the stairs seemed endless. He climbed and climbed, but the exit, with it's beautiful sky full of stars, never appeared to get closer.

Rabbit's breathing was fast and ragged by the time he reached the top. His head bent to watch the steps, he still stumbled, his feet automatically searching for another. He turned back to Eeyore. "We're here. We're out!"

But the donkey was immobile, half inside the door, half outside. He stared upward, eyes wide, a low moan escaping his lips.

"Come on," Rabbit said. "Let's see if we can find the portal. What's wrong? What are you looking at?"

He turned to glance at the sky.

And froze.

The stars were . . . wrong.

Some were red and bloated, pulsing with fire that somehow announced the death of civilizations. Others moved, spiraling across the blackness of the firmament, leaving traces in Rabbit's eyes that appeared to form scenes of unspeakable atrocities and nameless obscenity, impossible to quite make out, but leaving him feeling unclean.

Stars blinked on. They blinked off. A large red star disappeared to be replaced by an even bigger blue one.

The voices came from the stars. They whispered in his ears.

No. The words he heard, words from languages long dead, languages used by necromancers and people of dark, cold recesses long dead, came straight into his mind.

And while the pulsating stars of that living, breathing sky felt awful enough to break Rabbit's hold on his sanity, the true ugliness came from the words themselves.

They were words of death, of madness, of destruction.

They were commands to betray all he knew, to despise, to humiliate.

Words of debasement and dissolution.

Every star had its words. They jumbled together, a cascade of unwanted images and unhealthy demands. Rabbit tried to block them off, but to no avail.

He screamed, the sound joining Eeyore's moan. He clapped his paws against his head, hoping to create a barrier against the sounds, the images, the ideas that were sullying his soul with every evil known to those cold, dead stars and the inhabitants that had died when the earth was still young.

It was to no avail. The images filtered past his puny barrier.

After more moments of onslaught, Rabbit managed to marshal his thoughts for a fleeting instant. He recalled that the voices had started when he looked at the stars.

He closed his eyes.

Nothing happened. The voices still screeched in his mind, pushing aside Rabbit's own thoughts to try to drown each other out.

He opened his eyes again. As he stared helplessly into the burning, twisting sky, he saw there was more than stars up there.

Dark shapes flew among the lights. Rabbit tracked one. A bird.

An owl.

He flinched back, remembering the monster that had assaulted him in the level below. But a closer look showed that this owl was just a noble owl that looked just like the painting in Owl's home. If that was Uncle Robert, he was alive and well.

He glanced at another and, as he looked, the twin of the first owl burst into flame with a screech of agony that could be heard above the whispering of the stars. Another owl was caught in the talons of a flying demon, sagging limp and lifeless in its grip. Over there, on the other side of the sky, was another owl in fine condition. One had turned black and oozed some kind of slime. Another fell to the ground in four or five pieces.

A voice spoke. "Each of them took a different path." The tones were Eeyore's, sad and mournful. "Our path was perhaps the worst of all, for we were shown a part of the truth." One of Eeyore's eyes twitched, the fastest movement Rabbit had ever seen him make, though wholly involuntary.

But Rabbit had little capacity to wonder at his friend. Almost overwhelmed by the voices, he spotted one of the owls flying through the sky at a slow pace, carrying a heavy burden it its claws.

Rabbit looked closer and realized the form being carried was rabbit himself, torn and bloodied.

He reeled and, near fainting, stumbled over the short stone wall that surrounded the platform he hadn't realized they were standing on.

Rabbit fell, his scream gaining in pitch as he did so.

The ground arrived with bone-breaking force.

But the pain cleared his mind. He realized he was alive, even though it felt like his body was broken. The voices were hushed, drowned out by the immediacy of agony.

He tried to stand, and fell in a heap. If he wanted to leave that place, he would have to crawl.

He began to do so, not looking back and certainly not looking up. Each lurching half-step an agony.

But the clouds in the shape of pines were just ahead, and there, he'd find the portal.

Blue hooves appeared in front of him. He turned his head up to see Eeyore looking down.

"How did you get down?" Rabbit asked.

Eeyore shook his head sadly. "I never went in."

Was this one of the infinite Eeyores? Rabbit couldn't think through the fog in his head. He just nodded. "That was smart. Can you help me?"

Eeyore shook his head. "I don't have any hands. I'd tell you to hold onto my tail . . . but the pin holding it in would just pop out. If you can stand, I can probably support you."

Rabbit shook his head. "I'll just crawl."

A trick of the light before them told him that he would soon be back in the Hundred Acre Wood he knew.

He pulled himself through the shimmer.

———

Two months later, Rabbit, his wounds almost healed, sat in Owl's house, listening to the story of Uncle Robert.

Owl pointed to the painting on his wall. "And that's how my Uncle Robert died, trying to achieve his great goal."

"Yes," Rabbit whispered. "I saw him."

He whispered it to himself. No one heard him.

No one in the room, at least. The voices in his head, the whispers he'd brought with him, and whose dead language he'd learned to understand, all hooted and reminded him that none of that was important. The only thing that was important was that he stay close to his friends while he finished healing and finished sharpening the knives he'd gotten hold of.

Out loud, all Rabbit said as he surveyed the room holding Owl, Pooh, Tigger, Kanga and Roo was: "Could I have some more tea?"

For some reason, Eeyore never came to these things anymore. The blue donkey was avoiding Rabbit ever since they'd emerged from the Six Pine Trees together.

Did the donkey know something?

Rabbit didn't know. He also didn't know if the question was his or if it belonged to one of the voices.

But that didn't matter. There was no difference between Rabbit and the voices anymore.

In Which Piglet Discovers a Very Unpleasant Truth

Jaleta Clegg

"What is it?" Piglet poked the gray lump with a stick he had found in the woods that morning. He'd named it Dennis and it was a very good stick.

"Bother," said Pooh. "It's gotten out of the jar again."

"What's gotten out? I say, what is it?" Rabbit asked. "Probably a disease, that's what it is."

Piglet used Dennis to jiggle the lump again.

"I shall have to consult Christopher Robin," Pooh declared, then toddled off into the forest leaving Rabbit and Piglet alone with the lump.

"What's that, I say?" Rabbit said again. He hopped close and sniffed the lump. "Doesn't smell nice, not at all."

"I'm not sure what it is," Piglet replied. "Do you think it might be a woozle?"

"Can't say that I can say," Rabbit said, wrinkling his nose. "I've never seen a woozle. It looks like a strange mushroom to me. Yes, that must be it. I have a recipe for mushroom pilaf somewhere. Needs a fair bit of fresh oregano, though." And with that, Rabbit hopped away muttering about ingredients to himself.

Piglet stared at the lump of goo. He listened to the silent woods. The sunshine that had seemed so cheery just a moment ago now seemed too harsh, and somehow cold.

"At least I have Dennis to keep me company," Piglet said clutching his stick tightly.

The blob wiggled and wobbled, then stretched upward before bobbing back to the ground.

"Oh, dear me," Piglet clucked his tongue. "Dear, dear me. This is not a good sign. Not at all."

The blob shivered and wriggled and somehow looked like a fat balloon dog complete with wagging tail. It tilted its head to one side and gave a gurgly noise that might have been a playful bark.

Piglet poked tentatively at the blobby creature. It collapsed back into a puddle of goo.

"I say, Piglet," Owl's fruity voice came from the tree overhead along with a great flapping of wings. "What is that there? I say, what is that thing? Reminds me of my Great-Uncle Robert—he was a world-famous explorer, you know—and the time he had high tea with the Queen. It was a hot midsummer day, this was down in darkest Aferica in the country of Zumbeezee which is full of jungles and wild rivers with ferocious beasts."

"Owl, I don't think this is your Uncle Robert. Or the Queen. I think it might be a woozle."

Owl huffed and ruffled his feathers. "As I was saying, Piglet, and it might help if you would listen closely now, my Uncle Robert—"

The blob wobbled itself up into a lumpy approximation of Owl before jiggling around with a self-important air.

Piglet giggled.

"I say," said Owl, "I say, it might indeed be a woozle. Now, correct me if I am wrong, but I do believe woozles are dangerous beasts. Shouldn't it be in a jar or something? A containment, so to speak."

"I was just going to teach it to play Poohsticks," Piglet announced. He was usually the timid one but somehow the jiggly, friendly lump of goo made him feel brave and sure of himself.

"I should think that would be very dangerous of you, Piglet. Poohsticks is, after all, a most hazardous and treacherous competition involving multiple prongs of a deciduous nature." Owl harrumphed as he fluffed his feathers, preparing for a long speech on the risks of playing Poohsticks.

"But what if I enjoy danger?" Piglet asked abruptly.

Owl's train of thought was completely derailed. He forgot about using his large words and just blinked, like an owl should, with wide eyes and open beak. "You, Piglet? Enjoy danger?" He burst into loud laughter.

"Why ever shouldn't I?" Piglet turned his back on Owl to speak with his new friend, the one who didn't laugh at him, mostly because it hadn't talked. "We're going to the bridge to play Poohsticks."

The blob twitched and jiggled until it looked like Piglet in shape, a Piglet three times the size of the real one. Piglet, the small one that was pink and normally not brave at all, took the hand of the giant, gray blobby Piglet and together they marched off into the woods in search of sticks that were the perfect size for playing Poohsticks.

———

WINNIE THE POOH sang under his breath as he trundled along in search of the Marshy Bog. He was a bear of very little brains, and directions confused him. "Was it over that way by the Meadow or down by the Very Large Log? Think, think." He tapped the side of his head.

An orange and black blur bounded out from behind a bush and charged full tilt into Pooh. He tumbled head over tail until he bumped to a stop by a rock. Tigger crouched on top of him.

"Hullo, Pooh. It's me, Tigger."

"I know, Tigger, now could you please climb off my belly? I have an important errand."

Tigger bounced from Pooh's soft and fluffy tummy. He opened his eyes wide and whispered dramatically, "A secret importantous errand? I shall be honored to help you, right beside you all the way."

A new idea rattled in Pooh's head while he brushed himself off. He hadn't meant to invite Tigger along, in fact it would be best if Tigger were not there when Pooh visited with Christopher Robin. The idea blossomed and grew very quickly into a Very Good Idea.

"Quite," Pooh said as he resumed his trundle toward the Marshy Bog by way of the Very Large Log, "But not beside me. I have a separate secret errand just for you. You see, Piglet is watching the Creature of Insanity Incarnate. I want you to help him. It escaped its jar. Again."

Tigger stopped bouncing and became rather statue-like. "The C-I-I? Isn't that quite dangerific?"

"Very."

"And Piglet is with it?"

"Watching it, yes. It's still in blob form so he should be safe. But I would feel ever so much better if I knew you were there watching it, too. Rabbit is supposed to be helping, but we both know how Rabbit is."

"Flighty, that's what. Well, toodle-loo, then. I'm off to help Piglet!" But Tigger's call lacked his usual enthusiasm and his bounce was decidedly forced as he turned away. His tail tended to shiver instead of spring and his head swiveled side to side as if searching for danger.

"Bother," Pooh said when Tigger was out of sight. "Stuff and bother. It's not *that* scary. Now where was I? Ah, yes."

He began to sing the words to the song he made up as he walked. It was just a little walking song, something to keep him company until he found Christopher Robin and it went something like this:

> I used to love honey,
> But now it is funny,
> Pink and jiggly,
> Round and wriggly,
> I
> Love
> Brains.
> Eat them like candy,
> All fine and dandy,
> Rum-te-tum-tum,
> Dum-de-dum-dum,
> All
> For
> Me!

It wasn't very good yet, but he could keep working on the words. Because he was now a bear of very little brains. Many of them. As he sang the last line, he pounced on a hapless mouse clutching it tight in his paws.

The mouse stared up at him with huge eyes, trembling.

Pooh licked his lips and waited.

The mouse only quivered more.

"This is where you are supposed to beg me to spare your life," Pooh said helpfully.

The mouse's nose twitched.

"And call me Dark Lord Pooh."

The mouse said nothing.

Pooh shrugged then sucked the mouse in whole. He poked at his head until he felt the mouse slide upward to join the others in his head. He blinked but felt only a teensy bit smarter.

"Very little brains do not think well," Pooh said, "but at least they are better than fluff and stuff for thinking. The more I get, the smarter I become."

He bumbled off into the forest, singing his song.

PIGLET HELD the giant blob-Piglet's hand. Though it still wobbled, it was firming up and becoming more pink. Holding its hand and walking beside it made Piglet feel very brave indeed.

"You need a name," Piglet announced. "Do you have one?"

The blob stopped wobbling and walking. It stood still as stone.

"Oh, dear. Do you not want a name?"

The head oozed to one side then bobbed up and down. It looked expectantly at Piglet, though how one looks without any eyes was a mystery Piglet decided to solve another day.

"Then I shall give you one!" Piglet wriggled with excitement and feelings of great importance. No one had ever trusted him with such a grand task before. "How about Gertrude?"

The blob shivered.

"No? Well, perhaps . . . Bob?" Bob the Blob had a definite ring to it that Piglet rather liked.

The blob stopped moving and shrank in on itself until it was no longer Piglet shaped.

"I see. Not Gertrude or Bob." Piglet tapped his head, like Pooh did when he was thinking very hard. It didn't seem to help. Piglet had little experience as he had only recently begun to experiment with names. "Perhaps, Terrance or Ethel or Zendidemon?"

The blob retreated from Piglet, rolling under a bush.

Perhaps the blob didn't need a name after all, Piglet thought. He didn't want to lose his new friend so soon. "Maybe I should just call you Piglet-Too."

The blob stopped rolling and stayed very still.

"I should like it very much if you were like me," Piglet said. "I feel oh so brave when I'm with you. I never feel brave, not on my own."

The blob emerged and raised itself up, up, up, until it stretched into a very tall Piglet shape. Pink stripes bloomed across its surface until it looked very much like Piglet. Small eyes rolled in the face to their proper places.

"You shall be Piglet-Too, then." Piglet nodded firmly, although inside he quivered. Bravery seemed to be mostly pretending one was brave. "Shall we play Poohsticks?"

Piglet-Too tilted its head to the side.

"It's quite easy, really," Piglet explained. "We gather sticks of just the right size and shape, then we take them to the bridge and drop them in. Then race across the bridge to see which stick emerges first. It's a race for them." His voice trailed off. Poohsticks had seemed so exciting before, when Pooh had first invented it. Piglet had loved the thrill, but now it seemed somehow stale and small and not very exciting at all. He poked Dennis into a hole in an old log. Dennis was the right kind of stick for

Poohsticks and if Pooh had been standing there instead of Piglet-Too, he would have insisted that Piglet use Dennis for the game. Which meant that Dennis would be lost forever, floating away down the stream. Piglet had become rather fond of Dennis.

He found himself feeling something entirely new. It burned hot inside his belly, bubbling up at the thought of Pooh demanding he give up Dennis. He remembered other times such as the time Pooh let Owl take Piglet's lovely little house. Eeyore had offered Piglet's house to Owl when Owl's had blown down and Pooh had let him. Piglet had been about to speak up, and he *had* spoken up, but Pooh had insisted that Piglet should live with him. That had been a nightmare worse than the heffalump dream. Piglet finally moved out into a different house that was little more than an old stump full of creepy crawlies and damp. It was better than living in Pooh's house under the name of Sanders.

There were many other times when Pooh had decided things for Piglet despite Piglet not wanting those things. Had Pooh ever listened to Piglet? No.

The feeling burned, a bright new feeling that Piglet had never let himself feel before.

"I think I am angry," Piglet announced.

Piglet-Too bounced and jiggled.

"I am angry at Winnie the Pooh."

Courage flowed from the giant piglet-blob, loosing Piglet's tongue.

"He's bossy, that's what he is. And, and, and—" Piglet sucked in a long breath, "I will not stand for it anymore!"

"Oo-hoo-hoo-hoo!" Tigger's call echoed through the Wood.

Piglet's courage collapsed. "Oh, dear, oh, dear, dearie me. What have I just said?" He clapped paws over his mouth as Tigger bounced into view.

"Piglet, old buddy! Where is the elderitch abominablation?" Tigger's bounce ended abruptly at the sight of Piglet-Too. "This is not good. Not good at all."

Winnie the Pooh trundled along a fallen log. Mud splooped and splattered on either side. The Marshy Bog was not very large, rather it intimidated by being the most boggy bog in the Hundred Acre Wood. The mud was a rich black, full of peat and rotting vegetation and the stench of things long dead. The air above the swamp hung thick and dark and full of malevolence.

"Christopher Robin?" Pooh sang out, his feet thumping along the Very Large Log. He knew that the thing that would answer his call was not really Christopher Robin. The boy had gone away to school, promising to come back when summer holidays began. But he'd broken his promise. Christopher Robin had not returned, only a blond boy who resembled Christopher Robin. That boy had been called Chris by the pack of friends he'd brought with him. None of them had seen Pooh or Rabbit or Owl or Eeyore or any of the citizens of the Wood. It required a special kind of magic, a special kind of boy, to *see*, and Chris was no longer that kind of boy.

So Pooh had found the dark spirits of the woods and learned to cast magic. He'd created a construct of mud, twigs, leaves, and spirit that resembled Christopher Robin and answered when he called.

He'd also developed a taste for meat and brains, but that was neither here nor there.

"Christopher Robin, I need to speak with you," Pooh called. His feet touched the swamp. A bit of damp mud clung to his yellow-orange fur.

The apparition rose from the bog, assembling itself from whatever materials were handy. A frog dangled in place of one eye, the other a bit of bark. Two leaves made its mouth. A lupine in full bloom provided a nose. "Yes?" Its voice wisped like the thin breeze that barely stirred the heavy summer air.

"The Creature of Insanity Incarnate has escaped. Again. I may need, hmm, a larger pot as it were. And possibly a stronger sealing spell." Pooh bounced, enjoying the way the mud squished up and down and sent ripples across the bog.

The apparition swirled and bobbed. A fly buzzed into the nose then out the mouth. "You must devour that which exceeds the pot. To seal it within will require blood." The frog twitched a leg, sending mud dripping down like tears.

"More blood? I suppose I could find someone willing to bleed for me." Pooh tapped one paw on his head just below his ear. "Considering I'm stuffed with fluff, not blood and bone."

"That will change with time." The spirit's voice faded as it melted back into the ooze.

Pooh sat himself down on the log. "Who can I use this time? Think, think."

The very many little brains in his head churned and tumbled through dark thoughts, looking for the one that might resolve the problem.

PIGLET TRUDGED behind Tigger and Piglet-Too into the Meadow. Blue and white flowers nodded in the summer breeze. Tigger chattered away as he usually did. Piglet had not been able to wedge a single word into the conversation. And now Tigger was taking away Piglet's best friend, leading him by a roundabout path to the front of Pooh's cottage where Pooh and Rabbit and Owl no doubt lay in wait to trap him.

They couldn't stand the thought that little, frightened Piglet might not want to be little or frightened anymore. He wanted to be larger and braver. He wanted them to listen when he spoke.

The bright anger bubbled up again, a powerful wave that washed away Piglet's timidity.

"Silence!"

A cold wind whooshed across the meadow, wilting the flowers.

Tigger halted, eyes wide, mouth hanging open in stunned shock. "Did . . . Did you say something, Piglet?"

Piglet slapped his hands over his mouth. Had that shout come from him?

Piglet-Too bobbled and wobbled encouragement.

Yes, yes. That voice was his. That anger was his. Piglet puffed up his chest. "I said, that is, I shouted, yes, I said—"

"Well, spit it out, old chum. Don't stand there being obstinatorous."

"Shut up, Tigger!" Dark magic snapped from Piglet's eyes and reflected from Piglet-Too's jiggly form right into Tigger.

Tigger's mouth snapped closed. He sagged, the bounce gone from his tail. He became a very quiet Tigger, a very meek Tigger, a very obedient Tigger.

The anger mingled with the dark power in Piglet's belly. It became something else, a dark thing of slimy wriggles and slippery twitchings. Piglet-Too gave a loud Bloop, then grew to be four times larger than Piglet. Extra arms sprouted from its sides, long ropey things like snakes or an octopus's tentacles. Piglet stepped in front of Piglet-Too, craning his head to stare up into Tigger's face. He would have stared down his nose at Tigger but he was still very much a small pink Piglet. He would have to change that. He clutched Dennis tight in one fist.

Tigger shivered and shrank in fear. His lips worked in and out but did not open.

"That's better," Piglet said. "Now perhaps you will listen when I speak."

"Piglet?" Rabbit's voice came from the far side of the Meadow. "I say, Piglet, whatever are you doing? Where has that giant mushroom gotten off to?"

Rabbit bounced into view, hands clutching bouquets of wild herbs. He saw the giant Piglet-Too and his tentacles. He tumbled backward in shock. Shoots of green scattered around him. "What have you done? What is this, I say?"

"You will say nothing!" Piglet thundered in his squeaky high voice.

Rabbit's mouth snapped shut. His nose twitched furiously but no sound came.

"Now, perhaps we should take care of the real problem. We should go see," Piglet brandished Dennis, "Winnie. The. Pooh."

Piglet marched through the Meadow toward the Sandy Lane that led to Pooh's house. Maybe this time, he would take Pooh's house and make Pooh move in with Rabbit. Or perhaps move in to Piglet's old house with Owl. Let him listen to the constant blathering and endless nonsense stories. Piglet and his new best friend would take over the house under the name of Sanders.

He took Piglet-Too's slimy, blobby hand. A tentacle slid around his shoulders. He clutched Dennis tightly in his other paw. Between the stick and the eldritch horror, Piglet felt invincible, which was a strange, new feeling for him.

Piglet liked it.

Very much.

POOH TRUNDLED into the sandy spot in front of his house, brains buzzing with dark thoughts of honey pots and their new use as eldritch storage containers. He'd run out of honey a long time ago. The bees no longer hummed in the large old oak tree. They'd disappeared not long after the first summer without Christopher Robin, only that visit by the strange Chris-boy and his friends. The abominations had begun showing up not long after that. So Pooh had put his empty honey pots to use. His cellar was full of trapped horrors. At least they were supposed to be trapped. Some of them, like the Creature of Insanity Incarnate, tended to escape every now and then. As for honey, Pooh was left with a rumbly tumbly more often than not, one which he had learned to fill with less sweet but ultimately more satisfying things.

Leaving Piglet to watch over the blob had been a risk, but one that Pooh felt was safe enough. The thing wasn't very strong or very large and Piglet, little innocent Piglet, was so full of fear and anxiety that the thing wouldn't be able to corrupt him.

He paused near his Thinking Spot when he saw the parade headed his way. Piglet marched in front. A very large Piglet followed, wobbling about like a strawberry jelly. Behind them shuffled Tigger and Rabbit.

"Oh, bother," said Pooh.

Things had not worked out well. Not well at all.

"POOH? I MUST SPEAK WITH YOU," Piglet announced. He chopped off each word with a snap of his teeth. They were sharp carnivore teeth that hadn't been in his mouth that morning.

"Yes, Piglet? I see you have made a somewhat large and terrifying new friend." Pooh eyed the blob with foreboding. It would never fit in even his largest honey pot now. Devouring the excess would take a bit of doing, as it were.

"This is Piglet-Too. He's my friend. More than you ever were." Piglet clenched his anger tight. Pooh had wronged him so many times. It was time for payback.

"Piglet, I believe you are not thinking very straight. That is not your friend."

"Yes, he is. Quite a good friend, too. He lets me win at Poohsticks when I have actually won. He doesn't claim that all sticks are his sticks." Piglet squeezed Dennis tight.

Pooh tried to speak but Piglet was no longer meek little Piglet, timid little Piglet. He was angry and ferocious and full of bravery. Especially when Piglet-Too loomed over Pooh, dwarfing the yellow bear.

"You gave away my house. You never let me choose the flavor of my own birthday cake. You always tell me that whatever you decide is best. You never listen. And I am tired of it, Pooh." Piglet stomped his tiny little foot.

"And what are you thinking of doing about it?" Pooh asked in a very reasonable tone of voice.

"I am going to speak my mind, and you are going to listen." Piglet really hadn't thought this through.

"But Piglet, if we do not get that abomination back into the jar, it will keep growing stronger until it devours the whole Hundred Acre Wood, and then where would any of us live? You don't know what you are doing, Piglet."

Piglet stomped both feet. It made only a very small pitter-patter sound.

"We must do what is best. For all of us," Pooh said.

"You still aren't listening, you great lump of fluff and nonsense," Piglet shouted in his high squeaky voice.

"Now that is hurtful. My name is—"

"Winnie. The. Pooh." Piglet gnashed his teeth.

Rabbit and Tigger cowered as the giant Piglet-Too bobbled and wobbled in a most terrifying manner.

Pooh sighed. "Piglet—"

"Do you know how Christopher Robin chose our names? Do you?" Piglet demanded. "We are all named after what we are. Piglet," he slapped his sunken chest, "Rabbit, Tigger, Kanga and Roo, Owl." Piglet took a deep breath and stared into Pooh's dark button eyes. "*POOH*."

"And what of Eeyore?" Pooh waggled his eyebrows.

"Or the sound we make. *Whiny whinny*."

Pooh set his jaw. "That was hurtful and unkind. But since you are under the influence, as it were, I shall not hold it against you."

Piglet screwed up his little eyes and glared in a most frightful way. "I am so angry," he announced, "I shall do . . . something. Something beyond terrible. I shall . . . I shall . . ."

"Don't act in haste, my boy," Owl said as he fluttered to join the group. "That is, I say, that is a most auspicious looking jelly. Strawberry, perhaps? My Great-Uncle Robert was a mite too fond of jellies, as you may recall—"

"Shut up, Owl."

Stunned silence slammed into Pooh's Thinking Spot. Everyone stared at Piglet for a long, uncomfortable time.

"I say, Piglet, that was quite rude," Owl muttered. "Not polite at all."

"Piglet, you are not yourself," Pooh said.

"I am more myself than I ever have been." Piglet ran a pink tongue over the tusks that sprouted from his jaw. He felt larger than before, as if he grew new muscles.

Piglet-Too jiggled in agreement.

"I am quite afraid you have been possessed by the Creature of the Infernal Abyss," Owl said. "As we lose touch with reality and drift farther into the Dream-lands, I'm afraid to say it might become more common. Now as Timothy used to say—he's my mother's fourth cousin, thrice removed on her father's side—"

Piglet used words that had never been spoken in the Hundred Acre Wood. He wasn't quite sure where the words came from, only that they held power and fed the red fires in his belly. He felt quite older and more grown-up with each syllable.

Pooh nodded to Tigger. "It's time," he said.

Tigger pried his lips apart with one paw. "For Ultra-Top-Secret Emergency Plan H?" Tigger's tail gave a half-hearted sproing.

"I'm afraid so."

"No!" Piglet slammed his hands together. They were no longer small pink paws but large pink hooves. "No, no, no! You will not activate any secret plan!" Except it came out as "Oo ill ot" because of the large tusks and sharp teeth crowding his mouth.

"Quickly now," Pooh called, "before he becomes Boarlet instead of Piglet."

Tigger bounded up, up, up into the air; then came down, down, down right on top of Piglet. The small pink pig that was halfway to a large hairy tusker disappeared beneath black and orange stripes. Dennis bounced free of Piglet's hold and clattered away under a bush.

Pooh chanted in a strange unknown language as he rolled a large honey pot out from behind his Thinking Log. Rabbit shoved the wobbling tower of ectoplasmic jelly into the jar.

Owl quoted something that no one could hear over the squealing of Piglet and the shouting chant of Pooh.

Pooh finished the incantation, then slammed the lid of the honey pot in place. Blobs of Piglet-Too exploded around the clearing, quivering like slime molds and mushrooms. Pooh pressed the lid down with both paws. "If you please, Rabbit."

"Must I?" Rabbit shuddered, wiping his paws down his front in an attempt to remove traces of jelly.

"Yes, Rabbit, I'm afraid you must. Christopher Robin said it must be you. Again."

Rabbit breathed a long-suffering sigh, then stabbed his paw with a handy thorn. Red blood stained his pale fur. He smeared a symbol on top of the honey pot.

Piglet-Too gave a long howl that slowly faded into the distance.

Pooh thumped the honey pot with a satisfied smirk.

Tigger bounced free of Piglet.

Piglet, a much tinier, much pinker, much more humble Piglet, rose to his tiny feet. He quivered and shivered. Tears shimmered in his eyes. "But how will I be brave now without my friend?"

"I shall be your friend, Piglet," Pooh said, "As I always have been. And you shall share my bravery."

Piglet shrank smaller, standing with his ears drooping and his paws hanging dejectedly at his side. "I have made a terrible mistake."

"Cheer up, Piglet. All's right." Owl clapped a wing around the very sad Piglet. "You still have all of us, too."

"Even if I have been very rude to you?"

Owl waved his other wing in a magnanimous gesture. "In the past, dear chap. All in the past."

"Now, Rabbit," Pooh said, "I believe you have several good recipes? It's time for a Celebration and seeing that we have much to clean up and devour, we'll need some proper cooking."

Rabbit's ears perked up. "Cooking you say? I shall need some fresh thyme and possibly mint. You can pick that down by the stream. Mind you pick from the left bank, not the right. Or is it the other way round?"

Piglet listened to the bustle of activity from inside the muffling folds of Owl's wing. Everything was back to the Way It Was Before.

Or was it?

He was different in strange ways. Down deep inside where his feelings lived, there were new things growing, things he had never felt before. Strange and slightly scary and somehow grown-up feelings sprouted and took root.

He pushed Owl's wing away. "Pooh? I believe I need to speak with you. About strange things."

"Yes, Piglet, I believe you do," Pooh answered. He watched Rabbit and Tigger and Owl as they gathered the bits of Piglet-Too scattered about. Eeyore, Kanga, and Roo were in the distance with the rest of the inhabitants of the Hundred Acre Wood, all gathering in the Meadow for the Celebration. They hung banners and set flowers out. He waited until the others had moved away, busy about their chores.

The light in the Wood seemed stranger, more greenish-blue than before, more dreamlike.

"Sit here on my log in my Thinking Spot," Pooh said, "and I shall tell you about Christopher Robin in the Very Marshy Spot and the honey pots in my cellar that no longer hold any honey and the creatures that haunt our woods now that Christopher Robin, the *real* Christopher Robin, has forgotten us and the magic that keeps us alive. I shall share my secrets with you, my oldest and dearest friend."

"Am I really, Pooh?"

"Really what, Piglet?"

"Your oldest and dearest friend?"

"Forever, Piglet. Forever and a day, you will always be my oldest and dearest friend." Pooh sighed a long sigh. "Forever and eternally."

In Which Owl Reads a Story with Unintended Consquences

Leigh Saunders

It was a pleasantly gray morning in the Hundred Acre Wood when Winnie the Pooh stepped up to Piglet's door. He pushed away a dark vine creeping across the wood and knocked.

"Who is it?" asked a small voice. Pooh thought it must have been Piglet, for this was Piglet's house, and the small, nervous voice sounded like Piglet's.

But being a Bear of Very Little Brain, it was always possible Something Else had called out. There had been several Something Elses in the Hundred Acre Wood lately, so one could never be quite certain.

"It is Winnie the Pooh," he replied in his best Reassuring Voice.

"Is that really you, P-P-Pooh?" Piglet's small voice asked.

Winnie the Pooh opened his mouth to reply, but then he paused for a moment, scratching his head. "It was me when I said to myself, 'Pooh, it is a pleasantly gray day. You should go to see your good friend, Piglet.' As I have not stopped being Pooh that I know of, yes, I believe it really is me."

Pooh had barely finished speaking when the door flew open and Piglet rushed out, throwing his little arms around his friend.

"I heard several Something Elses scuttling around in the night," Piglet said after a moment. "I was afraid. I am glad you are you, and not a Something Else."

"I am not good at scuttling," Pooh said. "I would not make a good Something Else."

Piglet nodded. "And I am too small," he said. He jumped back toward his open door, startled by a bunch of dried leaves skittering past. "And much too fearful," he added, his already pink face turning a deeper shade.

"I think," Pooh said, "we should go to visit Eeyore."

"But how shall we find him? Piglet asked, looking up at the sky. "He is the very same color as the clouds."

Pooh raised a paw to his head, and pondered this a moment. It was true that the clouds were the very same shade of bluish-gray as their friend Eeyore. But as he stared up at the sky, a Thought occurred to him.

"To see the clouds," he said, "I have to tilt my head up. But when I speak to Eeyore, I tilt my head down, like this." He demonstrated, tilting his head down as though looking at Eeyore.

"With my head tilted just so, I cannot see the clouds. So any gray I see must be Eeyore."

Piglet jumped up and down in excitement. "You will have to point him out to me," he said, clapping his hands together. "For I am so small, I have to look up at everyone, and will not be able to tell him apart from the clouds."

And so, with that plan in mind, they set out through the Wood toward Eeyore's home.

Now, Eeyore lived in the far corner of the Hundred Acre Wood, in a bright meadow where the tall purple thistle flowers he liked to eat grew in abundance.

As Pooh and Piglet made their way toward Eeyore's Corner, from time to time, they saw one of the small, globular Something Elses watching them from the shadows along the side of the path.

"Do you think they see more with their six little eyes than we do with only two?" asked Pooh.

Piglet looked at one of the Something Elses, and the Something Else looked back at him, its bulbous gray body wobbling like a blob of gelatin as its six shiny black eyes all swiveled to stare up at him.

"P-p-perhaps," said Piglet, edging closer to Pooh. "But I wish they would use more of them to look somewhere else."

As Piglet spoke, another of the Something Elses moved out of the shadows, scuttling across the path ahead of them on its eight pointy feet. Five of its shiny black eyes slid to the side of its head to watch the pair, while the sixth eye faced forward to see where it was going.

When it reached the middle of the path it stopped.

Shifting its sixth eye so it was now staring at Pooh and Piglet with all of its eyes, the Something Else raised its large arms and clapped its heavy pincers together, the sharp, snapping sound making Piglet jump.

When a dozen more Something Elses emerged from the shadows, pincers raised and clapping as they scuttled across the road, it was all Piglet could do not to run away as fast as his trembling legs would take him. Pressing his hands to his ears, he hid behind Pooh, peeking out only after he could no longer hear the clattering of their pincers.

Finally, all but one of the Something Elses had disappeared into the shadows. The first one had waited, its eyes all bunched up on one side of its body and staring directly at Piglet. With a final loud *snap-snap* of its pincers it slid its eyes forward, then turned and followed its companions into the shadows. Leaves rustled and twigs crunched under their pointy feet as they scuttled away.

"Where do you think they are going?" asked Piglet, watching after them.

"They seem to like the shadowy places," Pooh said, as he and Piglet resumed their walk. "They are probably looking for the Shadowiest Place."

"How do you suppose they got here?" Piglet asked.

Pooh thought for a moment. "In the usual way, I expect," he said after a moment.

Piglet nodded solemnly, and after that they walked in silence for some time, though whenever Piglet happened to glance to one side of the path or the other, he was certain he saw shiny black eyes watching them pass.

The path to Eeyore's Corner took Pooh and Piglet past the tall chestnut tree where Owl lived, deep in the Hundred Acre Wood. As they drew near, they heard Owl's voice saying words they did not quite understand.

When they reached the small clearing in front of Owl's tree, they found him perched on a large branch and reading aloud from a very large book which was propped up in the crook of two smaller branches. They did not see Rabbit, though many of his Friends and Relations filled the small clearing along with quite a few Something Elses, all listening attentively. As Pooh and Piglet entered the clearing, the other small animals' heads slowly turned all at once, and a hundred unblinking black eyes stared at them.

"Maybe we should go," Piglet whispered to Pooh.

But Owl had spotted them, and before Pooh had a chance to answer, called out to them, "Halloo, Pooh!" and "Greetings, Piglet," he said. "Have you come to hear me read?

"What are you reading?" asked Pooh.

"It is a book Christopher Robin gave me a couple of days ago," Owl replied. "It is called the *Necro Comic Con.*" He tapped the pages with the tip of one wing. "It is dreadfully lacking in the sort of pictures one would expect to find in a comic book, and so was of little interest to Christopher Robin, but I have discovered that it is actually the secret history of my great-great-great uncle, Cuthbert Owl."

Owl paused then, fluffing his feathers and looking down at them expectantly.

Piglet noticed then that the Owl's eyes seemed much larger and much darker than usual, making him feel exceptionally small and vulnerable, which was a particularly uncomfortable feeling for a small animal such as himself.

"What a nice surprise for you," Piglet said, hoping it had been a nice surprise, and not one of those unpleasant sort of surprises that left you wishing you'd stayed in bed all day with the covers pulled up over your head. The many black eyes of the small animals watching them now were making him wish he'd done just that today.

"Indeed it was," Owl said with a happy hoot. Once again, he tapped the book with his wing. "I have not yet read all of his adventures, but there are numerous references to *Cth-hoooo-lu*—that would be Cuthbert Owl, of course—throughout the text."

When Owl said *"Cth-hoooo-lu"* all of Rabbit's Friends and Relations slowly turned their heads back toward him, repeating the word in unison.

A chill ran up the back of Piglet's neck, reached the top of his head, circled around twice, then turned and raced back down the way it had come. When the chill reached his feet, there was nothing Piglet could do, but follow it as quickly as he could.

"Goodbye, Owl," he said, raising one hand in a hasty wave as he began making his way through the assembly of black-eyed rodents

"Pardon me," Piglet said, squeezing past a pair of small rabbits.

And "Please excuse me," as he stepped over a group of mice who looked up at him with shiny black eyes.

"But won't you stay and listen?" Owl called out over the rodents' soft, whispered murmur of *"Cth-hoooo-lu."*

"Another t-t-time, perhaps," Piglet said. He slipped and squirmed out of reach of hands and tails and quills brushing against his pink skin as the smaller animals tried to grab him. "Oh, d-d-dear, Pooh, are you coming?"

"I am trying to," Pooh replied. "However, I am finding it somewhat difficult."

Piglet looked over his shoulder at Pooh. A dozen black-eyed mice had climbed onto Pooh's back and a hedgehog was wrapped around one ankle. Several of the Something Elses had scuttled out of the shadows, forming a ring around Pooh, while others were headed toward Piglet, their pincers clicking

The whispered murmur of *"Cth-hoooo-lu"* turned into a chant, growing louder each time the rodents repeated the word.

"Run, Piglet. Run!" Pooh called out.

As Piglet shook free of the last of Rabbit's Friends and Relations' grasp and dove into the Wood, he heard Pooh's muffled sigh:

"Oh bother."

Piglet ran all the way to Eeyore's Corner, only stopping when he tripped on a root and fell flat on his stomach. He lay there breathless for only a moment until the sound of scuttling behind him sent him scrambling back to his feet.

A second tumble sent Piglet rolling head over heels down a short hill with several "oofs" and "ohs" along the way.

When he finally came to a stop with his nose only an inch from a very Shadowy Place, his "oh, dear" came out in a whispered squeak as six shiny black eyes drifted together in front of him, a very small, very frightened Piglet reflected in each of them.

Piglet scrambled backwards as the Something Else scuttled forward, but as quickly as the Something Elses could move on their eight short legs, a frightened Piglet moved faster.

In one breath—certainly no more than two—Piglet was on his feet and once again running to Eeyore's as fast as his little legs would carry him.

Now Eeyore's Corner was the sunniest, most cheerful spot in the whole Hundred Acre Wood. A pleasant little stream laughed and burbled through a meadow of colorful wildflowers, and butterflies filled the air.

But when Piglet burst out of the trees and into the clearing, the heavy gray clouds that had blocked the sun for days seemed to have sucked away all of the color from the flowers. Gray petals drooped over gray leaves. A gray butterfly fluttered uncertainly toward Piglet, but when he raised his hand for it to land on, even his pink skin was tinged with gray.

"Oh dear, oh dear, oh dear," Piglet said. "It is worse than I thought. I'll never be able to find Eeyore. How I wish Pooh was here."

Piglet had been walking as he talked, holding his arms out in front of him in case he should run into anything in all the grayness. Still, he was very surprised when he walked straight into a large, soft, yet solid form that grunted slightly on impact

"Oh, Eeyore, is that you?" he cried.

"Thanks for noticing me," Eeyore said. "I'm just here munching on thistles, like I do every day at this time. Why anyone should be surprised to find me here, I really don't know."

"It's just that you're the same color as the clouds," Piglet said.

"And a lovely color it is, too," Eeyore said.

"Yes, yes. It is a lovely color for a donkey," agreed Piglet. "But I do think the sky should be a little bit bluer."

Eeyore nodded slowly and thoughtfully. "Perhaps," he said after a moment. "Purple thistles taste better than gray thistles, too. Did I hear you looking for Pooh? He isn't here. I am sure we would see a yellow bear quite easily if he were here."

"He's been t-t-taken by the Something Elses," Piglet said. "I don't know what to do."

"We should take him back," Eeyore said. He nibbled on a thistle, then asked, "Do you know where they have taken him? We will need to know where to look for him if we are to set out on a rescue."

"I last saw him near Owl's house," said Piglet. "B-b-but Eeyore, there are so very many of the Something Elses, and we are only two. How will we rescue Pooh?"

Eeyore thought for so long while he chewed his thistles, that Piglet was beginning to think he'd forgotten the question. But finally Eeyore swallowed the thistles and turned to look at Piglet.

"We'll need help. I suppose we should go see Rabbit."

And so, after snatching a last bite of thistles to chew as he walked, Eeyore headed down the path toward Rabbit's house, with Piglet walking quickly alongside.

RABBIT WAS VERY ANNOYED.

He had intended to work in his garden on what should have been a lovely summer day, but the gray clouds were so thick it was as though they were too heavy to remain in the sky and instead had fallen right on top of the entire Hundred Acre Wood, including Rabbit's vegetable garden.

In addition, almost all of his Friends and Relations had gone running off to listen to Owl read from some silly old storybook, leaving only the small, sleepy, littlest hedgehog to keep watch for the Something Elses that scuttled through the garden. The Something Elses were a problem, cutting leaves with their large clacking claws and poking holes in tender young carrots every time their sharp, pointy feet sank into the ground.

"If they came through and ate everything, I might understand," Rabbit said to the littlest hedgehog. "But I've never seen them take so much as a nibble. They just clatter along, poking and cutting things and staring at you with all those eyes while destroying a perfectly good garden. Well, I won't have it!"

The littlest hedgehog said nothing, just curled up in a ball and rolled after Rabbit as he marched off to his house.

Rabbit emerged a few minutes later, with a broom in one hand. He had strapped a washboard to his chest as a shield and placed a bucket on his head as a helmet.

The littlest hedgehog, wisely choosing to remain safely and securely inside, had declined the offer of a teacup helmet and a fork he could use to chase the

Something Elses away. Instead he made himself a little nest of blankets and pillows in Rabbit's large, overstuffed chair and quickly dozed off.

And so Rabbit returned to the garden alone to do battle with the Something Elses, sending them flying with mighty sweeps of his broom and the occasional kick when one of the creatures attempted to clamber onto his foot.

He had nearly succeeded in clearing his garden of the pesky creatures when Eeyore and Piglet arrived.

"Oh, my goodness!" Piglet cried as a Something Else sailed over his head and into the bushes beyond. He ducked as another came flying towards them, but this one didn't fly as far and landed right on the middle of Eeyore's back.

Eeyore reared up and gave a good shake that sent the Something Else tumbling to the ground. He then followed up with a good kick that sent it into the bushes with its companion.

"And a good riddance to you all!" Rabbit called out after them with a menacing shake of his broom. Then, clearing his throat and dusting his washboard, he smiled at Eeyore and Piglet.

"Oh, hello, Eeyore, Piglet," he said. Looking around, he added, 'And where's Pooh? I would have expected to see him with you." He ran an arm across his brow. "Would you like a cup of tea? It's early for tea-time, but chasing Something Elses is thirsty work. Too bad Pooh isn't here, or I'd offer him a little something as well."

"Pooh has been Taken," Eeyore said.

"That's why we've come," said Piglet. "We need your help to Take him back."

Well, Rabbit was so surprised at that news that he completely forgot about tea. He sat down right where he was and didn't know what to say for a full minute. When he finally recovered, he said, "I suppose you must tell me all about it."

So Piglet told him all about how he and Pooh were walking past Owl's house when the black-eyed Friends and Relations tried to Take him (unsuccessfully), but succeeded in Taking Pooh, though he didn't know why or where.

And when Rabbit removed the bucket from his head, Piglet climbed up on it and sat down, as it was a most useful bucket and just the right size for someone as small as Piglet to sit on while telling a story.

Piglet then continued, telling Rabbit the rest of his morning's adventure, running to Eeyore's house and finding him in the gray meadow.

"And that was when we decided to come here," Eeyore finished. While Piglet had been talking, Eeyore had been munching on some wilted carrot greens the Something Elses had left laying on the ground. But as this was the part of the story Eeyore knew best, it was only right that he be the one to tell it.

During the telling of the story, Rabbit had interrupted Piglet on three separate occasions to go and sweep away more Something Elses. Now that the story was done, he sat there looking beyond his garden and toward the part of the Hundred Acre Wood where Owl's tree grew.

"It seems to me," Rabbit said, his hand on his chin, "that the dark clouds are a little darker over there."

Then he turned and looked behind him. "And it is noticeably lighter in this direction."

"What does it mean?" Piglet asked.

"We must go to see Kanga." Rabbit said. "As Christopher Robin once said, a Kanga is Generally Regarded as one of the Fiercer Animals."

He stood and turned toward the lighter clouds. "The darkness is spreading from the heart of the Hundred Acre Wood. We will need Kanga's help if we are to rescue Pooh."

After leading them from the garden, and giving a passing Something Else a hard stare that sent it scuttling in the opposite direction, Rabbit said to Piglet and Eeyore, "Come, we haven't another moment to lose."

Kanga was having a Productive Morning. She had washed the linens and tidied her cupboard and put away the toys Roo had left on the floor.

She was humming to herself when she heard a tap-tap at the garden gate.

"Rabbit! Piglet! Eeyore!" she exclaimed. "My good friends, how are you on this fine, gray day? I have just set a tray of biscuits out to cool, and once I set aside some for Roo, you are welcome to join me."

"Roo is not here?" asked Piglet.

"No, dear," said Kanga, holding the door open for them all to come inside. "We were out walking early this morning and stopped by Owl's house. He was reading some silly story to Rabbit's Friends and Relations—something full of silly words that meant nothing to me. But the young ones seemed most entertained."

She brought over a plate of biscuits and offered one to Rabbit, Piglet, and Eeyore, who accepted them gratefully.

"As you may know, I am not fond of nonsense stories," Kanga said. "But Roo was amused, so I let him stay to listen to Owl while I came home to attend to my chores. It seemed harmless enough."

Piglet looked at Rabbit.

Rabbit looked at Eeyore.

With no one else to look at, Eeyore looked at Kanga. Swallowing his biscuit, he said, "Not that I wanted to be the bearer of unpleasant news, but it seems no one else wants to say it."

"Say what, dear?" Kanga asked.

"Pooh has been Taken by the Something Elses," Eeyore said. "And Roo is Potentially in Danger."

The biscuit on the small plate in Kanga's hand slid to the floor, followed by the plate itself. Kanga snatched up her broom and began to sweep up the mess, the expression on her face now quite stern.

Rabbit and Piglet backed slowly away from her, remembering the second part of Christopher Robin's warning about Kanga: Now that she knew Roo was Potentially in Danger, Kanga might become as fierce as *Two* of the Fiercer Animals, which was fierce indeed.

And while they still wanted her help to rescue Pooh, they also wanted to stay well out of reach of either her angrily twitching tail or the swift strokes of her broom.

"Now," said Kanga, once the mess was cleaned up, "I shall have to go and have words with Owl and find out what he has done with Roo and Pooh."

"Wait!" cried Rabbit and Piglet and Eeyore all at once.

Kanga, who was halfway to her door, stopped and turned back to them, tapping her foot faster and faster as they told her everything that had gone on before.

"So, you see," Rabbit said, "We must all go together if we are to have a hope of rescuing them and saving my Friends and Relations."

"Do we know what has caused their eyes to go black?" Kanga asked.

"I suspect it is the book Owl is reading to them," said Piglet. "He said Christopher Robin gave it to him a couple of days ago, and that was about the time the Something Elses showed up—"

"And when the sky began to turn gray," Rabbit added.

"Then we must persuade Owl to *unread* the book," Eeyore said.

Everyone turned to stare at Eeyore.

"If reading the book caused the problem," Eeyore said, his voice low and patient, "then *unreading* it should undo the damage."

"It makes a sort of sense," Rabbit agreed.

"But how to we convince him?" Piglet asked. "He is very proud to be reading a book about his great-great-great uncle. He won't want to stop reading it just because we ask him to."

Kanga smiled then, but it wasn't a friendly smile. It was a Fierce Animal smile that made the others back away from her again.

"Oh, I think Owl will do exactly what we ask him to," she said, exchanging her simple cooking apron for a sturdy gardening apron of heavy canvas.

"Now, let me look at the three of you." Kanga turned an appraising eye to Piglet, Rabbit, and Eeyore. Tapping a finger to her mouth, she went to a cupboard and rummaged around for a minute before coming over to Piglet.

"You are about the same size as Roo," she said. "And this is what he wears when playing at battle with the dragon flies in the meadow."

She placed a tin pot on Piglet's head as a helmet and hung a pair of baking sheets tied together with string over his shoulders so that one covered his back and the other his chest. A strip of cloth wrapped around his body and tied just under Piglet's arms kept them from clapping against him when he moved. Finally, she held out a wooden mixing spoon.

Piglet accepted the long-handled spoon and gave it a test swing.

"If I had been so well-armed when Pooh and I went hunting for Heffalumps, I would have felt much braver," he said solemnly. "Thank you, Kanga."

Kanga nodded in acknowledgement, then looked at Rabbit.

"I see you have done battle before," she said.

"I was evicting several Something Elses from my garden when Piglet and Eeyore found me," Rabbit replied.

"Well done." Kanga said approvingly. Then she turned to Eeyore.

"Hmm," she said, studying him. She moved around him, tilting her head. "Hmm," she said again. Then, "Yes, I think that will do."

She went into her kitchen, returning a moment later with a large box, a ball of string, and a sturdy colander. With Rabbit's help, Kanga opened the side of the box and arranged the heavy cardboard over Eeyore's shoulders and back, tying it in place with the string.

Then she plopped the colander on the donkey's head, sliding his long ears through the handles to keep it from slipping down and covering his eyes.

"There," Kanga said, stepping back to observe Eeyore. "Now you're protected. But I'm not sure what to give you to use as a weapon—"

"Don't need one," Eeyore said. "Couldn't use one if I did. Besides, I've got these." He reared up on his back feet and pawed at the air with his front feet.

"And these." He reversed position, leaning forward on his front feet while kicking out with both back feet. "They'll do fine. Always have."

"And look, Eeyore," Piglet said, pointing at his helmet. "Kanga's given you horns!"

Sure enough the colander's four short legs rose like a set of horns from the top of Eeyore's head.

"Imagine that," Eeyore said. "Me, a horned, armored donkey going into battle. Not a thing I expected to be doing when I woke up this morning, but there it is."

"I believe we are almost ready to march," Rabbit said. "Now, when we arrive, we will all have jobs to do."

Everyone listened as he made the assignments.

"Piglet," he said. "You are small and quick. You find Pooh and Roo and free them."

"And if Pooh and Roo have the black eyes and do not want to be freed?" Piglet asked.

"You'll think of something," Eeyore said.

Piglet looked uncertain, but he said "Ok-k-kay," trembling only a little.

Rabbit next turned to Kanga. "You are the largest and fiercest of us all. It will be your job to persuade Owl to read the book backwards and banish the darkness from the Hundred Acre Wood."

Kanga simply nodded, her grip on her broom and her fierce, frightening smile more eloquent than anything she might have said.

"Eeyore and I will distract the black-eyed Friends and Relations and the Something Elses," Rabbit said. "We'll keep them from interrupting the Important Work being done by Kanga and Piglet."

He placed a hand on Eeyore's shoulder. "There are many of them, and only two of us, but we are larger and stronger—"

"Still, we would be grateful if you did your Important Work quickly," Eeyore added.

"Agreed," said Rabbit

And so the four brave friends set out to rescue their friends and save the Hundred Acre Wood. With Piglet riding safely in Kanga's pouch and Rabbit and Eeyore marching quickly behind, they followed the path along the winding stream across the meadow and into the Darkness.

THE WOOD WAS DARKER than Piglet remembered. He had never been the sort of Small Animal who liked wandering the Wood at night. And now the thick, heavy clouds blotted out nearly all of the midday sunshine, making it dark and oppressive, with shadows full of glittering black eyes.

Their path ran alongside a stream that usually flowed lazily along with the occasional frothy tumble over clusters of rocks. But today, the stream was sluggish and black, oozing more than flowing, and the trees whose roots drank from it had dark lines running up their trunks and veining their leaves.

Eeyore took a nibble of the blackened grass at the water's edge and quickly spit it out.

"Tastes like despair," he said. "Even the gray grass in my corner only tasted like sadness."

"Stay away from the water," Rabbit advised. "There is something moving in it." He pointed to a shallow spot where the water pooled. They should have been able to see fish splashing in the water, but instead they saw dozens of long, shiny, wriggling black things curling through the water. Some were as thick as Kanga's tail while others were very thin.

"I cannot see where they begin or end," he said. "Nor can I tell if they are all separate creatures or part of Something Large."

There was a slurping sound behind them followed by a splash. They all turned to see several of the black things sliding across the path, each coiled around a struggling Something Else. The Something Large dragged the Something Elses into the water, which bubbled briefly before again going still.

"The Something Large likes to eat Something Elses," Eeyore observed.

"There are too many Somethings with no names in the Wood," Kanga said.

"And this one is heading t-t-toward Owl's house," Piglet said. "We m-m-must go faster." He wondered if the Something Large also liked to eat other Very Small Animals such as himself, but did not feel brave enough to ask the question out loud. As he huddled in Kanga's pocket, his wooden spoon suddenly seemed very small indeed.

"Shh!" whispered Rabbit pointing ahead to a gap in the trees. "We're getting close."

For the past few minutes they had all heard the rhythmic chanting of "*Cth-hoooo-lu. Cth-hoooo-lu,*" growing louder with every step. Now they could also hear the clacking of the Something Elses' large pincers.

The clacking followed a short-long-short, short-long-short tempo, matching the chant, and they found themselves matching their steps to the beat.

"Walk out of step," Eeyore said, nudging Rabbit in the back with his nose. Rabbit, who hadn't noticed that he was murmuring the chant under his breath, stumbled and fell into Kanga who spun around on her tail, her broom raised.

"It's like marching to the drumbeats," Eeyore said, his voice low. "Except that's just what we don't want to do. We have to walk out of step, or we'll fall into the pattern of their chant."

"Oh, yes," said Kanga, lowering her broom and reaching out a hand to help Rabbit up.

"Yes. Yes, of course," said Rabbit, hoping no one had noticed him chanting.

Piglet, whose head was nodding to the beat almost by itself, grabbed the handle of his tin pot helmet to make his head stop wobbling.

Kanga, Rabbit, and Eeyore crept forward, crowding behind the last gorse bush to peer over it at Owl's tree and the small clearing in front of it. Piglet, too low to see over the bush from his place in Kanga's pocket, carefully pushed the prickly branches aside to peek between the leaves.

The sky overhead, now that they could see it, was dark and full of churning clouds, as though preparing for a massive thunderstorm. Beneath the gray sky, it seemed the whole Hundred Acre Wood was gray, as if the color had faded away, leaving everyone and everything dull and listless.

Flowers drooped, leaves curled, and Rabbit's many Friends and Relations who were clustered close to the tree had lost their bounce. Even the globby Something Elses that surrounded them, clacking their pincers, rocked mindlessly back and forth on their pointy feet.

The sluggish black stream they had been following curved around the clearing and around behind the tall chestnut tree before continuing on through the Wood. Dark streaks reached out from the edge of the stream into the clearing, and any tufts of grass whose roots they touched had withered and blackened.

Heavy dark streaks reached up the trunk of the tree as well, and the leaves on the lower branches looked as if they'd been burned. The branch where Owl perched, only a short distance from his front door, was almost completely black.

"Eeyore and I will circle around to the other side of the clearing," Rabbit said. "We'll try to distract them long enough for the two of you to get to Owl."

"And find Pooh," added Piglet.

"And find Roo," added Kanga.

"All of that," said Rabbit. He turned to Eeyore. "Ready?"

"As if anyone is ever ready for this sort of thing," Eeyore said. He shook his head, brandishing his little horns. "But ready or not, there's no point waiting. It's just getting darker."

So saying, he moved forward, Rabbit behind him, sneaking around the clearing, creeping from bush to bush as they headed to the opposite side.

***

KANGA SCANNED the gathering of black-eyed Friends and Relations for any sign of Roo while she waited for Rabbit's signal. But there was no Roo-shaped animal anywhere to be seen in the rhythmically chanting group near the base of the big chestnut tree.

Roo had definitely been Taken, she was almost certain, and not turned into one of the black-eyed animals. Kanga wasn't sure which was worse. She just wanted him back safely in her pouch.

"Any second now," she whispered to Piglet. "Be ready."

She crouched low and waited. When the black-eyed Friends and Relations looked away from Owl, she would have only a moment—just time for two large jumps—before they saw her and tried to Take her as they had Taken Pooh and Roo.

And then Rabbit and Eeyore burst from the bushes on the other side of the clearing.

"Aha!" Rabbit cried out.

"Ah-ha," said Eeyore shaking his tiny horns enthusiastically.

As the Friends and Relations heads swiveled to look at them with their shiny black eyes and the Something Elses scuttled in their direction, Kanga gave a mighty leap.

She sailed over the gorse bush.

Touched down briefly near the center of the clearing.

Then leapt a second time.

Landing at the foot of the large chestnut tree.

"Owl," she called out.

Owl looked down at her. "Welcome, Kanga! I am glad you came to hear me read about my great-great-great, Uncle Cuthbert. We are having a wonderful time—"

"You must stop reading immediately, Owl," Kanga said.

"Why would I want to do that?" Owl asked, his tone shifting from friendly to harsh as he puffed out his chest and folded his wings across his chest.

"Look at his eyes, Kanga," Piglet whispered. "They seem very dark."

"Yes, I see," she whispered to Piglet. To Owl, she called. "Your story is bringing the darkness. Look at the sky Owl."

Owl looked.

"Those are your standard *cumulonimbus* clouds," Owl said. "The usual sort of clouds for a thunderstorm, which is why so many incorrectly call them thunderclouds—"

"These clouds are different, Owl," Kanga said. "The only way to clear them is to unread the book."

"I will do no such thing."

"They're coming," Piglet whispered.

Kanga had heard the Something Elses scuttling behind her. "Hold on," she told Piglet.

And even before she had stopped speaking, she leapt her mightiest leap from the ground to the first branch on the left. Then to the next branch up and on the right. And finally to the very large branch where Owl was perched.

"What? What? What are you doing here?" Owl cried in alarm. He flapped his wings and tried to step back, but one of Kanga's large feet pinned him to his perch and he could not move.

"Go now, Piglet," Kanga said. "I'll take care of Owl. Find Roo."

As Piglet scrambled out of her pocket, his baking sheets clattering, Owl flapped his wings at Kanga. "Release me!" he demanded.

"Unread the book," Kanga said, balling up her fists and punching at his wings as he flapped them at her.

"Unread the book, Owl," she said, "or I will pull out your pin feathers one by one."

While Kanga argued with Owl, Piglet hurried along the branch to Owl's front door. Ignoring the signs posted on either side of the door instructing him to knock or ring the bell, Piglet eased the door open and slipped inside Owl's house.

The blackness had made its way in here as well, streaking the floor and the walls and turning Owl's cozy house into a dark and dreary place.

Piglet tiptoed forward, holding the long-handled spoon out in front of him as he looked for any sign of a black-eyed small animal or a Something Else and where they might have hidden Pooh and Roo.

But there was no sign of anyone. The house was utterly and completely silent in a way that made Piglet more frightened rather than reassured.

"Pooh?" he called out in a Very Small voice. "Roo?" he said, trying to make his voice a little louder. "It's Piglet, c-c-come to rescue you."

A sound from the kitchen made him jump.

Was that a rattle, or the scuttling footsteps of a Something Else?

"Oh dear, oh dear, oh dear," Piglet said, his legs shaking so much he wondered if the sound he'd heard was actually that of his knees knocking together. "It is very hard for a Small Animal to be brave," he said. "But my grandfather, Trespassers William, would remind me that I have Important Work to do, so I must try."

Piglet moved cautiously up to the kitchen door, peeked around the edge and into the room, but once again, saw no one.

"Pooh?" he called out. "Roo? Are you here?"

A sound like "mmm-hmmm" answered him. And as he was turning around trying to find the source of the sound, there was a loud rattling and banging on a cupboard door.

Piglet jumped.

"Oh dear!" he cried. "Roo? Is that you?"

It had to be Roo. The cupboard was much too small to hold a large bear like Pooh. Almost immediately, there was an answering "hmm-mmm-hmmm-hmmm."

"I'm here to rescue you," Piglet said running over to the cupboard. But looking up at the tightly closed door far above his head, he murmured, "But how can a Small Animal such as myself rescue Roo?"

He looked around the house for something Useful, and spotted a chair tucked under a table near the window. With great effort, Piglet pushed the chair and pulled the chair away from the table and across the dark, stained floor and over to the cabinet.

When he finally climbed up on the counter, he found the cupboard door was firmly stuck in place.

"I'm coming, Roo!" he called. And then he tugged and tugged at the covered door.

Finally, after much tugging, the door popped open and Roo burst out. He landed in Piglet's arms and the two of them toppled backwards off of the counter and on to the chair, then rolled, laughing, on to the floor.

"You found me!" Roo cried. "Hey! You're wearing my dragonfly-fighting armor!"

"Yes, I did," Piglet said, "and yes, I am." While there still more to be done, he was Much Relieved to have found Roo and that Roo's eyes were laughing and merry and definitely not of the black and shiny sort. "But how did you end up in Owl's cupboard?"

"Owl told me to either sit still and listen or to go play Hide and Seek. So I found a perfect Hiding Place. Except the cupboard door got stuck and I couldn't get out. I was beginning to think no one was ever going to find me—"

"Was Pooh also playing Hide and Seek?" Piglet asked.

Roo shrugged. "Don't know," he said, jumping up and down. "I've been in the cupboard for the Longest Time and haven't seen anyone."

"If Pooh *was* playing Hide and Seek, and you were trying to find him, where would you look?" Piglet asked.

Roo raised himself up so he was balancing on his tail and looked around Owl's house.

"He could be behind that big chair over there," he said, pointing to Owl's overstuffed chair. "Or under the bed—I like to hide under the bed. Mama can never find me." He turned around a little bit more. "Or maybe he'd hide in that closet, there?"

Piglet thought that was the best of Roo's guesses and ran over to the closet. Peering in through the lock, he called out. "Pooh, are you in there?"

"Is that Piglet? It sounds like Piglet's voice, but there have been an awful lot of Something Elses in the Wood today," Pooh replied.

"It *is* Piglet," Piglet cried. "Oh, Pooh! I am so happy to have found you. I'm here to rescue you."

"Do you think you could hold off on rescuing me for another few minutes?" asked Pooh in a suspiciously sticky voice.

"No, it is time to rescue you now," Piglet said.

There was a key hanging from a hook on the wall next to the door. It was too high for Piglet to reach, even standing on his toes and stretching his hand as far as he could. But after three tries, Roo was able to jump high enough to knock it to the floor.

Piglet unlocked the door, and when he swung it open, he found Pooh sitting in the middle of Owl's pantry, with a smear of honey on his nose and a nearly empty jar of honey in his lap.

"It's not so bad being Taken when they lock you in the Pantry," said Pooh.

Piglet could quite understand why Christopher Robin often shook his head at Pooh, saying 'silly old Bear.' But there was no time for dallying now.

He reached into the pantry and handed Pooh a broom, then found a small tin pot and mixing spoon for Roo. "Come along," he said to them. "We've got Important Work to do."

—

Kanga had only pulled one very tiny feather from Owl's wing, just enough to let him know she was serious. But it was enough to convince him to unread the book.

"I am doing this under duress," Owl had said, puffing up his chest and blinking at her with his large, too-dark eyes.

"You'll be doing it under *water*," Kanga had told him, not sure exactly what 'duress' was, but certain Owl would not want to be dunked in the black stream. "Now unread."

And so Owl unread the *Necro Comic Con*, reversing one word at a time and turning the pages backwards as he reached the top of each one. Instead of the eerie *"Cth-hoooo-lu"* that had darkened his eyes and turned all of the Friends and Relations eyes black, everyone was soon chanting *"Lu-ooooh-cth. Lu-ooooh-cth."*

The blackness and all the wiggling creatures in the stream pulled back— though the dark water left a gray stain wherever it had touched, and the leaves and grasses remained winter-wilted until the following spring.

Before long, the small animals' eyes gradually lost their shiny black stare, and they wandered home strangely sad and confused, though none of them were ever quite sure why.

"But what about the Something Elses?" Rabbit asked.

He and Eeyore and Pooh, with Piglet's and Roo's help (under Kanga's supervision, of course), had gathered the blobby creatures into a squirming pile of clacking pincers and black eyes.

But their pincers weren't clacking as energetically as they had before, and all of their eyes had sunk sadly to the bottom of the globby gray creature's bodies making them seem somehow less menacing.

Several suggestions were made for where to relocate the Something Elses. Each spot suggested was far from the home of the individual making the suggestion as possible.

Most of these ideas were rejected by whoever lived closest to the suggested place.

When it seemed there was nowhere in the Hundred Acre Wood any of the friends thought might be a suitable home for the Something Elses, Pooh had an Idea.

"I suppose they could live in the Heffalump trap," Pooh said "No one is using it at the moment, and it is nice and shadowy down there. We could take turns looking in on them occasionally."

The friends looked at each other and then to the mound of Something Elses. One by one they slowly began to nod in agreement.

"They can come with me," Eeyore said when it was his turn. "Some folks prefer a cozy home, and some of us don't. There's room enough in my meadow. And I'll make sure the Something Elses stay on my side of the stream."

And so Eeyore became the Guardian of the Shadowy Things.

He took the Something Elses to his sunny meadow and built a little wooden house for them just like his own from some old boards that he leaned together until they just touched at the top. The Something Elses often crowded inside to rest in the shadows, clambering on top of each other in a mound full of pincers and eyes.

Over time, as the stream wandered out of its banks and the meadow became a Boggy Place with more thistles than flowers and most of the butterflies flitted off to another part of the Hundred Acre Wood, the Something Elses stayed because the old gray donkey was just the sort of gray they understood.

OVERHEAD, the dark thunderclouds had faded, and a light rain began to fall over the Hundred Acre Wood.

And from a large book that wasn't actually called the *Necro Comic Con* and which had been tucked into a wooden box and buried deep beneath Eeyore's house, the tiniest tendril of darkness leaked out . . .

The End?

In Which Christopher Robin Has Grown, and Tells a Story of His Own

Michaelbrent Collings

What?

A story?

Why I suppose there is time before we sleep, dear child—yes, though we are headed off to bed now, we can still tell it. Do pick up your toy swan, sweet child, the sound of its head bump-bump-bumping as you drag it along does wear on one.

What was that?

Oh, no—this is not one of *Those* Stories. This is rather a Happy Tale, with rather a Happy Ending . . . at least for some. And for some is better than for none, as your mother used to say, may the Great Lord bless her.

Where was I? Quite right—I was on the stairs. But where were *we*? And is the place we were quite the same as the one we are, and how does that altogether relate to where we are going? Those are indeed The Questions, dear child, sweet child.

But now to the story.

IT BEGAN in a place rather like this, I suppose: a bit cramped, a bit dark. It was a place with a long history, a place that had seen many generations grow and pass away, only to be replaced by still more generations, until a thousand generations had seen the place where our story occurs.

(What?

Why yes, I suppose a thousand generations is quite a lot of them. Though, since they belong to rabbits, the whole of it took less time than you would think. Only about six hundred years, in fact—which is still a long time, but far less than a hundred generations of humans, or even a single generation of mountains. It's all relative—yes, relative, just like your aunt.

But where was I?

Ah, the Rabbits.)

Quite a few of them had been born in this place, and quite a few had died. Not all of them, of course—some left the place before dying, and others did not die at all (though that is a story for another night, or even for the middle of day, given that it definitely is one of *Those* Stories). But six hundred years is a long time, and a thousand generations of rabbits had lived in this hole, until we came to today's hole, and today's Rabbit.

Rabbit was a nervous sort. He—

(Oh, you've met him, have you? Pray, tell me your impression of him?

Well bless my soul. You have met him. Though I must be honest that I'm not sure how, given how—

Actually, no, that's jumping ahead.

Regardless, since you and he are no doubt Fast Friends, I'll not bother recounting you with tales of his nervousness—of the time he screamed in the night until his friends came to his hole and found that the Heffalump he saw creeping into his bed was nothing but his own twitching feet, or the time he had An Attack when he thought he saw his great-to-the-tenth grandmother coming up out of the drain, scolding him for throwing away so much Perfectly Good Food. No, I'll not tell you any of that, for as you are already a great friend of Rabbit, you already know the stories.)

As I—

(No, I wouldn't mind. Not at all. If you've forgotten the stories, then of course I must tell them to you. Only watch your head, the ceiling gets a bit low at this part—better that we crawl. Just hold onto my ankle and stay close. No, you won't get lost. You can't, for if you did get lost then I'd be alone in the dark and where would that get us?)

As I was saying: Rabbit was nervous, which was why he jumped up quite high when there came a rather loud voice, shouting, "Is anybody home?"

The voice was warm, but stuffy, for the body it came from was warm and stuffed, and it was a voice Rabbit would know anywhere. So after he finished jumping in fright, he scuffled about, looking for Things and Sundries of all sorts— but most specifically for food, and trying to put it away before the voice came again. Which it did, quite suddenly:

"What I said was, 'Is there anybody at home?'"

"No," cried out Rabbit, for he was surprised at how suddenly the sound came into his hole, and how loud it was, and how much it threatened everything Rabbit held dear. Then, surprised at his own surprise, he followed up his "no" with a rather irritated, "You needn't shout so loud. I heard you quite well the first time!"

"Bother," said the warm, stuffy voice of the warm, stuffed bear. "Isn't there anybody here at all?"

"Nobody."

Rabbit was quite satisfied with himself, for he had come up with a Foolproof Ruse. Only, as we all know, the bear to which the voice belonged was not a Fool, but simply a Bear of Very Little Brain. And as Rabbit's ruse was not a Bear-of-Very-Little-Brainproof Ruse, eventually he found himself entertaining his old friend—

(Yes, they are old friends. Don't keep interrupting. Also, hold tighter to my ankle. If you do let go, there's every chance I shan't ever find you again, and we mustn't let that happen.)

Where was I?

Oh yes: entertaining.

Of course, as his friend came through the hole that led to the hole—which is to say, the doorway between Rabbit's world and that of his friend the bear— Rabbit had to clear away the traps he had been laying. He had heard noises, you see. Noises deep in the walls of his burrow, a skritch-skratch-skrutching sound like fingernails being shredded on the inside of one's skull. And though he knew the walls of his burrow were good and strong—they had lasted a thousand generations, after all, and might last a thousand more—and no such vermin could possibly dig through them, still he thought it must be rats. What else could it be? There had been no moles in the Hundred Acre Wood since the year Rabbit's own great-to-the-eighteenth grandmother had invited all such creatures over for tea and, after they drank the chamomile she gave them, the moles were never seen or heard from again.

(Yes, tea just like your mother's—on the cupboard shelf by the arsenic.)

So Rabbit, knowing there were no more moles, and knowing that rats are attracted to food (of which he always had a surplus), he knew that the sounds he heard must be such vermin, and that such vermin must be trapped. So he set out traps—first one, then five, then a hundred, then a thousand, which was one for every generation of Rabbit in the hole. He spent three long days doing it, neither eating nor sleeping the whole of the time, and then went to bed and awoke to find the traps all sprung, but not a rat in them.

Rabbit was a nervous sort—it probably came of being born in a place that had seen thousands of other rabbits within it, and had absorbed some of their energy. But nervous or no, he was a good host. He tried to be.

That is, perhaps, what I shall miss most about him.

So when his friend the bear made it known that he was coming in, Rabbit cleared away the traps, chop-chop, quick as you please. Then he set out his Best Silver and Finest China. None of which was necessary, for his visitor was only really interested in the honeypot, and once Pooh has a honeypot, he dispenses with all the niceties and simply moves the golden treasure from pot to mouth in as efficient a fashion as possible—which is to say, he scoops it up with his paws and shovels it directly into himself.

And that, as always, is just what he did.

Pooh made short work of the honey, then followed that up by consuming

six deviled eggs (far less Evil than you would think)
eight canapés (sweet)
three cakes (red velvet)
four canapés (savory)
two more cakes (pound)
five cucumber sandwiches (tangy enough they verged on Pickled)
and
one more cake (devil's food).

It was at this last that Pooh chuckled.

"What's so funny?" asked Rabbit, sounding irritable as only a nervous rabbit can when beset upon by a Bear of Very Little Brain but Very Great Tum.

"It's the devil's food," said the bear. He wrinkled his nose. "Don't you think it a bit much? To have devil's cake and deviled eggs in one sit?"

"Yes, it is," said Rabbit, brightening considerably. "In fact, I think you should—"

"I mean," Pooh continued, licking a very sticky paw, "one might Begin To Wonder, mightn't one?"

"What?" said Rabbit.

"What indeed," agreed Pooh. Then, before Rabbit could inquire, he said, "But I shall forgive you this indiscretion, dear friend. Of course I shall! Only do be a dear one and look about for a bit more honey."

"There is none," said Rabbit, in a rather harrumphy sort of way.

(No, I said harrumphy, *not* heffalumphy. *There's no need to fear such things here. And you can let go of my ankle. We'll have to keep crawling, but there is a bit of light. We'll just follow it—yes, and the sound as well. We'll follow them both!)*

"Well," said Pooh, "how do you know?"

"Because I know," said Rabbit.

"That's a rather tautological argument," said Pooh—which was quite the right word to use, though that was an accident, as Pooh thought the word meant "specious," rather than "pleonastic and reiterative." (Did I mention he was a Bear of Very Little Brain?)

But right or not, the word gave Rabbit pause—

(No, not paws. He had the same number of appendages at the end of the sentence as he did at the beginning, unlike his great-to-the-eighth grandfather Randolph, who ended up with far more appendages than he cared for, or could even maintain sanity through! Are you going to keep interrupting? Because if you do there is no way we'll get through the rest of Rabbit's story before we get to the end of ours.)

—and during that pause, Rabbit's friend had time to open up

three cupboards (dishware)
six glass jars (empty)
one tin of beets (avoidable)
a pantry (bare)

and

a bureau (antique).

It was at this last that Rabbit's pause ended, and his paws began to move. Waving them up and down in a manner reminiscent of a hummingbird, he shouted, "Hey, no! Hey, don't! Hey, stop!"

"You've made a great deal of hay," said the bear matter-of-factly (for the bear was not one to make hay out nothing), "but I wonder why." And so saying, he took a candle from off a nearby shelf (yes, very similar to the candle on that sconce over there, my child, now stop interrupting or I shall be forced to Issue Punishments), and shone it into the space within the bureau.

"You'll light my undergarments afire!" shouted Rabbit, wringing his paws in earnest terror.

"Nonsense," said the bear. "Everyone knows that Rabbits don't wear undergarments."

Surprisingly, this was absolutely correct—and is also one of the primary reasons you find so few rabbits in The Best Clubs. Perhaps because the bear *was* correct (or perhaps because of shame over the fact that he would never be permitted to join any of those clubs of which I have just taken notice), Rabbit fell silent. This gave the bear a chance to insert himself more fully into the bureau, casting about with his candle.

Now I must here point out that the bureau in Rabbit's hole was almost as old as the hole itself. No one is fully certain where it came from—such things are often Lost to Time—only that it had come from there centuries ago. Its age was apparent to even a Bear of Very Little Brain such as Rabbit's friend, and he leaned out to ask, "I say, what does this inscription mean?" but then leaned back into the bureau without waiting for reply.

It is too bad that he did not wait. Too bad indeed.

Had he waited, Rabbit might have told him that the inscription was "Magna Mater," a name for the protean figure known as the Great Mother. Thinking Men, he might have added, have long dismissed this figure as a creature out of myth, though there are still sects among the uneducated masses who give credence to Her existence—and to Her.

The bear, of course, would have understood none of that (any more than you can understand it, sweet child), but perhaps hearing such things would have encouraged him to Take His Leave.

But he did not hear. He did not listen.

He did not leave.

Those three things together led to the fourth: he found.

What he found is up for some debate. Some say it was a plate of solid gold that, when touched, became a golden manacle that shackled the bear to the bureau; and, further, that the bureau itself was a cage built to imprison The Great Goddess Herself and thereby shield all human life from the madness Her merest presence brings. Others say that it was a mass of thorns that, once touched, insert themselves under the skin until the pain becomes to great for aught but madness to bear.

Whatever it was, the bear touched it. He began to laugh—a wheezing, gaspy laugh like someone trying to blow a fly from their nose. Some say that is why the bear was called Pooh, because of that sound. But I think not. I think there must be some other reason, for "Pooh" is quite a Light and Silly Name, and there was nothing light or silly about that laugh.

(Speaking of . . . have I told you of the time that I was captured by the Hun and forced to stand at a wall where my hands were shackled above my head for days on end? My soldier-servant, a stout fellow called West, was with me as well, and when they finally loosed us from the shackles, my batman could not lower his arms at all and I woke that night to find him standing over me, arms still high in the air, cackling madly and calling upon things Dark and Final to save him. He laughed in much the same way our bear friend was laughing now, after finding . . . whatever it is he found, inside that old piece of furniture in a hole that had seen so many centuries of Life and Death and Things Unspoken.)

Rabbit was a good host. He really was! So when he heard the bear laugh like that, though his first impulse was to run and run and never look back, he instead turned to his friend and pulled him out from inside the bureau.

Pooh had been half-in the bureau and half-out. That fact was plain to see as Rabbit pulled him all-out and saw that the bear's upper part—the part that was inside the bureau—had turned white as a sheet on a ghost. The bottom part—the part that had been outside the bureau—was not white, but a kind of sickly gray. Phantasmic was the word Rabbit thought in that moment. And in the next, the word he thought was "GETOUT."

He did not know what had happened to his friend. Truth be told, he never actually looked in the bureau that Pooh had examined, because (again, truth be told), Pooh had been right: rabbits don't wear undergarments. And as the bureau was obviously meant to hold such, what reason then could he have for looking inside it?

Rabbit, as you may guess, was Very Proper. Part of this was upbringing, and part was inbringing. The upbringing was Rabbit's mother, who came from a very Prim and Proper colony of rabbits beyond the Hundred Acres, and who taught that Rabbits of Breeding did not look at—or mention, or even think of—such crass things as death, or suffrage, or undergarments.

The inbringing was Rabbit's father, who had lived in this self-same hole his whole life, and who toward the end of his life began to manifest some of the singular strangeness exhibited by many of those who are born where they die, and vice-versa.

Rabbit had tried to honor his mother's memory by never discussing or going near anything smacking of undergarments (or death, or the right of does to vote). And he tried to ignore his father's memory by never doing anything The Least Bit Strange, for fear that doing such a thing would crack open the dam that held back all things dark and insane in a family that had lived one place far too long.

Because of all this, Rabbit did not acknowledge his friend's queer aspect; or the fact that Pooh's laugh had become now a keening, mewling wail; or the drool that came from the bear's slack mouth. He just pumped the bear's soft (sticky) hand up and down quickly and said, "Wonderfultohaveyousosorryyouhave-toleavegivemybestttoPigletgoodbye."

(Yes, he said it just like that, in a single word that would give cruciverbal-ists an apoplexy and make typesetters faint dead away.)

Then he let go of Pooh's sticky hand.

Pooh, it must be said, did not leave. He did not move or say a word. He merely kept up that dreadful, maddening cry. It reminded Rabbit, suddenly and violently, of the sound his own dam had made, the night his father killed her. It was a Course, Ugly Thing—one that Rabbit sought only to forget (again, due to upbringing and inbringing), and Rabbit tried to forget it now. But the bright silver of the blade and the brighter white of his father's eyes, wide and staring into a place far gone—

And was the bureau open that day? thought Rabbit. *Did I come home early that day—early, because I didn't go to school but instead went to Old Man McGre-gor's intent on stealing carrots but instead he nearly captured me and I ran home so very afraid and wanting a kiss from my mother, a hug from my father but instead of either I came down into the hole to find that someone had opened the bureau, and someone had opened up Mother, and Father was half in one and half in the other, his feet and legs inside the darkness of the bureau, his hands and arms and trunk painted red with the lightness of Mother?*

(No, you mustn't run, dear boy. Stay close. Listen to the sound. Focus on the sound. Why yes . . . it does sound rather like a chant, does it not?)

Rabbit, as he thought all these things, pushed his friend to the hole that led out of the hole—which is to say, the doorway between Rabbit's dark underworld and the bright overplace of the Hundred Acre Wood. What would have happened, do you think, if he had gotten Pooh outside right then? Do you think it would have ended there? Would the bear's Natural Colors have returned and they would have laughed and made fun of the whole hole adventure, or perhaps—like Rabbit's dear mother, a bit of fresh blood in a bloodline long grown weary—would they have simply ignored it as a Thing Uncouth and Better Left Unsaid?

We shall never know.

Because Pooh, as you might remember, had eaten quite a lot. (Yes, now that you mention it, he ate exactly what you had for dinner. You are so smart, dear one; positively afternoonified!) So much had he eaten, in fact, it was rather like putting butter upon bacon: a bit too extravagant, a bit too rich. And together, that rich extravagance had conspired to create a Bear of Very Little Brain but Even Greater Tum Than Ever, such that he became stuck halfway out the hole, and halfway in.

Pooh was stuck.

So was Rabbit.

Neither of which might have been untenable, but it was then that Rabbit heard the scratching again. The *skritch-skrutch-skretch*ing of tiny claws on vasty walls, or of talons on bone. Rabbit scratched his own skull, right between his two rabbity ears. He did this to Help His Thinking—for he reasoned that such action might Inspire Thought—but also because, quite suddenly, the sound seemed to be coming not from within the walls of his burrow, but the hollow spaces of his mind.

So Rabbit scratched his skull and Pooh wailed in the hole that led to a hole. Outside, it grew dark. Inside, it grew darker still.

(Why yes, it has gotten darker in here as well. No, we can't stand up yet. No, it's not going to get any bigger—you'll understand why when we get there. But for now, why don't you take hold of this cord, the better for me to lead you with? Or—and this is a thought, a real daisy—why don't I just tie it around your hand so you can't let go of it? And the other hand for good measure? There we are!)

Rabbit kept scratching at his head until his yellow fur had been painted red, and the white of his skull showed through. Pooh, for his part, kept keening and moaning. But all good things must come to an end, as they say, and Rabbit eventually realized what a mess he was and went to the bureau to get a towel.

He reached in, and his fingers touched something. Something I daren't describe, but which you shall see presently. You shall know what Rabbit knew, what he felt in that moment. The feeling of the rats, now outside, now inside, now a part of him.

Yes.

It *has* been a while.

I'm sorry you're tired.

Here, let me carry you. I know! I'll take the rest of the rope and make a sling! I can carry you easily on my back that way—no, we mustn't stand up straight, not here in this place!—and you can rest your feet.

Just let me tie your legs. Must tie them, so you can't kick or esca—I mean, so you can't kick and accidentally fall.

No, I can't finish the story. Not yet. Not here.

Now.

In this place.

I was the one who found them, you know.

I found Rabbit, and I found Pooh. Well, I found what was left of them.

I was carrying my gun through the wood—always bring your gun, my father said, for you never know if you shall be beset upon by a heffalump or woozle, or even something darker and stronger than that. Not thinking of much, just of the beauty of the day, the clearness of the sky. All was blue and bright, save only a little black raincloud on the horizon.

And then I heard something. I didn't know what it was, only that I must follow it. And I did. I followed it to this very place, to this very hole. I found Rabbit inside, covered in bits of Sawdust and Felt. His eyes were wide and, though I didn't know it then, quite beautiful. He insisted it was the rats that did it. The rats that had eaten his friend.

And I thought, for a moment, perhaps it was. Surely no Rabbit would do such a thing. Surely no sweet creature could partake of strange meat never intended for consumption. Not Rabbit! Not Pooh!

I almost believed him. I almost believed it was the rats.

But then Rabbit began to laugh. He laughed and laughed—a horrible, terrifying, maddening, *lovely* sound. He laughed so hard he coughed, and he coughed so hard he gagged, and he gagged so hard he vomited. Piles of dark clots came up. I thought they might be blood, or some tumorous excrescence. But bending down I saw they were clumps of sawdust in bile. Bits of cloth in the humour.

I had my gun. My father always told me to take my gun in the woods, because what if I saw a woozle?

Or a far darker thing?

THIS IS something Rabbit and I had in common, even before that day: we both had mothers who Cared for Appearances. That's why I went looking for towels. That's why I went to the cupboard. Just looking for towels with which to clean up the mess, or for rags I could use to sop up the blood.

I found no towels. I found only—

(Yes, that is the bureau.

Yes, we are in the self-same hole.

Yes, I did discover the thing Rabbit found, and the thing Pooh found.

Yes, I do hear the rats.

Yes . . . I am so very, very hungry, dear child.
So very hungry, my sweet, sweet child . . .)

Six Glass Jars

Kary English

Three little cupboards and six glass jars
All stand empty in a pantry far
Out in the woods where the little ones play,
Roaming 'til dark at the end of the day.

Five little jars hold nothing but air.
One holds a lock of bright golden hair,
Out in the woods where the little ones play,
Roaming 'til dark at the end of the day.

Four little jars with one on its side,
Reeking a bit of formaldehyde.
In slides a thumb with the knuckle gone gray,
Out in the woods where the little ones play.

Jars three and four each hold an eye.
A brown one, a blue one that matches the sky.
The lids are on tight so they won't get away,
Out in the woods where the little ones play.

The woods have gone quiet but the cupboard's not bare.
Jars five and six have been polished with care.
The hunt's gotten harder with the children kept home
Save for a little lad who plays all alone.

He's got shiny buttons to fasten his coat,
And he sits near the pond with a tiny toy boat.
He sings little songs about piglets and bees,
And he can't hear the hunter o'er the wind in the trees.

Now the boat sails alone on the pond in the wood,
And the cupboard's locked tight, holding nothing that's good.
The hunter walks home in a night without stars
And puts one shiny button in each little jar.

Children, thought he, should stay in their yards,
If they don't want their buttons going clink in my jars.
For out in the woods where the little ones play,
I roam the dark near the end of the day.

In Which Pooh Is Reacquainted
with the Cult of Silence

Steve Diamond

"The cult is back, Detective Chief Inspector."

"Oh, bother," D.C.I. Pooh said. The words came out like a puff of smoke from one of his trademarked honey cigarettes. Heavy. Obscuring the air with its version of the truth. "Are you sure, Piglet?"

"It's back," D.I. Piglet repeated. "A runner just came in from the Floody Place. It's . . . it's bad P-p-p-p-pooh. Really bad."

Pooh closed his eyes, then reached up to rub at them with a paw. Three years. Three years since the last string of deaths. The time should have floated by, blissful and calm like a game of Poohsticks, but reality never came about with such simplicity. Rather, the years crept by, walking on the eggshells of dread.

"Who?" Pooh stood, strapping on the reliable Webley .455 Mk VI. He flicked open the cylinder and thumbed in six rounds. Each had a five-pointed star engraved in the point. Uncivilized bullets for uncivilized opponents. Ones he'd hoped to never use again.

"Pavel."

"He's the little porcupine who lives near Owl, isn't he?"

"He is. Was."

"Strange." Pooh holstered the revolver, then reached into his desk drawer to pull out a paw-full of extra ammunition. One could never be too careful.

"How s-s-s-s-so?"

Pooh shook his head, then hiked a thumb over his shoulder to the map of the Hundred Acre Wood hanging on the wall of his office. The outer edges of the map showed the tears from where it had been torn from a once larger map. "Why head all the way over there? Pavel kept to the woods. Strange."

"Everything is strange when it comes to the cult, Pooh. Everything."

"Everything," Pooh agreed. "Piglet . . . maybe . . . maybe you should sit this one out."

The small D.I. shook his head. "You know I can't, Sir. You know why."

"I know why." He opened his mouth to press his point, but saw fear mixed with determination on his friend's pink face. Piglet had never been one to back down from a fight. At least, not in the beginning. But the deaths three years prior had changed things. Piglet couldn't handle dark spaces anymore. He'd developed the stutter. But Pooh didn't know if his friend had truly lost his edge.

"I'll take the rifle," Piglet said with a wan smile. "I'll be alright. I owe it to . . . well . . . I owe them."

"Very well, D.I. Piglet. Very well."

THE HUNDRED ACRE Wood hadn't always been so empty. In fact, it hadn't always been called the Hundred Acre Wood. It had once been the Thousand Acre Wood. *A long time since I've thought that name,* Pooh mused.

The pair walked in silence, and the lack of sound put Pooh on edge. He should have opened his mouth, chatted with his best friend to ease both their worries. But no words came. No pithy phrases of encouragement. No witty joke to cut the tension hanging in the air.

The normally clear, blue sky had been taken hostage by dark clouds with pink, angry linings. A Heffalump's Sky, they called it. A bad omen, indeed.

The first one in three years.

A hundred acres. The last bastion of safety and sanity. The edges of their land had been under constant assault for as long as Pooh could remember. Perhaps eternally. So encroached evil; slowly, like an invisible snake encircling its victim until the moment it squeezed. By the time anyone realized the snake had them, escape wasn't possible. By the time the denizens of the Thousand Acre Wood realized their danger, they were living in the Five-hundred Acre Wood.

Then after the events three years earlier, the Hundred Acre Wood.

Everyone suffered loss. As Pooh glanced down at his friend, he realized some suffered more than others. Piglet's tiny shoulders hunched up against the chill in the air, and he'd pulled his overcoat close, flipping the collar high to hide his face.

Pooh didn't need to read minds to know his friend's thoughts. He thought of his sisters. Of his mother and father. They'd been the paragon of families in the

Woods. The tight-knit group everyone else looked up to. The kind of family artists painted to capture their likenesses as examples for all others.

Such perfection rarely lasted. Pooh never tired having a family of his own for that reason alone.

The Floody Place opened up ahead of the pair. Framed in the freakish light filtered though the Heffalump's Sky, Pooh felt an involuntary shiver creep up his spine. Maybe the runner had been mistaken. Maybe Pavel had succumbed to an accident. He lifted his eyes to the sky, willing the clouds to part. To give him hope.

The clouds turned deaf ears to him

Pooh took the lead, letting Piglet trail behind. *Better I see the scene of the crime first*, Pooh thought. The cattails swayed in the breeze, which grew stronger as they walked south. The wind always whipped up this way at the fringes of the Hundred Acre Wood. A warning, most thought. These days, most people avoided the fringes. There were always holdouts. Those who had homesteads or ancestral homes they refused to vacate, no matter the encroaching danger.

Pavel didn't fit into that category. He'd moved as close to the center of the Hundred Acres as he could.

Wet paths wove their way through deeper into the Floody Place, twisting and doubling back on themselves. They would have led strangers astray, but not D.C.I. Pooh. He'd walked these paths with Christopher Robin for years before the boy had vanished. His disappearance had been everyone's first real clue that not all was right in the Wood.

Pooh sniffed the air. Brackish water and rotting wood made up the majority of the scents . . . but not all of it. As they walked ever deeper into the swamp, the coppery smell of blood grew stronger.

Their wet pathway doubled back again, then suddenly opened up to a small clearing. On any other day, the clearing would have been a discovery worth celebrating. Though still damp, grass covered the clearing's ground, green and fresh. A large log from a fallen tree rested peacefully on the right side of the open space, a single yellow flower growing out from one of its knots. A perfect thinking spot. Staring at that log reminded Pooh of something. What that "something" was, he didn't know. It flitted at the edge of his conscious thought.

He pushed it away, choosing instead to focus on the horror in the center of the clearing.

With a deep breath, Pooh looked down at what remained of the porcupine named Pavel.

The gentle little fellow never stood a chance. Though Pooh still didn't know why Pavel had traveled so far away from his home in the woods, that detail could be left for rumination at another time. Under the Heffalump's Sky, all that mattered was the death of another resident of the Hundred Acre Wood.

Whomever had reported the death had the right of it. The scene looked all too familiar. This definitely had the fingerprints of the Cult of Silence.

Pavel lay in the center of a circle drawn out in the earth. The staging never changed, though the location always did. Whether in soggy grass, or the undergrowth of the woods, or the soil of a farm, the symbol never changed.

Dug unto the ground, maybe by someone's heel, or with a thick stick, Pooh knew once they moved Pavel's body, they'd see the full picture. Two curves, like seams of a baseball, would show near the outer edges of the circle. Those two lines would touch the ends of an inset eye. Pooh took another breath, hoping it would calm the honeybees in his stomach. It didn't.

"Bother," he said, voice barely above a whisper. He cleared his throat. "Okay. Piglet, I need to know who reported the crime." When no response came, Pooh looked over his shoulder and found the young D.I. staring at the mutilated body of the porcupine. His friend's eyes held a far-away quality, as they looked not at the scene, but at the past.

Piglet blinked, shook is head, and sniffed back the tears threatening to escape. "S-s-s-s-sorry, P-p-p-p-pooh. I, uh . . . I got lost for a minute." He tapped his head. "Up here. Pavel's the same size . . ."

"I see." And Pooh *did* see. The corpse looked awfully close to that of Piglet's father. It was the size more than the actual appearance. The poor D.I. had probably imagined his father splayed out just like the porcupine. "Piglet, you can still—"

"No." Piglet's words had a sliver of steel in them. Just a sliver, but steel all the same. "The uh . . . the one who reported it was Breeze. The bear. She's the p-p-p-p-painter. I guess she was out here looking for a scene to paint and stumbled on . . ." Piglet trailed off and waved a hand at the display.

Pooh looked around the clearing, and at the end opposite the fallen log, near another pathway, lay an abandoned easel and a sodden, blank canvas. The story made sense, at least on the surface.

Now the part Pooh had dreaded.

He took his time walking to the clearing's center, eyes scanning for footprints. As with the other scenes, there were none. The Cult left nothing behind other than their symbol and a body. They'd been dubbed the Cult of Silence for leaving nothing behind . . . not even a whisper. Even walking slowly, Pooh stood at the border of the symbol too quickly for his own liking. His feet stopped right at the outer edge, unwilling to cross the threshold of their own accord.

Up close, the smell of death drifted to his well-trained nose. There were two things Pooh could recognize by smell with absolute accuracy: honey, and blood. Unfortunately, it took a lot longer to dispel the scent of the latter.

The porcupine lay on his back, eyes staring sightlessly into the heavens. Hopefully the heavens where he now lived. They would be a far sight better than here in the Wood. The little animal's arms were raised above his head, palms overlapping and held in place by a single, sharpened stick. By itself, the stick wouldn't have been enough to immobilize the little guy, even knowing Pavel's timid nature. *Post-mortem, then. Bother, and double-bother.* Pooh wanted this to be anything but the Cult of Silence, but the scene seemed determined to thwart him.

Likewise the porcupine's feet were staked into the soft ground. His body perfectly filled the inside of the cultish circle, hands touching the top of the inscribed lines and feet the bottom. All the poor boy's quills had been plucked and left in a neat pile in the bottom left of the circle. His organs formed an equally tidy pile in the upper right.

Everything about the death came across as clean. The cut vertically opening the whole torso. The slice in the neck—the likely cause of death. The lack of blood spray. Not for the first time, Pooh wondered if the denizens of the Woods had been killed elsewhere, then brought to their ultimate location to pose. In the beginning, both he and Piglet had thought as much, but the theory never rang true to the D.C.I.

In his gut, Pooh knew they were posed where they were killed. Somehow, the killer—or *killers*—controlled the scene. But how, he didn't know.

Pooh stepped into the circle, then gently reached down, running his paw over Pavel's eyelids to close them. No more would the porcupine have to see this cruel world. No more would he suffer. Next, Pooh lifted the hands, stake still skewered through them. Then he slid the carved stick free from the flesh. As he'd expected, and just like all the deaths those years ago, the stick was neatly whittled to remove all bark and off-shooting stems. Its lower end sharpened to a wicked point, the wooden spike had passed easily through the victim's palms. Pooh set it softly on the damp grass, to the lower left of the circle.

Pooh's paws hovered over the gaping body cavity for a moment, shaking. He could do nothing about that emptiness. Instead he crossed Pavel's arms over his torso, obscuring most of the red hole. Pooh pulled the stake from the feet and lay it next to its blood-stained twin.

Standing, the D.C.I. moved to the body's left side and bent down to roll it. Even though he knew what would be there, he had to make sure. As he slid his hands under the body, Piglet's own appeared near the corpse's feet. Pooh's friend said nothing, and he hadn't heard the little fellow approach. Together, and without a word, they rolled the body over.

Pooh saw two things. First, red meat where a large patch of skin had been flayed from Pavel's back. Just like all the others. Then he saw an eye, dug into the grass and dirt, staring up at them. Again, just like all the others.

"No mistaking this S-s-s-s-sir. The Cult is back." Piglet looked over his shoulder in the direction of the center of the Woods. "We need to warn people. Tell them to watch out for each other."

"You're right, of course. But I have to say, Piglet . . . I . . . I just don't know what the goal is here. These are obviously sacrifices. But to who?"

"Or *what*?"

Pooh nodded in acceptance. "Indeed, Piglet. A very good clarification. Who, or what, benefits?"

"I don't know, P-p-p-p-pooh. I just don't know anymore. And this body isn't t-t-t-t-telling us any stories. Not any good ones, at any rate. Maybe we—"

"Hold that thought, Piglet." Pooh reached down into the grass and plucked a small, fluttering object previously hidden in the grass pressed flat under the body."

"What is it, Pooh?"

Pooh held up a feather. A distinctive feather. An *owl's* feather. "I'd say it's our first real clue in three years."

———

No one liked visiting Owl.

This hadn't always been the case. Pooh thought back over the last several years. When had the change come? When had wise, old Owl become the creature of darkness? When had madness overtaken that denizen of the trees? Once, years ago, Pooh had made the regular trip into the woods to visit the old codger. Back when Christopher Robin still came 'round.

But that boy hadn't come by in years, leaving the Woods to suffer in his absence. He'd disappeared at least a year before the Cult killings. Simply left one day, and never returned.

Pooh pushed thoughts of his old friend away.

Owl.

The once sunlit canopy of branches no longer held the feeling of hope and knowledge. At least . . . at least not the knowledge Pooh or any sane bear would seek. Owl had taken to locking himself in his treehouse, beak buried deep in old tomes filled with arcane symbols.

No, the sun no longer touched these trees. It failed to penetrate the dense leaves above, and the forest floor now resembled more of a hedge maze of brambles and fallen logs. The once clear pathways now looked more like the forest ground after an apocalypse.

And perhaps, Pooh thought, *that's exactly what the Hundred Acre Wood is going through.*

"Piglet," Pooh said, "has the world ended, and we just didn't notice?"

Piglet didn't answer for a long time. They wound their way through the trails. It seemed to Pooh that all the trails in the Woods were trending this way. Winding, overgrown, and not necessarily leading to the destination a traveler wanted.

"To be honest, Pooh. I think my world ended three years ago. I'm just caught in the current . . . like a floating stick."

"I'm sorry, Piglet. I didn't mean to dredge up those memories."

"You hardly have to try these d-d-d-d-days." Piglet smiled, small and sad. "I never really forgot, you know? It's hard to forget."

"Piglet you don't have to—"

The diminutive D.I. held up a hand to cut Pooh off. "No. Let me g-g-g-g-get this out. Pooh, you never forget something like that. Coming home from a nice walk to find four circles carved into the soil of the garden. One for each member of the family. Mother, father, and both sisters. Just like what we saw in the Floody Place. For months—*months*, Pooh—I saw that scene every time I closed my eyes. Then it was every week. Then every month. I hadn't relived that nightmare for months, Pooh. And then today . . ."

Pooh didn't say a word. This was the most his friend had spoken about that fateful day in . . . well, ever.

"The Cult of Silence," Piglet finally continued. "I wish they weren't so silent. I wish they made noise. Without sound, without warning . . . it makes them so much worse. I wish . . . I wish Christopher Robin were here. Maybe he'd s-s-s-s-see something we are missing."

"I wish he were here too."

The overgrown undergrowth led to the base of a massive tree and the start of a grand, wooden staircase leading up into the dark above.

On rickety, rotting steps they climbed. Wooden planks creaked with the slightest pressure, and fragments of wood flaked and fell away. At the start of the climb, Pooh hardly noticed. But the higher the two walked, the more the prospect of falling intruded on the bear's thoughts. He paused to rest, leaning against the trunk of the great tree, then took a moment to look down. Maybe the light played tricks on his perception, but from where he stood, he saw only darkness below. Above he saw the same. No ground below, yet no sky above.

Just unrelenting darkness.

"P-p-p-p-pooh . . . I feel like these stairs have multiplied on us." Piglet's voice didn't raise above a whisper. Out of fear, or maybe dread, Pooh couldn't be sure. But his small friend had the right of it.

"I think it's a spell of some sort, Piglet. The last time I was here, Owl was practically swimming in old grimoires. I didn't think much of it at the time . . . but now . . . but now, I don't know."

"Do you think he's . . . you know?"

Pooh shrugged. "Maybe. But something is bothersome." He stepped away from the edge overlooking the void below, crossed his arms, and tapped at the side of his head. "Think, think, think. Think, think, think. Piglet . . . how many murders were there three years ago?" A painful question to ask the D.I., but a needed one.

Piglet frowned and sat down on the step. "Let me s-s-s-s-see." He counted out on his fingers, the number reaching higher than Pooh would have liked. "I think . . . nineteen? Plus the one today makes twenty. And we d-d-d-d-don't know if the deaths three years ago marked the first set of sacrifices. Back when it was the Thousand Acre Wood, folks just disappeared. We always assumed they moved away, but what if they didn't."

"I find I agree with you, Piglet. What if the Cult of Silence has been around for years and years. And the Wood used to be so big, we never found the bodies? And we never knew a cult existed because they were so . . . so . . ."

"Silent?" Piglet supplied the word when Pooh trailed off.

"Yes. But Piglet, surely Christopher Robin would have known?"

"Maybe." The D.I. stood, and looked up at the spiraling staircase. He shifted the rifle slung over his shoulder. "I just d-d-d-d-don't know anymore, Pooh. Do you have any smokes on you? I could use one."

"Piglet, you don't smoke."

"I do today."

Pooh nodded. He could hardly blame the little fellow. Reaching into the inside pocket of his trenchcoat, Pooh pulled out a small bundle of cigarettes. Dried carrot leaves from Rabbit's garden mixed with granulated honey. Pooh had hand-wrapped them himself with paper marinated in aged honey-ale he stored in his basement. The good stuff. Christopher Robin had never approved of the habit, but the boy had lost all rights to judge when he'd stopped visiting.

He passed one to Piglet, then stuck one into the corner of his own mouth. He patted at his coat pockets, heart sinking as he feared he'd left his matches at the office. A small rattle in his breast-pocket drew a sigh of relief. He fished out the small box of matches, and shook it again. The sound resonating from the inside seemed feeble. Fragile, even. When Pooh slid it open, he saw only six tiny sticks remained.

Striking one on the tree, Pooh held it out to Piglet first, then lit his own and took a deep drag. The burn of the honey felt good in his lungs. He held out the cigarette and studied its glowing tip. Somehow it reassured him. He puffed out a perfect smoke ring: the only thing perfect in this otherwise imperfect day.

Piglet pulled hard on his own smoke like he'd done it a thousand times before. Like he had the same, long habit Pooh could never quite kick. The D.I.'s eyes held deep bags under them, and his tiny hands trembled. But the honeyed smoke seemed to calm his frayed nerves. Piglet nodded once, and Pooh took it for the signal that his friend was now prepared to soldier on.

Whatever the cause—smoke, honey, or the moment taken to clear their minds —the darkness above resolved, and the endless stairs stopped their multiplying. Three times more around the trunk led them to a wooden porch anchored to the great tree with large, metal spikes. *Have those always been metal?* Pooh peered closer and saw bizarre runes etched into them. *No. Definitely new. Bother. This doesn't bode well.* He held his paw to his lips to indicated the need for silence, and drew his Webley. Piglet pulled the slung rifle around, bracing it against his shoulder.

The front door to Owl's treehouse stood partially open, dead still. Pressure built around Pooh's ears, cutting off even the minutest of sounds. He reached out and passed his paw through a low-hanging branch of leaves. Nothing. No sound at all. He looked down at his companion and tapped an ear, then held up a paw in question.

Piglet should his head.

Pooh's eyes darted about. High, low, behind. With no sound, the worry of being snuck up on clawed its way to the front of his awareness. The whole house felt like a crypt. Motionless in eternal slumber. But Pooh wasn't fooled. He knew, when it came to otherworldly nightmares, the dead rarely kept still for long.

He pushed the door open the rest of the way. It could have squealed, but he'd never have known. Inside, Owl's home lay dark, illuminated only by the feeble light from outside and the tiny flickering flames from a few candles surviving on the last life of their wicks. Pooh wished they'd thought to bring torches, but Owl's home had always been so bright before. Or at least it had always seemed that way. The once tidy abode now had every surface covered with scatted papers and tomes. Stone tablets engraved with nausea-inducing symbols lined the walls, and the wall themselves had other runes, words, and flowers carved into them at every level. The flowers depicted were the same as the one in the stump at the murder scene.

With his off-hand, Pooh waved Piglet to cover the left side of the room while he took the right. The black mouth of an open door further in pulsed sickly yellow, just for a moment. The two friends froze, firearms raised. Yellow light shone dully again, not bright enough to be seen outside the home, but somehow still bright enough to illuminate the room beyond.

A pedestal. A large tome—bigger than Pooh himself—sat open on it. So large was the book that even the figure of Owl standing between the investigators and the book stand couldn't completely block their view.

Owl stood motionless, yet in the moments lit in yellow, his feathers stirred in a breeze unfelt by the D.C.I.

Pooh crept up on his old friend. Old habits and scars bubbled up to the surface. Paranoia and stress from old conflicts and horrors in the past. Normally, Pooh would have shoved them down like all soldiers do. But today he let those feelings push away the dread of putting a bullet in the back of Owl's feathered head.

Pooh didn't know what gave them away. Perhaps the squeak of a floorboard he couldn't hear in the unnatural silence. Maybe both he and Piglet were breathing harder than they realized. Or maybe Owl had a spell set in place to warn him of all manner of intruders. Whatever the cause, Pooh's heart froze when Owl's head slowly turned completely around to stare at them, locking both the detectives in place.

Once, Owl's feathers—the same feather Pooh held in an evidence bag inside a coat pocket—had shone in both sun and moonlight. Lustrous and golden-brown. Neatly groomed with nary a feather out of place. But now . . . now Pooh could scarcely recognize his old friend. Those once-neat feathers looked drab in the low light. Broken and frayed ends tangled together.

But Owl's eyes were worst of all. They'd once been pools of wisdom and wit, deep with color. Now, they were nothing but black mirrors.

Until they lit up with yellow sickness.

The horrible, unnatural light leaked from Owl's eyes. Tears of madness and pain. Pooh felt tears spring into his own eyes as he fought against some eldritch force attempting to keep him frozen. Maybe this was how all the other victims had been taken without conflict. Without a sound. *The Cult of Silence, indeed.*

Owl's mouth opened, moving as words spilled from it. Pooh couldn't read lips, even at the best of times, and no one could read beaks. Even as Pooh's pistol raised inch by inch, something in him screamed to stop. To *listen.*

In Pooh's experience, a good detective made their own luck. Hard work and harder observation led to finding clues a lesser investigator would have missed. Pooh hadn't always been the best. Christopher Robin had taught him a thing or two, but nothing compared to the school of experience. He'd failed at more investigations than most other detectives had ever been involved in.

Call it luck, or maybe he'd been aware of what he was doing at an instinctual level, but at that moment his cigarette saved him.

The burning stub of honeyed paper caught the edge of his lip, searing his flesh. The pain of the moment jolted Pooh from the spell holding him in place. Sound crashed down on him in a cacophonous avalanche. Not just the words now being spoken by Owl, but all the sounds of the past few minutes since ascending to the top of the outer staircase. Each and every earlier sound hit at once in a flood, threatening to drown him.

Ears ringing, Pooh dropped to a knee. To his left, Piglet still struggled against the sorcerous mechanism holding him in near stasis.

As Pooh's ears cleared, Owl's words clarified, though they sounded like they came from a great distance.

"I'm sorry, Pooh. I'm so sorry. I can't . . . I can't hold him back any longer. Can you hear me Pooh?"

Owl's words didn't match the movement of his beak, and though no actual tears streamed down Owl's face, the sounds of weeping filled the room.

"Owl?" Pooh's own voice came hoarse, like he'd been screaming. Maybe he had.

"Pooh? Pooh, can you hear me? You must run. You must take everyone and run. He's coming."

"Who is coming, Owl?"

The distant howling of wind threatened to carry Owl's voice away. "Pooh? I'm so sorry. I tried. I tried to hold him at bay. I tried to keep him away all these years. I tried all the right spells. Ones filled with light. But none worked. So I resorted to his own magic. It kept him away at first. But really it just allowed him in."

"Who, Owl? *Who?*"

Though unshown on Owl's face, Pooh swore he *heard* a sad smile. "I can barely hear you, old friend. But you are here all the same, and for that, I am grateful. Who? Another time I'd make an owl joke at you . . . but I'm afraid my time is short. He comes Pooh. The Prince. The Prince in Yellow. To rule over the Wood. To make them his own for ever and ever. To stay young forever and prepare the way for the King."

Pooh stretched a hand out to grab the owl.

"No! You mustn't!" Owl's sharp voice arrested Pooh's movement. "I've tried to keep back the summoning as long as I could. I left you a clue. But I can't keep him away anymore. Pooh . . . please . . . end me before it's too late."

"End you?" Pooh stared up at Owl, knowing what was being asked. "I . . . I don't know that I can."

"Then you doom everyone here. You'll all end up like poor Pavel. I had no choice, Pooh. My body is not my own anymore. It's *His*. He made me take that poor porcupine to the Floody Place. There is a great, dark power there. I'm the Cult of Silence, Pooh. Me. I—"

A great scream tore from Owl's throat, ripping into the darkness. The yellow pulsing came quicker now, signaling the approach of this Prince in Yellow who so terrified Owl.

Time slowed to a stand-still for Pooh. He saw the single tear at the corner of Piglet's eye. He saw the unhallowed wind stirring Owl's feathers even harder than before. He saw, in his mind's eye, the Hundred Acre Wood consumed in yellow fire, and its denizens laid out in rows.

"Please," Owl's voice whispered, even as his beak moved in phrases summoning destruction.

Pooh raised the Webley, and fired all six shots into Owl's body.

It should have ended there.

Pooh looked up at the treehouse. Light now flooded the woods, and the undergrowth no longer pressed in on him or Piglet as they walked slowly away. A normal length staircase climbed a largely average tree. At the impact of the sixth shot, the spell broke, and Piglet fell to his knees. Owl slumped forward, his body covering the arcane tome, blood painting its open pages and the wall behind.

"Pooh, wait." Piglet stopped in the middle of the trail. "We just . . . we just left him up there."

"We did."

"Doesn't he deserve better? He may have killed Pavel, and there's even a chance he killed my family . . . but . . ."

"But what, Piglet?"

"But it wasn't his fault. If we believe his words, he was controlled. He was our friend P-p-p-p-pooh. Our f-f-f-f-friend."

Pooh sighed and looked up again at the house. In truth, Pooh meant to come back after taking Piglet home. Not to bury his old friend above, but to burn it all to the ground. Death carried more permanence when reduced to ash.

But maybe his small D.I. was right.

"What do you have in mind, Piglet?"

"I'll go collect some flowers. The yellow ones he so liked. Go put them on his body. Maybe we can come back later and bury him. Dismantle the home. I doubt anyone should live there anymore."

"Very well, Piglet. Go gather the flowers. I'll wait here. I . . . I'm not sure I can go up those stairs again."

Piglet smiled and wandered off into the woods.

Pooh found a nearby log and sat on it. His legs nearly gave way as he sat down. He pulled out the Webley and studied it as it sat in his hand. He'd never dreamed he'd one day have to turn it against a friend. But it had been for the best.

Hadn't it?

Even though the case was closed, it didn't feel finished. Something nagged at Pooh's detective sense. The Prince in Yellow. It had an ominous sound to it.

Yellow.

Pooh's grow furrowed in thought.

Flowers.

Yellow flowers.

As Piglet had said, they were Owl's favorite. And he'd left them at the murder scene, and drawn them on his walls. Pooh thought back to the other murders. He couldn't be positive, but he thought he remembered a yellow flower at each scene. A calling card? A clue?

Yes. A clue.

Think, think, think.

What had Owl said there at the end? *I left you a clue.* Pooh had thought it to be the feather. But what if the real clue had been the flower? A clue that should have pointed Pooh to Owl years ago. Because he loved those flowers so much. They'd been Owl's favorite ever since the day Christopher Robin had—

Pooh's eyes went wide.

"Oh . . . oh no. It wasn't Owl."

At that moment, Owl's house exploded outward in a flash of putrid yellow light tinged with black lightening. The shockwave lifted Pooh and threw him back dozens of feet to crash into a gnarled tree.

Pooh's head swam from the impact, and he had trouble blinking the stars from his eyes. Debris rained down around him, lighting the surrounding foliage in dirty, yellow flames.

"Silly old bear."

Ice seized in Pooh's veins. Those words. Words he'd longed to hear for three years, but which now filled him with terror.

Pooh's vision cleared, and when he looked up, haloed in yellow was the floating form of Christopher Robin. He wore a cloak that looked to be made from stitched together pieces of cloth. Pooh blinked.

Not cloth. Not cloth at all.

Skin.

In the shimmering heat coming off Christopher Robin, Pooh saw the skin and pelts of all the animals who'd died as sacrifices. He could pick out who each patch had once belonged to. He even saw a patch that still had the porcupine quills on it from poor Pavel. Pooh'd never understood the flayed skin, and he and Piglet had never shared that detail around. But now Pooh understood. In that cloak, he saw dozens of victims, including those which they'd all assumed had moved away.

Why had they all assumed as much? Because in many cases, Christopher Robin had said so.

"No," Pooh said. "This can't be true."

"Don't be silly, Pooh." The boy's voice was light. Jovial. His eyes glowed bright yellow under the hood of the cloak. "It *is* so good to see you again, old friend. I've missed you terribly." Christopher Robin floated lower to the ground, but his feet never touched the soil beneath. In his hand, he held Owl's head. "Poor Owl. He didn't realize I'd made him my vessel."

The boy coughed then, wet and thick, and when he wiped his mouth with the corner of his cloak, red blood stain his lips. Pooh's old friend still wore the light blue shirt he'd been dressed in the last time they'd seen each other three years earlier. But red, spreading splotches marred the blue of the fabric. Six red stains, in total.

When I shot Owl, I shot Christopher Robin. Six shots, but twelve hits on old, beloved friends.

The boy grimaced in pain. Pain a self-styled god shouldn't feel.

"Sorry, Pooh. Your trusty, old Webley. A good pistol. Any sooner, and you would have killed both me and my vessel."

"His name was 'Owl.'"

"So it was, my old friend." Christopher coughed again, more violently. "As it was, I fear you wounded me."

Pooh drew the pistol and pulled the trigger as fast as his paw would allow. Nothing happened. In the aftermath of Owl's death, he hadn't reloaded. "Bother."

"A good try, old bear. And you might have finished me off. I had hoped to have you with me, Pooh. Ruling beside me, forever." He lifted on corner of the cloak. "These sacrifices are just the start, but we can both live for eternity, Pooh. Just you and me . . . at least until my father, the King in Yellow, comes."

"I'm afraid not," Pooh said.

"A pity," the boy said. "Then I'm afraid I'll have to make a sacrifice of you, silly old bear. You'll have to suffice. After all, coming all this way, using all the blood split in my name . . . well, to let myself die would be a terrible waste." Christopher stuck out his bottom lip in a small pout, but then immediately brightened. "Fortunately, you're here all alone. Just for me."

Alone? So he didn't see us through Owl's eyes?

"I didn't want to involve anyone else coming here," Pooh said.

"Imagine my surprise upon waking up, and finding my best friend waiting for me. Almost like it was meant to be. Aren't you happy to see your best friend here again, Pooh?"

"I only have one best friend," Pooh said, a grim smile forming on his lips. "And I'm afraid you aren't him."

"What do you mean I'm—"

The roar of Piglet's rifle interrupted the boy, and a corresponding chunk of meat blew free from Christopher's chest. Red blood sprayed, covering Pooh's face. The boy hit the ground, clawing at the massive wound.

Pooh got to his feet and limped to the boy's side. His yellow eyes bored holes into the bear.

"P-p-p-p-pooh . . ." Christopher said. "You . . . you . . . silly . . . old . . . bear . . ."

Piglet's small shadow fell over their old friend. A thin line of smoke drifted up from barrel of his rifle. His face emotionless, and him lips set in a thin line, Piglet pointed a steady, unwavering gun down at the boy's face.

Without a stutter, Piglet said, "This is for my family, *old friend.*"

He pulled the trigger.

Pooh and Piglet limped away from the woods. Red flames washed away the yellow ones brought by their old friend, and new enemy. No one would set foot in this area of the Hundred Acre Wood again.

Neither spoke, but Pooh saw his truest friend walking with more steel in his spine.

They walked until they found Pooh's favorite thinking spot, and sat against the log there. He pulled out his last remaining honey cigarette, broke it in half, and gave a piece to Piglet. The D.I. took it, smiled and held it out for Pooh's match.

Pooh took a drag of his own, and blew out the smoke. The blue smoke rose up and away.

Up into the retreating Heffalump's Sky.

In Which Pooh Discovers the Secret of the Hunny

Joseph Capdepon II

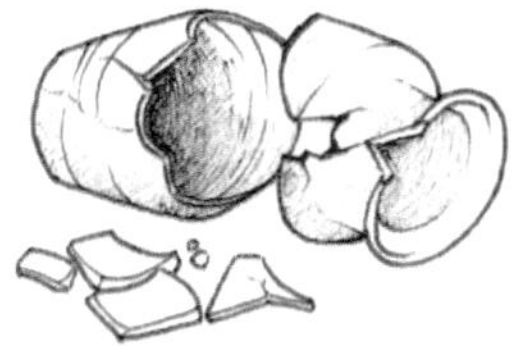

I woke up on the floor, my face sticky, a half-remembered nightmare filled with a bone-numbing buzzing clawed at the back of my mind. I grabbed the hunny pot next to me and pulled it close. My paw dipped into it and came back empty.

"Oh bother," I groaned.

I pushed myself to a sitting position and looked around the room. I couldn't remember how I ended up on the floor, or back here, or where my hunny had gone. I grabbed another jar and shoved my face into it. Empty. All of them empty. I licked the rims of the jars, taking every little bit of crystalized hunny off them that I could.

"You've done it now, Pooh Bear," I muttered. I stood up and kicked at the empty jars. I missed and found myself back on the floor. I had to get up and figure out what happened last night. I picked up one of the empty jars and clutched it tightly in my arm. I needed more hunny, and I knew who I could ask about what happened.

Heavy clouds hung over the Hundred Acre Wood, turning the world grey, and created odd, threatening shadows. I stopped, the door behind me open, the empty hunny jar pressed hard against my body, and stared out at the cold, grey woods.

"I don't know," I muttered to the hunny jar. "What if Piglet isn't home? What if he's at Owl's or Eeyore's?"

The empty jar stared back at me in silent accusation.

"No, you're right. Piglet doesn't go out on his own. He'll be waiting for me. Then we can go get more hunny together!"

A short walk later, I found myself in front of Piglet's door. I knocked and no one answered. The empty hunny jar stared at me, and I scowled. Where was Piglet? I knocked again and called out his name, but still no answer. I decided to try the door knob and it was unlocked. How very odd. Piglet never left his door unlocked. He was too frightened of Heffalumps coming in uninvited, even though Owl told him that he didn't have to worry about Heffalumps, as none lived in the Hundred Acre Wood.

I pushed the door open and walked inside.

"Piglet! Where are you? I need your help!"

I heard a noise coming from his cupboard and investigated. Inside, wrapped in a blanket, with a frying pan held in his paw, I found Piglet.

"Pooh! Oh dear, I'm so glad it's you," Piglet cried. "It was terrible. I didn't know what to do."

"What are you talking about, Piglet? What's so terrible?"

I pulled Piglet from the cupboard and we made our way over to his chairs.

"The Heffalumps! They came! I knew it. Owl lied. The Heffalumps do exist and they're here, in the Hundred Acre Wood."

"When did they come, Piglet?"

"They were here before you got here," Piglet said. He looked around his home, his eyes wild. I gripped the empty hunny jar, worried that Piglet would hurt it. I couldn't let him hurt the precious jar. What would I carry the hunny in?

"I didn't see any on my way here, Piglet. There's nothing out in the Wood except trees, grass, leaves, and the wind. I'd have seen them if they were here."

"That's what you think, Pooh. They are here, in the shadows. Hiding and waiting." Piglet grabbed an unlit lantern, lit the wick, and placed it in a corner of the room where there had been a slight shadow. "I won't let them get in this time, Pooh. If there aren't any shadows, they can't get in."

I looked around for the first time since I'd walked in. There were lit lanterns everywhere. Piglet had tried to cover every part of the room with light to keep the shadows away.

"Do you want to go with me for a walk, Piglet? There's no shadows outside. You can come with me to Owl's."

"No shadows?" Piglet walked over to the window, pulled the curtain back, and looked outside. "Yes, Pooh, I can do that. What do you need from Owl?"

I showed him my empty hunny jar.

"I need more hunny. I've run out."

"But Pooh, you know how and where to get hunny."

"There were problems last time, Piglet. Don't you remember? Owl said the next time I needed hunny, to come to him and he'd help me. I'd hate to get stuck again."

I waited while Piglet readied himself. I felt my hunger as it grew. I'd looked around his pantry for any hunny, but Piglet was never one for the hunny. He hungered for other things. We exited Piglet's home and walked into the wood toward Owl's.

While I had been in Piglet's, the clouds had gotten heavier, and the sky threatened rain. I looked back, half expecting a Heffalump to pcp out from behind a tree and grab Piglet or myself, but it never happened. I couldn't shake a feeling that maybe Piglet had been correct and the Heffalumps *had* come.

We entered the clearing around Owl's home. I paused for a moment and stared at Owl's home. Something was wrong. Piglet felt it because he stopped next to me, and his body shook in fear.

"Pooh . . ."

There was a shadow in the doorway of Owl's home. Something large. Bigger than Owl and decidedly not Owl shaped. I couldn't move. I tried. I tried to turn and run.

"Piglet, run!" I shouted. Piglet looked at me, his eyes sad, and he smiled.

"I told you they were here, Pooh."

Darkness overwhelmed me.

W*HAT? Where am I?* I remembered trees and Piglet.

It had to be a dream. I found myself back in my home, in bed, but I could not remember how I had gotten there.

I got out of bed and tripped over an empty hunny jar.

"The hunny!" The words seemed loud in my room, and I cowered back from them as they echoed off the walls.

I searched the room for hunny, but all of my jars were empty. I did not find one drop of that delicious golden liquid inside any of them. I must have licked them clean, as not even a drop remained inside any of the jars.

This all felt familiar, as though I'd done it before. I must have eaten all of the hunny last night and fallen asleep. I looked for my coat and picked up one of the jars.

"Piglet will help. We'll go to Owl and he'll tell me how to get more hunny."

I stepped outside, and the world was gray and dreary. It looked and smelled like rain. I went back and grabbed my raincoat and an umbrella. Piglet hated getting wet.

Before long, I found myself outside Piglet's home. I stomped up to the door and banged on it with my free paw.

"Piglet! Hey Piglet, it's Pooh!"

"G . . . g . . . g . . . go away, Pooh!" Piglet cried from inside.

"Piglet, what's wrong? Let me in." I tried his door knob but it was locked. "Come on. It's Pooh, and it looks like it is about to rain."

"No, Pooh, I can't. I can't do it." Piglet cried. "Go away. Leave me alone. If you don't, they'll come."

"Who's going to come?"

"The Heffalumps. They are out there. I need you to leave me alone, Pooh. Go away. Please, go away."

I stared at his door, the empty hunny jar held tight against my body.

"Piglet . . . Piglet, please let me in." I knocked on the door. Pressed myself against it. "Piglet, it's going to rain, and I forgot my umbrella. Will you let me in before I get wet?"

Thunder rumbled in the distance, and I heard a squeak from inside. The door opened and a disheveled Piglet stood in the doorway, his eyes wide and bloodshot.

"Piglet, what's wrong," I began, but he pushed me away from the door and slammed it behind him. We stood on his door step as the rain began to fall.

"You've got to go, Pooh. Go to Owl, before it's too late. I can't. Not again. Not again. Please don't make me."

I looked at him, confused. I didn't know what he was talking about, but I could tell that fear had gripped him tightly.

"What is it, Piglet? Why can't you what? I don't understand."

He looked at the hunny jar in my arm, and his eyes went wide. He grabbed for it, and I moved backward out of his reach. He stumbled and fell to the muddy ground.

"It's the hunny, Pooh. You've got to stop eating the hunny."

Stop eating the hunny? He had to be mad. How could I stop eating hunny?

"Piglet, I think you need to go lay down. I think you may be sick. I'll go to Owl and see if he will come check on you. He'll know what to do."

Piglet backed up to his door and opened it. The flicker of lamplight inside spilled out around him.

"You do that, Pooh. Go find Owl, but I'm not going. They won't get me again."

He backed into his house and closed the door. I heard him lock it and lock it and lock it. Thunder rumbled overhead, and I looked up as the rain slapped me in the face. Whatever had been wrong with Piglet, I could deal with later. Owl would help, but first I needed more hunny. My stomach rumbled at the thought of that thick, golden liquid. I opened my umbrella and started toward Owl's house.

The rain beat against the umbrella as I walked up to Owl's house. A warm light shone inside, and I saw Owl standing at a window watching the rain. I raised my umbrella in greeting, but Owl turned away and disappeared. A moment later, he appeared at his door and opened it.

"Well, you silly bear, are you going to stand in the rain, or will you come inside?"

I walked inside, left my umbrella by the door, and found my way to one of the comfy chairs Owl had. A fire roared in the fire place, which pushed back the chill I felt from my walk in the rain. Owl walked over and looked at the hunny jar I still held in my arm. He stood next to the fire and stared into it.

"Oh, Pooh, what have you done?"

"I'm not really sure I know what you're talking about, Owl." I looked around and thought that maybe I had broken something on my way in, but everything looked like it always had. I'd tromped water and some mud in, but Owl didn't get upset over such things.

"You've eaten it all, haven't you, Pooh? Every last drop."

"The hunny? Of course I have. I need more." I held out the jar, it's emptiness a challenge to him.

"I saw." He touched it with one of his wings. "You've eaten quite a bit of it, haven't you? Every jar you had, I imagine."

"All of it. I need more, and I know you could help me. Piglet wouldn't come though."

"No, I imagine he wouldn't," Owl said. "He should have, as this would have been much easier, but we will make do, won't we."

Owl motioned for me to follow him, and I did. We walked to the back of his house and out the door into the dusk. Lightning tore across the sky and thunder rumbled, but the rain had stopped. Owl moved off into the darkened wood and I followed.

"Do you remember the way, Pooh?" Owl called to me. "Do you remember where the hunny is?"

I look up and the shadows had gathered around Owl.

Darkness engulfed me.

I jerked awake, the empty jar of hunny held tightly against my body. I looked around, my eyes blurry, and discovered I was not at home. I did not know where had I ended up, but a noise interrupted my musing as someone banged at the door.

I found myself at Owl's house, but I could not remember what happened. We'd talked about hunny and Piglet and then darkness had overwhelmed me.

"Owl? Owl!" I called out as he would never leave me alone, but he didn't answer me. Someone banged hard on the door. When I pulled the door open, Piglet stood there, the rain dripped off him, his feet and legs muddy.

"Pooh, where's Owl?"

"I don't know, Piglet. I woke up on the floor. We were talking about hunny, and then I woke up. Do you think he went to get me hunny? I'm getting so very hungry."

Piglet pushed around me and walked around Owl's house. He looked into the closets and cupboards, under the bed, behind doors, and finally sat in one of the big comfy chairs with a defeated sigh.

"It doesn't matter," Piglet muttered. "They'll take us all, and there's nothing we can do."

"What are you talking about?" I asked Piglet. He turned to me, his eyes wide with anger and fear.

"Idiot bear," Piglet stood up, his face screwed up in rage. "Don't you get it? Don't you remember it? Any of it? It's your fault. You and that damnable hunny jar."

Piglet lunged for the hunny jar, but I turned and he bounced off of me. I stepped back as he picked himself up from the floor.

"Piglet, what's wrong? Why are you acting like this?"

"I hoped that Owl would have fixed it, but I guess he didn't. What happened to Owl, Pooh?"

"I don't know!" I screamed at Piglet. "I was here, we were talking about hunny, and then everything went dark. I woke up on the floor with you pounding on the door."

"What'd you do, Pooh? Where's Owl?"

Piglet had moved toward me, his timidity gone, his face screwed up in a rictus of rage. He charged me, and I brought the hunny jar down on his head as he passed me. It bounced off with a dull bong, and I almost lost hold of it, but it did not break. Piglet sprawled on to the ground with a grunt and lay still. I didn't know what had gotten in to him, but he had never acted like that before.

I found some rope, used it to tie Piglet up, and then sat in one of the chairs and waited for him to wake up. I heard his breathing change and he started to snore. I thought about taking a nap, but then Piglet started to stir. His eyes opened, and I could see the confusion in them.

"Pooh, what's happening? Why am I on the floor?" He struggled against the rope. "Pooh, why am I tied up?"

"It's okay Piglet, I had to. You tried to attack me."

"What are you talking about? I wouldn't attack you."

"Piglet, why else would I tie you up? You showed up here at Owl's, started screaming at me, then tried to attack me."

"Can you untie me Pooh?" he asked. "I . . . I don't know what happened before, but I'm good now."

I hugged the hunny jar close to myself and watched Piglet. He looked like the Piglet I knew, the one who helped me find hunny, and all of our other adventures we had gone on over the years. I stepped toward him.

"I don't know Piglet. Why'd you get so angry with me? What is it that Owl was supposed to fix?

"I'm not angry with you Pooh. You don't understand what's happening, or what's been happening. That's why it chose you, but we've got to stop it, and you have to help."

"Who chose me for what?" I asked. "I wake up, and I try to get more hunny. That's all I know. You won't help me, so I came to get Owl's help, and now he's gone and you're here. What is going on, Piglet?"

"Not who, Pooh. What," Piglet said, saddened. "You've got to let me go, Pooh. Hurry, before It gets here. Before it starts it all again."

"What are you talking about, Piglet?"

I heard a noise behind me. Piglet's eyes grew wide, and he strained against his bonds. I turned, and shadows exploded into the room. As the darkness engulfed me, I heard Piglet wail in terror.

When I woke up, everything was different. Piglet's wail of terror still echoed in my ears, and I found myself outside, the night sky clear. I looked up and stared at the stars. The ground felt soft against my back, and for a moment, I forget everything as I looked up at the stars. But then I felt it pressed against me. The cold hardness of the hunny jar. The empty hunny jar.

I pushed myself to my feet and picked the jar up. The emptiness of it mocked me. I could taste the hunny if I closed my eyes. That sweet, thick nectar covered every inch of my tongue. I was outside of Owl's, but I don't remember coming here, but I do remember Owl as he stood there and talked to me before the darkness overwhelmed us both.

"Owl!" I shouted, but Owl did not answer. His home looked empty. "Piglet?"

The empty house seemed to stare at me, and Piglet's wail echoed in my head again. I saw him, frightened, terrorized, and I did not know what to do.

"No, I'll find Piglet at home I'm sure. Curled up with a book and a cup of tea," I whispered to myself. I repeated it, louder, as I had a hard time believing it. I ventured into Owl's home, but found no one there. No signs that anyone had been there, and no hunny. I left and headed to Piglet's.

When I approached, I could see the flicker of light behind his curtains. I knocked on the door and stood there, but no one answered. I tried the door knob, and the door swung open. I took a step inside and fell to my knees, in pain. Piglet's wail of terror pierced through my head, so loudly that I almost dropped the empty hunny jar. I jerked back out of his home, and it stopped.

"Piglet?" I called. "Piglet, are you in there?"

I took a hesitant step inside again, but this time no wail sounded as I stepped over the threshold. I walked farther in, but Piglet did not appear to be home. A lone lamp sat on his table, casting shadows that moved with every flicker of the flame. I stood transfixed and watched them dance on the walls.

As I watched, they began to change, to take more solid shape. I probably should have run, but the thought never crossed my mind. Why would I run away from something that could not harm me? Piglet's wail of terror pierced my mind at that moment, and it knocked me out of my hypnotic state. I could see the danger in those shadows now. The sharp edges. The deep darkness of them. I could feel myself beginning to fall into that darkness.

The hunny jar started to slip from my grasp, and I jerked awake. The shadows were normal again. Simple things cast by the light of the lamp wick. I pulled the hunny jar tightly against me and looked for more lamps to light. I'd make sure the house would be cozy and welcoming for when Piglet returned from whatever errand he had gone out on.

I awoke several hours later, having fallen asleep in his chair. The clock on his wall chimed and chimed and chimed, twelve times.

"Piglet?" I called, but no one answered. Piglet did not stay out late like this. He should have been home, snuggled into his bed. He should have woken me from my slumber in his chair and sent me on my way home. "Now where would you be, Piglet? Did Owl come back, or did you go over to Kanga's or Eeyore's?"

I decided to head back to my own bed for the night, as none of the others would be very happy if I showed up in the dead of night on their doorsteps, even if Piglet were there. My bed beckoned me, with its soft mattress and warm blankets. I blew out the lamps and made sure Piglet's front door locked behind me, then headed to my home.

My front door stood open, and I saw light flickering inside. I knew I had blown out the lamps when I left, so someone had visited me. I approached and pushed the door open.

"Hello?" I called. "Who's here?"

"Pooh?" I head Owl call from inside. "Is that you?"

Owl stood in the middle of the room.

"There you are," Owl said. "I see you still have the hunny jar."

"What happened Owl? Where did you go?"

Owl paced around the room, his wings rustling in nervousness. I sat in a chair, watching him.

"You silly bear," Owl said. He stopped and stared at me. "You don't remember any of it do you?"

"Piglet said similar to me. I don't know what either of you are talking about. All I've wanted since I woke up is hunny. I'm so hungry, Owl. So very hungry."

Owl looked at the empty hunny jars that littered the floor and at the one that I held gripped tightly to my body.

"Yes, the hunny jar. The same one you had earlier when you showed up asking for my help. Why that one, Pooh?" He gestured to all of the empty jars littered around the floor. "Why not one of these?" He stopped, picked up one of the jars, then dropped it. The world seemed to slow down, and I watched in horror as it fell. Watched it hit the ground, watched as the cracks expanded through it, watched as it exploded into a hundred pieces.

A sharp pain exploded in my head, and I screamed. Owl picked another up and dropped it. Another explosion of ceramic as it broke. Another sharp pain exploded in my head. I kept the one in my arm gripped tightly against my body, and watched helplessly as Owl destroyed every jar that littered my floor.

"We've got to change it, Pooh. Stop it—and I think I know how—but you're going to have to give me that hunny jar."

I looked down at the jar in my arm and up at Owl.

"No," I said. I backed away from him. "I need it for the hunny."

"You don't need the hunny Pooh. That's why this all happens. You need to stop and the only way is letting it go. Give it to me, and then we can fix everything."

"I can't," I said. I looked behind me at the door.

"Pooh, don't. We need to stop this, and I need you to help me stop this."

"Stop what, Owl? You haven't explained to me what we are going to stop."

"Give me the hunny jar, Pooh, and I'll explain everything. I'll explain why all of this has been happening, but you have to give me that jar." He reached out. I looked down at the jar, up at him, and then at the door.

"I can't." I ran. He couldn't catch me before I made it out the door. I pulled it shut and heard him slam into it. I ran as hard as I could toward the woods. I glanced back and the door opened. Owl stood silhouetted by the light of the lamps, and I heard my clock as it chimed one.

"This will be easier if you'd help me, Pooh," Owl cried. I watched in awe as he spread his wings, and launched himself into the air. I ran into the woods but I could hear him above me, the steady whoosh as he followed me.

"Pooh, it has been so long since I've flown in the night," Owl called down to me. "It is wonderful to fly again, but it hurts my old bones. Stop, and this will be easier."

I ran through the woods, deeper into the trees, and hoped that Owl would not be able to follow. I stopped to catch my breath, listened, but did not hear him above me. I stopped running and continued at a brisk pace through the woods. Before long, I found that my feet had carried me to Eeyore's home.

"Eeyore?" I called. I walked closer to his stick house and called again, a bit louder. I peeked in, and the house stood empty. A crash echoed in the night behind me, and I spun around. Shadows exploded out of the woods, rushed across the ground, and engulfed me.

Darkness.

THE BUZZING HURT MY HEAD. The incessant, unending buzzing. I sat up with a start, panicked until I touched the hunny jar. I looked around, confused as to where I found myself. Soft light filled the room from a number of lamps on the table near me.

"You're finally awake," Kanga said from behind me. I turned around and she stood there, her face stern and a bit sad.

"Kanga!" I cried. "How?"

"I found you asleep outside of Eeyore's," Kanga said. "You wouldn't happen to know where he is?"

"No. You haven't seen Owl or Piglet have you?" I stood up and pulled the hunny jar against my body. Kanga stared at it and me.

"Not since yesterday," she said. "Where've you been, Pooh?"

"Here in the Wood," I said. "With Piglet, until he disappeared. Then with Owl, but he's mad at me. I've been trying to get more hunny. I'm terribly hungry."

"You were muttering about hunny while you slept," Kanga said. "I tried waking you, but you wouldn't, so I carried you here."

"You don't know where I can get more, do you? I . . . I can't remember. I tried, but I can't. Why can't I remember where the hunny is? Why won't any of you help me find it?"

Kanga backed to the door. It opened, and Owl strode through.

"You're our friend, Pooh Bear. Let us help you," Owl said. "Give me the jar, and we can fix all of this."

"Listen to Owl," Kanga pleaded. "Before it's too late."

"No," I shouted. The shadows on the wall seemed to grow as my anger did. "Leave me be. Why won't you help me? All I want is hunny. Take me to the hunny, and I'll give it to you."

Owl and Kanga looked at one another, their faces filled with sadness.

"We can't do that, Pooh," Owl said. "The hunny is the problem." Owl lunged at me, his wings spread wide, with Kanga behind him. I curled around the jar and waited for him to hit me. We fell to the ground in a tangle of arms, legs, and wings. We rolled about on the ground for a moment until I disentangled myself and stood.

"If you won't help me, I'll find it myself. I know where the bees hide," I shouted at them and ran.

Outside, the sky had lightened as dawn approached. I'd been out all night. I shuddered at the memory of the shadows that had exploded out of the woods before I had passed out, and wondered what they had been.

I ran from Kanga's toward the woods. I stopped and stared at the shadows cast by the early morning sun, and pain ripped through my head. Had the shadows attacked me? I remembered the shadows. I remembered as they came, then the darkness.

What were the shadows? Why were they attacking me?

"I do wish Owl wasn't mad at me so he could help me answer these questions," I said to the hunny jar. "Also, that he'd help me fill you back up. I'm worried that if I don't get some hunny soon, I'll perish." I looked around and decided to head to the last place I remembered there being any hunny: the old tree where the bees had had a hive and I had gotten stuck. There had to be hunny there.

I watched the sun rise above the trees, the first time in days that I'd seen the sun or felt it's warmth on my face. The jar felt cold against me and reminded me of what I had to do. I needed to go, find the tree, and see if hunny still filled the inside. I would wiggle my way in and eat every last bit of that golden liquid.

My feet carried me to the clearing where the tree had stood. I stood there and watched the sun touch the top of the tree. I heard a buzzing and stood there frozen. The world dimmed around me, and I thought I saw shadows leap from the tree toward me, the buzzing growing in intensity. I blinked, and the shadows and buzzing disappeared. The tree stood there, sunlight illuminated it, but I did not see any bees buzzing around. I walked across the clearing to the tree, the jar held against my body.

"Hello?" I called, as though the bees would answer me. Nothing stirred in the tree. I drew closer and it looked empty and dead. I walked up to it and knocked on it. A hollow thud filled the clearing. I stepped back as a crack ran up the tree where I had hit it. I turned and ran.

Behind me, I heard it tear itself apart. I stopped, turned, watching the tree as it fell. The tree screamed as it tore apart, as it crumbled to the ground. I watched my dream of hunny fall to the ground, rotten and crumbled onto the forest floor.

"Oh, bother," I said. I stared at the ruined tree and then felt the hunny jar slipping from my fingers. I watched in horror as it fell to the ground. It bounced, rolled across the ground, and stopped. I sighed in relief, only to gasp in terror when a piece of the tree fell onto it, smashing it into thirty pieces.

"No!" I screamed and lunged forward, but too late. I fell to my knees and tried to put the pieces back together but they wouldn't stick. How would I get hunny now? I stood up and looked around. The world seemed darker now that the jar had broken. I stumbled out of the clearing, not sure where I would go.

I found myself back on the path to my house. I passed by Kanga's, but I saw neither feather nor tail, and it looked as though no one were home. Soon the path brought me by Eeyore's, and though his his little stick hut looked knocked over, I did not stop to investigate. The only place I wanted to be was home, in my bed, to mourn the loss of my hunny jar. I passed by Owl's without a glance, as at this point, I worried whether he would fly down and berate me about whatever he and Kanga were going on about.

Piglet's door stood open when I passed, and perhaps they were all there, but I did not stop as I was sure they would not want to see me. No, I would not stop and have Owl shout at me again. Something pulled me toward my home. I could hear it in my head, a buzzing. The same buzzing I remembered hearing when the shadows came and the darkness overwhelmed me.

It grew louder as I approached my home, but still no shadows attacked me. I felt it inside of me and it made my bones ache. My eyes burned and felt as though they would melt out of my face. I saw things in the sky, in the trees, in the grass. Terrible things. Fantastic things. Things that hurt my head if I stared at them too long.

I approached my door and placed my paw on the knob. The buzzing stopped, I pulled the door open, and stepped through.

I can't . . .not right. Where was I?

The smell. It was everywhere.

Hunny.

I saw it. I wasn't in my home, or was I? I remembered. I remembered the bees. They'd came from the sky. From my dream of a bruised sky. They'd arrived and made a home in my house, or was it in my head? I remembered.

They hungered. They needed to feed to make the hunny. The sweetest, most golden hunny that had ever passed between my lips. I needed more of it. I needed all of it. I had wanted to drown myself in it.

Their Queen. She showed me what I needed to do.

I didn't want to see, but I had to watch. I had to watch if I wanted the hunny. I had to see, so I opened my eyes and I stared into Her's. She stared into me and I fell.

Piglet was first. He didn't struggle long, but he understood. He looked into her eyes and he saw what I saw. The endless night that comes, but how we can be safe from it. She will make us all safe from it. In the hunny. In the Great Comb.

Piglet. My poor Piglet. He struggled but he understood. I saw him in encased in the comb, his face a rictus of terror as I walked deeper in the nest. What sights he must have seen before She saved him from terrors and pain much greater than he would have understood.

I walked further into the hive, deeper into the comb, where I heard the call of Her. I gave Piglet one last glance and moved on. The Endless Night would come and he would slumber safely in his comb until the universe would be born again in a bright new dawn, by Her.

I heard Her song more clearly now. I had been away from the hunny for too long. Out in the world, as I tried to save the rest. I remembered it all now. Everything came back with a rush. Owl had tried to break my connection with Her. He wanted to rescue Piglet and Eeyore. I had been so close to having Rabbit, but Owl had stopped me at the last moment. He had taken the hunny, denied it to me, broken my link to Her, but She had always come back for me.

I walked on until I came to the great chamber where She lay. The worker bees watched me as I approached. The smell of the hunny overwhelmed me and I plunged face first into a pool of it at her feet. I could feel Her in my head as it passed my lips. Her song cleared away the last of the cobwebs, the darkness that had threatened to keep me from her.

The buzzing changed though and I spun around. Owl, Kanga, and Rabbit stood there, in the hive, flaming torches in their paws. The bees buzzed about agitated. The Queen, her song changed, to something sinister, dark, full of death and pain. I felt the change in the air.

"Pooh, we tried helping you," Owl said, saddened. "We tried to show you the way, but you wouldn't listen. You could have stopped all of this but you didn't."

"You don't know what you are talking about, Owl!" I shouted to him. "Don't you understand? Can't you see Her beauty? She came to protect us. To keep us safe."

"Safe from what?" Kanga asked. She moved forward a couple of steps, but kept the torch held tight and above her head. She pointed to where Eeyore lay, encased in the hunnycomb. "How is that keeping us safe?"

"Eeyore will be safe from the Endless Night when it comes. She will keep him safe, and Piglet, and all of you as well, if you let her. Then when She defeats It, the world will be reborn, and so will we."

"You're mad, Pooh," Rabbit said from behind Owl. He shook and looked scared, but he held his flaming torch tight and high.

"It's got to end, Pooh," Owl said. "This thing is not here to help. Don't you understand? It is here to feed on us. To make us into its hunny, so it can trap others, and feed on them."

I stepped forward, anger flooded through me at his words.

"You fool, Owl," I spat. "You've always thought you were smarter, better than the rest of us, in your cozy home with all your books. I tried bringing you to Her the easy way, the way that Piglet and Eeyore came, but obviously you don't want that. So be it."

I ran toward them and the bees attacked. I didn't watch them as they took Rabbit, as my eyes were locked on Owl. We slammed together and tumbled into an oozing wall of hunnycomb. The hunny dripped over us, and made us sticky. I grabbed Owl and pushed him deeper into it. I could see the panic on his face.

For a moment something odd happened. I could see through his eyes. The hunny covered us both, from top to bottom. It invaded our ears, mouths, and noses. We were connected. My mind cleared and I could see what he saw.

My mind rebelled in terror at what it revealed. The horrific image of what the Queen looked like through Owl's eyes. The darkness that played about the edges of the hunnycomb. I could smell the stench of decay, of death all about me. I could taste it in the hunny, and for a moment, I stared into a pit of utter darkness that threatened to pull me in, then our connection broke, and everything returned to how it had been.

I stumbled back from him, out of the hunny. Owl picked himself up and struggled out of the hunny, trying to get it off. I looked about but could not find Rabbit. Kanga stood her ground, a number of dead bees around her feet.

"What . . . what was that?" I stammered.

Owl looked at me with pity in his face.

"The truth, Pooh," he said. "What I've been trying to tell you. To show you, so that maybe we can stop it."

"You're wrong. That can't be the truth. She showed me the truth. She showed me what was coming."

"Lies," Owl said. "All of it. Help us stop them. Help us stop Her!"

I looked up at the Queen and back at Owl. I flashed back to what I had seen when the hunny had connected us. The horror of what she was. The death all around. No, that couldn't be the truth, could it? What had I done? Piglet and Eeyore.

"Piglet . . . Eeyore," I whispered. I saw the truth of everything and my soul broke. I gasped and a wail erupted from me. I could hear the Queen behind me agitated, the increased buzz of the workers around us. I grabbed a torch from Owl and turned.

"I'm sorry," I said.

"It's okay," Owl replied. He looked at Kanga who nodded her head. "Do it Pooh. End it all."

I lifted the lit torch and charged. The workers buzzed down at me, but the fire kept them away. I dodged their stingers, and swung the torch at them. A few I managed to set ablaze, and they buzzed off with what sounded like screams, their burning bodies bright in the dim hive.

I reached the Queen and lifted the torch, but I hesitated.

"Nooooooo," a voice whispered in my mind. The word echoed in my head. I looked up and She looked down at me. I could hear a voice behind me, that screamed at me to toss the torch into her. To set her aflame as I had the worker bees, but I couldn't.

Buzzing filled my head, my mind, and for a moment I found myself elsewhere, and I floated in a sea of hunny, the Queen above me. I watched in fascination as her stinger extended down and pierced my chest, but I felt no pain.

Then darkness engulfed me.

I OPENED my eyes and I found myself on the floor next to my bed, an empty jar held hard against my body.

"Oh bother."

In Which We Are 666

Lee Allred

"Bother," said Pooh. Brass .455 cartridges tumbled to the floor. Fingerless mitten-paws were just not up to loading Webley service revolvers, but Pooh was the only reloader Christopher Robin had.

Christopher Robin was too busy shooting to reload, and the boy's father, A.A. Milne, sat very pale against the wall of the House at Pooh Corner and bled through makeshift bandages even as the Beast's poison slowly killed him.

Christopher Robin peered out the curtained window. "Here come more of them!"

The young boy steadied the heavy pistol in his hands—a selfsame conjured twin of the pistol Pooh now loaded—and desperately fired all six rounds at the corpse-white giant maggots crawling toward them.

Bullets punctured two of the chthonic servitors, turning them into flaccid flesh bags dribbling out pus and ichor.

The rest continued undulating forward.

Pooh snapped the cylinder closed and exchanged his pistol for Christopher Robin's empty. Pooh had only managed to load four shells this time, but even a bear of very little brain knew four were better than none.

And bullets were their only hope of stopping the maggots.

The maggots *and* their master, the Beast.

Because once the Great Beast 666 had swallowed up Pooh and his friends, nothing could stop him from doing the same to the Hundred Acre Wood and the wide world beyond.

Earlier that day in London
March 1927

ALAN ALEXANDER MILNE exited the National Liberal Club in as foul and blustery a mood as the weather overhead. The city reeked of chimney smoke and damp from the Thames. Horns blatted as motor traffic chugged by.

Milne was everything a *Times* reader might picture a playwright-novelist to be: lean of face and figure, a tweed jacket under a dun greatcoat, a briarwood pipestem clenched in his teeth. The ideal in everything but expression. Anger flushed Milne's face.

He usually lunched, when he lunched at all, at the Garrick Club, London's club for actors and playwrights. But ever since Milne published his Pooh book, dining there became an ordeal. The Garrick might have ironclad rules against conducting business inside its walls, but that didn't prevent shop talk.

Actors require plays to act in; that's just how actors are.

And if one is arguably England's foremost playwright and one is writing Pooh and poem books instead, one isn't writing England's foremost plays for actors to act in. Verdict: Milne should forego Poohing.

Playwrights, on the other hand, require theatres to produce their plays in and there are only so many theatre buildings standing; that's just how playwrights are.

So, if one is arguably England's foremost playwright and one is writing Pooh and poetry instead of England's foremost plays, then one isn't engaging more than one's fair share of theatres in both London and New York. Verdict: Milne should Pooh even more. Pooh unceasingly.

So, the Garrick was out. So was lunching at home. Milne's otherwise darling wife Daphne was once again planning to completely redecorate the Milne's London house. One cannot enjoy one's lunch with wallpaper samples continually thrust under one's nose.

Hence the National Liberal.

But what Milne had failed to remember was that the National Liberal had no ironclad rules against conducting business.

And Pooh was Business. Big business.

A little man in woolen underwear (figuratively but perhaps literally, too) had offered Milne a thousand pounds for every story in Milne's new Pooh book that featured Christopher Robin wearing children's woolen underwear. Immediately afterward, an American soap maker had pushed an equally absurd offer of a thousand pounds for every Pooh story that featured bubble baths.

In other words, Milne stood to gain an easy two thousand quid writing a Pooh story in which Christopher Robin took a bath while wearing wool flannels.

Ridiculous.

Before any more offers surfaced, Milne bolted down his undercooked meal and beat a hasty retreat far from the madding club.

Now he stood on the curb outside, hoping Burnside, his chauffeur, would pull up with Milne's motor before it started to rain.

And here it came now.

A vivid blue Italian Fiat in a sea of coal-black British-made Vauxhalls and Alvises.

Milne had purchased the Fiat not because he was a fiend on flashy motor cars. Indeed, he was hopeless with automobiles; he'd gone to the expense of hiring a chauffeur because (as he liked to tell his friends) Milne was "the only man in Sussex for whom cars did not start." Rather, Milne—called "Blue" by his family and friends—had purchased the Fiat simply because it *was* blue.

The Fiat pulled up to the curb, but Burnside wasn't behind the wheel.

CIVILIAN CLOTHES COULD NOT DISGUISE the ramrod military-bearing of the mustachioed imposter. Milne knew this asthmatic scarecrow with wireframe spectacles: Colonel Vernon Kell. He'd worked under him during the War.

Memories of France and the War came flooding back.

The trenches. The dead. The dying. The putrefying. The flies and the rot.

Frail flesh withering in the rivening guns. The horrors of the grave and the Horrors beneath.

Beneath Earth, beneath Reality.

"Get in," Kell snapped. Kell's wheezing voice brought Milne back to reality.

He made no move to obey. "I've told you before, Kell. I'm through with the Section."

"The Section isn't through with you, though" Kell said.

The Section was never *through with you.*

Milne resignedly climbed in. Kell eased the Fiat back into traffic.

Milne refilled his pipe, more to give his hands something to do than anything else. "What is it you want, Kell?" he asked, puffing it to life.

"A man will call on you in the next few days," he said. "No names, you'll know him. I want you to meet him."

"One of yours, I take it?"

Kell snorted. "That's the question, isn't it? Is he ours, or the Germans', or is he in business for himself? Be a good chap and find out for us, Milne. There's a good fellow."

The spymaster turned the Fiat down a dark, narrow alley that stank of kitchen refuse and drunkards' vomit. Midway down the alley, Kell stopped the vehicle and switched the engine off. Pistons stuttered to a stop, their clatter echoing off grimy brick walls.

"Why me? I'm not an agent." Milne asked. "France aside, I was never more than a glorified typist for your Section. Let the Section handle it."

Kell twisted around to face Milne. "It's not the Section he's coming to see. It's you. We have to play the hand he deals." He then produced a Webley pistol and a cardboard carton of ammunition for it. He held them out to Milne. "That doesn't mean you needn't take precautions. Take these, keep them with you at all times."

A gun for *him*? A gun for A.A. Milne, the pacifist so reluctant his fellow *Punch* magazine staffers had had to white-feather him into the War. The Army officer who crawled across No Man's Land at the Somme with an unloaded pistol, because he hated the very idea of having to fire one? The man who cowered in the caverns of France and froze when faced with the Horror that crawled out of it—

Milne pushed them away. "I'm not shooting a man for you, Kell."

"Whoever asked you to shoot a *man*?" Kell asked.

"Then what am I shooting at?"

Kell's jaw set. " 'We wrestle not against flesh and blood, but against principalities, against powers, against the rulers of the darkness.' " The words from Ephesians were not Kell's own, of course, but were all the more powerful for the borrowing.

Again, Kell held out pistol and carton of shells. "You'll need them."

"I don't see how. I've plenty of paperweights already," Milne said, but took the offending items and shoved then into the pockets of his greatcoat, if only to speed Kell on his way.

It did.

Kell opened the driver's side door and stepped out. "I won't bother wishing you good luck. I'm not in the luck business."

Then he vanished into the welcoming shadows.

Milne sat, reluctant to slide himself behind the wheel. Electric starter or not, the obstreperous Fiat would never start for *him*.

"I'll drive you, sir," a voice from the alleyway said. Burnside, Milne's chauffeur.

Of course. He's one of Kell's men. Kell wouldn't just leave Milne unwatched, would he. Not someone who'd gone down the Staircase.

Milne glared at his driver. "I'd fire you, Burnsides, but anyone I'd replace you with would just end up another Kell man, wouldn't he?"

"I shouldn't wonder, sir," Burnside said. A single press of the electric starter and the engine purred instantly, easily as it never did for Milne. "Home, sir?"

THE FIAT STOPPED alongside the curb outside Milne's Mallord Street house. The drive had given Milne time to regain some calm. He even managed a slight smile as he exited the car to face the welcoming bright blue doorway of his home, flanked by blue plant pots. Another little joke that only family shared.

Their son Billy—christened Christopher Robin but never called such by the Milnes—when he'd been an infant learning to speak had turned "Milne" into "Moon." His wife Daphne had immediately dubbed her husband "Blue Moon," for the rarity in which Alan graced the nursery with his presence.

The blue Fiat clattered away, heading for the hired garage Milne rented space at. He knocked the dottle of his pipe and turned to the welcoming blue door to his home. He'd deal with Burnside later. Burnside and Kell, himself.

Milne went to open the door when a smudge of yellow chalk on the lintel caught his eye. Kids, perhaps, although they'd have to be ruddy tall kids to chalk up there. The gas man perhaps. He shrugged and pushed open the door.

With Daph constantly redecorating the house, its interior was never the same three weeks running. Currently, the entry hall was painted chartreuse? Olive? Some ghastly green color that must be all the vogue among Daph's Mayfair set.

She'd then carpeted the downstairs in black, a poor choice. Flecks of white tobacco ash from Milne's pipe led a trail to his writing office in the back of the house. The hall staircase leading up was runnered in a Kurdish pattern suggesting Gordon at Khartoum, although it'd take a stouter man than mighty Gordon to stomach the colors of the front parlor, currently done up in painful marigold and burnt orange. Milne derived secret pleasure in confining uninvited guests there. Reporters and Inland Revenue agents and soap makers who wanted bubble bath.

Daph didn't seem to mind. She kept her writing desk in the parlor where she answered Pooh fan letters as Milne's fictitious secretary "Celia Brice."

Milne went to remove his greatcoat and hang it in the hall closet when remembered the heavy pistol in its pocket. He shrugged the coat back on. He'd hang it in his office where Billy couldn't get at it.

A scuffling noise came from the parlor. "Daph?" Milne called.

A man's voice answered, high and reedy yet somehow sinister. "Come in, Milne. I've been waiting for you."

Kell had been right. Milne knew his visitor instantly on sight. All England knew the corpulent, scrofulous toad seated before him.

Aleister Crowley. Pervert, pederast, pretend-mystic, and wickedest man in the world. The Beast 666. Self-proclaimed.

Crowley sat sprawled on the padded-leather chesterfield. He wore a scarlet silk turban on his bald head and a purple cape embroidered with gold astrological symbols draped over his ill-fitting black suit.

He stared at Milne with deep-set eyes. That Mesmer trick wasn't going to work on Milne.

"Where's my wife?" he demanded.

A diffident wave of a corpulent hand, bejeweled with gold rings set with gemstones. "Out, I suppose. Our business doesn't concern her, so it doesn't really matter."

"And my son?"

"Doing whatever little boys do in their nursery. Playing, I suppose. Myself at that age, I strangled cats."

"I well believe it."

Crowley sighed. "Oh, do take off that coat and sit down. I'm getting a crick in my neck looking up at you."

Milne pointedly did not sit, did not remove his coat.

Crowley sighed again. "You really are the most ungracious host, Milne. A ward sigil chalked on your door, everyone in your household—even down to your hired Nanny—with Second Names to prevent direct castings. I don't know how I should have ever gained entrance past the ward spell if you hadn't been so obtuse as to leave me clue on your porch. 'Blue,' indeed. Kell must be slipping."

"Certainly he's slipping if he hasn't arrested a traitor like you yet."

"Traitor?" Amusement quirked one corner of Crowley's mouth upwards. "Oh. You must mean that Irish thing during the War. Done on Kell's express orders."

"I doubt that very much." Crowley had run a newspaper for New York's Irish called *The Fatherland,* equal parts pro-German propaganda and Celtic Druid tomfoolery.

Crowley shrugged "Doubt away. Kell will use any weapon he can against the Staircases."

Milne started. *Staircases? Plural?*

Crowley tilted his head and smiled a shark's smile. "Oh. I see. You thought the Staircase you and Kell dealt with in France was the only one in the world?"

Milne felt his knees buckle. He sat down in Daphe's desk chair. *More than one gateway?* More gateways to Hell spewing crawling Horrors?

"Germany, with the help of Irish Celtic druids, was on the brink of finding their own Staircase in 1915. I tricked the Irish into recruiting me, supposedly to help in their magic research. My 'help' set the Germans back ten years. But only ten years. And their new Thule Society isn't as gullible as the Kaiser's men. They'll find it." He smoothed the folds of his cape. "And if Germany has a Staircase, we must have one as well, if only to serve as deterrent."

"And this involves me how?" Milne asked, voice shaking. Surely Kell wouldn't send Milne back down another Staircase. Not after he'd failed so abjectly the first time . . .

Crowley tented sausage-like fingers. "It seems you're the one man in England with the means to locate a Staircase here in England."

"Me? But I—!"

"It's all in your silly book about that bear."

Upstairs in the nursery, Christopher Robin was taking his nap.

Winnie the Pooh sat very quietly on the bed, not that he could move on his own anyway. Not in the nursery, of course, except maybe enough to topple over onto the floor. It was boring sitting quietly.

Eventually Christopher Robin woke. "Hullo, silly old bear," the boy said, reaching out for Pooh.

Nou, Christopher Robin's Nanny, lay asleep in the adjoining room, taking her own nap on the day bed. That meant Pooh and Christopher Robin had to play quietly, which Pooh felt was a shame as all the fun games required noise.

Christopher Robin diffidently played with his toy soldiers until both he and Pooh heard the sound of the front door opening,

"Oh, good!" Christopher Robin said. "Blue's home." Now, Blue was a silly thing to call a father, but Christopher Robin did it anyway.

"Daph?" Pooh heard Father-called-Blue call from downstairs. But instead of Mrs. Blue answering, a stranger's voice did. A man's voice. And not a very nice one at that.

Pooh didn't like it at all.

Christopher Robin clapped his hands. "Oh, good! A reporter or somebody. Maybe they'll take our photographs again."

Pooh didn't enjoy getting his photograph taken. He didn't understand photographs—Pooh was a bear of very little brain. He didn't like flash bulbs. They hurt his button eyes.

"Let's listen in," said Christopher Robin.

There was a secret spot on the staircase in the Milne house, a certain stair where if one sat on it, one could hear plain as day everything said in the parlor.

Christopher Robin's father said that it had to do with the acoustics of the circulation vent, but the vent wasn't made of sticks at all, but of iron grillwork.

Dragging Pooh along by the ear, *bump bump bump*, Christopher Robin slid on his bottom down one stair at a time until he reached the magic stair.

The stranger and Christopher Robin's father talked Grown Up Things. Something about a Staircase—not the one Christopher Robin and Pooh sat on, of course.

The visitor had just said something about "your silly book about that bear"— Pooh's ears perked up when he heard himself mentioned—but then the visitor's voice stopped short.

Suddenly, it was if Pooh could feel the man's gaze upon him through the wall, feel the heavy pressure of his blazing eyes. If only Pooh could run from those eyes!

The stranger spoke again, but in a new Voice, one deeper, broader, one with a tone of command. Pooh wanted to obey it even though the Voice was meant for Christopher Robin, not Pooh. Lucky for Pooh, he couldn't move.

"When we were very young," the Voice of Command said, boring its way into Pooh's very little brain, "we listened at doorways to things we shouldn't."

The Voice knew they were spying on them. It *knew!*

"But now that we are 666," the Voice continued, "we've put away childish things *and obey our elders!*"

Christopher Robin jerked to his feet, his eyes glazed and his jaw slack. Jerkily, as if asleep, Christopher Robin descended the stairs, dragging Pooh, *thud thud thud,* along in the boy's somnambulant wake.

The boy shuffled into the parlor. The stranger awaited, bald and fat and cruel. His eyes glowed red and darkness and shadow—solid and slimy and shifting as treacle jam—coalesced about him. The stranger pointed his fat finger at Christopher Robin.

"You asked me what means you have to find the Staircase. Milne? *Here he is!*"

Their drive down to Ashford Forest was a waking nightmare. No sooner had Milne's son fallen under Crowley's Voice than Crowley used it to snare Milne as well.

Milne vaguely remembered being hustled into an ugly black Vauxhall 5-seater saloon parked outside. It seemed to Milne in his muzzyheadedness that Crowley was both driving up front and sitting in back with Milne and his son. Impossible, and yet it was.

The backseat Crowley wore a turban while the driver wore no hat at all.

Driver Crowley asked if Milne had been searched. Turbaned Crowley sneered. "Him? The famous *Punch* pacifist? Carry a weapon?" Milne was thus vaguely reminded of the great metal lump of a pistol in his greatcoat pocket. Milne managed somehow to press his thigh a little harder against the door padding. Firmer contact with the cold steel of the revolver seemed to clear his mind a bit.

Not that that helped much. Milne still could do nothing but sit as ordered while they drove south. Turbaned Crowley droned on and on about things beyond Milne's ken. Crowley, it seemed, wanted to boast.

"The ancient Egyptians called it *Ka*, the Thelemae *Aiwass*. The doubling of the soul, of a person, place or thing. Creating a *selfsame*." Turban barked in laughter. "And sometimes, that results in a True Will—a selfsame greater, more wondrous, more powerful than the original."

A mewl escaped from driver-Crowley and Turban Crowley laughed again. "A case in point. In creating me, my useless Originator ceded all his powers to me, his double. I think he regrets his choice."

On and on the car drove in the rain. The shadows of early evening darkened. A helpless Milne, possessing no more volition than the Pooh bear clutched in the chubby hand of his mesmerized son, could do nothing but sit and obey.

Night fell by the time the Vauxhall finally coasted to a stop. Gravel crunched under the wheels. A few last flecks of rain from the spent storm dripped upon the windshield.

"Get out," The Voice ordered and Milne and the boy obeyed.

Milne could neither turn his head or move his eyes. From what he could see in the automobile's headlights, they stood at a trailhead leading into a forest.

"Ashdown Forest," Crowley provided. "But at the opposite end from your weekend farmhouse which I imagine is crawling with Kell's men."

Again, he used the Voice. "Follow." Milne and Billy Moon followed, Pooh Bear held in the boy's arms.

Crowley led them to the forest edge and halted. He then pantomimed pressing his palms against an imaginary wall blocking entrance into the forest.

"There," Crowley muttered, finding some unseen spot in the invisible wall. He reached for the boy's hands, but finding them full of Pooh Bear, shoved the stuffed animal at Milne, ordering him to take it.

Crowley then guided the boy's hands, pressing them on the indicated invisible spot in the air.

Crowley stepped back to look at the tableau, then nodded at Milne. "It takes a powerful magician to create an Aiwass," he explained, as if Milne had agency to listen. "But a small child of sufficient imagination can as well—or did you think *all* imaginary friends are only imaginary?"

Milne was having trouble thinking anything at all.

"Take a child," Crowley continued, "a child such as your son here, possessing an exceptionally vivid imagination, coached and encouraged by an adult trained in the arts of imagination such as yourself. Such a child can construct an Aiwass of an entire forest. A selfsame so powerful it contains a Staircase.

"Yes, Milne. The Hundred Acre Wood is as real as you or I and exists outside your books. It exists every time your boy steps into Ashdown Forest."

The turbaned mystic raised both arms high and began chanting, nonsense syllables spewing forth in rhythmic cadence in a voice that deepened and grew, like a pulpited vicar in full bay.

A circle of light sparked from the boy's splayed fingers.

The light coalesced, growing into a full circle ten feet across. The blurred light came into tight focus, showing a portal into a daylit world beyond: a forest, but not the natural Ashdown Forest of birch and beech and willow that Milne knew, but the scratchily-penned ink and watercolor landscape of E. H. Shepard's illustrations—the Hundred Acre Wood itself.

"Follow," ordered The Voice as Crowley walked through the portal.

Milne and his son followed, shuffle-stepping from reality into the realm of fiction.

* * *

Earlier that afternoon
Offices of Punch *magazine, London*

Ernest Howard Shepard hurried through the doors of 10 Bouverie Street, almost an hour late for the Wednesday editorial lunch at the famous Table. Shepard had been touching up in watercolors the illustrations for the second and hopefully last of A.A. Milne's blasted bear books and had lost track of time, ending up in such a rush that India ink still stained his fingers.

He'd barely shrugged off his rain-sodden overcoat when he bumped into Platt, the Table's Chief Steward, dithering in circles like a headless chicken.

"Oh, Mr. Shepard!" Platt blathered. "Thank goodness you're here! It's just awful! First that horrid man carving into the Table and now this Army man. And they're all sitting around the Table dead, just dead!"

"Who's dead?" Shepard demanded, hanging jacket.

"*Everybody*," Platt wailed. "The *entire* Table."

Shepard pushed past him into the Table room.

It was true.

The entire editorial and creative staff of the magazine lay sprawled across their dinner plates. Portraits of former *Punch* editors and owners and illustrious contributors hanging on the dark paneled walls leered down at the victims.

Unlike Platt, Shepard had served in the trenches in the Great War. Dead bodies no longer bothered him. Besides, these bodies didn't look particularly dead. They were still breathing.

"Merely sleeping, Captain Shepard," said a thin asthmatic stranger in a trench coat. "Waters of River Lethe. Administered in aerosol form, I'd imagine."

The words were so much mumbo-jumbo, but the asthmatic didn't look a fool. "You have the advantage of me, sir," Shepard said stiffly. "You know my name but—"

The asthmatic flipped his wallet open, displaying a warrant card listing him as one Colonel Vernon Kell, Military Intelligence. The warrant card only served to puzzle Shepard all the more. What was someone like Kell doing at *Punch?* "You're from military intelligence?"

"You might say I *am* military intelligence," Kell said. "And this isn't the first time we've met. Think back to the south of France, 1918."

Shepard remembered. His battery of siege artillery had been yanked from the Italian-Austrian lines and shuttled by train to back to France. A weedy little major ordered them to set up in the middle of nowhere hundreds of miles from any front. Shepard had sat there without explanation for two days, then that major ordered them to pack up and return to Italy. Kell must have been that major, though hanged if Shepard could remember his face.

"But what's this all about?" Shepard asked.

"This. Look here." Kell ran his fingers across a newly-carved set of initials. The huge oval table was scarred all over by the carved initials of Punch luminaries over the years. Owners, editors, publishers, writers, artist. Shepard's initials were carved on there, too.

The carving Kell spoke of were brand new: a barely-legible triplet of the numeral six carved almost on top of Shepards own.

"Six-six-six," Shepard read, and immediately he felt a strange sort of unseen power crackled from the gouged numbers, pulling at Shepard, tugging at his mind.

Kell nodded, seemingly oblivious to any eerie pull from the scrawl. "666 The Mark of the Beast. A Beast in human form. Aleister Crowley."

"Crowley?" Shepard breathed. "*That* charlatan?" How dare *that* man desecrate the Table! "I'll have Platt get somebody to buff that out immediately."

"You'll do no such thing," Kell snapped. "That carving's a stroke of luck. The only luck we've had in this sorry whole affair. It might just make it possible for you and I to scotch Crowley and maybe, just maybe, save Alan Milne and the rest of the world."

After putting one of his trenchcoated men to guard the carving, Kell hustled a very confused Shepard outside to Kell's waiting automobile, a sleek-looking Alvis built for speed. Its driver was wasted in the Army; he should have been in the racing circuit, the way he swerved through the rain-slick streets of London, pushing the powerful engine to its limits, speeding them out of the city in nearly no time at all.

Wipers clacked back and forth in metronomic monotony. Shepard could still feel its pull. If anything, the pull grew stronger the further south they traveled out of London. "That carving," he asked, "why did you call it luck?"

Kell chuckled sourly. "Because it's Crowley's first mistake. Yes, yes, I've bungled things badly—I thought he'd be a week longer getting here from Germany, I thought he'd hit at Milne's country farmhouse instead of their London home—but Crowley boobed as well. He thought Milne still worked for *Punch* and he went there first."

Shepard snorted. "Milne hasn't worked at *Punch* since the War started. Old Man Lucas didn't want a pacifist on staff."

"Crowley wasn't to know," Kell said. "An accomplished mystic scholar he may be, but not up on current events. He barged in at the Table expecting Milne, and when he didn't find him, settled for hexing you as a sort of backup insurance."

"Hex?" Shepard asked. Kell acted as if that charlatan Crowley actually had real magic.

And yet, Shepard felt that carving's pull.

"That carving links you to Crowley," Kell said, then smiled.

Shepard knew that smile. He'd once smiled it himself. At the Somme, at Passchendaele, at Mentello Hill, while his hand on the lanyard of a 60-pounder as enemy infantry foolishly advanced across open ground.

"With you and Crowley linked," Kell continued, "we can follow him. Where he goes, we go."

Windshield wipers swept once, swept twice, swept three time.

"And where are we going?" Shepard asked.

"Ashdown Forest," Kell answered. "And from there, the Hundred Acre Wood."

Hundred Acre Wood
On the same day, but a somewhat blustery one

THE MOMENT CHRISTOPHER ROBIN's father stepped into the Wood, Pooh felt that old familiar feeling come over him again. He could move again! He was alive again!

Pooh promptly squirmed out of Mr. Milne's arms so as to walk again on his own two fuzzy little legs the way Pooh bears should

His squirming seemed to confuse the glassy-eyed Mr. Milne; the man made to keep walking, but couldn't advance.

Then Pooh noticed that it wasn't his squirm that was confusing Mr. Milne, but his overcoat.

The overcoat's coattail stretched tautly, hanging horizontally from the other side of the portal. That coattail was stuck.

Something big and lumpy in the hip pocket—something iron and steel, Pooh could feel it!—prevented passage through it. Mr. Milne, his eyes glassy under the spell of the Voice, heaved in near-mindless desperation, managing to tug the coat and its contents free and all the way through.

As it fell free, the coattail swung and—*thud!*—swatted Mr. Milne's leg. The impact of the metal object seemed to clear Mr. Milne's glazed eyes somewhat.

Pooh didn't understand why it would, or how the Grown Ups had managed to find their way into the Wood with Christopher Robin and himself, but then Pooh knew himself to be a bear of very little brain.

THE MOMENT the pocketed pistol whacked his leg, the fog blurring Milne's mind lifted substantially. The compulsion to obey Crowley still held sway, but lessened. And while Milne couldn't move of his own volition, at least he could think again.

And what he had to think about!

He, Alan Milne, was actually in the world of his own book. A wonderland that looked exactly like Shepard's scratchy drawings, only three-dimensional. Instead of solid colors, pastel hues blurred like watercolors, ran past their borders like ink washes. The real Ashdown Forest was a veritable panoply of tree varieties; this Wood contained only the scraggly-limbed things Shepard unartfully bodged on his canvas.

Milne didn't care for the man's art—Old Man Lucas, the fathead!, had forced Shepard on Milne—but Milne knew the success of the Pooh book was because the public loved Shepard's scratches. It was a pity the man couldn't draw real trees, especially now that Milne walked among them.

Milne's son Billy—no, Christopher Robin, for in this world Billy could *only* be the Christopher Robin of the books—shuffled ahead of Milne, displaying none of the sense of wonder a small boy should have walking through the insides of an actual book.

If only Milne could find some way of freeing both himself and his son. He could think of none.

———

CROWLEY LED them further into the wood, not even glancing at their strange surroundings. *His* eye was on whatever prize he sought inside this imaginary wonderland.

The group continued down the path, through a dense clump of Shepard trees whose arching branches cathedraled overhead. Eventually, they emerged in open ground again and approached a very odd, very familiar wooden bridge.

It took Milne a moment to realize what was odd about it. This was the Poohstick bridge! The very bridge upon which Milne and Billy had stood hundreds of times tossing Poohsticks into the river and racing their makeshift boats under the bridge.

The Poohstick bridge here in the Wood looked just like a real world one. It wasn't some illustrated construct of Shepard's. Shepard, after all, hadn't finished the illustrations for this part of the book yet.

Crowley, who couldn't possibly know of Poohsticks, still stopped on the bridge anyway. "Yes, this is the divination place. I can feel it."

He turned to face his shuffling captives. "I sense the Staircase, but will need divination to find it. My original knew that going in." The turbined Aiwass laughed a cruel, haughty laugh. " 'Staircase for Britian'. That fool still harbors vestiges of patriotism. 'Staircase for me!', is what *I* say. With one under *my* control, I'll rule not only Britain, but the entire world!"

The madman laughed again as he dangled a sea-shell necklace, bronze medallion depending from it. He studied its swing. "Hmm. Divinations usually require the reading of entrails, but this says I should toss an item in the water instead. What to do?"

The corpulent Aiwass laughed. "Why not both? Two birds with the same stone knife." He snaped his finger and produced a long, wickedly-jagged dagger of the blackest obsidian. Poisonous ichor dripped from its blade. "I'll carve out your entrails, Milne, and toss them over the bridge. *That* should produce the desired effect."

A crook of Crowley's finger and Milne felt himself helplessly shuffling forward. Forward into impaling himself on the dagger.

Milne struggled desperately, but he could not resist. Closer and closer the blade loomed.

Abruptly, Crowley waved Milne away, ordered him to stand aside.

"No, no. Not you, Milne." He snapped. "I'll use the boy. I don't need him anymore now that I'm inside, and children's entrails are purer, more powerful."

Another crook of a finger, and now it was Christopher Robin shuffling toward the deadly blade.

NO! Milne screamed in his mind. *Not my son! Not Billy!*

He redoubled his frantic efforts to free himself, not for himself now, but for his son. In his desperation, his physical body actually managed to shudder and sway.

The swaying knocked the iron pistol against his leg again. It grew warmer, it grew hot. Hot as fire. The runed shells in the opposite pocked burned even hotter.

Writhing now against that heat, Milne's spasms grew into viclent convulsions. With one final, terrible paroxysm, Milne broke free of the Voice's control.

Crowley, startled, turned his attention from the boy.

"How are you resisting me?" he demanded in The Voice. The words staggered Milne, slowed his movements to a crawl, but did not completely stop Milne from plucking the Webley from his pocket, swinging it up in slow motion, and cocking the hammer.

Crowley screamed in frustration. "I'll gut you, *then* the boy!" he railed. He raised his knife hand high in the air to strike Milne down, confident he could beat the wobbly Milne to the kill.

But Crowley hadn't reckoned on the one member of the party everyone had forgotten.

As a stuffed toy, Pooh weighed only a pound or so. Inside the Hundred Acre Wood, though Pooh was *almost*-flesh-and-blood and so had *almost* the weight and heft of a similarly-sized British bulldog.

Pooh leapt with all his beary might at their tormentor, slamming into the backs of Crowley's knees. buckling the corpulent man's legs.

Crowley staggered.

Unfortunately, Crowley staggered forward, plunging the poisoned dagger into Milne's shoulder.

Milne screamed in pain, even as—reflexively—his finger pulled the trigger, firing point blank into Crowley's chest. The impact flung Crowley backward, slamming him off-balanced into the bridge's low, wooden rail.

The magician toppled into the river, impaling himself on his own dagger in the fall.

Eldritch energies, evil and palpable, swirled around Crowley as the current carried him away. The energies grew and grew, threatening to engulf the entire river including the bridge and those who stood upon it.

"Run!" gasped a wounded, bleeding Milne. He somehow managed to grab his son, free at last from Crowley's control. Pushing his son forward, Milne fled.

———

BOTHER, thought Pooh.

Things hadn't gone as Pooh had planned. True, he'd stopped any stabbings, and true, the fat man had fallen off the bridge.

That hadn't been a good thing, however.

Blustery black lightings crackled from the floating flat man and Pooh's cloth fur stood on end.

This was bad.

Mr. Milne, his shoulder oddly red and wet, was dragging Christopher Robin away. "Run!" he kept gasping.

But Mr. Milne was running the wrong way.

Pooh may be a bear of very little brain, but even Pooh knew when trouble threatened the place to run was back home, not toward that scary Heffalump hole. There were scary things down there.

"No! *This* way!" Pooh insisted, tugging on Mr. Milne's coat. "We need to go this way." His beary mitten-paw pointed in the direction of the House at Pooh Corner.

———

CROWLEY CAME TO. He awoke to agonizing pain. He found himself floating the river, gutted like a fish upon his own knife, his energies dissipating into the ether.

He immediately stopped their outward flow and drew them back in.

He felt his wound. The jagged blade had carved a ragged hole in his belly. Loops of intestines, as if pulled by an unseen hand, suddenly squiggled out from the gaping wound.

Crowley cackled with laughter, headless of his pain. He'd needed entrails for his divination and now his very own were serving that purpose. His entrails pointed the way to the Staircase.

Crowley somehow kicked his way to the bracken-covered bank and crawled ashore. He rolled over onto his back and begun stuffing his intestines back where they belonged. Once, done, his magicks closed his wounds.

Shakily, Crowley got to his feet, whole again if not hale.

First. he would wrest control of the Staircase from its Slug'gg'oth guardians. Then he would set those chthonic hordes against Milne and his son.

Crowley's control of the Staircase would never be absolute as long as those two lived to thwart him.

MILNE RESTED an arm against the hollow tree Pooh used as his house and caught his breath as best he could. The house looked just as Shepard had drawn it in Milne's book: a thick-trunked tree with a Pooh-sized door. a coil-spring door bell, and a sign reading "Sanders" tacked above them.

Milne grimaced. "I'll never fit through that door."

The door suddenly double in height.

His son smiled shyly, looking at the hand he'd just waved like a magic wand.

"It worked," the boy said wonderingly. "I can double things, just like that man said."

That wasn't exactly what Crowley had said, but close enough. It had worked, hadn't it? Milne let his son help him through the newly embiggened door.

The house's interior was much bigger than the tree outside.

Empty hunny jars filled much of it, but the interior space was large enough to hold a kitchen, a dining table, and a fireplace. A cheery fire blazed, warming a pan of Coddleston Pie.

Christopher Robin rummaged in the kitchen cupboard till he found a first-aid kit. "In case Pooh skinned his knees," the boy explained, overlooking the fact that a cloth bear would be better served with needle and thread. He set about to clean and bandage his father's stab wound as best as a boy could.

The boy's best should have been enough that, with a little rest, Milne might have regained enough to lead his son back to the real world, but chemist shop Mercurochrome could do nothing against the ichor's poison and Milne felt himself grow weaker. Even so, Milne might manage yet.

Too bad any such hopes were suddenly dashed.

Crowley's Voice rang through the Hundred Acre Wood. "I'm alive, Milne," it announced. "But you won't be for long."

A pause.

"Where are you, Milne?" the Voice demanded. "I can sense you but I cannot see you. Show yourself. *Come to me.*" The Voice commanded, but Milne and his son were immune to it now.

"You resist me?" it asked. "No matter! I've control of the Staircase, Milne. You know what it holds beneath. I'm sending them up to play. They're coming for you, Milne, you and your son."

And then, as if he could see them, Milne *felt* the horrid things emerge from the depths. Giant, undulating slug-like horrors.

Pooh waddled to look out the window—the inside of Pooh's house had a nicely-curtained window, even if the tree trunk outside lacked any such.

The little bear bleated in fear. "Heffalumps! Crawling out of the Very Deep Pit!'"

Christopher Robin rushed over. "Those aren't Heffalumps," he said, trying to keep his voice from shaking. "But what are they?"

"Slug'gg'oths," Milne said.

"A nasty name."

"A nasty name for a nasty thing." Milne could feel them squirming closer, could all but see the hideous cloud of flies weaving about them, a murmuration of millions swirling in dark impenetrable clouds, the buzzing, *buzzing*, BUZZING.

Milne mind started sliding into madness again, just as it had in France.

Standing at the Staircase maw, futilely standing by the field telegraph staring at the copper wires leading down as Kell's handpicked team was devoured one-by-one until none were left, cowering as the first of the slug'gg'oths came crawling out toward him, stopped only by Kell unloading his pistol into it as Milne cowered helplessly—

Milne shook himself back to sanity, back to the present.

Kell might not be here to save Milne again, but Kell's pistol and the carton of those special shells were here! Milne dug them out of his pockets.

His face fell.

Only twenty-four shells, the box read. Even at one bullet per horror, not enough for what they faced. Then he snapped his fingers.

Selfsame.

He held out the carton to his son. "Can you selfsame these bullets like you did the door?"

"Make them bigger?" the boy asked with a frown.

"No, make more of them. Double them. Make two boxes. Keep doubling more as we shoot them off so we don't run out."

Christorpher Robin smiled. "I think so," he said and waved his hand. The one box became two. Another wave of his and he doubled a second revolver into existence as well. "So we each have one," he explained.

Milne coughed weakly. "I'm afraid you'll have to do all the shooting, son." He looked his son in the eye. "You do remember how?"

The boy nodded. Milne had let him shoot the little bulldog pistol he kept at the farm a couple time, plunking tin cans and such.

Milne coughed again. "While you're shooting off one pistol, I'll be reloading the other. That way you'll always have something loaded." If he *could* reload in his weakened state. Milne could barely even sit upright.

"I could do the reloading," Pooh offered. "If you show me how.

"You better be get started," Christopher Robin said, aiming the revolver out the window, "because *here they come!*"

Milne rested as his son shot and shot at the crawling horrors. The boy hit more often than he missed, but it was a losing battle.

"Bother," said Pooh, fumbling at reloading.

"Here come more of them!" his son—ever the brave little solider—wailed. He looked almost on the verge of tears. The boy couldn't fire fast enough, couldn't keep up with the ever-increasing numbers Crowley sent.

No hope for them after all, no way to even—

A sudden fusillade of shots sounded from outside. Bullets slammed into the flanks of crawling terrors. Confused, the survivors broke and slithered back into the wood.

A few seconds later Kell and that foolish old Shepard came bursting through the doorway, pistols drawn. The asthmatic Kell wheezed like a grampus.

"I told you'd this is where they'd be," Shepard said. "I drew the place, didn't I?"

With two grownups at the window to shoot, Christopher Robin took over reloading from Pooh. "Bother," said Pooh. Pooh sat himself down next to Mr. Milne, feeling just as unneeded.

Maybe he really was nothing more than a silly old bear.

The not-heffalumps were slow coming back.

Instead, the Voice called out:

"Very clever, Kell, using Shepard to find your way in. But too clever by half. You in turn led me right to Milne. 'Sanders,' indeed. I couldn't See him with that Second Names confusing my Sight, but I have you now!"

"You have nothing!" the bossy man with glasses who'd arrived with Mr. Shepard yelled back.

The Voice yelled back in turn. "No more games, Kell. No more fooling with mere Slug'gg'oths. I should have brought out the Cuttlefish to begin with."

The bossy man's face went white and he blurted a Very Bad Word.

The very ground itself started to quake. Trees began to topple and it seemed the entire forest starting tilting to one side.

Pooh staggered as best he could over to window.

Up from the Heffalump Pit rose the most tremendous creature Pooh had ever seen. Big as a house, big as a tree.

The thing's bottom jaw was nothing but a mass of writhing octopus tentacles, each as long as a crocodile. Bat-wings fluttered from its back. Inky poison lubricated the fish-scales covering its green-gray body.

And riding atop its bulbous head like some mahout, sat Crowley, his purple cloak fluttering triumphantly like a flag.

The creature lumbered forward, knocking aside trees with every step.

Shepard and his bossy friend emptied their pistols as fast as they could pull the trigger, but the creature didn't even slow its pace.

"No use," the Bossy Man said. "We can't shoot fast enough and the boy can't reload fast enough."

"There's got to be way," Mr. Shepard said and started shooting again.

Got to be a way.

Pooh stroked his chin. *Hmm,* he thought, and *hmm,* he said.

"I know I'm only a bear with very little brain," he said at last, "but why selfsame bullets going *into* the gun? Why not selfsame bullets coming *out* of the gun?"

Mr. Milne looked at Pooh with a look of respect he'd never given the bear before. "A machine gun!" he shouted. "Son," he said to Christopher Robin, "double, triple, hundredfold the bullets as they come out the barrel."

Christopher Robin said he'd try.

The Bossy Man took aim and pulled the trigger a single time, but instead of just a single bullet fired, a stream of bullet fired. A continuous stream ripped through the air. Hosing down the approaching creature with the never-ending bullets, the Bossy Man aimed where the creature was tender: its eyes, its mouth, and its tender pink gullet.

Jaw-tentacles fluttered as the Creature roared in irritation. He balked at continuing forward.

Crowley roared with his Voice, kicking and trying to goad the creature forward, but that only shifted the creature's rage to the pesky ant riding atop its head.

The Elder God reached up and flung Crowley to the ground, stomped on him, then scooped up his mangled body and tossed it away.

Free of Crowley's control at last, the Cuttlefish turned and slowly shambled back down the Staircase to return to its ancient slumbers.

They'd won.

THEY FOUND Crowley's mangled body past the Six Pines, way up on the knoll Nice For Piknicking. It lay on a soft bed of moss and lady fern.

" 'We wrestle not against flesh and blood, but against principalities,' " a weary Kell said, staring down at the mangled piece of meat. " 'Against powers, indeed.' "

Milne took a long drag from his pipe. "So much for Crowley's selfsame. What about the original?"

"He has his uses," Kell shrugged, pouring green liquid from a whiskey flask on the corpse. The liquid foamed like a bromide antacid as it came in contact.

Milne snorted his disgust. "And the Staircase?"

Kell re-stoppered his flask. "Can't be accessed except through your son's imagination and little boys don't stay six forever."

"And the German Staircase?"

"A snipe hunt for Crowley to keep him spying on the German mystics. Nasty bunch, even without a Staircase."

The wind soughed over the knoll.

"So, when are you coming back to the section?" Kell asked.

"Never."

"Can't sit around doing nothing forever, Milne."

"Writing *isn't* nothing."

"Wasn't writing that saved your boy. It was the Section and the pistol we handed you." He looked Milne in the eye. "Go ahead. Pretend Evil doesn't exist. Write your silly plays and books. Or you can come back and do *Something*. Like we did here. Nobody else around to do it."

Kell turned and started down the hill.

Sighing, Milne wandered over to where Christopher Robin and Pooh stood next to Shepard as he sketched the Wood. You really could see it all from here.

"Kell called my work Nothing," he told Shepard.

Shepard shrugged. "Compared to what we saw today, I suppose it is."

The artist put away his sketch book. "So you're going back to him?"

Milne tousled the blond hair of his son, the son that had come ever so close to being slaughtered by ancient Evil. "I suppose I have to," Milne muttered. A bit firmer he added: "I'm not going to do Nothing any more."

"Ever again?"

"Not so much," Milne looked down on the receding form of Kell. "They don't let you."

Wind in the Wood

Kary English

Nobody told me,
Nobody knows,
Where the wind comes from,
Where the wind goes.

Bombs all around me,
The woods are on fire.
My backpack is filled
With explosives and wire.

The bombs are like thunder,
The bullets are bees.
Innocence shattered
By cannons and screams.

Who comforts the soldier
When the wind blows?
Nobody told me.
Nobody knows.

In Which War Comes to the Hundred Acre Wood

Lehua Parker

Soaring over the French countryside in a C-53 Skytrooper, trapped between a moonless night sky and rolling woodlands, Corporal Billy Moon sets his jaw against the teeth-rattling roar of the engines. As the scent of burnt cinnamon toast blows through the cargo hold, he prepares for the sharp sting of a Nazi bullet.

Thigh or chest, he wonders, calculating ground angles and calibers. He shrugs. *Doesn't matter. Dead is dead. Anywhere but the face. No mum should see that.*

Parachuting behind enemy lines, it's likely Billy won't live to feel his boots touch ground, but that doesn't stop Allied troops from counting on him to hiccup Hitler's war machine. His mission: neutralize Pont Forêt des Rêves Bleus, a small bridge on an insignificant road leading to salvation. In his pack are explosives he knows shouldn't detonate until he wants them to, but he's seen stranger things in war.

Bullets that buzz like bees. Elephantine tanks that stomp and crush. Relentless soldiers with weasel faces on fast motorcycles rampaging villages. Young children left lying in mud, their warm woolen mittens far from their stone-cold bodies. Ashes and smoke and everywhere, everywhere, the fetid stench of charred flesh, vomit, and blood.

He closes his eyes, clasps his hands, and massages the webbing between his thumbs and forefingers.

This is real, he thinks. *This is now.*

At the signal, he jumps.

At first, there's just the whistle of wind in his ears, higher pitched than the engines, but blessedly quieter than the bone shaking Skytrooper's hold. He looks toward his toes and counts, praying his chute opens when it's time to pull.

The clouds he parts with his boots are like nothing he's ever seen. Sticky, humid, and sour as mildewed socks, it's like sliding down a dragon's gullet. The bilious green clouds strobe and flash as Billy fall, fall, falls into the devil's cauldron. He holds his breath and tries not to think about sparks and the payload in his pack.

What hell-spawn is this?

Don't breathe; don't breathe; don't!

He's lost the jump count.

Oh, God. Was that thirty? Forty-five?

His lungs are dying. He has to take a breath.

It won't be a bullet that gets me.

Panicked, he pulls the rip cord early, too early. There's a twinge in his thigh and another along his collar bone as the ropes twist and tangle. His parachute doesn't fully open.

He kicks and flaps his arms, tugging on each line, desperately trying to remember his failsafe training, but he's falling fast, too fast. There's no way he's on course.

Sorry boys, he thinks. *I tried; I really did.*

He clenches his jaw. *This is going to hurt.*

And then he realizes: *I'm not dead yet.*

With Herculean effort, he whips his body sideways. The maneuver springs the lines free. His parachute billows as his body passes through the last of the toxic clouds.

All the way down, wafting over the deep black woods, he searches for the bridge. It's impossible to spot in the darkness—the only light comes from cancerous sparks arcing across the clouds above. He aims for what he hopes is a clearing, but at the last moment a stray breeze pushes him back to the woods. He tumbles through branches until his parachute hangs lifeless, caught in a tree that won't let go.

Billy tries not to think about the harness straps strangling his bladder as his boots sway mere inches from the ground. Near midnight when he jumped, dawn now creeps in on little cats' feet through the woods. He no longer feels his toes.

Stupid pilot, he thinks. *Typical Trinity College-reject for sure. The drop was off; I knew it the moment I cleared the clouds.*

In the waking light, Billy scans the meadow, his eyes moving, moving, moving.

God, I need to wee.

For the millionth time, he kicks his feet, trying to shake himself free. He pushes off the tree trunk, and it buzzes angrily. Sharp jabs strike his neck, shoulder, and knees. Billy blows his breath hard and fast, trying to keep the swarming bees from stinging his face.

Bloody, bloody bees.

One inch or a hundred feet off the ground, Billy isn't going anywhere without his knife. He can just make it out, a faint shimmer in the grass near the roots of the tree where he'd dropped it hours ago.

Billy sighs. *I'm a bee-stung corpse hanging in a tree.*

Sorry, boys. I tried. I really did.

"Good morning, Christopher Robin," says a small voice behind him. "Are you after a bit of hunny for breakfast? If so, I would very much like some too."

Billy freezes. Whatever this is, it's not the Nazi kiss he expects.

"Um, Christopher Robin? I can't help but notice that you don't have a hunny pot. Would you like me to fetch one? Hunny is awfully hard to carry in your paws, especially for two."

Shocked, Billy swings wildly, twisting to see behind him. Bees skim his nose and threaten his ears in defense of their hunny, but all he wants is to face the voice in the woods. "You speak English?" he hisses.

"Of course, silly. I'm an English bear."

Bear, Bear, Bear. Billy's mind reels as it parses through the pre-mission info dump. "Résistance?"

"Resistance? No, we're all pretty accommodating here," says the voice. "Well, except for the bees. They don't like to share their hunny. I must say, you're not a very convincing rain cloud, Christopher Robin. Rain clouds don't kick. No wonder the bees are angry."

"Bear, my knife. Do you see it?" says Billy.

"Yes, I do. It's next to the hunny tree."

"Get it. Cut me down. Hurry!"

Just past his left boot, Billy sees a fuzzy brown mitten reach for his knife. With a couple of snicks and a few grunts, Billy finally falls all the way to earth. He moans as blood rushes into his legs; a million spider prickles spiral through his thighs as he staggers to his feet. Unzipping his fly, he takes a wide stance and rests his head against the tree.

Bliss.

"Are you all right, Christopher Robin? You took quite a tumble."

After a very long time, Billy zips his trousers, takes a deep breath, then turns with his hand out. "Thanks, mate . . ." His eyes travel down, all the way down,

down, down to the small brown bear standing next to him, round and full of fluff. The bear's head comes just above Billy's knees.

The bear looks up and blinks his black button eyes.

Billy screams.

The bear jumps back.

Billy slaps his hand across his mouth.

The bear covers his mouth.

Billy closes his eyes.

The bear closes his eyes.

Billy opens his eyes.

The bear says, "Is this a new game, Christopher Robin? Is it like Simon Says? May I open my eyes now? I can't see what you're doing with them closed."

"How . . . what . . . ?" stammers Billy.

"Who, why, where?" giggles the bear as he opens his eyes. His brown plush fur looks oh, so squishable, so delightful; his ears curve away from his round face. His nose is black velvet and twitches in the breeze, but it's his mouth that captures Billy's attention, pink on the inside without hint of tongue or teeth. He can't stop staring as the bear says, "Now about the hunny. Do you have any? I've got a terrible rumbly in my tumbly, Christopher Robin."

"Why do you keep calling me that?"

The bear stretches out his arms. "Christopher Robin? Because that's who you are."

"No, I'm Corporal Billy Moon."

"No, you're Christopher Robin. I've known you forever. Well, almost forever." The bear wrinkles his nose. "You're a year older than me."

"Nonsense. I'm Corporal Billy Moon, 53rd Parachute Regiment, British Army!"

The bear grins. "You're not a Para, Christopher Robin. Paras are all grown up."

Billy lifts his chin. "I am a Para! See? On my shoulder, the patch, right here: *Utrinque Paratus!*"

"Oh, Christopher Robin," chuckles the bear. "You're definitely *not* ready for anything."

"I am so!" Billy insists. "I'm Corporal Billy Moon! I am ready. I have an important mission: neutralize Pont Forêt des Rêves Bleus. People are counting on me."

"Oh," exclaims the bear, "I see! It's an Army game! Well, if you're Corporal Billy Moon, then I'm Commander Pooh!" The bear scratches his head. "Is Commander higher than Corporal? I think so. Hmmm." He looks up. "Does this mean I'm the boss of you?"

"You're not the boss of anything," Billy huffs.

"Oh. Better just call me Pooh Bear, then," says Pooh Bear.

Billy reaches up and jerks his parachute. It doesn't budge. He shakes the ropes dangling like strange fruit, but it's useless. There's a bee sting along his neck swelling like botfly larva beneath his tender skin. He idly scratches it as blood seeps into his collar.

The parachute doesn't matter, he thinks. *The Nazis already know I'm here. Nothing matters, except the bridge. If I don't stop Hitler from crossing the river, everything is toast.* He checks his watch. 08:03. *There's still time.*

He swings his pack off his shoulders and does a quick inventory: binoculars, detcord, explosives, compass, map, radio. He fiddles with the radio dials, but there's no signal, not even static.

Busted.

"Would you like your knife, Corporal Billy Moon?" asks Pooh Bear.

"What? Oh, yes." Billy sticks it in the sheath on his belt and shoulders his pack. "Thank you, Pooh Bear. You've been a big help. You can go now."

"Go where?" asks Pooh.

"Isn't there somewhere you have to be?"

"Oh, we're both exactly where we need to be, Corporal Billy Moon."

Billy swings his arm, encompassing the meadow, sky, and tree. "And where, exactly, is that?"

Pooh laughs. "Why, wherever we are, Corporal Billy Moon."

Billy winces. "Please stop calling me that!"

Pooh says, "What?"

"Corporal Billy Moon," he mutters.

Pooh tilts his head. "But that's your Army name. We have to play by the rules."

"Paratroop . . . never mind," Billy sighs. "Call me Billy. Just . . . Billy."

"Okay, Billy." Pooh clasps his paws behind his back and starts to rock. "Billy, when do you think—"

"Quiet, Bear. Let me think."

Pooh looks to the sky as he nonchalantly waves away a bee. "Are you still thinking, Billy?"

"Shhh."

"Are they big thoughts?"

"I'm not telling you again," says Billy.

"Telling me what?" asks Pooh.

"Oh, good grief," says Billy. "This is worse than being stuck in the tree."

"Sometimes humming helps when I have to think big thoughts. Would you like me to hum for you, Corporal Billy Moon?" Pooh begins to hum, then bursts into song. "Oh, hunny is a secret treat, just for you and me—"

Billy covers his ears. "For the love of all that's holy, Pooh Bear, stop! Stop!"

Pooh Bear ducks his head and kicks at the dirt. He sniffles a bit.

Softer, Billy says, "I mean, we can't call attention to ourselves. We must be quiet."

"Why?"

"Nazis."

"Who?"

Billy looks at Pooh Bear, really looks at him for the first time, and sees how butterflies flutter about him, how the sun shines on his sweet face, how his button eyes twinkle.

He really has no clue. What English speaking pocket of France doesn't know about Hitler and Nazis and Résistance and Allies?

He's a bear. A small, wee bear.

I'm losing my bloody mind.

Billy caresses the tender webbing between his left thumb and forefinger. He pauses just for a second, then twists viciously.

Ow, ow, ow!

I felt that!

He looks at the red spot on his hand and feels it flush and swell. He pokes it once more for good measure.

"Billy?" says Pooh Bear, "did you forget you were telling me about the Nazis? I forget what I'm doing sometimes, too. Is it time to get hunny now?"

Real or not. Dead or not. Crazy or not. I still have a mission. People are counting on me, and this creature can help.

Billy squats and takes Pooh Bear's paw. It's softer and squishier than he even imagined, and he has to stop himself from burying his face in Pooh's warm belly. *Home,* he thinks, *home and chocolate chip cookies with tall glasses of milk.*

"Pooh," he says, "may I call you Pooh?"

"Oh, of course, Billy. That's my name. Well, Winnifred Edward Bear and Pooh Bear for short, but just Pooh will do."

"Thank you, Pooh."

"You're welcome, Billy."

"Pooh, there are bad people coming," says Billy.

Pooh gasps, paws to his cheeks. "Woozles?"

"Er . . ."

"Don't tell me it's Heffalumps! Or no, it's Jagulars, isn't it?" Pooh covers his eyes and shakes his head. He whispers, "Spotted or Herbaceous Backsons? Oh, no, I can't bear it." Pooh shivers and quakes.

How.

How do you explain tanks and guns and bombs that fall from the sky?

"It's more complicated, I'm afraid," Billy says.

"Why are the bad people coming, Billy?"

"They want . . . they want what you love most, Pooh."

"My HUNNY!"

"More than your hunny. But don't worry, Pooh. I'm here to stop them."

"Thank goodness, Chris—I mean, Billy!"

"To stop them, I need to see them coming. I need a place to survey the area, a high place where I can see a long way. Do you know of such a place?"

"Of course, Billy. There's a hill just beyond the meadow. You can see everything from there, Kanga's House, Rabbit's Burrow, Owl's Tree—even Eeyore's Gloomy Place. I'll take you there."

"No, Pooh. You've done enough."

"But I haven't done anything at all!"

Billy licks his lips. "Pooh, listen to me. You need to run. Gather your friends and go as far away from this place as you possibly can. It's not safe for soft things."

"Oh, Billy," Pooh grins. "You can't do this alone. Friends are friends through thick and thin. We'll face the Heffa-woozl-lars together."

Lying on his stomach, tucked among bushes and grass just below the hilltop, Billy peers through his binoculars. *Either the mission brief was screwy, or I got dropped in the wrong place. Nothing makes sense. Where's the front line? No smoke, no dust, no motorized sounds at all. How can I blow a bridge that doesn't exist?*

Bored, Pooh makes daisy chains for Piglet to wear as Tigger does what Tiggers do best.

"Can I wear your helmet? Please, oh pretty please," bounces Tigger.

"I told you no. Helmets are for soldiers," says Billy. "Stop asking."

"Aren't we all soldiers?" asks Tigger, pulling himself up to his full height and saluting. "Major Tigger reporting for duty!"

Pooh says, "I think only Billy Moon is a soldier—"

"Paratrooper," Billy mutters.

"And we are merely—"

"A wonderful thing!" shouts Tigger. "Say, do you see them, Christopher Robin? I mean through those glasses of yours? Can I take a look?"

Pooh says, "Remember, it's Billy Moon," and weaves another blossom into his garland. "Hand me those dandelions, Piglet. I'll use them, too."

"That'll be nice, Pooh."

"Thank you, Piglet."

Tigger scoffs. "Billy Moon, Christopher Robin—it's all the same to me. But hey, whoever you are, para-somethin'—tell me more about them Heffa-woozl-lars. Are they as big as skyscrapers with sharp, shiny teeth?"

"Oh, no, Tigger," says Piglet. "They can't be that big. N-n-nothing that big could possible fit in our Hundred Acre Wood."

"I don't care how big they are; I'll fight 'em. I'll rip their noses right out of the middle of their faces. I'll squash their stubby tails with my mighty paws. Nothing's gonna steal our hunny!" says Tigger. "Lemme show you how it's done."

"Eeek," squeaks Piglet. "Tigger, you're so fierce!"

"First, you gotta sneak up behind them, real slow. Then, when they least expect it, you pounce! You grab their little ears and jerk 'em back. And when you have them on the ground, that's when you—"

BOOM!

BOOM-BOOM-BOOM!

"What was that?" shrieks Piglet.

Billy doesn't need his binoculars to see the air in the meadow below rip apart, the edges flickering green-gold and shiny like asphalt in August. A shockwave flattens trees and grass into a wide dirt road. For a split second, he sees clearly: German tanks rolling from nothing into the woods; soldiers on motorcycles, guns slung on backs; canopied trucks loaded with barrels of fuel and soldiers, always more soldiers. Billy blinks once and it's gone; only clouds of dust and the rushing sound of death on the march remain.

"The Heffa-woozl-lars," he breathes. "There're here."

"Let me at 'em," shouts Tigger. "I'm not scared."

Pooh sets down his flowers and stands. "Heffa-woozl-lars are loud," he says. "There's so much dust."

"I can't see anything," says Piglet.

"It's better that way," Billy says. "We don't need to see them to follow their tracks."

"Are they coming for our hunny, Billy Moon?" asks Pooh.

"Not if I can help it."

Piglet covers his nose and mouth with his scarf. "How will we stop them?" he mumbles.

"What?" says Pooh.

"I-I s-s-said, 'How will we stop them?' They're headed straight to Kanga's house."

A DONKEY'S TAIL?

It's the first thing Billy Moon sees when they stumble out of the woods and into a new clearing. Crumpled and rumpled, a sad gray sting with a thumbtack on one end, the tail sits in the middle of deep Heffa-woozl-lar tracks squashed in the mud.

Billy says, "Don't look."

"Oh, you found it. Hooray!" says Pooh, picking up the tail by its thumbtack and flicking off dirt. "Look, everyone—it's Eeyore's tail!"

Piglet claps and Tigger bounces. "Oh, ho!" Tigger crows. "That'll cheer the old guy up!"

"We've been looking for it for ages," says Piglet. "Hooray, hooray, hooray!"

"Let's show it to Kanga," says Pooh and turns to the left. "Oh. Oh, no!"

Where Kanga's house stood is a pile of broken sticks and a couple of bashed mailboxes tumbled in a heap. Rising from the rubble is a broken broom, the straw bending every which way.

"Kanga?" calls Piglet. "Roo?"

"Stay here," says Billy. "Don't move."

Shifting through the debris, beneath a stained frilly apron Billy finds a scarf. As he gently pulls, stuffing oozes. Stuffing, stuffing—so much stuffing, *oh God, the stuffing*, with bits of brown velvet and chunks of plush fur and black stitches torn loose and lying tangled in the cold, damp earth.

For a split-second Billy sees chestnut hair in a fermière's kerchief, but when he blinks in disbelief, the image shimmers with green-gold light and morphs into slender kangaroo ears and tufts of milk chocolate velveteen, softer than a kitten's paw.

Billy blanches, and try as he might, he can't help himself. He retches and retches, but his stomach is empty and the bile burning his throat doesn't mask the stench of hot steaming stuffing simmering in mud.

But stuffing doesn't stink, Billy thinks. *There must be something more.* He swallows hard, then turns back to the rubble and begins rapidly tossing boards this way and that.

Buried beneath a scrap of stripped wallpaper, a severed paw peeks out of a teeny blue shirt—*a child's shirt*—and Billy can bear no more. He collapses in the Heffa-woozl-lar caterpillar tracks, weeping for the tender things of the world.

Heffa-woozl-lars. Bloody, bloody Heffa-woozl-lars.

"Billy," calls Pooh. "Billy. Don't cry. We'll build a new house. Things can go back to exactly the way they were."

"Kanga and Roo would love a new house," says Piglet. "Especially one with a bigger porch—ooo—with a new porch swing! Can you imagine how fun it will be to swing on the porch and drink lemonade in the summertime? Roo will love it. Don't you agree, T-Tigger?"

"Sure, Piglet, ol' pal. It'll be good as new. We'll build it together!" Tigger turns to Billy and spots the tears leaking from his eyes. "Hey," he says, "hey." He crawls to Billy and curls in his lap. "If it's all the same to you," he whispers, "I'll stay right here until your bouncitivity's back. I lost my bounce once—Rabbit hid it from me —but not really. I just thought that. Your bounce is still inside you, Billy Moon. You just have to grab it with both paws."

"There's a r-r-rabbit leg over th-th-there," Billy stutters, "and owl feathers and s-something blue and purple and floppy next to the b-b-broom."

"Why Billy Moon, you sound just like Piglet," laughs Pooh. "Doesn't he sound like you, Piglet?"

"Oh, yes, Pooh. He d-d-does," says Piglet with a wide smile. "You and me— we're the same, Billy M-M-Moon!"

"No," Billy says, shaking his head until his helmet rattles. "We're not, and nothing will ever be the same again."

Tigger follows his gaze. "That?" he says, pointing to lumps of pink velvet snout and the scrap of pocket-pouch ripped along its seams. "Is that what's worrying you, Billy? That's nothing, nothing a bit of thread and needle can't fix as good as new."

Billy covers his face as his shoulders shake. "The world's not safe for soft things," he moans.

Tigger reaches up, straightens Billy's helmet, and pats him on the head. "Nonsense. You're Corporal Billy Moon. People are counting on you. Just remember to bounce like a Tigger. Bounce, bounce, bounce! So! Much! Fun!"

Billy grabs the webbing between his thumb and forefinger and pinches it white. Through snot bubbles he says, "It hurts, Tigger. It hurts too much."

Tigger turns Billy's chin toward Pooh and Piglet who are standing by the edge of the clearing and marveling at Eeyore's tail, how it floats like a kite in the breeze.

"It's like a sail, Piglet! Do you think that's how Eeyore lost it? Did it sail away on an adventure?"

"Oh, Pooh! We've got lots of lumber and nails now. Let's build a boat and sail like Eeyore's tail to the moon," says Piglet, clapping his paws with glee.

"The moon?" chortles Pooh, "like Billy Moon?"

"Oh, y-yes!" says Piglet. "E-exactly like that."

"That reminds me of a hum: What fun, my chum! We'll sail away, and float all day, all the way to the moon," sings Pooh.

"From Eeyore's tail, we'll make a sail, and fly away to the moon," sings Piglet.

"Hey, now that's the ticket," says Tigger, patting Billy's back. "Come sail away with us, Billy-me-boy, all the way to the moon."

"The moon? We can't go to the moon! Why would you say that? Can't you see the stuffing, Tigger? There's so much stuffing all around us—too much!"

"Why, of course I can! Stuffing's what Tiggers do best!" says Tigger. "But I'm thinking maybe something's bothering you, Billy-ol'-chum." Tigger taps his head and spins a slow circle on his tail.

"Is it me, Billy Moon?" asks Pooh. "Am I the bother?"

Piglet shoos a butterfly fluttering about Billy's head. "Is that better, Billy Moon? It was the butterfly, wasn't it?"

Billy hangs his head.

Madness.

It makes the most sense.

"I know!" shouts Tigger, springing over Pooh's head. "It's Eeyore's tail, isn't it?"

Billy sighs. "No." He pauses to watch Pooh sniff a rosebush and begins to nod to himself. "Yes," he says, "yes, it's the tail. It's not a sail, and it's not a kite."

"I know! Why don't you leave Eeyore's tail with me and Piglet? We'll make sure he's all together—and Rabbit and Kanga and Roo and Owl, too. We'll mend them good as new."

"What an e-excellent idea, Tigger," says Piglet. "I've got a button eye. I think it goes with Eeyore's tail."

"Perfect!" says Tigger. "I spy Roo's hindquarters up in that tree. And there's Owl's beak. All we need is some thread."

"Kanga's sewing basket," says Piglet. "It's right over there."

"Got it!!"

"But stuffing never goes all the way back," mumbles Billy. "And how will you know whose stuffing is whose?"

"Aw, what's a little stuffing between friends?" Tigger gathers a warm pile in his arms and sets it next to Piglet. "You worry about the oddest things, Billy Moon."

"Pooh?" Billy says, rubbing a bit of fuzz between his fingers.

"Yes, Billy Moon?"

"Are you okay with this, Pooh?"

"Okay?" Pooh looks to the sky. "So many puffy, fluffy clouds. That one looks like a dragon. The sun is shining. Kanga will get a new house. Later, we'll build a boat." He pauses. "But there wasn't any hunny this morning, and I dearly love hunny. That was a disappointment." Pooh shrugs.

"I don't know what to do, Pooh."

"Do? Don't be silly, Billy Moon. You do what you came here to do," says Pooh.

Billy wipes his face, leaving a clean streak on his chin. "What's that?"

"The thing you can't remember. It's on the tip of your tongue," says Pooh.

Tigger bounces over and sticks out his tongue. "Is it dere?" he mumbles.

"I don't see anything, Tigger," says Pooh.

"No letters or words? Are you sure?"

"N-n-nothing," says Piglet.

"It's gotta be around here some place," says Tigger.

And then Billy remembers.

Pont Forêt des Rêves Bleus. Heffa-woozl-lars. Bee-bullets and bombs.

"The bridge," he says. "I have to get to the bridge."

"The bridge to Christopher Robin's house? Why didn't you say so? Everyone knows the way," says Tigger. "Hey, Pooh, good buddy, ol' pal. Corporal Billy Moon here wants to go to the bridge."

"Why?" asks Pooh as he sorts through ragged wisps of softness. "Is this Roo or Eeyore? I can't tell."

"Just put it in the pile, Pooh Bear. We'll s-s-sort it out as we sew," says Piglet.

Billy asks, "Pooh, the bridge, the one called Pont Forêt des Rêves Bleus. Do you know where it is?" He spits the last of the bile from his throat and shake, shake, shakes his arm. There's a bit of fur clinging to his wrist that won't let go.

"'Course I do. It's just over there."

"Pont Forêt des Rêves Bleus? It's through those trees?"

Pooh nods. "Where else would the Hundred Acre Wood Bridge be? Just past the Sand Pit on the way to your—I mean, Christopher Robin's house." Pooh chuckles as owl feathers float just out of his reach. "Silly Owl! Stop playing games."

"I found Roo's foot!" says Piglet. "Ooo! Here's another one. Oh, but I think it's Kanga's. It's too big to be Roo."

"Bring them over here. I've got Roo's arm and shirt," says Tigger. "This is going to be great. I love stitching things back together. "

"Are we going to play a new game, Billy Moon? Is that why you want to go to the bridge?" asks Pooh, carrying half a wing and a few tail feathers to Tigger.

"Ah—"

"Poohsticks!" claps Piglet. "That's what you play on the bridge."

"Oh, I love Poohsticks!" says Pooh Bear, hugging his tummy. "My very favorite. Well, after hunny, of course."

"Me, too!" says Piglet. "May I c-c-come along?"

"No," says Billy as he rises from the mud. "This kind of Poohsticks is strictly for two, Piglet. Besides, you're helping Tigger."

"Saaaay, that's right, Billy Moon," says Tigger. He dusts his paws. "Yeah, Piglet and me, we'll tidy up the place a bit. Hand me that shovel over there, will you, Piglet? The one next to Kanga's broom."

"Are we making a new garden now? Is it for Rabbit? Are we planting more carrots?" asks Piglet.

"Right as rain you are, Piglet," says Tigger. "Right as rain."

Pooh tilts his head. "Even though we're going to play Poohsticks, Billy Moon, we're still playing Army, aren't we?"

Billy adjusts his pack. "We most certainly are, Pooh Bear." He bites his lip, flicks a bit of thistledown from his pants—*so much stuffing*—and checks his compass against the sun. "Lead on, Commander Pooh!"

"Right this way, Corporal Billy Moon!" says Pooh. He turns and takes two steps, then stops. "Er. Should we march, Billy Moon?"

Billy hitches up his trousers and squares his shoulders. "I think it's best, Commander Pooh."

"Right. Hep, hep, hep, hep, left, right, left, right," calls Pooh as he heads through the woods.

Tigger sighs. "Hand me Eeyore's tail, would you, Piglet? Gosh, these needles are difficult, but you can't sew an eye until you thread one. Piglet! Is that what they mean by 'an eye for an eye'? Get it? Heh. So. Much. Fun!"

FOR ALL THE space it takes up in Billy's imagination, Pont Forêt des Rêves Bleus is a very ordinary bridge with a little wooden railing and simple stone walls. Bubbling merrily, the stream flows beneath it cold and clear. Looking down from the bridge you can see mossy river rocks, reeds along the bank, and ducklings paddling by.

It's not wide enough for a tank, Billy thinks as the paces off the bridge. *It's really just a footpath.*

Pooh says, "We need Poohsticks. Shall I look for some?"

Billy lies on the path and slides his head and shoulders over the edge of the bridge.

"I don't think you'll find a Poohstick there, Billy Moon."

"Right here." Billy pats the bridge. "That's the spot."

"But Billy," says Pooh, "Billy! That won't work." He shakes his head and scuffs his toe. "That's the wrong side of the bridge."

"What? How is there a wrong side?" asks Billy as he comes to his feet.

Pooh throws his paw into the air and marches to the east side. "You have to drop your Pooh stick on this side," he says and runs across the bridge to the west side, "so you can see it come out this side. But you can't just drop it willy-nilly. You have to count to five."

"Why five?"

Pooh wiggles his paw. "Because that's how many fingers Christopher Robin has." He tilts his head to the side. "Are you getting this, Billy Moon? Poohsticks are complicated." He brightens. "I know; I'll find a stick so I can show you." Pooh starts to ramble off to the bushes flanking the bridge.

Billy hastily slips off his pack. "No," he says, "we don't want any of these old sticks. I've got just the ones we need in my knapsack."

"Will they float under the bridge? It's important that they float," says Pooh.

"They'll get the job done," says Billy, slipping his helmet off and wiping his nose on his sleeve.

"This is an odd way to play Poohsticks, Billy," says Pooh. "It's not much fun."

Billy picks up his helmet as he steps back to admire his work. The explosives are set; the detcords are run. All that's left is to light the fuse.

And then?

The rendezvous?

The bridge is real. The farmhouse must be, too.

"Billy?" asks Pooh. "Are we ready to play?"

Oh, God. The small, wee bear.

"Pooh, you must make a choice," says Billy.

"Hunny," says Pooh Bear. "The choice is always hunny."

Billy feels for the bruised spot between his thumb and forefinger and caresses it. "Look, Pooh. Things are going to change real fast, real soon. You need to choose which side of the bridge you want to be—the north side where your friends are or the south side with me."

"Why, with you, Chris—*Corporal* Billy Moon! Always with you," Pooh cries as he waddles over and slips his paw into Billy's hand.

So, so warm and soft. Like whiskers on kittens.

"Pooh, you understand that the bridge is going away, right? If you're on this side with me, I don't know if you'll ever see Piglet or Tigger again. And I . . ." He looks to the clouds, white as fresh laundered sheets in a summer's breeze, and sighs. "I don't know where I'll be after."

Pooh tugs once, twice, thrice on Billy's hand. "Then I'm definitely staying with you," he says. "Otherwise, you'll be all alone in the world, and I couldn't possibly bear that."

"Silly bear," says Billy. "If you're sure."

Pooh looks up with his big button eyes and smiles. "I'll never leave you."

Billy's eyes water. He blinks and clears his throat. "Right," he says, releasing Pooh's paw. "Then on to it. Would you like to strike the lighter?"

"Oh, may I?" Pooh claps and twirls around.

"Yes," Billy laughs. "In fact, there's a rule that whoever lights the fireworks must wear a helmet. So, Pooh," he says as he plops his helmet over Pooh's head, squishing Pooh's ears just a bit, "this is for you!"

"Eeeee!" squeals Pooh. "I get to wear the helmet, too?!"

"Here, hold the lighter. It works like this—flick this part. Great! Exactly that. Careful, careful—don't catch your fur on fire—just snap the lid shut to extinguish it. Perfect."

"Oh, Billy Moon, that was so thrilling!" Pooh walks to the detcord trailing over the edge. He waves the lighter. "Do I just—"

"No!" shouts Billy.

Pooh looks up, startled.

Softer, Billy says, "We'll light it way, way over there where it's safe. That's why the cord is so—"

BOOM!

BOOM! BOOM! BOOM!

The Heffa-woozl-lars have come.

From the midst of an oily cloud of vile green smoke, the first tank rolls through, swinging its turret like an elephant's trunk. It's caterpillar tracks mow down the bushes next to the bridge as it impossibly widens until it's fifty feet wide and skyscraper high.

"Light the cord, Pooh!" screams Corporal Billy Moon. "Do it now!"

There's just enough time to see the lighter fall from Pooh's paw before Billy has to turn and run.

The blast sends Billy stumbling, his cheeks slashed by branches and his back pelted by gravel. It's loud, louder than the hold of a C-53 Skytrooper or the sound of crashing through trees. From the corner of his eye, he spots a paratrooper's helmet as it rolls past, singed brown cloth and sawdust spilling and spinning.

And still the Heffa-woozl-lars come.

There's no time to grieve or even think. There is only time to run, run, run as a weasle-faced soldier on a motorcycle races to get ahead of him. Billy scrambles up a hill, turns, and sees a white clapboard house with a swing.

The farmhouse!

As Billy leaps across the porch, the air about the door shimmers green and gold. A dragon roars behind him, his breath humid and fetid as it musses his hair, filling his mouth with the taste of burnt cinnamon toast and wood ash. Billy grabs the doorknob. It twists in his hand.

He crosses the threshold.

And all is white and still.

A single butterfly dances in front of Billy's nose. He follows it to a child's bedroom.

"Why, Christopher Robin!" says Pooh from the table.

Piglet holds a cup as a rabbit pours tea. Tigger is munching on cucumber sandwiches, while an owl and a donkey converse with a large kangaroo. A joey peeks from her pouch. "Hooray, hooray, hooray!" shouts the joey. "It's Christopher Robin at last!"

"We've been w-waiting for you!" says Piglet.

"Enchanted, my boy, simply enchanted," says the owl as he holds out his wing.

"Would you like some tea?" asks the rabbit.

"It's not very hot," says the donkey, "but it tastes all right."

"Especially with hunny!" chortles Pooh.

"Home," breathes Christopher Robin. "I'm finally home."

A Request

If you liked this anthology, please take the time to leave a review on the site where you purchased it and/or on one of the social media reading sites like Goodreads. Tell your friends that you enjoyed it. Suggest it as reading for your local book club. Request it at your local library (or more than one local library). This helps others learn more about the book and gets the word out.

Please use the #horroratpoohcorner and #hemeleinpubs tags on social media.

Thank you for your time, and thank you for reading this book!

Find more exciting books to read at hemelein.com.

HEMELEIN PUBLICATIONS

About the Contributors

Lee Allred is the award-winning author of several dozen fiction stories for professional markets such as Asimov's Science Fiction and Pulphouse magazines. His works are found in dozens of book anthologies. He has also scripted comic books for Marvel, DC, IDW and Image Comics, including such books as *Batman '66*, *Batman Black and White*, *Fantastic Four*, *FF*, *Bug! The Adventures of Forager*, and *Dick Tracy*. His novella, "For the Strength of the Hills", was named a Sidewise Award for Alternate History finalist.

A great love of history and historical detail infuses all of his work, whether he's writing steampunk, vampire tales, alternate history, or military sf. Allred served three rotations in Iraq as part of Operation Iraqi Freedom for the United States Air Force. After retiring as a Master Sergeant, he settled down to a writing life. Learn more at leeallred.com.

Gustavo Bondoni is an Argentine writer with over two hundred stories published in fourteen countries, in seven languages. His latest books are *Ice Station: Death* (2019) and *The Malakiad* (2018). He has also published three science fiction novels: *Incursion* (2017), *Outside* (2017) and *Siege* (2016) and an ebook novella entitled "Branch".

His short fiction is collected in *Tenth Orbit and Other Faraway Places* (2010), *Virtuoso and Other Stories* (2011), *Off the Beaten Path* (2019), and *Thin Air—The Cosmic Crime Fiction of Gustavo Bondoni* (2023). In 2019, Gustavo was awarded second place in the Jim Baen Memorial Contest, and in 2018 he received a Judges Commendation (and second place) in the James White Award. Learn more at gustavobondoni.com.

D.J. Butler has been a lawyer, a consultant, an editor, and a corporate trainer. His novels include *Witchy Eye, Witchy Winter, Witchy Kingdom,* and *Serpent Daughter,* the modern fantasy novels *The Cunning Man* and *The Jupiter Knife* (with Aaron Michael Ritchey), the time travel novel *Time Trials* (with M. A. Rothman), and the science fiction novels *In the Palace of Shadow and Joy, The Gray Lords,* and *Abbott in Darkness,* all from Baen Books. He won the Whitney Award for Best Speculative Fiction Novel and the AML Award for Novel for *Witchy Winter,* and the Dragon Award for Best Alternate History Novel for *Witchy Kingdom.*

His middle-grade steampunk fantasy adventure tales, *The Kidnap Plot, The Giant's Seat,* and *The Library Machine,* are published by Knopf. Other novels include *City of the Saints* and the *Rock Band Fights Evil* series from WordFire Press, and *The Wilding Probate* from Immortal Works. Dave organizes writing retreats and anarcho-libertarian writers' events, and travels the country to sell books—he's visited nearly half of all Barnes & Noble stores! He plays guitar and banjo whenever he can, and likes to hang out in Utah with his children. Learn more at davidjohnbutler.com.

A Texan by birth, and temperament, Joseph Capdepon II grew up reading everything he could get his hands on. After high school, where he would read the day away when he could, he went into the lucrative career of retail, then construction, because working in the hot Texas summer was much more preferable than being shouted at by angry customers.

After a few different construction jobs, he finally found his niche, and is out of the heat, working in the office, the air conditioned office, working hard on designing fire alarm systems. After some prodding from friends, he started writing, publishing his first short story to the *Grantville Gazette Universe Annex.*

He's been working furiously, pounding away at keyboards, putting words down, and weaving stories he hopes people will enjoy. He continues to churn out words from his home north of Houston, with his lovely wife, and his amazing standard poodles, daughter, chickens, two ducks, and one quite serious goose.

He is taking care of business, one word at a time.

Jaleta Clegg was born some time ago and has filled the years since with plenty of make-believe. She writes science fiction adventure, fantasy of all flavors, and silly horror. When not writing, she enjoys playing with yarn, cooking weird vegetables, designing costumes and quilts, and generally messing around. Learn more at jaletac.com.

MICHAELBRENT COLLINGS is an internationally-bestselling novelist, produced screenwriter, and speaker. Best known for horror (and voted one of the top 100 Greatest All-Time Horror Writers in a Ranker vote of nearly 20,000 readers), Collings has written bestselling thrillers, mysteries, sci-fi and fantasy titles, and even humor and non-fiction.

In addition to popular success, Michaelbrent has also received critical acclaim: he is the only person who has ever been a finalist for a Bram Stoker Award (twice), a Dragon Award (twice), and a RONE Award, and he and his work have been reviewed and/or featured on everything from *Publishers Weekly* to *Scream Magazine* to NPR. An engaging and entertaining speaker, he is also a frequent guest at comic cons and on writing podcasts like *Six Figure Authors, The Creative Penn, Writing Excuses,* and others. He is a mental health advocate and TEDx speaker.

Find out more about him at WrittenInsomnia.com.

STEVE DIAMOND is a horror, fantasy, and science fiction author for Baen, Wordfire Press, Gallant Knight Games, and numerous other small publishers. He was the founder of Elitist Book Reviews, has been a professional editor, a publisher, an accountant, a bookseller, an art director, and pretty much any other job you can find in the realm of publishing.

He's been nominated for awards as both a reviewer and an author. Steve lives in Utah, has a family, smokes a lot (BBQ, not the other thing), listens to all sorts of music (except country), loves sports, hates sharks, loves video games, and thinks horror is like bacon – it makes everything better.

MEREDITH DILLMAN is an artist inspired by nature and the myth and magic of fantasy. She is known for her colorful watercolors which blend Art Nouveau, fantasy and Asian art influences. Learn more at meredithdillman.com.

Jessica Douglas has been a professional artist for over 25 years. She has shown in galleries and museums all over the world and works in a wide range of mediums, though she specializes in mixed media utilizing gemstones. Her husband, Shawn, makes the paints that she uses in her art.

When choosing a subject matter, Jessica tends to be drawn to the fantastical because it stretches her creativity and pushes her to think outside of the box. She currently resides in Utah. Learn more at submergedstudio.com.

Kary English grew up in the snowy Midwest where she avoided siblings and frostbite by reading book after book in a warm corner behind a recliner chair. She blames her only high school detention on Douglas Adams, whose *The Hitchhiker's Guide to the Galaxy* made her laugh out loud while reading it behind her geometry book.

Today, Kary still spends most of her time with her head in the clouds and her nose in a book. To the great relief of her parents, she seems to be making a living at it. Her greatest aspiration is to make her own work detention-worthy.

Kary is a Hugo and Astounding finalist whose work has been published by *Galaxy's Edge*, *The Grantville Gazette*, *Wordfire Press*, *Writers of the Future*, *Star-ShipSofa*, *Daily Science Fiction*, and *Tor Nightfire*. Learn more at karyenglish.com.

Nebula Award winner Esther M. Friesner (Ph.D. in Spanish from Yale) writes sf, fantasy, and a bit of horror, which comes to over 40 novels and more than 200 short stories. She is a poet, a playwright, and the editor of several anthologies, best known of these being the Chicks in Chainmail series she created for Baen Books. She is also the author of the Princesses of Myth series of young adult novels from Random House.

Esther is married, a mother of two, grandmother of two, harbors cats, and lives in Connecticut. She has a fondness for bittersweet chocolate, graphic novels, manga, travel, and jewelry. There is no truth to the rumor that her family motto is "Oooooh, SHINY!"

Her super-power is the ability to winnow her bookshelves without whining about it. Much.

Julie Frost grew up an Army brat, traveling the globe. She thought she might settle down after she finished school, but then she married a pilot and moved six times in seven years. She's finally put down roots in Utah with her family—a herd of guinea pigs, three other humans (though two of them don't live with her), and a "kitten" who thinks she's a warrior princess—and a collection of anteaters and Oaxacan carvings, some of which intersect. She enjoys birding and nature photography, which also intersect. Utilizing her degree in biology, she writes werewolf fiction while completely ignoring the physics of a protagonist who triples in mass. She also writes other things, on occasion, as the fancy strikes her.

Her short fiction has appeared in *Monster Hunter Files*, *Writers of the Future*, *The District of Wonders*, *StoryHack*, *Unlikely Story*, *Stupefying Stories*, *Weird World War IV*, *Straight Outta Dodge City*, and too many other anthologies to count. Her books are available at various online retailers. She whines about writing, a lot, at agilebrit.livejournal.com.

Jonathan Maberry is a *New York Times* best-seller, five-time Bram Stoker Award-winner, anthology editor, comic book writer, executive producer, magazine feature writer, playwright, and writing teacher/lecturer. He is the editor of *Weird Tales Magazine* and president of the International Association of Media Tie-in Writers.

He is the recipient of the Inkpot Award, three Scribe Awards, and was named one of the Today's Top Ten Horror Writers. His books have been sold to more than thirty countries. He writes in several genres including thriller, horror, science fiction, epic fantasy, and mystery; and he writes for adults, middle grade, and young adult. Learn more at jonathanmaberry.com.

Leila May is an up-and-coming artist with a knack for the macabre. She is experienced with multiple mediums, and has been creating fantastical art for over a decade.

Joe Monson worked at many different jobs before trying his hand at writing and editing fiction. He co-edits the LTUE Benefit Anthologies series with Jaleta Clegg, and oversees the Legacy of the Corridor publication series. He has edited almost two dozen anthologies and collections and has a number of other anthologies and collections in various stages of planning and completion.

He has written several short stories and is currently working on the first novel in a space opera adventure series. Joe collects science fiction and fantasy art, but not as much as Paul (as if that was even possible). Joe lives in the tops of the mountains with his lovely and talented wife, their three amazing children, and their pet library. Learn more at joemonson.com.

Jody Lynn Nye is a *New York Times* and *USA Today* bestselling author of fantasy and science fiction books and short stories, many of them with a humorous bent. Before breaking away from gainful employment to write full time, Jody worked as a file clerk, bookkeeper at a small publishing house, freelance journalist and photographer, accounting assistant, costume maker, and technical operations manager at a television station. Since 1987, she has published over 50 books and more than 200 short stories across the speculative fiction spectrum.

In addition to her writing, Jody has taught in numerous writing workshops and participated on hundreds of panels at science fiction conventions covering the subjects of writing and being published, spoken in schools and libraries, taught fantasy writing at Columbia College Chicago, and she runs the two-day writers' workshop at DragonCon.

Since 2016, she has judged entries for the Writers of the Future contest, the world's largest science fiction and fantasy writing contest for new authors. She is now its Coordinating Judge.

Once a lifelong Chicagoan (though still a Cubs fan), Jody now lives near Atlanta with her husband Bill Fawcett—a writer, game designer, military historian and book packager—and three feline overlords: Athena, Minx, and Marmalade. Learn more about her at jodynye.com.

Lehua Parker writes speculative fiction for kids and adults that often explores the intersections of Hawaii's past, present, and future. Her published works include the Niuhi Shark Saga trilogy, Lauele Universe Stories, Lauele Chicken Skin Stories, and Lauele Fractured Folktales, as well as plays, poetry, short stories, and essays. *One Boy, No Water* (Niuhi Shark Saga #1), was a 2017 Hawaii Children's Choice Nene Award Nominee.

As an author, editor, and educator trained in literary criticism and advocate of indigenous cultural narratives, Lehua is a frequent presenter at conferences, symposiums, and schools. Her hands-on workshops and presentations for kids and adults are offered through the Lehua Writing Academy. She is currently the Lit Coordinator for PEAU (Pasifika Enriching Arts of Utah).

Originally from Hawaii and a Kamehameha Schools graduate, Lehua now lives in exile in the high Rocky Mountains. During the snowy winters, she dreams of the beach. Learn more at lehuaparker.com.

Janci Patterson writes romantic comedy, epic fantasy, young adult urban fantasy, and contemporary young adult novels. She is honored to have co-authored novels with Brandon Sanderson, James Goldberg, Lauren Janes, and Megan Walker. Janci lives in Orem, Utah, with her husband, Drew Olds. When she's not writing, she can be found customizing Barbie dolls, playing geek games of all kinds, and watching reality TV. Learn more at jancipatterson.com.

Cedar Sanderson's long and checkered career started with being paid in plants. Since then, she's come to prefer money, and has tried many ways to earn it: balloon twister, face painter, children's librarian, scientist, cosmetic chemist, author, artist, and many more.

A born researcher, Cedar's passion for reading metamorphosed into writing, fueled by her long interest in history, infectious disease, food anthropology, and human behavior. After her four children had reached a suitable age, Cedar returned to higher education and obtained a Bachelor's of Science in Forensic Science and Investigation with minors in Chemistry and Molecular Biology, which enabled her to finally display the credentials to match her passion for scientific research.

Currently she writes for a living with facts, and on the side she writes fiction for fun. Author of ten novels, countless short stories, and a children's book, she has also edited an anthology, and illustrated five coloring books. Learn more at cedarwrites.com.

When not writing speculative fiction for a living—her day job is writing computer software manuals—Leigh Saunders enjoys writing "social science fiction," stories that focus on people—or "things" that are also people—and how magic, futuristic events, or advances in technology impact their lives. A 1993 Writers of the Future finalist, Leigh returned to fiction in 2010 after a long hiatus, with her short fiction since appearing in a variety of anthologies and collections. Her novels range from heist-style space opera to epic fantasy.

To learn more about Leigh and sign up for her occasional newsletter, visit her online at leighsaunders.com.

ALEX SHVARTSMAN is a writer, anthologist, translator, and game designer. His adventures so far have included traveling to over 30 countries, playing a card game for a living, and building a successful business. Since 2010, he has sold over 100 short stories to a variety of magazines and anthologies, including *Nature*, *Analog*, *Strange Horizons*, *Orson Scott Card's InterGalactic Medicine Show*, *Galaxy's Edge*, and many others.

He won the WSFA Small Press Award for Short Fiction in 2014 and was a finalist for the Canopus Award for Excellence in Interstellar Fiction in 2015 and 2017. Alex edits *Unidentified Funny Objects*, an annual anthology series of humorous science fiction and fantasy short stories. He's also the editor of *The Cackle of Cthulhu*, *Humanity 2.0*, *Coffee*, *Dark Expanse*, and *Funny Science Fiction* anthologies. His translations from Russian have appeared or are forthcoming in *The Magazine of Fantasy & Science Fiction*, *Apex Magazine*, *Samovar*, *Amazing Stories*, and other venues.

Alex resides in Brooklyn, New York with his wife and son. Learn more at alexshvartsman.com.

A Nebula Award winner, Hugo Award nominee, and winner in the Writers of the Future Contest, ERIC JAMES STONE has had stories published in *Year's Best SF 15*, *Analog*, *Nature*, and Kevin J. Anderson's *Blood Lite* anthologies, among other venues. His debut novel, a science fiction thriller titled *Unforgettable*, was published by Baen in January 2016.

One of Eric's earliest memories is of seeing an Apollo moon-shot launch on television. That might explain his fascination with space travel. His father's collection of old science fiction ensured that Eric grew up on a full diet of Asimov, Heinlein, and Clarke.

While getting his political science degree at Brigham Young University, Eric took creative writing classes. He wrote several short stories, and even submitted one for publication, but after it was rejected he gave up on creative writing for a decade.

During those years, Eric graduated from Baylor Law School, worked on a congressional campaign, and took a job in Washington, DC, with one of those special interest groups politicians always complain that other politicians are influenced by. He quit the political scene in 1999 to work as a web developer in Utah.

In 2002, he started writing fiction again, and in 2003 he attended Orson Scott Card's Literary Boot Camp. In 2007, Eric got laid off from his day job just in time to go to the Odyssey Writing Workshop. He has since found a new web development job.

Eric lives in Utah with his wife, Darci, and their children, Honor and Link. Learn more at ericjamesstone.com.

⁂

Brad R. Torgersen is a multi-award-winning science fiction and fantasy writer whose book, *A Star-Wheeled Sky,* won the 2019 Dragon Award for Best Science Fiction Novel at the 33rd annual Dragon Con fan convention in Atlanta, Georgia. A prolific short fiction author, Torgersen has published stories in numerous anthologies and magazines, to include several best of year editions.

He is named in *Analog* magazine's who's who of top *Analog* authors, alongside venerable writers like Larry Niven, Lois McMaster Bujold, Orson Scott Card, and Robert A. Heinlein. Married for over 28 years, Brad is also a United States Army Reserve Chief Warrant Officer—with multiple deployments to his credit—and currently lives with his wife and daughter in the Mountain West. Learn more at bradrtorgersen.com.

Additional Copyright Information

www.ingramcontent.com/pod-product-compliance
Lightning Source LLC
Chambersburg PA
CBHW021502110726
47899CB00001BA/256